CIVIL & STRANGE

CIVIL & STRANGE

Cláir Ní Aonghusa

HOUGHTON MIFFLIN COMPANY

Boston · New York

2008

For information about permission to reproduce
selections from this book, write to Permissions,
Houghton Mifflin Company, 215 Park Avenue South,
New York, New York 10003.

www.houghtonmifflinbooks.com

Library of Congress Cataloging-in-Publication Data
Ní Aonghusa, Cláir.
Civil and strange / Cláir Ní Aonghusa.
p. cm.
ISBN-13: 978-0-618-82936-1
ISBN-10: 0-618-82936-9
1. Rural conditions — Fiction. 2. Ireland — Fiction.
I. Title.
PR6064.I123C58 2008
823'.914 — dc22   2007009422

Book design by Melissa Lotfy

Printed in the United States of America

MP 10 9 8 7 6 5 4 3 2 1

For Aengus and Cormac

CIVIL & STRANGE

One

AFTER MONDAY MORNING MASS, Beatrice Furlong makes her way toward O'Flaherty's shop. She was never a one for weekday Masses, but now she's like a machine with an unforgiving program. Routine and regulation are what save her and sustain her through each day.

She's a tall, slim woman, dressed in jeans, a light jacket, and walking shoes. Her hair is an indeterminate brown, and the fine lines on her skin are beginning to deepen a little. Despite this, she looks younger than she is.

Still cool with dew, the morning feels clammy, and the roofs and windows of the cars parked on the street are misted heavily. Traffic through the village of Ballindoon, which takes workers to their jobs in the surrounding factories and towns, is beginning to taper off.

"A fine start to the day," James O'Flaherty says when she pays for her paper, bread, and plums. James, a balding, heavy-set man in his late sixties, is barely five eight in height. He has an unsettling habit of running his tongue across the front of his yellowed teeth, then working their edges with a cocktail stick, while talking to his customers. Why he can't floss in the bathroom before opening his shop is a mystery to her.

"You heard about the Tuohy business, I expect?"

She catches a note of suppressed animation in his voice. "No, what?"

"Hanged himself in the garage yesterday. The wife found him late last night. He's left her with two young children." He breaks the cocktail stick and drops it into the bin. "God rest his soul," he says by way of a pious afterthought.

Her body sends intense shooting pains to the top and base of her skull. More than eighteen months have passed since Beatrice's son, John, took the farm shotgun out of its locked cupboard, went into the old hay barn, smoked a cigarette, aimed the barrel of the gun at his head, and pulled the trigger. That week he had been on his own on the farm, as Beatrice was staying with one of her married daughters in England. It was days before what was left of his body was found.

"That's terrible," she manages to say. "What age . . . was he?"

"Just shy of forty. He was in here the other day buying stamps."

It's cruel to tell her like this, but then James O'Flaherty's unsubtle curiosity won't be denied. She remembers him the way he was years ago at dance halls and festival marquees. He got one or two local girls into trouble before he settled down with Mary Ann Ellis from the next parish. After his superficial charm and good humor evaporated, Mary Ann found herself living with a dour, insensitive, and casually cruel man. There were no children. After ten years of this, Mary Ann suddenly cleared out their bank account, packed a few suitcases, left the house, and, it was rumored, absconded with a man to Chicago.

Beatrice puts her groceries into her shopping bag, shoving them in roughly without regard for the ripe plums. "You have your news now. You're set up for the day, James," she says in a matter-of-fact way.

"Indeed I am. Indeed I am," he agrees, with an oily smile.

Outside the shop she steadies herself, raises her shoulders, and hurries out of the village.

That same August afternoon, Ellen Hughes struggles up Ballindoon's main street in the gusting rain. With gleeful ferocity, a downpour sends streams of water rushing along the sides of the streets and floods the drains.

Ellen's wet hair is pasted to her scalp. She keeps her head down to shield her face against the weather. Sneakily, the wind whips up her long summer skirt, causing it to billow above her knees like a sail. She uses her arms and hands to clamp down the material and catch the escaping pieces of cloth.

Her lips are dry, a cold sore swelling the center of the upper lip. Since the separation from her husband, she has been plagued by bodily eruptions, mouth ulcers, pimples on her nose and chin, and the cold sores that keep her company on a regular basis. "Viruses," her doctor in Dublin said. "They can erupt when a person is under stress or run down. Keep the lips moist."

She turns down a lane and makes her way into a walled garden, to a detached house set back from the other houses. As suddenly as it began, the cloudburst ceases and the sun appears. Wet surfaces gleam in the dappled light and water gurgles as the drains clear.

The door lock is stiff and capricious and has defeated her on many occasions, so she knows she must slide the key in at a particular angle and apply a precise pressure to open it. Eventually she hears the click and glide of the mechanism, and she's almost catapulted into the hallway when the lock yields.

She has known the house since her childhood, when she and her late father visited it. His maternal cousins, a retired teacher, and a nurse, Sarah and Mollie, spent a good part of their lives there. Their youngest sister, Peg, who held no professional qualifications of any kind, never vacated the parental abode even briefly. She left school at the earliest opportunity, worked for years in a local shop, but then gave that up as she was expected to keep house and devote herself to the care of her increasingly infirm mother. Old Mrs. Hamilton—Mam, as they called her—willed the place to the eldest, Sarah, with the stipulation that it would provide a home for each of the sisters during their lifetimes.

The cousins ran the house with military precision. Ellen remembers the smell of polish, the sheen on the kitchen range and the roaring, smoky fire in the living room. She can see bleached net curtains fluttering in a breeze from an open sash window. Every Thursday afternoon the cousins launched an assault on the two downstairs rooms, clearing furniture and books into the hall, brushing and vacuuming the carpets, wiping down skirting boards, bookshelves, and doors, dusting and polishing each piece of furniture before returning it to its original place. In the kitchen, the cooker, fridge, table, chairs, and old-style top-loading washing machine and roller were moved so that the floor could be washed, with food and storage cupboards emptied and cleaned three times annually. In later years, Sarah blamed Mollie for their zeal. She had worked in English hospitals for decades and never shook off a manic enthusiasm for cleanliness.

For much of the year the cousins supplied flowers for the church altar. Ellen can almost see the profusion of flowers, shrubs, and trees in the garden. In the spring and summer months they spent the better part of the day working the garden, obsessively weeding, trimming, feeding, and mulching flowers and shrubs, repositioning plants, digging potatoes, and shaking out onions to dry, their wide-brimmed straw hats bobbing up and down under trees and weaving through tall shrubs and vegetation.

After her father's sudden death from a heart attack when she was nine, Ellen was afraid that she would never visit Ballindoon again, but her mother, Kitty, continued the tradition of depositing her with the sisters for holidays.

Kitty was never a great driver and, dreading the long, slow journey back to Dublin, she was forever in a hurry. She wouldn't countenance staying over for a night and always had an excuse for not sitting down to eat the meal the cousins had prepared. Once the cousins had taken charge of Ellen's case, Kitty would relinquish control, confining herself to a quick pat on her daughter's shoulder before making her getaway. Admiring her outfit and commenting on changes in her appearance, the cousins would lead Ellen into the kitchen to partake of dinner under their approving eyes.

The trio of sisters were strict in ways, keeping her in each morning to help with clearing up and preparation of dinner for the middle of the day. Then, in the early afternoon, following the washing up, when the last plate had been put away, one of them would say, "The rest of the day is your own," and off she'd run on her adventures, pausing only to flit back in for tea.

The sudden expanse of freedom was a release for Ellen. She had weeks of running wild through fields on the outskirts of the village, marching up unexplored paths and roads, and the utter delight of skipping down the laneway to the river for a swim, bathing togs wrapped in a towel. On her return from gallivanting, she would call, "Uh-hoo!" like a strident cuckoo, and locate Sarah and the others from their answering trills.

Now the building radiates the intense cold of a place long unlived in and the stench of neglect. Tidemarks of damp stain the wallpaper. Repulsed by perspiring plaster, it is cellotaped here and there in an attempt to hold it in position. The windows are covered in grime, the carpets are filthy, and the floors sag. The upholstery on the chairs is threadbare and stained. Everything is covered in dust.

On her first official visit, following her purchase of the house, Ellen had been met by the fetid odor of rancid grease, damp, and rust in the kitchen. It took her two days to wash down the walls, scour the appliances, and scrub the floor.

Outside, gathering clouds threaten another heavy shower. As she sits in the darkening room her imagination overlays the various odors with the scents she remembers from her childhood.

She has been in the village for the last three days, passing by some of her former haunts, but keeping to herself. She feels invisible, ghostly, and likes the sense of being a mysterious character in a narrative.

A vehicle turns into the driveway. Then the engine cuts out and a door is slammed. Footsteps crunch on the gravel and the doorbell rings. She can't bring herself to move. The doorbell rings again and a face appears at the window. With a sigh she stands up and goes to open the door.

The stooped figure of a tall man stands before her, his face in shadow, obscured by a cap. A cigarette glows from his lips. "Hiya there, Ellen," he says.

She stumbles in surprise. "Uncle Matt!" she exclaims.

"It took you long enough to answer," he carps. "I thought the place was empty."

"I'll switch on the light," she says, and he follows her in. She watches him look around. "Grim, isn't it?" she says. "I was remembering how Sarah, Mollie, and Peg would sit here in the evenings until twilight and let the room get dark. They'd talk for hours in the shadows, and I'd sit and listen, not opening my mouth for fear they'd remember I was there and send me to bed. They were always very sparing with light."

He rubs his hands together. "They were sparing with heat, too. Lots of condensation here."

"It's the damp and the thick walls. I tried to light a fire in this room but the chimney smokes. We'd be better off in the kitchen. I gave it a good clean-up so it's just about presentable. Who told you I was about?"

He gives a bark of laughter. "Old Denis Foynes has been trying to place you since you arrived. Terry Fitzgibbon pointed me in this direction, although I half guessed where you'd be. How long are you about?"

"I came last Friday."

"And is this another of those flying visits?"

She grimaces. "I'm afraid not. I'm staying this time."

He shakes his head as if in wonderment. "Despite everything I said, you went and bought this wreck."

She laughs. "I didn't like any of the new houses. Too big or too cramped, and pretty soulless. I can leave my imprint on this place. When the auctioneer showed me around, I did a lot of sighing over its dreadful condition. The poor man couldn't believe somebody was finally interested in buying. He was thrilled to offload it."

"I wonder where the money you paid for this place will end up?"

"Theo Hamilton left everything to a charity."

"That was the strangest thing out. It's beyond me why Sarah willed this house to that cousin in America."

"Old Mrs. Hamilton and Theo kept up a correspondence. She was very fond of him and had some notion that he wanted to retire to Ireland, so she directed Sarah to leave him the place. The will was made before I was born. By the time Sarah died, I was married and had my own setup."

"Be that as it may, you've burned your bridges. It's a big step, Ellen. What does Kitty make of all this?"

"What she feels is very let down. She's disgusted that Christy and I have thrown our hats at the marriage. She's pretty traditional that way. Lie in the bed you made, and all that. She's given me a good few tongue lashings. In fact, she's out with me."

"It's a cod trying to live your life to please other people. You're blessed not having children. I know your mother was very taken with Christy but I could never understand his attraction. He was very good at sucking up to her, but he seemed pretty wishy-washy."

"You never said."

"It wasn't my business to tell you who to marry, no more than it's my place to say that you're mad to go to the expense of renovating this."

"I'm sentimental about this house."

"Exactly. You need your head examined! Anyway, how is the ever-youthful Kitty?"

"Very well. She's in Italy on a painting trip."

"Next thing she'll be moving down here to live with you."

Ellen laughs. "That wouldn't be Mum's style. Actually, she did suggest that we pool our resources to buy an apartment in Dublin. That's when I first thought of making the move."

He smiles. "Ballindoon would never be grand enough for that lady. But you're a different kettle of fish."

"I like the idea of having a connection with the village. Terry Fitzgibbon recognized me the second time I was in her shop. Apparently, I used to play with her sister."

He tries the back door. "Is this unlocked?" When she nods, he puts his shoulder to it and pushes it open. He peers out into the garden. "You'll have your work cut out for you clearing this." They walk halfway down the overgrown path. "The way the garden falls back behind the house is very attractive. Does it stretch to the river?"

"All the way."

He views the house from every angle. "It's not bad really, but it's a bit cramped."

"They fed crowds in their day," she says, "packed us all in, you and Julia, Stephen and Colum, Dad, Mum, and me on our visits. I don't know how they managed."

"The miracle of the loaves and fishes." He follows her indoors as raindrops start to spatter down. "What are your plans? You're hardly going to live in it the way it is?"

"It needs damp-proofing, rewiring, and replumbing."

"And bloody central heating. Have you funds?"

"It went very cheap, so yes."

"After all my trouble driving you about to show you other places," he grumbles. "And you didn't tell me your decision."

"I knew the choice wouldn't please you, and I felt I'd bothered you enough already."

He snorts. "My only brother's only child — my sole connection to Brendan — and you didn't want to bother me! A courtesy call wouldn't have killed you." He stamps the stub of his cigarette into a cracked tile on the kitchen floor. "Who's going to do the work on the house?"

"I don't know really. I've heard of a builder in the —"

"— I'll give you a few names. There's a fellow up the mountains who did work for me. He's good, very particular." He winks at her. "Local knowledge is a great thing. You should move fast. You're living in awful squalor." He places a carrier bag that contains a bottle on the table. "Brought you a present," he says.

"What's that?"

"Open it up and see."

She unpacks a bottle of whiskey. "You won't have to be embarrassed if somebody calls. You can offer them a drink," he says.

"I can take a hint as well as the next woman. Sit down and I'll pour us a glass each. All I've got is water or lemonade."

"Water is just the ticket." He looks big in the room, menacing almost, his eyes taking everything in. He can't settle. He jiggles his knees and taps the table with his fingers. As she rinses and dries glasses, he gets up and prowls about again. "How can you live here?" he asks. He opens the fridge. "Does this thing work?" She nods. He laughs harshly. "Ancient, isn't it? You might get money for it as an antique."

"It keeps the butter and milk and a few frozen peas but not much else."

"This house is like a time capsule, isn't it? How did those women manage?"

"It was fine years ago. Of course, it was lived in then." She finds a jug for the water and pours whiskey into the glasses. "Sit down and take your drink," she orders.

"I suppose you'll be getting an architect in to design the alterations."

"I've done that, and he's drawn up plans."

"You're not serious!" He takes a sip of whiskey. "No doubt you'll be having the obligatory conservatory out the back. They're very fashionable."

She smiles, abashed. "Well, yes, I will!"

"This should be interesting," he says, deadpan. "I'm going to enjoy the transformation. Show us the plans."

She runs upstairs and fetches them, and he spreads them out on the kitchen table. "What's wrong with this table?" he asks, shaking it. "It's rocking."

"It's old and unsteady. You'll have to make do."

He nods and checks the plans. "French doors for the conservatory?"

"Oh, yes."

"You're better off. The sliding patio doors are a godsend to thieves. They can remove them. No trouble to break in. Saw a program about house security on the BBC the other night and you'd be amazed how simple it was."

"You hardly need security in a place like this."

"Rural Ireland isn't the place it was. Gangs travel the countryside looking for places to rip off. There have been two break-ins in the village over the last year or so, a shop and pub only to date, but some house will get done eventually."

"So the twentieth century has arrived."

"What century are you living in? It's the twenty-first century by my reckoning. Course I could be wrong, being ignorant and backward and all that."

"None of that nonsense, Matt. You may have left school early, but you've picked up all you need to know."

He throws her one of his rare grins. "The only reason I'm sucking up to you is that a few books will come my way if you settle down here. I'm assuming you still read. I remember your mother complaining to me you always had your nose stuck in a book. She could never find you for the washing up and household chores."

9

"I'd hide in the bathroom! That used to drive her wild. She wasn't in the cousins' league when it comes to housekeeping, but she wanted things neat and tidy. Housework was never my strong point, although I'm better now."

"What I always liked about you," he says, and pours a good measure of whiskey into each glass, "is that, even when you were older, grown up really, you still didn't give a damn whether the house was falling down about your ears. The cousins used to go on about how you wouldn't or couldn't see what needed doing. You had them mesmerized."

She blushes. He's being ironic, she presumes.

"You'll have to buck up now though," he says, handing her a glass. "The women down here have a points system for housekeeping that will keep you on your toes."

"I'll sign up for the opt-out clause."

"So, no change there." He continues to study the plans, asking occasional questions. Then he rolls them up and hands them back to her. "Shouldn't be too bad," he comments. He raises his glass. "Here's to a successful venture."

"Thanks. I might need your advice now and again."

"In order to disregard it? But you could try me," he adds when he sees her crestfallen look.

She goes to refill his glass. "No thanks. I'm driving," he says, and stands up. "These chairs are riddled with woodworm. Most of what's in this house is only fit for a skip." He pauses at the door. "How'll you manage during the building work?"

"I'll rent out a little place down the street. It's very cheap."

"You could rest with us."

"I'd only get on your nerves."

"Since when did you get on my nerves?" he asks, reprovingly. He looks about. "I don't remember seeing a phone on my way in. Did they get one in the end?"

"No, they didn't."

"Now there's a funny kind of meanness for you. Always down to the public phone box to make their calls, battling down the street in all weathers when there was no need. Could never understand it myself."

"They thought it was a luxury they couldn't afford."

"Bollocks. They were just too mean."

"I'm getting phone points put in most rooms."

He snorts. "From one extreme to the other, eh? I suppose you'll take the eye out of us with your designer this and designer that, trying to show us all up with your new fads."

"You know me better than that," she admonishes.

"I'm just trying to annoy you. Come up for dinner on Sunday, two o'clock sharp," he says. His invitations are always abrupt.

"I might take you up on that."

"We'll expect you. Remember, on the dot of two. Julia's a stickler for time."

She thinks about her uncle as she makes her way to his house. He's known as a quiet man although he's involved in community affairs, a member of the Parish Council, and the Tidy Towns and St. Patrick's Day committees. He has a reputation for speaking only when he has something to say, but he always says what's on his mind. She's seen photographs of him in his youth and, despite the awkward poses, forced smiles, and strange clothes, it's clear how handsome he was. Traces of his former attractiveness linger on his face when it's in repose.

Julia answers the door, greets Ellen with a quick, ducking embrace, like a bird's wing brushing against the cheek, and flashes a formulaic smile. Julia isn't unpleasant or bad-tempered but she holds herself aloof. She keeps physical contact to a minimum. She has been known to move as if to shake a person's hand but then not touch them.

As a child, Ellen tried to make an ally of Julia, but Julia warded her off. She didn't encourage Ellen to visit the farm, and on the rare occasions that she issued a face-saving invitation—as if there were a risk of cross-contamination—she generally arranged for Ellen's younger cousins to be at friends' houses. Almost the only occasion at which Ellen could be sure of running into her cousins, barring the occasional unexpected encounter on the street, was Sunday Mass.

Matt lets Julia make most of the conversational openings, and there's little sign of his usual teasing quickness and comments. Now and again a quirky smile flickers against the edges of his mouth.

"Come in. Sit down. You must be perished with the cold. I didn't hear an engine. Did you walk up?" Julia says.

"I'm between cars."

"How long is it since you were last around? You must see great changes."

"I can't get over all the little shops that have closed down."

"That's the way now. Somebody retires and nobody in the family wants to take on the business. Ballindoon is lucky to have a butcher at all. Lisdonnell lost theirs when the poor man died. The shop is standing empty."

Matt shakes off his torpor. "Our small population doesn't make it worth anybody's while to buy premises," he says, as he hands her a glass of whiskey. "Most people do a weekly shop at the supermarket and use the local stores to top up. It's terribly easy to get into Killdingle these days. The traders in the town send out a bus on market day. They want the business. It picks people up at eleven and drops them back at half past three."

"Thanks for the chocolates," Julia says. "I'm not much given to chocolates but your uncle likes them. I'm more into baking. I like a nice fruitcake."

"I'll remember that next time."

"Are you a good cook?" Julia asks.

"Not great at baking or desserts. I'm better at main courses."

Matt looks up. His eyes glint. "Our Ellen doesn't do much in that line. Kitty used to claim that any boy would do better than her in the kitchen. Isn't that right, Ellen?"

"That was ages ago, Matt!"

"I must give you a few recipes," Julia says absently.

"I won't be doing much cooking for a while. The place I'm renting has two rings and a grill."

"There must be more than that," Matt says.

"It's cheap because it's primitive, and it won't be for long."

"I suppose," but he doesn't sound convinced.

They sit down to the meal and, as she eats Julia's food, Ellen begins to think her own cooking skills not too bad after all.

Two

AYS LATER every church pew is taken and the choir gallery is crowded for Dan Tuohy's funeral Mass. The organist to the back of the gallery can't see over the heads of people. She has to rely on those to the front to alert her to the priest's signals to strike up for the next hymn or prayer.

Beatrice is in the last row of seats to the side of the altar. She can see Stella Tuohy and her children some of the time. For the most part Stella sits quietly, eyes downcast, a child to either side of her. Dan's two sisters sit rigidly to the edge of the pew like security guards. All three women look grim, as well they might, reflects Beatrice. She blesses herself as the coffin is wheeled down the aisle to the front door, genuflects in the direction of the altar, and hurries toward the side door.

"This must bring it all back," a voice says behind her as she dips her right index finger in the holy water font outside the door.

She forces herself to turn and face Brenda Finnegan. "Hello," she says.

All five-foot-three of Brenda strains up to look into Beatrice's face. "My heart goes out to you," she says, giving Beatrice's arm a sympathetic squeeze.

Beatrice is always wary of Brenda and her predilection for gossip, but she smiles as if touched by the expression of concern. "Terrible, isn't it," she says. "I'm just thinking of the poor man's wife and family."

"I was in the house last night," confides Brenda. "You should have seen her; well, heard her. She was in an awful state." The tone of Brenda's voice is unsettlingly brisk.

Unable to bring herself to call to the Tuohy household the previous night, Beatrice had persuaded Simon, her farm manager, to deliver apple tarts she had baked.

Nan Brogan joins them and they exchange greetings. "Do we have any idea why he did it?" Nan asks.

"There's talk of bad debts," Brenda says.

"Wasn't there a bit of a scandal about him and the young Galvin boy years ago?" asks Nan.

"That was nothing but loose talk," Brenda says in one of her occasional forays into setting the record straight.

Something in Beatrice snaps. "I hate that kind of tittle-tattle," she says. "People speculating when they know nothing, making up what they can't know and salivating over it all. It's disgusting."

"You heard me defend him," Brenda says hotly.

"I was only saying what I heard," Nan says in an offended manner.

"Well, that doesn't mean you have to repeat it."

"God, you're getting very hot and heavy," Nan says. "Keep your hair on."

"The way stories take wing here just sickens me," Beatrice says. "Don't think I don't know how they blackened my John's character, when his only crime was not being up to things." Not being able to cope with the life his father forced on him, and letting the only girl he cared for go because he hadn't the guts to propose to her, she thinks. For a moment she's half afraid that she has spoken her thoughts aloud and glares fiercely at the other two.

She's aware that Nan and Brenda are staring at her openmouthed. Instantly she's sorry that she said anything at all.

"You're overreacting, Beatrice," Brenda says quietly. "We're all bemused by Dan's death. Nobody can figure out why it happened."

"What are we all? Hyenas? Feeding on the kill? Can't we leave people alone?" bursts from Beatrice. She watches the women exchanging looks and nods, takes in a quick gulp of air, and steadies herself.

"There, there, don't go on so," Brenda says in an infuriatingly gentle tone. She strokes Beatrice's arm. Beatrice has to struggle with herself not to push her away. "It's not so long since you had to — had to . . ." Brenda falters under Beatrice's cold gaze. There's satisfaction in seeing her words extinguished, like the spluttering gasps of a dying engine. For moments there is silence. "We all feel for you. This must stir it all up again," Brenda says eventually.

"I'm not going to parade my emotions for your benefit. I try to keep all my crying private, the way I live my life," Beatrice says thickly.

"You weren't so full of yourself the day of John's funeral. There were tears then. You think you're beyond reproach because of what happened but you're not. Nobody is," Nan says coldly.

The words slice through Beatrice like a knife and she wishes she could press a button that would transport her to another place, any place other than here, but she's stuck in this accursed village with these two harpies at a depressing funeral. "Who's beyond reproach, Nan? Let him who is without sin cast the first stone. Remember that? 'There's so much good in the worst of us, and so much bad in the best of us, that it hardly behooves the most of us to talk about the rest of us.' That was one of my father's sayings. Good, isn't it?" she snaps. Brenda is tugging at Nan's sleeve, trying to pull her away, but Nan can't leave for fear she might miss something interesting.

Beatrice walks quickly to catch up with the crowd as it leaves the church grounds for the adjoining graveyard. She reaches the plot as the gravediggers reposition the funeral flowers on the dug earth and set the coffin on planks covering the hole in the ground. People cough and make way for the priest and altar girls. Nan takes her cue to wiggle and push her way to the front of the throng, dragging Brenda with her.

As soon as the priest opens his breviary, Beatrice forgets her irritation with Nan and Brenda the way a person forgets a swatted fly. She's transported back to John's burial, the gash of the opened grave, the hushed crowd, and how she found herself reading the inscription on her husband's tombstone over and over again. She listens to the drone of the priest's voice and loses track of time. The silence of the day and the hush of the crowd as the coffin is lowered into the grave, the tantalizing beauty of the countryside, covered in a fine mist, reactivate the pain in her heart and the feelings of loss she usually works so hard to suppress. She's conscious of glances directed at her as the priest finishes his prayers, shuts his book, and the gravediggers cover the hole with a wide plank.

Father Mahoney stares into the crowd. "Dan's family has asked me to thank you all for coming and to invite everybody to attend a buffet lunch in Hegarty's pub," he says.

Father Mahoney walks toward Beatrice, who doesn't notice his approach. "This must be a very sad occasion for you," he says. "Very lonely."

"It's difficult, Father."

"Would you like me to fetch you a plate of food?" She shakes her head. "My door is always open, Beatrice, if you ever need to talk."

"I know that, Father. It's very good of you."

He massages his forehead as if he has a headache. "I have to admit that I'm at a loss," he says. "I know we're given all sorts of explanations — the loss of spirituality, the emptiness of life in a materialistic society — but what really drove your John to end his life, or what made Dan kill himself? They lived in a strong community. The family structures were in place. What was at the nub of their despair?"

She doesn't feel able for Father Mahoney's blunt comments, however well-intentioned. "I'm as much in the dark as you, Father. Maybe they thought their lives were hopeless?" She shrugs. "There's really no way of knowing."

"Yes, but . . ."

She realizes from the thrust of his jaw that he wants to launch into a conversation on the subject and her courage fails her. She knows that he's only trying to do his job, but today she can't handle his grim earnestness, his pedantic and humorless attempts to come to terms with the concerns of his flock. He's a pleasant man, if taken in small doses, but she just has to get away from him. "I've changed my mind. I think I will grab something to eat," she says, and edges past him toward the table.

At the buffet Beatrice finds herself next to Brenda, who is busily loading two plates with quiche and salad. Out of the corner of her eye, Beatrice sees the bony outline of Nan's head craning on its long neck as she waits for Brenda to join her.

"I see you escaped Father Mahoney," Brenda says. "He can be a bit hard to take. Could you pass me that plate of sausage rolls?" Robotically, Beatrice passes her the plate. "Thanks very much." Brenda slips away to join Nan, who has secured a corner spot for them.

"I'll fill that for you," Lily Traynor, the caterer, says, and whips away Beatrice's plate. It returns laden with savories, salad, and rice.

"Thanks, Lily."

"Let me get you a drink," Lily offers. Beatrice shakes her head.

"No ifs or buts now, you're going to have a glass," Lily insists. "Red or white?"

"A glass of white, please."

"Time was you'd never have turned down a drink, Beatrice Furlong," a voice at her shoulder says.

She always does a double take whenever she encounters Matt Hughes. Of course, she notes mechanically, he's still a handsome man. "I have a splitting headache, Matt," she says. "I feel like 'Exhibit A' here. They're all feeling very sorry for me."

Lily passes her the wine. "There you go," she says. "I'll call up next week, and we'll drive across to Waterford and have our lunch out."

"I'd like that, Lily. Give me a ring."

"Pay no heed to all that attention. It's of the moment," Matt says, guiding her away from the crush at the buffet table. He smiles. "I hear that young fella you have on the farm is gettin' on well. I'd say you were glad to have him during the foot-and-mouth scare."

She's grateful to him for being so low-key. "It was like living under siege. Well, you know that yourself. Simon was great. He stocked up on feed for all the animals and found places to keep the calves when we weren't allowed to sell them on. I'd have been lost without him."

"The vigilance here seems to have paid off. We got off very lightly compared to Britain."

"One case of infection. Still, it was tough on everybody."

"I'll grant you it was hard. So, you're happy with yer man?"

"He's a godsend, but he's only biding his time with me." She realizes that everything is going to lead back to John, but she can't help herself. "I look at Simon and I think of poor John, and how a farm was foisted on him when it was the last thing he wanted. Then I see what Simon does and what he's capable of. He's a natural, only he'll never be able to afford his own place. It's a crying shame."

"This business with Dan must bring it all back again."

"That it does. It's always on my mind . . . John urging me to go away and stay with Paula that week. And I nearly didn't go . . . but he was in great form. And all the time . . . all the time, he . . . he planned to . . ."

He squeezes her shoulder. "I shouldn't have mentioned it. I didn't mean it to tail back to . . ."

"Sure, it's grand, Matt. My biggest trial since his death has been those two leeches" — she nods to a corner of the room — "attaching themselves to me."

He grins. "You mean your very good friends Nan and Brenda?"

"Don't talk to me. It's been hard trying to fend them off, and I haven't always got the better of them."

"Nan's the real problem. Brenda wouldn't be so bad — she has some humanity — but she's easily led. Odds on that they'll find poor Stella Tuohy more interesting now."

"That would be a relief, but I wouldn't wish it on her."

He lowers his voice. "I was full sure that your Andy would turn up at John's funeral. I didn't say anything at the time but . . ."

"He's not in touch with anyone, Matt. I used to hope . . . but . . . I've more or less given up. I don't know where he's working. None of us even has an address."

"Ah, eaten bread is soon forgotten."

Her voice is subdued. "A friend of one of the girls met him a few months ago on a plane trip in the U.S. . . . so he's . . . you know . . . still alive. It's been nine years, Matt, nine years."

He edges her into an alcove and they sit on low bar stools. He faces into the wall and angles his body to act as a shield so that he's looking at her but keeping the world at bay. Her plate of food lies untouched on the circular table between them.

"It's cruel, isn't it, the way things can turn out?" he says quietly.

"You're telling me," she says, almost on a sob. She realizes that he's signaling somebody but she can't work out what he's up to until Lily suddenly appears with another glass of wine. "That's the business," she says gratefully to Lily.

"Whatever you need, girl."

"And you mean to say that there's been no communication whatsoever from Andy?" Matt muses. "I wouldn't have believed it. The fight was with Jack, wasn't it?"

"It was with all of us in the end. He fell out with his father but he blamed us all."

A shadow falls across them, and Beatrice looks up to find Julia peering down. "Hadn't we better be going?" she says coldly to Matt. She acknowledges Beatrice with a barely perceptible nod.

"In a moment," he says. "In a moment."

As Matt leaves, his place is taken by Lily, who has delegated table duties to one of her minions. "Eat up," she urges Beatrice. "No slacking on the food front. You need to keep up your strength."

The commercial activity in the village is divided between Fitzgibbon's well-stocked mini-supermarket, O'Flaherty's news agent and general grocery with post office, Hickey's butcher, O'Hara's hardware store, Mitchell's takeaway and sit-in, Rafter's chemist (closed on Wednesday afternoons), Kennedy's car-repair garage with petrol pumps, Fennell's dilapidated three-storey guesthouse, and five pubs.

When Ellen visited this place as a child, many of the houses were derelict and had fallen into ruin. The breaks between buildings contained overgrown sites, lush with weeds and coarse grass. Now most of the ramshackle houses have been renovated or knocked down and rebuilt, sometimes in the old style of narrow, single-fronted terraced houses, more times on a grander scale — tall, wide, double-fronted residences with imposing hall doors and side entrances. Bit by bit most of the overgrown plots have been bought up, tidied, and built on, cosmetic implants that enhance the previously gap-toothed streetscape.

The principal village streets form the shape of a crude Y, with offshoot lanes and side streets, and an old-fashioned square of three-

and four-storey houses set in its groin. The meandering river inter-
sects each stretch of street. Ellen's house is in the tail, a little up from
the commercial center. When she exits from her little side street she
faces the Catholic church, the girls' primary school, and a sloping
green space. Where the river undercuts the left arm of the letter,
at another end of the village, there was once a thriving Protestant
church that fell into disrepair and ruin when its congregation dwin-
dled to nothing. Astride the river is the Protestant graveyard, full
of elaborate tombs from the eighteenth and nineteenth centuries,
with a few plain graves, hollowed and sunken, outlining the shape
of long rotten coffins, as if corpses might at any moment suddenly
sit up and take a turn about the grounds.

After Ellen's arrival in August, the staff in Terry Fitzgibbon's
shop take the best part of a month to progress from "helloing" her
to exchanging comments on the weather to inquiring about the
progress of renovations to the house to, eventually, calling her by
name. Terry introduces Ellen to her husband, the elusive Bart, co-
owner of the shop. "He wouldn't know you," Terry laughs. "He's a
blow-in."

"We'll be up one day to see how the work's progressing," Terry
says. "I always liked Sarah's house. It was a shame to have it idle for
so long."

The next time Ellen goes in for the paper and bread, Terry says,
"I took a peek in the windows of your place last night. I like the extension and conservatory. You'll have a great view."

Ellen bows to the inevitable. "Would you like a guided tour?"

"Yes, please." Terry and the girls seem to take Ellen to their hearts.
They volunteer tendrils of gossip when handing back change. She
learns that the post-office job is up for tender, that somebody or
other — she rarely knows who — has died, that such-and-such a person is ill, or rumored to be ill, and that a pub a mile outside the
village is up for sale. She always knows if a car accident has taken
place on a main or by-road. Unfortunately, Terry presumes her to
be cognizant of the history of whatever person or event is being discussed, as if, fully formed like Venus, she arrived in the village with
complete knowledge. If she says, "I'm not certain I know them,"
Terry is sure to comment, "You do. You've just forgotten. Ask your
uncle."

"Careful of what you let slip around here," Matt warns on one of his visits to the rented house he calls "Ellen's pen." "Play it civil and strange."

"Play it what?"

"Be polite, but be extremely wary, and keep them at arm's length."

"That's a new one on me. But why do I have to be so careful?"

"How can I put it? Don't be too eager to give out information. Your every word will be scrutinized. You have to be careful the way you phrase things because what you say is likely to be misinterpreted. You'll be quoted as saying things you never said. I'm serious," he says grimly. "There's a core of hardened gossips ready to pounce on any unwitting newcomer. It's only sport to them, and they're all stirred up by your arrival."

"I can't understand how they're so interested in me and my doings."

"It's recreational, happens in all small communities. They know now that you're not here on a fleeting visit. That opens up tracts for conjecture." He draws on his cigarette. "Not being a complete outsider will give you a bit of status, but it also means you'll be subject to harsher scrutiny than a blow-in."

"There's none of this in the city. Nobody gives a damn."

"It's known here as neighborliness."

"I've been asked when the renovations are due to finish, whether I'm putting in central heating, if I'm damp-proofing the place, what the kitchen extension is for, how I intend to use the conservatory, whether the house needs a new roof, and where I'm thinking of buying my kitchen."

"See? Be wary of them. And what about your job? Have you ditched it?"

"Oh gosh, no. I took a year to get sorted out. I'm on the lookout for a subbing position."

"You can't get away from bread-and-butter issues. That's a cross we all have to bear. But, Ellen, you're a demon for staying in. You're too young for that. I don't see you out and about. I expected to come across you in one of the licensed establishments."

"The pubs?" She sighs. "To tell you the God's honest truth, it feels peculiar to walk into one on my own. Poked my nose into a place one Saturday night and it was full of noise, smoke, and teen-agers."

"That'd be Murphy's, haunt of the young pups. Call into Hegar-ty's tomorrow night and I'll stand you a pint."

Nothing easier, she thinks. However, without his presence, she knows that her confidence would ebb away quickly.

He drains his cup, rounds up the last crumbs of cake with his in-dex finger, presses them into a lump on the plate, brings them to his mouth, and swallows them. "That's good for a shop cake," he says. He stretches and stands up. "Better head up to the house for supper. Why haven't we seen you in a while? I'm partial to a bit of company, and the house is way too quiet with the boys grown up and gone."

Unmentioned is Julia's obvious lack of welcome the time Ellen turned up uninvited at the farm. Her silences or monosyllabic an-swers were eloquent. She wasn't overtly rude and never said any-thing that could be pinned down. There was never a moment of crisis as such. She offered Ellen tea, but she was a very preoccupied hostess, constantly slipping away to complete this or that chore and leaving Ellen, as Matt would put it, in "glorious isolation."

Two weeks have passed since that occasion and, when they meet in a shop or on the street, Julia has taken to saying, "You must call up." Ellen smiles noncommittally, but when, one Saturday night, Julia rings and crossly issues an invitation to the following day's din-ner, Ellen accepts, if only to please Matt.

"Come in. Sit down," Julia says at the door. As per usual, every-thing about her smile is calculated. The lips measure their grip on the expanse of the mouth. The performance is obedient to the teeth and confines itself to the area of the jaw.

Matt is an enigmatic presence at the table, hunched in on himself and particularly subdued and deferential. He doesn't make eye con-tact with Ellen. Julia bustles about the kitchen, lifting lids on pots and pans. Her manner toward her guest is formal and forced, as if humoring a tedious dignitary. She gives the impression of fighting her own inclinations. She and Matt must have had a disagreement before Ellen's arrival, and Ellen will never know if her invitation arose out of a battle of wills won by Matt, or if they compromised with a tradeoff.

"How are the renovations going? Are you managing the hardship?" Julia asks as they start into a meal of tough roast beef, overcooked vegetables, and underdone Yorkshire pudding. Matt passes the gravy boat to Ellen, and she pours some of the lumpy liquid on the meat and potatoes.

"My needs are few. I'm living out of packets and tins at the moment."

Matt laughs. "That'll be no hardship to you. No cooking!"

"You can stop those digs. I've already told you how improved I am in that regard. I had to when I married," retorts Ellen crossly. For an instant she's scared they'll ask about her marriage, but mercifully nothing is said.

"And are you really determined to live here?" Julia asks, breaking the silence into which they have lapsed after the main course.

"Oh, yes. I intend to make a go of it."

"Well, that's quite extraordinary," declares Julia, springing to her feet and removing the plates.

"What's extraordinary about it? People are moving out of the cities every day," Matt says brusquely.

"Nothing," Julia answers impassively as she sets dishes of apple tart and ice cream in front of them. "It's just such a turnabout from the way things used to be. The drift was always toward the cities."

"It's a new world," Ellen says wanly. She forces herself to swallow mouthfuls of dessert. She's had about as much as she can take. "I'd better make a move," she says a little later, pushing her empty dish away.

"Have tea or coffee before you go," Matt says, and Julia gets up to put on the kettle.

After the meal Julia takes her on a tour of the back garden. It's a conventional space with lawn, bedded shrubs, and a path, with a gate leading into a walled vegetable and fruit garden. The vegetable garden is well tended, and the apple and pear trees have been stripped of fruit. "We supply all our potatoes, vegetables, and salads from here," says Julia.

"Do you grow onions?" Ellen asks, remembering sacks full of onions tumbled and laid out to dry in Sarah's garden.

"Onions, scallions, cucumber, tomatoes, lettuces, the lot."

"And you work it all on your own?"

"He prepares the beds and I do the rest." Matt is referred to as "he" or "your uncle" and never by name. "That's where we store the apples," Julia says, pointing at a shed. "The pears have to be eaten when they're ripe, but I've boxes and boxes of apples wrapped in newspaper."

"It's all pretty impressive." Julia doesn't answer. Ellen senses her withdrawal from the conversation. Perhaps she finds her husband's niece boring, or maybe she feels that her duty is done. She has given her ration of talk and attention. It has been metered, invoiced, and paid for.

It's a miracle of sorts that they produced children, but of course that was Hanora's influence, his mother choreographing events, orchestrating the tune Julia played during brief truces that Matt, never a natural combatant, mistook for peace offerings. Much as the bull obliges the cows, while there was need of him, Matt had played his part in producing the heir and spare.

He often imagined that he would leave Julia once the boys had grown up. He'd picture various ways of breaking the news to her. Even more pleasurable would be to disappear from her life without warning.

His mother used to tell an old story about the man who did a runner the day of his marriage. The wedding party had been walking toward the bride's house when the man hopped over the ditch. Nobody took much notice. There were no toilets in those days and people often did their business in fields. When he failed to turn up at the bride's house, they sent two men down to search for him. He was never seen again in the locality. Years later somebody claimed to have run into him in New York. The woman kept her married name and called herself his wife till the day she died. Matt liked that story, although he knew there was precious little chance of him ever escaping to New York. If he ever got away, London would be as far as he'd reach. In the recesses of his heart, he knows this is a pipe dream. He didn't want to be a farmer in the first place but now he'll never be anything else.

This weekend Stephen is down. They're clearing the table and stacking the plates in the sink after a late dinner. Julia pours a kettle of hot water over the dishes. She has inveigled Stephen into doing the drying up. "Your father has got very fond of the gargle," she says suddenly. Matt has taken to driving down to Hegarty's each night and looks forward to these outings. This is her first comment on this new practice.

Stephen flashes his father a quizzical look. "That's right, son," Matt says. "I've turned into an old soak, incapable after a few pints, staggering home drunk every night. Sad, isn't it?"

"It's a dangerous business when somebody suddenly develops an interest in drink. God knows what the repercussions will be."

Trust her to try to make mischief between them. He senses Stephen's unease. It's obvious that he doesn't want to be drawn into his parents' squabble. "Don't worry, son. Two pints each night aren't going to kill me."

"But what if it turns into a habit? What if he starts to drink more?"

"That's nonsense, Julia. I've always been a very regular sort of fellow, moderate in my habits, and I don't see any need to change that. The company in the bar helps me relax after a day's work."

"You never needed to until now."

"Look at it this way, Stephen. I've no interest in those television soaps your mother likes to watch. The winter nights can be very long. I don't want to take up golf or card playing. There's little on the box to interest me. I enjoy a quiet chat and a drink in the snug. Then I come home and have a little read."

"Alcohol has ruined many a life," she says.

"Don't concern yourself about it, Julia. I'll go down to the pub for a couple of hours every night, and that's all there is to it. Do you want a lift, Stephen, or do you fancy taking your own car?"

Stephen smiles. "Hang on while I finish here. I told some of the guys I might meet up with them tonight."

"Give us a shout when you're ready."

Stephen's just thirty, but Julia treats him like an eighteen-year-old. Matt guesses that she will put pressure on Stephen to stay in the house. She'll suggest that it's too late to go to the village or complain about being left on her own.

Stephen comes down to Matt's office. He looks tense. "She's annoyed I'm heading out tonight," he says glumly. "She's going on about hardly ever seeing me."

"Tell her we'll be back in an hour or so. She'll want to watch her soaps on the TV and then she'll have to see the news. There won't be much talk while they're on. We'll be back soon after. It's as close as makes no difference."

Stephen has already gone to the back porch to fetch his jacket. Matt hears him telling Julia he'll be back after the news.

"There was no call for you to interfere," she says when Matt enters the kitchen. "He was quite happy to stay at home before you spoke up."

"What harm does it do, Julia? He wants to see his pals. It's seldom enough they all turn up on the same weekend."

"It's not asking much to have him stay in. It's not often we see him."

This is how they wage war with each other over their children. She always has an agenda that he tries to save them from. She's still angling for one of the sons to take over the farm. She always said it was unnecessary to educate each boy beyond the Leaving Certificate. Once, when Stephen was in his first year at university, Matt overheard her suggest to him that his father was disappointed the boy showed no interest in the farm.

"He may do as he pleases," he'd said, emerging from his office. "Son, you go and get your education. I never got a chance so I won't deprive you of yours."

She held a hand to her throat as if recovering from a fright. "Sure, if he takes the farm, there's no need to waste three or four years clocking up some degree he'll never use."

"Do you want the farm, Stephen?" he asked, and saw the answer in the boy's dumb misery.

"There's no way he wants it," he said. "What's more, he's entitled to his feelings."

Later that night Julia came into Matt's bedroom. She stood at the door and said, "What sort of fool are you? They're all saying what an eejit you were not to keep him at home and train him in. You'll regret this education. He'll think he's too good for the place if you give him too much scope."

"Keep him under wraps, you mean? Force the farm on him? He'd resent it later. It has to be a free choice."

"You and your nonsense about choice. What say had you in the matter? Did it make any difference? Wasn't it good enough for you?" she said, talking quickly, almost shouting. "It gave you a livelihood and a good life. Why throw it all away? And what was the point of all those years building it up?"

"They're all good questions, aren't they, Julia? Tell me if you ever figure out the answers."

She turned on her heel and went into her own bedroom.

He lay in the bed thinking about it that night. Unlike most of Matt's contemporaries, his children could stay in Ireland, find work, and live in their country. They weren't labeled "export only" and cast off. He remembered the boys in his own class, few of them getting any sort of proper tutoring, the majority of them hauled out of school at fourteen by their parents, many emigrating to the States or Britain, and one or two to Canada. Only three out of an original class of thirty-two finished second-level education.

A decade later he still thinks he was right to give Colum and Stephen opportunities, even if it means the farm will be put up for sale after his and Julia's deaths. "Come on, Stephen, chop, chop," he says. "We'd better hit the big smoke."

He reverses the car out of the garage and Stephen hops in. The car lights illuminate the nearby road. He goes gently to save the car's suspension from potholes in the tarmacadam. "Was she on about the farm again?" he asks.

"She mentioned it, yes. She doesn't feel the same as you about it."

"And never will. I was forced into this life, son. Maybe, if I'd come to it of my own volition, I'd have been happier. I'm not saying I was miserable, but I would have liked to have finished my schooling."

"You're self-taught, Dad, and well read. I work with people who know less than you, and that's at third level. I'm not joking!"

"But I might have done something else. Brendan was the favorite to take over the farm, but he had other ideas."

"The way you tell it, he went into the priesthood to escape Granny. Didn't he leave his order after her death?"

"Before she died. He never told her."

"What!"

Matt sighs. "Your grandmother was what's called a domestic tyrant. When someone made a stand against her, it was done indirectly. We discovered that Brendan had opted out of the priesthood when he made it clear that he wouldn't be officiating at your grandmother's funeral."

"And what did he do after?"

"Lived in cheap digs in Dublin and worked his way through an arts degree. He ended up a teacher, like Ellen. She's living in the village these days, come back to the old sod. Have you come across her?"

"Not unless she ventures into the pool room in Murphy's. That's usually where I hang about."

After a protracted silence, Stephen says, "You know it's unlikely that either Colum or I will opt for the farm, don't you, Dad? You understand. We're settling into our lives."

Matt stops the car outside Hegarty's, pulls out a packet of cigarettes, and lights one. He inhales deeply. "Why do you think I invested so much in your education? Because I never got the chance, and I didn't want either of you to end up in the trap I found myself in. Your mother's all agitated about succession and tradition but, not to put too fine a point on it, I couldn't give a monkey's." He throws a wry look Stephen's way. "Don't worry about it, son. *Que sera sera,* eh? It'll be a nice nest egg in years to come. You could make a packet out of selling on to developers. What else is going to happen to land with farming going down the tubes?"

"Doesn't it make you sad to think that way, Dad?"

"What's sad? I'm beyond sad, son." He exhales smoke on a shuddering sigh. "Anyway, it's all economics now, isn't it? You should know that. Ways of living, communities, values, people, none of that matters any more. We're all being sold on."

Stephen shifts uneasily in the passenger seat. "Don't write anything off yet," he says. "If I were to marry . . . it's different when you've children to rear. Your priorities change."

Matt looks amused. "Throwing me a bone, son? You're a terror for excavating. Stop digging. Let it lie." He opens his door and nods toward the pub. "I'll be in there. If you decide to stay on in Murphy's, give us a shout."

Stephen gives a snort of laughter. "You know that's not an option, Dad. Meet you in about an hour."

Saturday night merges into Sunday and the day passes at a galloping pace. All too soon Stephen will have to leave. In the early hours of Monday morning, Matt comes down in his dressing gown to see him off. Stephen plans to break the journey with a stop for breakfast.

Matt watches the dark swallow up the taillights of the car as it turns onto the road. The house feels as cold and lonely as a heath as he pads through the kitchen in his slippers on his way back to bed.

Julia passes Ellen on her way out of the store. "Hello, Ellen," she says.

"Hello, Julia."

Julia sits into the car and drives off in the direction of home.

"Your uncle's wife is a very close woman, nearly impossible to get to know," Terry confides. "How do you get on with her?"

"She's quiet," Ellen says diplomatically.

"There's a story there."

"There's always a story, Terry." No doubt there is, but Ellen doesn't want to hear it.

"I'll tell you regardless," Terry says, as though it goes against her nature. "Years ago your uncle was great with another woman. There was a big bust-up, and she ups and marries another. Next thing Matt's walking down the aisle with Julia. Did you know that?"

Ellen feels Terry's eyes on her. "No, I didn't." No point in pretending otherwise.

"Your uncle was a bit of a lad in his youth, a real charmer, had all the women trotting after him."

Ellen dips her head to hide her expression. "You live and learn," she says. "You never know who people will end up with." Why *did* he marry tight-lipped Julia? "Who's this other woman?" she asks.

"She's a nice person, but she's had tragedy in her life, terrible tragedy. She comes down for Mass every day."

Ellen knows that Terry is itching to tell her about the tragedy, but she gathers up her bags and makes for the door. "See you tomorrow," she says, brandishing a smile like a shield.

When she reaches her house, she finds a message from her

mother on the answering machine. Kitty has returned from her trip to Italy and is off to London for two weeks.

Ellen sighs and rings Kitty. "You're traveling a lot these days, Mum. When are you coming down to see me?"

"Oh, that place gives me the shivers. I can never relax there," Kitty says. "Why don't you come to Dublin and see my new apartment?"

"I'll be up soon." Ellen doesn't tell her mother that her nickname in the village is "The Duchess" because of her infamous grand ways.

Three

O
N THURSDAY EVENINGS they drive to Killdingle to do the shopping. Matt pushes the trolley up and down the supermarket aisles and Julia fills it. He has little interest in any of the items. Occasionally, she consults him about a purchase, and he'll usually say, "Whatever you like" or "Take it if you want it," but mostly it is she who decides. He carries the shopping bags out to the boot of the car. On this particular outing, on the journey home, she asks if he'll drive her to the local hospital the following morning. "I'm being admitted for tests," she says.

It's the first mention of this. "Nothing serious, I hope."

"I've been feeling under par for a while now and suffering from stomach pains."

In a display worthy of her, he says nothing for a while. He's trying to remember if he noticed anything different of late. Then, "I'm sure it's nothing to worry about."

"How can you know that?" she snaps.

He sneaks a look at her profile and, sure enough — but it's probably his suggestibility — she looks thinner in the face. He allows himself the luxury of imagining her being absent from his life, of a void in the space she occupies, of there being no need to contend with her.

"Perhaps you have an ulcer," he says eventually, for the sake of making a comment.

"Maybe that's all it is." Does he imagine her turning in his direction? Does he feel her gaze on his face? He won't place a hand on her hand and feel her withdraw it from his grasp. Words and silences are what lie between them now. He looks resolutely ahead, his hands resting lightly on the steering wheel, watching the beam from the car's headlights shine on hedgerows and ditches, lighting them up like a scene from a film. As the images flick by, he feels his body grow numb, but underlying this sensation is a growing excitement. He wills himself not to look at her for fear she'll see and understand his feelings.

It's only when he reaches home and walks into the house that he realizes he has the place to himself. Except for the time Julia left home for a fortnight to nurse her dying mother, or the few days she spent in hospital after each of the boys was born, she has always been an uncompromising presence in his life.

She has left a casserole on the hob for dinner the next day. Like everything she makes, it will be competent but unexciting. Eating her food is a deadening experience; the taste buds remain untitillated, the appetite unsatisfied. He has always marveled at how she never mastered the art of cooking.

Julia always guards the fridge, cooker, and sink like a terrible Medusa, her frizzy hair rising if anyone dares to approach them. Matt finds it strange to be free to open cupboards, and to look into the fridge to see what he might find. He takes out some bacon, sausages, and eggs, fills the kettle and switches it on, places a pan on the hob, cooks up a fry, butters bread, and makes tea.

Without her presence, without her particular denseness or rigidity, he finds himself talking to some cartoon version of him and her as he eats. "There now, Julia," he says, "take it easy, would you? It's just chewing. It's not a crime." Or he turns to her place at the table and says, "Nothing wrong with reading at the table. It isn't as if we ever talk."

He's watching some late night film and has dozed off when the phone rings. The newspaper falls to the ground as he gets to his feet to answer the call. His reading glasses slide down his nose, where they perch precariously. It's his wife's sister, Mona, asking if he'll drive her in to see Julia the following day.

"You think she'll require that?" he says a little lamely, realizing that, left to his own devices, it would never occur to him to visit his wife. She didn't mention anything about expecting him. He had deposited her at the door of the ward and anticipated a phone call to summon him to collect her.

"Sure, you have to visit. It's awful to be in hospital if nobody calls," Mona says. Her voice is as sharp as her sister's when she's annoyed, although he has formed the opinion that she's more yielding than Julia.

He waves goodbye to some of his anticipated time alone. There's little point in offering resistance. He'll be worked on and worn down. "Right so, when do you want to go in to see her?"

"When's visiting?"

He has to admit that he hasn't a clue, and then waits while she goes off to ask her family if they know the times. He hears her footsteps recede and tap-tap back again on the linoleum floor in their hall. Mona tells him tartly that he may pick her up after tea. He puts the phone down realizing that he has been managed again.

From then on he visits his wife every evening, cottons on to what the form is by paying attention to what other patients receive. He brings in whatever she needs, a fresh nightdress, a cordial or fizzy drink, some grapes. It's a quiet time on the farm and he has become a dab hand at shopping, cooking, and laundry.

Sometimes he brings a magazine, usually one suggested to him by a shopkeeper. Magazines are almost her only reading matter. He hardly ever sees her look at a national newspaper, except to peruse the deaths column. International news is of no interest to her. He guesses that she has only the haziest idea of what goes on in the world. He wonders what politicians she votes for in general elections, as he has never heard her express a political opinion of any force. In that respect she's a chameleon, echoing whatever's being said at any given time. Any books she ever bought were textbooks from school or university lists, or inappropriate books that, because of their titles or the wheedling talk of a shop assistant, she had decided would be useful for the boys' "education." She was ambitious for her sons, but her ideas on education were a mystery to Matt for years until he finally concluded that she regarded it as a process or contrivance that had to be endured in order to render a person employable. The tools of that engagement, the books, were encumbrances that could be disposed of when the desired outcome — the requisite certificate, diploma, or degree — was achieved.

Thus their younger son, Stephen, discovered — much to his annoyance — that she had stripped his bedroom of posters and books shortly after he graduated from university. Not only had she thrown out his textbooks, but also his football and music magazines and his collection of thrillers. When he broached the subject with her, she dismissed his anger, claiming she had cleared out "all those books" that had "clogged up the space" in his room. Something in her craved this emptiness, this absence.

Matt keeps his reading material locked in his office for fear she will sweep it all away and consign everything to the fire or waste bin. He gives strict instructions that she isn't to throw out anything from his desk or bookcase lest it relates to farm accounts. On many occasions she has asked him to "go through" the books and to "clear out the rubbish" and he has always ignored the plea.

She does, however, have a fondness for the *Southern Chronicle*, the local newspaper, but curiosity and envy fuel her interest. She scours the pages for photographs of events or personalities and uses many of the stories as fodder for gossip and snide remarks. She believes anything she reads, and it's a fruitless exercise to try to persuade her that some of the reports are biased or unreliable.

So, when he brings her one of those magazines — with their baffling mix of interviews with celebrities, knitting patterns, recipes, gardening and household tips, photos of the homes of movie stars, quota of romantic fiction, readers' letters, and comments — he waits to see if she will pick it up and look at it. For the most part, except for necessary practical exchanges, she ignores him and watches the television in the ward, and he sits beside her in silence for up to an hour.

When the novelty of bringing her magazines wears off, it feels uncomfortably like a parody of gift giving and, as she seems indifferent to anything from him, he arrives empty handed one evening. She appears not to notice.

Ellen is visiting the house at night. The plastered walls and cement floors are drying out. The last of the workmen are finishing the electrics, and the understairs toilet has to be plumbed in. Every downstairs room is strewn with builders' equipment. Moisture in the air causes the windows to steam up. The house is cold because the central heating system has yet to be tested and turned on. She has ordered oil from a local supplier.

It's irksome as well as pleasurable to call in to the property. She enjoys wandering about, but she's itching to have the place to herself. Jerry, the builder, has promised that he and his crew will be out within a week. At night she claims ownership of a part of her territory. She has plugged in the old fridge and kettle, reinstated the table and chairs in the extended kitchen, and colonized the living area with crockery, cutlery, a jar of instant coffee, and packets of tea and biscuits. A rickety electric heater makes feeble efforts to disperse stickiness in the air. She has no kitchen as such, only the plumbed-in old sink unit and the ancient and partially functional electric cooker.

The week Julia is away for tests, Matt takes to popping in on his way back from evening visits to the hospital. She'll hear the rap of his knuckles on the window and she'll either rush to open the door or call out, "It's on the latch." They'll sit down in their coats, first to a cup of coffee for her and tea for him, and then she'll produce the bottle and fetch glasses from the windowsill. In her mind they resemble a raddled old couple in pre–central heating days, slipping into an illicit sheebeen pub in some remote part of the west of Ireland to drink *poitín*. All they need is the packet of Woodbines, the stale smell of unwashed bodies and clothes, companionable silence broken by an occasional conversational exchange, the sheen of ancient mirrors on the wall, the crackle and glow of a turf and wood fire, and the soothing dark of stained pitch pine furniture with its tincture of dust.

She's not given to daily consumption of spirits but drinks to keep Matt company. She wonders how a man once so disciplined and abstemious has come to rely so heavily on alcohol. She's convinced that not a day passes but he imbibes one, two, or more drinks. He doesn't drink to excess — she has never witnessed him drunk — but it's an important ritual for him. Until the alcohol appears, he sits uneasily in his seat, fidgeting with anything at hand and hunching his shoulders. His relief when she produces the bottle and glasses is palpable. He goes almost as far as to smile as he lifts the glass and slugs back the first few gulps of the dark liquid. When the alcohol starts to take effect, she can see the tightness in his stooped shoulders loosen. He stretches out his limbs, crosses his feet at the ankles, and is disposed to talk.

"How's Julia?" she might ask. It takes courage to mention the topic as Julia is almost a taboo subject with him.

And he will reply, "Much the same," "a little better," or "not so good tonight," until one evening he announces, "She came home this afternoon."

Ellen takes this as an indication that Julia is well, until he lets slip that chemotherapy sessions are to commence in a few weeks' time. "I thought she was in for tests?" she says.

"That's what she went in for, but something showed up on a scan, I think, and they extended her stay. They wanted to explore that, do more tests and take a few biopsies. She's at home to recover and let everything heal before she starts treatment."

Ellen decides against asking what type of cancer Julia is suffering from — she suspects stomach — as she's fairly certain that Matt will skirt the issue. He can be infuriatingly vague. "So, will she have to go back into hospital?"

For a moment, from his look, she thinks that he's going to tell her he hasn't a notion, but then he says, "Once every three weeks she'll go in for a session of chemo."

"They must think she has a chance."

He shakes his head. "It's cancer of the pancreas and it's very invasive. It's gone into the liver — that's why she was yellow. Mona thought she had jaundice. She'll be getting what's called palliative chemotherapy. It could improve her quality of life, or extend her time a bit, and it gives her peace of mind. She feels that something's being done."

"I should pay a visit."

"No, no, she doesn't want visitors, except immediate family."

"Do Stephen and Colum know?"

"I've told them — and she says — that there's no need for them to come down every weekend. It's not as if they can do any good," he says despondently.

"The prognosis isn't good then."

He looks irritated. "No, but who knows? You hear stories of condemned people surviving, and those expected to survive shuffling off."

"Julia didn't object to you coming out tonight?"

A frown indicates that her questions are on sufferance. "Mona came over. The two of them are as thick as thieves, so I left them to it. They don't want me about."

He's always itching to move away from the topic of Julia and her health, and a lighter note enters his voice as he relates this or that story, scandal, or controversy, as if they are treats that he has stored away to reveal or allude to during his visit to Ellen. In turn, she fills him in on the tittle-tattle of her encounters with others. He wouldn't dream of telling Ellen that she's a comfort to him. She wouldn't admit that, but for his visits, her days would be solitary.

"Are you a Mass goer?" he asks one night.

"You've seen me at church."

"Yes, but did you go when you lived in Dublin?"

She takes a sip of whiskey. "Of course."

"Tell the truth and shame the devil. I'd be surprised if you went at all."

She regards him through narrowed eyes. "Here it's expected."

"Lots of them don't bother. The church is half-empty of a Saturday night and it's almost deserted at the Sunday Masses, except in summer when people are home or visiting."

"I suppose I go for social reasons, hoping someone will talk to me, and generally somebody does."

"And they know who you are?"

"They know that I'm one of the Hugheses. Yes, I get lots of small talk."

"You still haven't given a proper answer."

She shrugs and looks away.

"I'm not going to strike you down if I don't like your response," he says.

"It's a generational thing. It's difficult to know what to say to you."

"I know what's wrong," he says, topping up his glass. "You can remember the days when it was dangerous to give a straight answer, when everybody had to dissemble. You think you have to fob me off, don't you? Amn't I right?"

"You think you're the only one can ask questions," she complains. "Are you religious?"

"That's a good one. Am I religious?" He sits back in his chair and regards her. "What do you think?"

"If I knew, would I be asking?"

"If neither of us answers," he muses, "we have a stalemate. I asked first, why don't you answer first?"

"I'm not at all religious," she says crossly. "I believe in some sort of god but I can't stand the church, that is, the organization. When I lived at home with Mum, I went, but after that no, except for work-related stuff. Here, it's the done thing."

He nods. "About what I expected you to say."

"And you?"

"Me? It's so deeply ingrained, such a habit, that it would be difficult to break away from it now. It was pounded into us when we were children. We got it at home. We got it at school. There was no escaping it. Life was steeped in rituals and procedures. There's part of me attached to some of the ceremonials, but do I believe?" He takes a rhetorical pause. "I have to say I reject a lot of it," he continues. "You straddle different generations, mine who got roped in because there was no avoiding it, and the young ones nowadays who couldn't care less. They never go near Mass, unless for a wedding or funeral. For some people my age, religion explains the meaning of life. That doesn't apply to me. I stumble when confronted by certain articles of belief." That habit of reticence and concealment is so embedded in him that this is the first time he has trusted her with any revelation.

She wants to match his openness. "I've shrugged off a good deal of it," she says carefully. "Subversive teachers helped to feed the doubts — but parts, the sexual morality — which I know is rubbish — dog me, can't shrug it off so easily."

"Right." The bemused expression on his face makes her think that she has taken openness a degree beyond what he can tolerate. "That's just one example," she ventures.

"No, no, that's obviously a large part of it," he says gamely. "When they've got you by the balls, your heart and mind will follow!"

"I came in on the tail end of that stuff being taught, but it's all out the window now."

"Right," he says guardedly.

"And I think we'd better change the subject," she declares with a laugh.

"What would your father make of all this, I wonder?"

"You knew him. I haven't a notion."

"He told me he left the priests because he couldn't take the celibate lifestyle. When he came across your mother working in the university library — she had just qualified as a librarian — he laid siege to her. She was a looker, very well got up, which made a change. The clothes people wore then were very drab."

The doorbell rings and they start. "Are you expecting someone?"

"Damn," she says. "Just when it was getting interesting."

"You'd better answer in case it's important."

She can't imagine who it might be. Except for Terry and Bart's tour of the house, her only visitor has been the postman. Suddenly she wonders if Mona has sent down for Matt and hurries out. When she opens the door, a stranger, a tall young man, faces her. She has to crane her head to look up at him. In addition to his strong physical presence, she's immediately aware of a distinctive characteristic, like a surfeit of energy or an electrical current.

"Saw a light," he says, and extends a hand.

"And you are?" she says, holding back.

"Didn't your builder tell you to expect me? I'm Eugene O'Brien, the kitchen maker."

"Oh," she says, remembering. "Jerry said you might call."

He grins. "Now, will you shake hands?"

She is almost afraid that his touch will carry a charge. Then, sheepishly, she places her hand in his. "Sorry."

He steps in. "That little house you're renting was in darkness so I chanced my luck here when I saw the light. God bless all here," he says when he enters the kitchen and sees Matt at the kitchen table.

"Do you know Eugene?" she asks Matt.

He nods. "He made a kitchen dresser for our place the year before last."

Eugene extends a hand and Matt shakes it. "Am I interrupting? I can come back at a more convenient time." He's whippet thin and, now that she can see him properly, he looks ridiculously young. He's relaxed, and exudes a freshness and vigor that's very engaging. She hadn't anticipated the kitchen man being attractive.

"I'd better make use of you now you're here," she says. She has learned from experience that local tradesmen are difficult to source. It's tricky to get them to call to a house, and even trickier to get a starting date out of them. They make promises they have no intention of keeping. Her builder has flagged this man as the best at his job, but she's not prepared to take any chances.

"Well, I'll be off," Matt says abruptly.

"Don't go," she urges, reluctant to lose him. "This shouldn't take long."

"I'll only hold up proceedings. You'll be yapping on about whether to use this wood or that wood and the look of things, and I've no truck with that talk."

"Eugene just has to make a few measurements, then go off to make a plan and work out an estimate. Isn't that right, Eugene?"

"Well, I'll need to measure the space exactly. Matt's right. I can't give you a plan or an estimate unless I know what style of kitchen we're talking about. You'll have to give me some guidelines."

"That's one area where I don't have an opinion," Matt says. He finishes his drink and gets to his feet. "Buy a sink unit at the hardware shop, find a place for it, plumb it in, wire in a cooker and a fridge. Bob's your uncle and that's your kitchen," he adds as a parting shot.

"There's more than that to it, Matt," she grumbles as she escorts him to the front door. "Will I see you tomorrow night?"

He smiles as he puts his cap on his head. "Depends on whether Mona calls over. She's my escape ticket."

"I'll expect you."

Eugene hands her one end of a measuring tape and directs her to stand at the edge of this and that wall while he extends and retracts the tape a few times. When he turns his head toward her, the light catches his features at a particular angle, and suddenly she notices the thin, faded scar running from temple to chin on one side of his face. All that remains is an indentation and a difference in the pigmentation of the skin. She draws in her breath.

"Didn't you spot that till now?"

"What?"

"My calling card."

"It's very faint, but how did you get it?"

"Years ago I was ambushed by a gang on my way home late one night, and they were just getting stuck into me when a taxi came round the corner. The taxi saved me, and the driver took me to hospital."

"That's awful. Was it . . . How did it affect you?"

"Was it traumatic, do you mean?" He shakes his head. "It needed stitches. I was a bit nervous for a few weeks, slow to venture out on my own, but I got over that. There's a lot you can shrug off when you're seventeen."

"I'm sure you could have it treated cosmetically."

He snorts. "There was a time when the look of it bothered me, but now I think I'd miss it if it weren't there."

"It's not that noticeable. I don't think it'll affect your prospects."

"Prospects? That's a word rarely heard nowadays. I thought it was women who worried about their prospects."

"Stop thinking in stereotypes," she scolds.

He watches her quizzically. "That's something I can't be accused of." He closes the tape measure, jots down a few figures in a little notebook he keeps in his shirt pocket, paces up and down and roams about the kitchen, as if getting the feel of it.

"So Matt is your uncle," he says suddenly.

"He's the only one I have. My mother's an only child."

"I didn't realize you had connections here."

She laughs. "Will having connections improve the price?"

He looks straight at her, and she's disconcerted by the clarity of his gaze. "You'd never know," he says, as if he means something else. He has presence, what's called charisma. Strictly speaking, he couldn't be dubbed handsome. His features are sharp but regular, his eyes a dark brown, his nose slightly prominent, and his chin solid but not excessive. With the exception of the slight distortion of the scar tissue, he has good skin, which reminds her of her own blotchy complexion. She estimates that he's probably eight to ten years younger than she.

She feels exposed, sensitized to him, as if stripped of a protective layer of skin. It's probably the whiskey. She hopes that he's unaware of the impact he's having on her.

As he jots down a few additional notes, she notices his elegant hands. He has the long slender fingers of a musician.

"So, what have you in mind for this kitchen?"

She laughs wryly. "I haven't a notion. I hoped you might help me out. You know what works."

"Well, for example, if you're going for wood, do you want hard or soft wood?"

"Hard. I know that much."

He grins. "That's a start. Firstly, I'd suggest putting the sink by the window. The hob would work in the corner and . . ." He pauses. "Look, why don't I draw up a draft plan and base the estimate on a few different woods? I'll bring along samples next time. We'll take it from there."

"Jerry said you're particular about your work so that's a great recommendation."

He grins. "That's a lot to live up to. Jerry's a bit of a perfectionist. I'll drop in a rough estimate in a few days. It'll be reasonable. It won't be city prices. Ask anyone about my work and they'll tell you it's good. Okay so?" He rams his notebook into his shirt pocket and grins. "That's it for now."

"I'll see you out."

"Right. We'll talk again soon."

The house feels deprived of his presence when he's gone. She clears the glasses from the table and rinses them under the tap. The window panes need cleaning. Everywhere needs cleaning. Each time she sweeps the floors more dust descends. Jerry has told her that it will take a year for the newly built parts of the house to dry out completely.

It's a Saturday night and suddenly she decides that she can't face the pokey bedroom and gruesome bathroom in the rented house. The builders won't disturb her on a Sunday morning.

None of the upstairs lights is working. She carries a basin of cold water up in the dark and goes down again for a torch, matches, and a small old paraffin heater. On her third journey, she makes up a hot whiskey and fills a hot-water bottle she found in a cupboard under the sink.

In the bathroom the white of the new toilet and shower unit gleams in the moonlight. Her illuminated reflection flickers in the mirror above the sink. From the window she can see the shadowed backyard. She washes her teeth, rinses her mouth, and spits out the water.

She carries the whiskey and hot-water bottle into her bedroom. The moon ducks behind a cloud and her eyes take a while to adjust to the darkness. The floorboards are bare, the windows are without curtains, and the bed is a silhouette. She lifts the dust sheets carefully and places them in a corner of the room. The streetlight isn't working but it doesn't matter. It's all right. Everything's all right. She knows her way by touch. She knows every inch of this house.

Beatrice lays her buckets under the tap on the uneven cement floor. From the open door behind her comes the *chug-chug* of the milking machines, snuffling snorts and occasional moans from the cows.

The sleeves of her jacket are spattered with dirt. Her boots leave tracks of mud on the floor. Outside, cow dung intersperses with pools of water, making a patchwork pattern in the sludge. She's indifferent to the strong smell. Over thirty years of living with that odor has immunized her against it.

Behind the run of buildings is the hay barn. In the weeks and months following John's death, she used to become almost physically sick if she had occasion to visit this place. She would torment herself by wondering what his last moments were like. A dull pain would suffuse her body if she tried to imagine what he might have been thinking about as he smoked his final cigarette, what convinced him to pull the trigger, and how long it took him to die.

When their third child was born, she was delighted to have a son. John had been full of promise as a child, a handsome, cheerful boy, at ease with himself and always willing to help with the farm chores. In his teenage years his vulnerability became apparent. When the school summoned Jack and her to a meeting, they learned that he'd been skipping classes on a regular basis. Teachers had caught him coming out from town pubs or gaming halls on more than one occasion. That encounter exposed John's disastrous academic performance and that he didn't have a single friend in the school. *"You half-wit,"* his father shouted when John arrived home that day. *"What sort of idiot have I as a son?"* He didn't speak to John for months after that. And he didn't speak to Beatrice for a number of weeks. He blamed her for any failings in their children. *"How come you weren't on top of this?"* he demanded. *"You're responsible for rearing them and you've fallen down on the job!"* She had given up trying to answer his accusations and steeled herself for another of his campaigns against her. Silence and patience were her allies. Reproaches and recriminations only fueled his antagonism.

John swaggered about, deaf to all Beatrice's entreaties to him to talk, but she suspected that something in him had broken. Because the second youngest in the family was the least capable of her children, she held a special place for him in her heart, always wishing she could put his world to rights.

John was thirty-three when he killed himself. He had walked out of school on his fifteenth birthday, taken a job in one of the milk processing factories outside Cork, and worked there for more than a decade. His older sisters, Paula and Niamh, qualified as a solicitor and a doctor. They went abroad to find work, and eventually married and settled in England. The youngest, Andy, left home abruptly after a clash with his father escalated into a row and forced the cancellation of a meal to celebrate his graduation from Cork University.

Following Andy's departure and Jack's death after a major stroke, it was left to Beatrice to tell John that the farm was his to work. He attended classes at an agricultural college but never took to farming. He neglected the paperwork and struggled with the day-to-day organization and upkeep of the farm. For years Beatrice had to witness his failures. Soon after his father's death he began a steady line with a pretty young nurse whom Beatrice thought might be the making of him, but he dithered over asking her to marry him. The woman gave up on him and married a returned emigrant who owned and managed a highly successful restaurant in a local town. John became even more remote. Beatrice dared not speak to him at times.

When Lily's husband, Damien, recommended Simon for the job of farm manager — the deal struck at the kitchen table shortly after John's death — she knew that she would have to find a way of coexisting with the barn. She has developed a knack of not looking at it by directing her eyes to a point above the structure and ensuring that her gaze never lingers on it.

The weather is mixed in an Irish fashion. A gentle breeze ruffles her hair. The sun shines. Moistness mists the air. Her gaze follows the contours of the landscape. On days like this, even through a gossamer film of rain, it's pleasurable to let her eyes run along the rim of the hills, over the sharp incline of the mountain ridges, and deep into the gully of the valley. She can make out faraway houses and cottages nestling in the steep hills. The hazy sun reflects off a distant metal roof. She imagines the buildings peopled by families, although she knows that those farms are probably in as much trouble as the ones on this side of the valley.

Simon opens a gate to the backyard and herds the cows away from the buildings. Soon it'll be time for them to winter indoors, but they're having a remarkable run of mild weather this October. Simon whistles as he runs after them. "Hoo-hup! Hup hup," he shouts. The collie barks at the cows, and they pick up their pace, cantering into the field, sliding across mud, slithering and skidding into one another.

She rinses the buckets, scrubs them with disinfectant, and hangs them from hooks on the wall of the shed. Then she hoses her boots and the floor with water, steps into a disinfectant tray, turns off the tap, and all is stilled. She hears the silence. It vibrates along her body. A drip from the tap explodes into a bucket. In the distance a cow lows.

Simon returns. She hears him flicking switches, followed by the clang of a metal gate. The automatic scraper bursts into action and Simon comes into the shed carrying more buckets. "I'll finish up here," he says. She can just about hear him over the noise of the scraper. He's different when he's working. No jokes, no winks, no teasing asides, his expression fixed, his eyes absorbed. She likes this serious side.

"I'll put supper on," she says.

"See you in a while, Bee," he calls after her. *Call me Beatrice* she wants to say. Simon's penchant for abbreviations is almost his only flaw.

In the porch at the rear of the house, she hauls off her boots, pads across the kitchen in a pair of old woolen socks, and runs upstairs to change out of her work clothes. Back in the kitchen, she pokes and stirs up the range and busies herself setting the table, slicing bread, boiling the kettle, and warming the frying pan. She turns on the radio to listen to the six o'clock news, cracks eggs into a bowl, and chops onion and bacon to cook.

Twenty minutes later she goes out into the lower yard and rings the old school bell to alert Simon that she's about to put the meal on the table. He hurries down to the house, removes his boots in the porch, comes into the kitchen, and washes his hands at the sink.

He sits at the table, snatches a slice of bread from the breadboard, and butters it.

"I heard Julia Hughes is out of hospital."

"I wonder how she is."

"Not so good. She's starting treatment, but I think they don't hold out much hope." He takes a mouthful of omelet. "Spot on, Bee. No one can best you in the cooking stakes."

She laughs. "It's nice to have someone about to appreciate it."

"I hit the jackpot, Bee, when I landed here. You must be the best cook in the county."

"No need to exaggerate."

"I'm serious. Lily Traynor is your only rival and, to my way of thinking, you have the edge on her. Your strawberry pavlova is better than hers."

"Lily has won awards for her cooking, Simon. I don't think I'm in the same league."

"You never put in for those awards. That's all." He gives her a knowing look. "Now, just between us two, old Julia was a disaster in the culinary department. It'd put you in bad form. I don't understand how her family tolerated it."

"God, Simon, where's your Christian charity? It's not up to us to judge people. Julia could be dying."

"I know, I know. Just an observation."

"And less of your 'old Julia,' if you don't mind. She's younger than me."

"Well, she never looked it. Age is just a number, Bee. It's attitude, attitude and attitude that counts. Some people are never young."

"In Julia's house, when she was growing up, the servants did the cooking. Her mother didn't know how to boil an egg."

"You'd think she'd have picked up some know-how over the years."

With a shake of her head, Beatrice asks, "What did Julia ever do to you? You really have it in for her."

"She didn't approve of you taking me on. She made that clear."

"Oh, you had words, did you? That's not surprising. It's just Julia's thing about blood and local connections. It's all family with her. She's very strong on that."

"I hate that primitive stuff about bloodlines. She's no one to talk. Neither of her sons would touch the farm."

To change the subject, Beatrice asks, "Is Angie coming up? Are you two going out?"

"Not tonight. I'm going out on my own."

She collects the dishes, scrapes off surplus food, and stacks them on the draining board as she runs the hot water. "I haven't seen Angie in a while. Did you have a falling out?"

Simon throws her an impatient look. "These things run their course," he says.

Her heart stutters a beat as she squirts washing liquid into the hot water and begins the washup. "You *have!* What a shame. I'm very fond of Angie, as you know."

"Well, you mightn't be seeing much of her from now on," he says in a closed-down fashion.

"You're not serious."

He says nothing, but the tilt of his jaw is stubborn. There's a coldness to his manner that she never noticed before. It surprises her. She has always taken him for an easy-going man. Up to this, there has never been a cross word between them.

She wipes her hands on the kitchen towel and turns to face him.

He looks forbidding, hostile almost. "Sorry, Simon. It's none of my business. I'll say no more."

"No harm done," he says abruptly. He drums his fingers on the table as if playing a tune on a piano. When he straightens up, he throws her a combative look. She returns the look with a smile. He starts to hum and slams the door after him as he exits the room.

Four

LTHOUGH THE DAY is bright and the November sunshine looks inviting, it's no longer possible to sit out in Paula's back garden. The chilly air and shortening days have forced people to retreat into their houses. Beatrice visualizes Simon clipping hedges about the farm. He will have brought in the cows to winter them, she thinks.

Paula and Niamh are in the kitchen preparing Sunday dinner. Their husbands are watching one of the sports channels, and the three children have disappeared upstairs, no doubt to torment themselves with a game on the Play Station. She listens for sounds of discord but all is quiet.

Beatrice is banned from the kitchen-cum-dining room, and she's flicking through the lifestyle section of one of the English Sunday newspapers. Although the gathering is in her honor, and even though the English sons-in-law are attentive to her needs, she is bored. She would far prefer to be chopping, cooking, and chatting in the kitchen with her daughters, but she understands that this is their idea of giving her a treat.

Niamh appears at the door. "Here is where you're hiding," she says. She joins her mother on the couch and slouches against the backrest. "We're almost ready to go," she announces.

Paula calls the men and rounds up the children. Barry heads for the dining room to sort out the children's drinks. Niamh's husband,

Rob, wanders into the room where she and Beatrice are ensconced. "How's the birthday girl?" he asks in his broad Yorkshire accent, rocking on his heels, a grin on his big square face.

"Bearing up. Keeping the show on the road," Beatrice answers with a smile. With each daughter's marriage, she was disappointed that they had chosen to marry Englishmen. It lessened the possibility of either returning to Ireland. It also meant—or so she thought—that she would never be able to talk to these men as she would to Irishmen. However, once she got past the English accents and the different cultural backgrounds, she became fond of her sons-in-law. They are obliging and courteous, and she hasn't found the gap in understanding between them difficult to bridge. Niamh lives and works in Hull, although the two girls started their careers in London. Were she asked which son-in-law she prefers, she would probably opt for Rob by a short head, because of a more natural affinity between Yorkshire and Irish people. However, she can never forget the support from Barry and Paula at the time of John's death. When the phone call that brought the news came through, Paula rushed home from work and, shortly afterward, Barry arrived and immediately booked tickets to Cork Airport for all of them. After the funeral, Paula and the children stayed on an extra week. She might not have come through that crisis without them.

"Okay, Mam, we're ready for you," Paula says. The grandchildren, Conor, Sheila, and Robert—Robert delighted to be a part of festivities in his aunt's house—lead Beatrice into the dining room to her place at the head of the table. Paula ladles out soup, Beatrice's favorite, red pepper and carrot. The children aren't fussy eaters except for Conor, Paula's eight-year-old, but even he picks up his spoon and tucks in.

Later, when Niamh brings out the birthday cake—a customized Gateau Diane—Beatrice is relieved to see that only six candles have been lit. "One for each decade," Paula says with a grin. Always a little plump, and quite overweight after the births of her children, a dramatic weight loss transformed Paula after the trauma of her brother's death. She became better looking and even seemed taller.

When lunch is over, Barry and Rob load the dishwasher and disappear to watch more football. Beatrice sits at the table with her daughters. Niamh and Rob stayed over the previous night so the house is crowded, but the grandchildren are happily watching videos in the second downstairs reception room, and there is a natural lull after the meal.

"We should make your birthday an annual event," Niamh says. "We don't get together often enough."

"See how we feel next year," Beatrice says. It's not something she admits to, but she's always a little glad to get away after a spell in either of her daughter's houses. She never relaxes enough to fit in properly and suffers a queasy homesickness if parted from the farm for more than a week.

"Imagine, Dad would be seventy-five if he were still alive," Paula says.

"Seventy-five next January," Beatrice says.

"Did the age gap matter?"

"It wasn't a problem. I would have been considered young to be getting married at the time, but he was about average for a man."

"Was it a big romance?" Niamh asks.

Beatrice laughs. "Not as such, although Jack was quite keen."

"And you, were you keen?" Paula asks mischievously.

"I didn't know what I was doing. It was like a dream. A lot of my life was like that, took me by surprise."

There's a long silence in the room, and Beatrice realizes that her daughters probably think that she's referring to John. Or Andy. "Nice surprises, mostly," she says. "Like my children and grandchildren. I've had a good life."

"But Dad was difficult. I don't know how you put up with him," Niamh says. "He was no help."

"He wasn't any different from most men then. Your husbands are a new breed."

"Yeah, part adolescents, part sports fanatics," Paula says with a laugh.

"But much more active as parents," Beatrice says quickly.

"That's true. We wouldn't tolerate what you went through with Dad."

"He wasn't a drunk and he didn't beat me. By the standards of then that was good going. And he had his moments. You two know that." She has often thought that Jack was what used to be called a "good enough" person, possible to get around but limited in ways.

"He was more mean than generous," Niamh says. "I know you say that's because money wasn't plentiful, but he could have been easier on us. And as for what he did to Andy . . ."

"Nothing's perfect," Beatrice says. "I think you have to try to make the best of what you've got."

Their reaction surprises her. "Make the best of it!" screeches Paula. "Can you imagine!"

"That sounds so sad, Mam," Niamh says. "Who'd want to have to do that!"

The builders have ceded control of the house to Ellen. She roams about, prowls through rooms, admires the smooth plasterwork on the ceilings and walls, runs a hand along surfaces, opens, closes, locks, and unlocks the new windows and doors, delights in the numerous power points, and marvels at the sanded and varnished floorboards. She plans decorating schemes, jots down colors for the walls, and wonders how to furnish the rooms. On the upstairs landing, now brightened by a new roof window, she pauses. This is her domain.

She has a bed, a table, and chairs, and some furniture that was worth salvaging from the house. There are four telephone points, each connected and operating. A computer has been ordered. A television has been delivered. It sits in its box in the conservatory. She decides to ring various friends to tell them her news, but the first number she tries is busy and the second connects her to an answering machine. She slams down the phone.

She paces bare floorboards, clatters up and down the stairs, unable to keep still, incapable of relaxing, powered by energy she can't contain. She is diverted repeatedly by this or that feature of the renovations, a child in thrall to a plethora of new toys.

Eventually she finds that she is tired. She is surprised to discover the day's light is fading. She hasn't eaten since morning, and still she has no appetite. In the early hours of the following day she finally falls asleep, and wakes much later to discover that she left all the lights in the house on.

Matt calls — he hasn't seen the house since the big clear-up — and she shows him about. He's unimpressed by the details she's most proud of — the technical aspects of the house — good use of space, maximization of brightness, clever and practical lighting. "What's the use in getting into a lather about all this stuff — a house is a house, that's all," he says dismissively. Almost grudgingly he concedes that the finish on the plasterwork is excellent. He shows no interest whatsoever in the proposed kitchen, lighting a cigarette and inhaling as she tries to explain the outline sketches, exhaling smoke and waving away the plans and asking her how she could possibly imagine he'd ever care about such niceties. "It's women who find those things interesting," he declares. "They're always buying pricey magazines and watching makeover programs on the telly. Why does the appearance of a place matter? Who gives a damn?"

"Don't be a sexist bastard," she chides, but she knows he isn't. She's cast down by his reaction although she tries to make light of it. "I thought you'd be impressed," she confesses. "A lot of thought went into making the place work."

"I can see that it has been well done, but I've no curiosity about the finer points. You're wasting your time trying to stir me up over them," he says. "I'm more interested in function than appearance. I'd be hard put to tell you the colors of the carpets, curtains, and furnishings in my own house."

She's disappointed but perhaps she should have known. His sense of aesthetics extends no further than the books he enjoys reading, the music he appreciates, and the paintings and sculptures he admires. By the standards of his generation, he's a cultured man, widely read, politically aware, and sensitive to cultural matters. Taste is an adjunct to prosperity, she reflects. He grew up in a time when money was in short supply, when basic survival and comfort were important, when the look of something was secondary to its cost.

"I suppose you don't want to drink a celebratory toast?"

"Oh no, I'll drink to it all right. I'll drink to a job well done. Don't expect me to fall in love with it, that's all. *Sláinte is fadshaol*," he says, as he raises his glass and clinks it against hers.

She nods wanly. "Good health." Her enthusiasm for her little palace has suffered a blow. She sips her drink in a subdued fashion, barely able to hold up her end of the conversation.

"They made a fine job of it," he allows as they sit in the extended kitchen. "This room has brightened up nicely. It'll look well when you slap a lick of paint on the walls."

She's finding it difficult to maintain her equilibrium. She hadn't realized quite how dependent she is on his approval, and how she courts it. As if he realizes his gaffe, or senses her despondency, he rouses himself. "I haven't really looked at the place properly," he declares. "It's hard to absorb it all in one go. I'll take another turn about." He redoes the tour of downstairs on his own. She sits at the table and knocks back her drink. She has no intention of being mollified by this pseudo-interest in the restored house. "It's grand. Transformed. It does you proud," he says on his return. "Now, don't be disappointed if I don't bow down and adore the kitchen when it arrives," he jokes.

"You needn't worry. I won't mention it. I won't even draw your attention to it."

"No getting into a huff now! Sure, you'll have to mention it. There's no avoiding that." He holds out his glass for a refill. "Don't expect too much of me these days. I can't see past my nose," he says gruffly.

"I know it's silly of me to be so pleased by the place. It's just the relief of having it finished."

"And being able to live in it. That's great."

"How's Julia?" she asks as she sees him out.

He squirms as if a part of him itches. "She's not getting any better."

"Is she worse?"

"She's not responding well to the chemo. It makes her very sick. They took another scan and it looks as if the cancer's spreading. They may stop the treatment, although they're talking about taking her back in for a blood transfusion."

"If they stop, does it mean they've given up?"

"Washed their hands of her, you mean? Well, yes." He sighs. "There have been all sorts of meetings with consultants and doctors. They suggest placing her in a nursing home or even trying for hospice care, but she won't hear of any of it. She expects to be looked after at home, and Mona has been roped in to help. That's all very well, but Mona has a family, and the youngest boy is still at school. Nevertheless Julia is dead set against hiring nurses. She won't let the palliative care team near her. Says there's no call for them. But there will be need of all these people soon. I can see changes in her every day. She's going to need a lot of looking after, and the farm won't run itself. We won't be able to keep going—how do they put it?—twenty-four seven."

"How long can this go on?"

He throws up his hands in an exasperated gesture. "How long is a piece of string?"

"This must be a very invasive cancer, it's so fast acting."

He massages one of his temples as if trying to rub away a mark. "Ellen, she's dying. Barring miracles, she can't beat this. I'm sick to the back teeth of being told these amazing survival stories—people who confounded the medics—but the odds are against her." A bleak expression hardens his features. "Not that she's ready to die." He makes a face. "When the medics say that she knows her own mind, it's not a compliment. They mean that she's contrary and difficult. She's not making it easy on anybody, least of all herself.

"Those palliative care people," he continues, "they're very keen on the idea of making a good death. They want to ask her if she believes that she will survive. They expect people to face the end and talk about it, but that doesn't square with Julia's frame of mind. She's denying the whole thing. She can't get out of the bed unaided. She has no appetite, even for the liquid stuff, and she's fading away. Nevertheless, the other day she told Mona she was going to beat this!"

"They say that people with a positive frame of mind live longer."

"They say a lot of things, Ellen, and most of it is tripe. There's a medical condition. She's deteriorating. There's no denying that."

"No, I agree. It's grim." She wonders if she dare hug him, but she's fairly certain that he'd rebuff her.

"I'd best be off," he says. "No rest for the wicked."

"Drop in again soon," she says. "I'm willing to lend an ear anytime. You can say whatever you like. I don't mind."

He snorts. "What would I say?"

"Oh, you could give out about things, complain, whinge if you want. That sort of stuff doesn't bother me."

He throws her an incredulous look. "I'm not in the habit of whinging, as you put it, and I don't intend to start now."

"All this buttoning up, the stiff upper lip, doesn't help anybody."

He tilts his head and drags his fingers through his hair. "I'm no good at that sort of talk. You know that." He strides off, his shoulders hunched against the day.

Maureen is already in situ when Ellen reaches the restaurant. "Just as well we're having an early bird," she says. "The à la carte prices are way over the top." It's the best part of three months since they last met, and in the intervening time Maureen has dyed her hair an unbecoming blond. Ellen wonders what Maureen's students make of her new hairstyle. She clamps her mouth shut on a comment.

"Did you bring photos?" Maureen asks. "I'm mad to see this house. I've heard so much about it over the phone."

"How's everyone at work?" Ellen asks.

"I can't believe how the school year is flying. Midterm was over before I realized it had started. You're well out of it, Ellen. What I'd give to be able to take time off like you."

"It's very odd not seeing all of you every day. I'd better get my act together and find part-time work but, honestly, I've been too taken up with the renovations."

"Well, we can't get used to you not being about at break time or lunch. Jane and Nesta send you their love. They want us to meet up for a big night out soon. You should come up and celebrate Jane's birthday in a few weeks. It'll be Christmas before we know it, so don't let it go too long, Ellen. Come up on the Friday, and we'll all hit the town. Will I put your name down for the staff's Christmas dinner?"

"No, no. That'd be really weird. It's too soon to be coming back. But tell Jane and Nesta I miss them every day."

A waitress brings a bottle to the table. "I took a chance on the red, Ellen. You like red, don't you?" The waitress pours a tasting amount of wine into a glass. Maureen brings the glass to her nose and sniffs. "That's fine," she says. "You can pour away." Maureen examines Ellen's photographs in a perfunctory fashion. "The conservatory worked out well. It doesn't have that added-on look, and you've made a good job of the kitchen space. But I'm no good at the visuals. I don't get any idea of the rooms from bare floors and plastered walls. I want to see it when it's furnished and done up." Maureen turns her attention to Ellen and scrutinizes her. "You've perked up!" she declares. "Last time we met, you had a cold you couldn't shift and you were on antibiotics. You're looking a lot better, more like the Ellen of years ago. The country air must agree with you. Maybe being away from Kitty helps?"

Ellen smiles. "Everything's okay at the moment. I felt pretty rough at first but that's gone."

"Definitely you needed a change of surroundings." Maureen breaks off to give her order to the waitress and waits for Ellen to give hers. "How long is it since you phoned me about the split? It must be heading up to a year."

"A year next week."

"You were in the throes of the breakup then, but you're well on your way now. And wasn't I right when I said that it was the best thing that could happen?"

Ellen nods. "The hard part wasn't breaking up — although it was bloody difficult at the time — no, the difficult bit is finding a replacement life."

"How did you stick it out for so long? That's what I don't understand."

"Why didn't I leave? I thought about it lots of times, but whenever I worked up enough courage to go — maybe he sensed what I was up to — he'd make an effort, and I'd feel that I'd better give it another chance. And that's the way it went on for years and years. Looking back on it, I think I must have been depressed."

"Probably. Maybe Christy isn't a bad man, but it was definitely an unhealthy situation. He really did you a favor by finally bailing out. What gets to me is that when you and he socialized he'd be all over you. Nobody would ever have guessed how it was. I knew things weren't right because you lost all your joie de vivre."

"I got bogged down in it," Ellen says with a grin.

Maureen laughs. "It swallowed you up. You've no idea of the changes in you these last few months. You're back to smiling. You're laughing again. You used to look so serious, so severe."

Ellen shrugs. "See," Maureen says. "You look taller these days because you're not hunched in on yourself."

"You're seeing stuff that isn't there, Maureen."

"I wouldn't say it if it weren't true. Tell us, have you made up with Kitty?"

"We're civil to each other. She's being gracious and forgiving."

"I was amazed the way she took it. Considering what you told me about the men in her life, I thought she'd take it in her stride."

"Christy was good at playing the attentive son-in-law. She wouldn't believe that he was utterly different at home."

"'He left his fiddle in the hall.' That's a phrase my father used about men like him. You have the distinction of being the first person on the staff to separate, to do it openly."

"It's not top of my list of achievements but it beats being in a dead marriage. If two people were ever mismatched, it was Christy and me."

"What did you think you were getting into?"

"I think I bought into that excitement he seemed to generate. I made the mistake of thinking it meant something. All his predecessors were such duds — kids really, fellows moping about, wasters — that they made him look good. I didn't love him and I wasn't in love with him, but I didn't realize that. How does any twenty-four-year-old know what they're doing? I was sleepwalking, Maureen. I wasn't awake."

Much as she doesn't know what Maureen's marriage is really like, it strikes Ellen that she can't convey to Maureen what being married to Christy meant. He wasn't a stupid man but he was shallow, with no close emotional connections to anybody. During their years together he evinced not the slightest interest in her or her inner life. How would she express the loneliness of being his wife?

However, Ellen is resistant to divulging these details to others. Huge areas of experience are so private and personal that they're impossible to discuss with other people. Revelations are embarrassing. All a friend can do is act as a sounding board, because they daren't comment or criticize. Even if regretted, confessions can't be retracted. They leave a stain that won't ever be washed away.

Unannounced, Eugene O'Brien calls to her house one night, catching Ellen makeup free, and wearing a misshapen old navy woolen jumper, tracksuit bottoms, and dilapidated trainers. He's even taller than she remembered, and the scar lends him a buccaneering air. She takes in his fresh jeans, crisp white shirt, and brown leather jacket. He looks as if he detoured to see her on his way out to a social event.

She steps back, and next thing he's in her kitchen, an invader, even though she had no intention of admitting him. "Decisions, decisions," he says, rubbing his hands together. "That's why I'm here." She's conscious of him taking in the spread of Saturday newspapers, a plate of crackers and cheese, and a half-empty bottle of red wine on the table.

"Decisions?" she asks.

"You said to call about the kitchen. Is this a good time?" His smile reveals the whiteness of his teeth.

About as bad as could be, she thinks, but she has no excuse with which to fob him off. For reasons unknown, she can't make even the most basic decision concerning the kitchen. "I was just chilling out," she says, indicating the mess on the table. "I suppose there won't be a better time."

He's brought his bag of tricks, the samples, color charts, suggestions, photographs, and specifications. "If you're sure?" he asks.

"Yes, yes, why not? Let's bite the bullet." She gathers up newspapers, dumps them on the floor, and clears a place for him at the table. He plonks down his wares, looks up at her, and grins. "Tea or coffee?" she offers. He raises an eyebrow. "Or a glass of wine?"

"Wine would do a treat."

She finds a second glass as he sorts through his stuff. "You're well prepared," she observes.

He orders her to sit beside him, tops up her glass, fills his own, and lays his products out on the table. "Have a look at these," he says, indicating photographs. He encourages her to sift through the bundles of pictures and diagrams and to extract anything she likes, reaches across her to point out examples, saying things such as, "I thought this might appeal" or "That would look well."

"I may lose concentration," she warns, but he guides her seamlessly through his interpretation of what might please her. In the end, he sketches an impressionistic mockup on the back of one of the brochures. When he presents her with this, she realizes how well he has understood her.

"How about we go through it one last time?" he suggests.

"You're very bossy," she complains. "Do we have to? I was told you weren't pushy."

"Who's the woman who keeps changing her mind? I don't want you going off on a different tack once I've started to make it. Know what I think the problem is?"

"What?"

"You think you should deny yourself the things you like, but you still hanker after them."

He's too bloody attractive, she thinks, much better looking than her first impression of him, and she likes him more each time they meet. This is his third time in her kitchen. For their last meeting, he had prepared an estimate and talked her through everything, but she felt becalmed, disengaged, out of it, so much so that he made his excuses and left.

"There's so much choice, too many kitchens," she complains, aware that this is probably a tactic to hold his attention. "This must be a killer for you, this dithering woman, the client who doesn't know her own mind."

"I'm used to it," he explains cheerfully. "It's a big decision. Some people just want the model they saw in a showroom or magazine or something that was on the box. Lots of people haven't a clue. They're like kids in a sweets factory. They can't tell you what type of oven they want, where they want it, or how much they're going to use it." He shows no sign of impatience, seems to even enjoy the exchanges.

"I'd like to keep my options open in case I ever turn into a cook," she volunteers, and is disconcerted to find him looking baffled.

"Don't you cook?" he asks.

"Well, yes, but only when strictly necessary."

He shakes his head at her. "Aren't you ashamed of yourself, woman?"

She laughs and then hears her laughter. It's arch, flirtatious. She feels obvious and false. Suddenly she's disgusted by her vacillations. Of course he's not interested in her culinary prowess but feels that he has to humor her. "Look, I'm going to finalize everything," she declares.

"You're the boss," he says, with an infuriating, knowing grin.

She avoids his eyes and tries to damp herself down. "You're very dedicated, Eugene. You should be out on the town on a Saturday night, not here with a client."

"I'm perfectly happy as I am."

She sits back in her chair and rattles it off. "Okay, here goes. Separate hob and oven — I want a separate grill, too — the mix of wood and metal you suggested, and damn the expense. Cherry wood units, the granite worktop, the larder, saucepan drawers, and the corner carousel. Put a figure on it."

"Sure?"

She nods.

He scribbles figures, tots them up on a calculator, writes down a sum of money, and slides the page to her. She glances down. "Not as bad as feared. Right, I'll go for that." She knows that in the city a similar kitchen would be beyond her means. His amused gaze snags hers. "Word of honor. I won't change my mind again. I promise. On my oath."

"One final time, if you wish."

"That way lies madness," she says, and he laughs.

"Good. We'll fix on that." They shake on the deal.

She expects him to gather up his stuff and go, but he seems inclined to chat. He tops up her wine and drinks some of his own. She likes him being in her kitchen, sitting beside her and concentrating on nobody other than her. He's an exotic presence, somebody who, under different circumstances, she would allow herself to be interested in.

"Tell us, how did you land here?" he asks. "I know you're related to Matt, but that's all I know."

"It's a long story. My marriage broke up so I was . . . well, I was mad to get out of Dublin . . . and, somehow or other, here is where I ended up."

"You bolted."

"Yes. I came here to establish an independent republic. But I'm familiar with this house, spent summer holidays here when I was a school girl, months at a time."

"How come?"

"Well, my father's cousins lived here. After he died my mother used to leave me with them during holidays. It gave her the freedom to go away, and I used to have a great time. I had the run of the village, could wander anywhere and do as I pleased. I have very fond memories of this house. It was always special."

They discuss the notion of freedom, the lack of restrictions when she — and he — were children. She discovers that he's younger than she thought, twenty-six to her thirty-eight, which to her confirms him even more definitely out of her reach. She rattles on about how confined and controlled a lot of city kids are, chauffeured and monitored, their parents afraid to give them free rein for fear of encounters with murderers or sexual deviants. "They're not allowed to disappear for hours on end."

He wants to know why she didn't stay up at Matt's place. She skirts about the immovable obstruction of Julia. "Just happened that the cousins offered to take me — I was a great favorite with Sarah — for a week it was supposed to be originally, but I got on so well with them that it turned into a month. It stretched even longer in other years. I was in my element here." She talks about Kitty. "You haven't met my mother. Well, mothering wasn't exactly her thing. She couldn't resist the opportunity to offload me, suited her right down to the ground. Kept the two of us happy. We weren't at each other's throats all summer. It was a godsend."

"So you never stayed at your uncle's?"

"No but, of course, I visited. They had sons, but they were younger than me." She comes to a halt, feeling as if there's a subtext to all of what she's been saying, not something she likes to face, the question of why her immediate relations, her mother, and Matt — not Matt, Julia really — weren't keen to take her on, and why it was left up to more distant relations to look after her. "My summers," she says. "Such summers. But what about you? Tell me all about you."

"Me?"

She smiles. "Don't think you can grill me and get away with it. You're not from around here. What's the low-down?"

"I'm a Wexford man, born and reared in Enniscorthy."

"So, why are you living here?"

He shrugs. "Followed a woman, followed a job, a bit of both really. The woman came to nothing. The job went well and I decided to set up on my own. I bought the plot of land and had a house built, converted an old shack into a workshop."

"No ties to the place?"

"My move here was accidental."

"Will you move on?"

"I've lived outside Ballindoon for more than three years now. Sometimes I think I'll end up somewhere else. Other times I reckon I'll stay put. I do very well here. Business is good."

She empties the last of the wine into their glasses. "I'm inclined to fret about the decision to come here, worry that the whole thing's a big mistake," she admits. "I haven't settled, don't feel I've taken root. It's probably why I messed you about with the kitchen."

"If you decide to sell up, the kitchen's a great investment." He catches a skeptical expression on her face and speaks emphatically. "That's not just sales patter. You may as well have everything up to standard. This is a grand house, it'll be brilliant when it's finished. Whatever happens, you'll get more than your money back. Only thing is, if you do change your mind, won't it be next to impossible to break into the property market in Dublin?"

She shudders. "I've been over this a hundred times. Could I afford to return if I wanted to? That's all murky territory."

He regards her in a quiet way. "Don't they say that there are only decisions and consequences?"

She hugs her arms close. "I'm so full of doubt these days. I really don't know what I'm at."

"You mean to say that you aren't on the hunt for husband number two?"

She squeals with laughter. "That's the last thing I'd want. I'm allergic to husbands. I've had enough of them. One was enough."

He watches her with amused calm. "You'll be okay," he predicts. "Starting over is hard. It's quite an adjustment. You have to give yourself time."

"You're sickeningly wise for your years," she jokes. "I'm much more lost."

"I could be lost too. Did you ever think of that?" He stares straight at her and she's taken aback. She can't believe this.

"That's highly unlikely," she says skeptically.

"You think?"

"Well, yes, I do."

"But what do you know about me?" he asks disconcertingly. He drains his glass. "Let's stroll down to the pub for a celebratory drink. It's the least we deserve. We sorted the kitchen tonight."

It's age-inappropriate to be with him, she reminds herself. How will she sustain the farce of her disengagement in his heady company? She'll make a false or revelatory move, let slip a predatory disposition, and they'll hit an impasse. It's not as if she hasn't been trying to establish a prudent distance between them. She has demonstrated her sensitivity to the disparity in their ages, dropping phrases like "When you get to my stage" or "In years to come you could find," and so on, and it's hard work. Her reflex nervousness kicks in. Just when she thought she had salvaged her poise, she has come unstuck. "Oh. Oh. I don't know," she says.

"Why not? Unless — unless *you're* fixed up tonight?"

It's a question of who's being predatory. Does he sense her loneliness? Is it out screaming in the world, obvious to everybody? Perhaps he's showing a professional friendliness? She can't have it. She won't. She's well able to trot out some patter. "Oh, it's past my bedtime, way past it, Eugene. It's very good of you to offer, but I've held on to you for far too long. I'm not fit to be seen tonight. Go and relax over a pint with someone more . . ." She stops herself from saying "your age" and says "more congenial."

His smile looks forced, as if her refusal annoys him. "I'm talking about a drink, one drink. It's not a big deal. Look, you don't have to talk down to me. Just speak to me as you'd speak to anybody else."

She's dumbstruck. There's a standoff, his eyes glinting with anger, hers wide with surprise. She drops her gaze and feels the treacherous heat rising on the skin of her neck and face. Different scenarios flash through her mind—she could cancel the order for the kitchen and expel him from the house—she could make a play of being offended. No, no, neither of those. She can't. It's not in her, and it isn't what she wants. She hadn't meant to sound condescending. She didn't intend to patronize him. What can she say to break the tension?

Finally she manages to look up. "I'm sorry. I didn't mean it the way you took it. That stuff—the business about age—was supposed to be a running joke. No harm intended."

He looks away. "Good. Fair enough. Thanks. We'll work on an equal footing from now on."

"Honestly, I'm not in the humor for going to the pub. I haven't got my public face on. It's bad enough you catching me like this—"

"This?"

"Slumming it. Disheveled. No makeup."

"What's wrong with you? Why do you need makeup? You look fine to me."

She laughs. "No disclaimers," she says. "My skin's not good. I'm a mess. And I've nothing else in except whiskey or coffee."

"Coffee will do nicely." He tidies his samples into the bag he brought.

"Remember, there's no obligation. You don't have to be polite."

He sighs exaggeratedly. "Are you still banging on about that?"

"God, sorry. I'm always making assumptions. And I shouldn't. I don't know you well enough."

He catches her hand and squeezes it, which adds to her confusion. "Relax, would you? It's no big deal. Once we're straight with each other, I won't miff easily. You don't have to be on guard with me."

She wonders what would happen were she to place her free hand on top of his? What if he were to respond? She's as bad as any inexperienced adolescent hooked on sensory excitement. She knows how these thoughts hatch and why she's in this delusional frame of mind. She blames it on the gristle of loneliness that has lodged in her innards.

She withdraws her hand and hopes her face is inscrutable. Thank God he can't read her thoughts. He might feel sorry for her. The idea of his pity is enough to shrivel her insides. How terrible to be so needy, so incomplete in herself that she'd even think of—well, what would be so awful about it, really, except for how it might be interpreted?

But she revives, makes coffee and gives him an accelerated tour of the house. His manner is restrained as he follows her in and out of rooms. In the conservatory he comes to life and heads straight for the open crates on the floor. He bends down and examines the contents of the first crate. "Books," he says. "It's full of books." He reaches into another crate, bundles some volumes together, lifts them out, examines their titles, skim-reads some of the blurbs on the back covers, nods as if he has satisfied himself on some issue. "Educated reading," he says, almost dismissively. "All fiction, is it?"

"History and politics as well." She feels as if she's lining up character witnesses to defend her against reproach.

He bestows a conspiratorial smile on her, returning the books to their boxes. "Our house was always full of books," he says. "Mum and my aunts are into reading in a big way. Dad's a fan of Westerns and thrillers, and I take after him. I'm annoyed if I don't figure out the plot before it's given away. I used to read political stuff, even considered joining a political party once. What am I saying? I went along to a few meetings."

"Which party?"

"I'm too ashamed to say," he says, as though choking down a laugh at his former self. "Anyway, I copped myself on. Know what I found out about politics?"

"I've no idea."

He frowns. "I used to think the stakes were big. Actually, the stakes are too small. It's all compromises and sellouts. Depressing stuff."

"I can't visualize this serious you," she says playfully.

He frowns. "I'm supposed to be apathetic because of my age, right? You have to think beyond the stereotype, Ellen, beyond the surface. Isn't that what you said? You decided certain things about me the minute we met, didn't you? One, that I wasn't a reader and two, that I wouldn't be interested in politics. Right?"

"I wasn't being serious," she says crossly. "And I'm not the big baddy. Okay, maybe there was a bit of lazy thinking. Look, I promise not to typecast you, but you have to promise to do the same for me."

She's taken aback by the warmth of his smile. "Deal. Atta girl," he says, to her disgust.

"I'm not a horse," she snaps.

"But you are spirited."

"I should hope so." She looks at her watch. "Is it that late? It's time to throw you out."

"Tonight was very enjoyable," he says at the door.

"Really? Golly gee, thanks," she says lightly in a mock-American accent.

"You could do with some bookcases."

"Bookcases?"

"For your books."

She shakes her head. "I've lost the habit of reading. Wish I could get back into it. It's a great way to pass the time."

He leans forward and kisses her on the cheek. The air thins. She pulls away, realizing too late that it's not a pass, but she's beyond reciprocating. "How very continental," she says.

"It's a great way of getting to kiss women without giving offense."

"Goodnight, Eugene."

He grins at her. "I'll leave you to your hot-water bottle. Don't forget to take out your false teeth before you go to bed."

She makes as if to hit him, and he laughs and dodges her blow. "You're a bad bastard," she calls after him, then shuts the door and leans back against it.

As she washes up, she notices that she's humming. It could be interesting getting to know Eugene. But, didn't Matt suggest that he's involved, or was involved, with a woman? She's sure he told her Eugene was living with a partner. "'Partners,'" Matt had said. "It's a tricky word. They're all living with partners these days. Time was when a partner was a business associate. Now partner can mean anything. You're nearly afraid to ask, especially if a fellow's partner is another fellow!"

Naturally, Eugene has a woman, and no doubt she's a fresh young thing. Ellen isn't susceptible to him. She understands the situation. He was playing her, oiling the exchanges between them, and consolidating her commitment to the kitchen.

Five

EATRICE IS IN THE MIDDLE of chopping vegetables for a stir-fry when Mike Hogan, the stone mason, calls her out from the house to admire his handiwork. She wipes her hands on a dishcloth as she follows him to the side of the house. She has watched him shape the new wall, steps, and raised bed over the last couple of days, but finds that she is unprepared for the finished product. Without telling her, he has created a seat on the lower wall of the raised bed. "Aren't you the one?" is all she can say as she views it.

Mike, a hunched, thin, balding man in his mid-fifties, hangs back as though anticipating a reprimand. "Do you like it?" he asks shyly.

"Like it?" she echoes. "I love it!" Mike has curved the finish on the top of the rear wall and made flat ledges to the sides and front of the new structure. The ledges and steps are made from Liscannor stone, but the supports and walls are built with local sandstone and limestone. "You're a treasure," she says and walks up past the new planting bed to the wall that now borders the existing lawn and shrubbery, exactly as she planned and he has executed it.

"So you're pleased?" he says quietly.

"Pleased? I'm delighted and so impressed. You're one of the wonders of the world, Mike! You must be kept busy these days."

"There's great call for walls and garden features. Over the last few years it's become a fashion to put a stone façade on entrance porches or a section of a house. Some people face the entire front in stone."

"I've seen that, although some of it doesn't look great."

"It needs the right stone, local stone, for the best impression."

She turns to him. "And you've managed to finish in time for dinner. Come in and wash your hands. I'll call Simon."

He protests, but she waves aside his politeness and insists that he join them. She pours three glasses of whiskey and fills a small jug with water. "We'll celebrate a job well done," she says with a smile.

Mike, always retiring, runs his fingers through what remains of his hair and smiles shyly behind thin lips and bad teeth. "I'm glad you're happy," he says, nodding. In the old days, he'd have twiddled a flat cap and touched his forelock in deference to her and the powers that be.

"Go out and admire Mike's handiwork," she says to Simon, when he ducks into the kitchen for dinner. This morning she warned him that dinner would be in the middle of the day.

"That's great skill," Simon says on his return. Mike's bobbing head and frozen smile convey his agonized delight.

Beatrice knows they had better temper their enthusiasm or Mike will take off, finding the praise too much to bear. "Here's to a job well done," she says, diluting the whiskeys according to each man's taste and filling her own glass to the brim. *"Rath Dé ar an obair."*

"Sit down, Mike," Simon says. "Beatrice likes you coming to the house because you're a great grubber."

"Waste not, want not," Mike says, glowing red spots on his cheeks the only indication of his pleasure.

"Have you met the new arrival in the village?" Simon asks Mike when Beatrice produces upside-down pineapple cake after the main course.

"Who's that?"

"Ah, you must have seen her about, Matt Hughes's niece, the one who did up Sarah Hamilton's old house. She was lucky with the builders. Jerry and the lads went at her house hammer and tongs. They're great workers."

"They musta had five men working on it the first month," Mike says, his tongue loosened by whiskey, flattery, and conversation.

Beatrice makes tea. "They started at eight sharp every morning, six days a week. I knew she was about and I called a few times, but she wasn't to be seen. I was certain I'd run into her, that we'd bump into each other. How is it I never came across her at Mass?"

"You go Sunday morning. She goes Saturday night," Simon says.

"Brendan, her father, was a fine man," says Beatrice.

"I was only a young lad when he died, but I can remember my father traveling to the funeral in Dublin," Mike says, accepting a helping of cake.

"Glasnevin Cemetery, wasn't it? He'd be about seventy if he were alive today."

"At the time it seemed strange he was buried up there but it makes sense. His wife didn't want much truck with this place. Ah, it was a shame. Brendan was a character. He had a lot of spunk, much more go in him than Matt."

"Yes, very different in personality. Outgoing, and much more ambitious, knew his own mind," Beatrice says. "They used to say that their mother had a vocation for one of her sons to be a priest, but that the wrong son got the vocation. Mind you, Brendan didn't last long after his ordination. Lord knows what happened. It all came out at Hanora's funeral."

"It was great gas, Simon," Mike says. "We were all waiting on Brendan to say the Mass but he had left the priests. Bit of a scandal, you know. Next thing we heard that he was teaching. I think he had trouble finding a permanent position but finally he got a job in a Protestant school. When he eventually turned up, he had a wife and baby in tow. After that he used to come pretty regularly. He'd bring Ellen. They stayed with the Hamiltons because Julia was against having him in the house."

"Julia?" Simon asks.

"There was terrible tension. Julia was very hot on religion. Matt tried to put his foot down but it was a waste of time. She'd have worked against him and spoiled any holiday."

"So she was like that even then. And Ellen?" asks Simon.

"She used to come —"

"I know, spend the summer holidays here. Terry told me."

"Ellen was lovely, the grandest little girl. Everyone knew that she was a favorite of Matt's. He'd bring her some little treat whenever he called to the Hamilton's. She'd come up here to play with Paula and Niamh. Never a bit of bother. Did you say she's on her own?"

"So I heard."

"I thought she married. I wonder what happened? Anyway, I'll redouble my efforts and make a point of calling to see her."

"Mostly she keeps herself to herself. Supposedly, she's a great woman for going on long walks. No problem to her," Simon says.

Beatrice sits down and pours tea. "I used to think nothing of walking miles. There are wonderful routes around here, some she probably doesn't know about."

The novelty of the house wears off. Ellen tires of staring down at the overrun garden from the conservatory. She has visited numerous furniture stores and seen nothing that pleases her. She has toured garden centers and come away empty-handed.

A cloud of inertia descends on her. She's restless and contrary. She has hit a trough, a rough of anticlimax. It manifests itself as an ache and resides in the general area of her stomach.

The days seem endless. The nights are long. She craves company but she doesn't want to see anybody. Julia's situation has deteriorated and Matt can't escape so easily from the farm at night. On his now infrequent visits, he's often taciturn or preoccupied. He hunches his shoulders a lot and loses track of conversation. When he speaks, he hints at doctors, nurses, and other presences in Julia's sickroom. Ellen offers to call up at the farm but he always says something like, "Probably not at the moment" or "Don't bother, there's no point" or "Wait to see how it pans out." She offers to help in practical ways. She could cook meals, do laundry, ease his and Mona's plight. He shakes his head, turns away, and doesn't reply.

Ellen is bewildered by his determination to distance her from the source of his distress. She knows that hardly anybody manages to see Julia, who seems to have remarkably few friends. Visitors are turned away or given the runabout, informed that Julia is tired or resting or weak.

"Let's not talk about it," Matt says. "I get a bellyful of it all day long."

Ellen feels disconnected from herself. The ghost of her past, of being one-half of a couple, haunts her. Christy may have been a peculiar husband but he took her places and loved social occasions. He was constantly on the go, gathering and scattering all before him, with a special knack for drumming up a crowd. He always had tickets for this or that event and a wide circle of interesting acquaintances. Ellen enjoyed attending events he organized and looking out for photographs in the following day's papers. She liked to meet people who were well known publicly, even if such moments were fleeting. The stimulation of these proceedings served to disguise the vacuuming silence at the core of their relationship. The private Christy turned himself off and shut down all conversation.

Why does she stir this pot every so often? She knows how miserable she was when she was with him and shudders at the memory of their grim intimacies. Nevertheless, she's suffering withdrawal symptoms, as if she's lost a limb. The space this hypothetical limb occupied aches and tingles until the sensation becomes almost unbearable. Did she stay in that relationship because the alternative of being alone was too threatening? The best thing she ever did was to give him the boot when she discovered his girlfriend. The thrill of autonomy gave her a real rush. So, why this sudden faltering?

During the day she can trot off to the grocery shop, visit the post office, call into Terry's store, browse in the chemist's, finger knickknacks in O'Hara's hardware, purchase petrol at the garage, visit the health clinic, walk out from the village in any of three directions or, should she so wish, drive into Killdingle and browse through a greater array of stores.

Most of the village shops close at six. Terry stays open until half past seven, nine on Thursdays. James O'Flaherty takes an old-fashioned half-day on Wednesdays. Occasionally, Ellen approaches the group of sullen young people that lurks outside the takeaway, asks them to move aside, and waits to push past while they shuffle out of her way with practiced slowness.

In Dublin she was never stuck for a place to socialize at night, meeting up with friends for a drink or a meal, going to the cinema or theater, accompanying Christy on one of his lunches or dinners, looking in on exhibitions or turning up at various launches, and either hosting dinner parties or attending them as guests. She had to start a diary to keep track of it all. It wasn't necessary to survey life from a distance, so to speak, as is the case in Ballindoon. Now she has to face this void.

Her boredom threshold is low. She turns on the TV. Her finger works the remote as if it's the trigger of a gun, blipping and killing anything that displeases her. She flicks from station to station and sighs in exasperation. The channels are strident with "reality" television or game shows. What happened to the sorts of programs she used to watch? Has television changed, or has she? Has she simply outgrown it?

She unpacks books, leaves them on the floor of the conservatory, hesitates over them, extracts a few from the tumbled bundles, flicks through the pages, and drops them back on the floor.

Now and again her restlessness at night becomes so acute that it drives her out to Hegarty's pub. She's been there with Matt but she has to brace herself before she enters. She opens the door, makes her way in, inhales the fumes of alcohol, feels the heat of the room, and notes the scattered groups. Invariably, teenagers are playing a game of pool in the back room.

Heads turn. Eyes scan her. Sometimes she acknowledges what may be mumbled greetings with a vague nod and brief smile. She slinks toward the bar, orders a drink, avoids eye contact, sees where she can sit on her own, sinks into a seat, huddles into herself and opens a newspaper or book with studied calm. She forces herself to read — usually the same extract over and over — but rarely lasts longer than the first uncomfortable drink. With a quick nod in the direction of the barman, she exits. It's as if none of her adolescent insecurities actually ever went away, merely lurked about, in anticipation of another opportunity to ambush her.

It's all nonsense, of course. The bar staff knows her. Why does she imagine eyes following her? Why does she flinch if she overhears laughter from a group? It's her silly brain, hard-wired into attitudes and expectations from her childhood, the origins of which can be traced back to fault-finding attentions from her mother — for whom so little of what Ellen represented was right — and the equally restrictive adulation of Sarah, Mollie, and Peg, who looked for perfect behavior, and who were wounded — not too strong a word — by hearing any adverse reports on the minor deity they had cultivated. Enviously, Ellen notes how young girls swagger about, confident, fearless, and almost arrogant. She's the one who's in-hibited, who's lost courage, stupidly trying to second-guess others' opinions of her, expecting at any moment to hear a repressed snig-ger behind her, ready to turn and find . . . what?

A man, any man, can walk in unencumbered, sit at the bar, and consume numerous drinks with little scrutiny. A woman's right to this freedom is qualified. It could look as if she has a problem with alcohol, or she might be judged to be sexually needy, slipping into a pub in the hopes of nabbing a man to trot up a dark lane with for a quick coupling. She doesn't make the rules, merely operates within their confines. Useless for her to deny that she's "asking for it" or "mad for it," and that she merely wishes to sit in the company of others. She must be cognizant of all the implications and interpre-tations of her behavior. She longs for an uncalculated, incalculable freedom — primarily from herself.

One Saturday afternoon Ellen is returning from a walk to a local lake when the temperature suddenly drops, the wind rises, black clouds whoosh in and darken the sky, and the heavens open as if somebody unlocked the sluice gates of a reservoir. The torrent is relentless and she's buffeted by a sharp-edged wind. She's dressed for rain but within a few minutes her feet are squelching in her boots. Her jeans are soaked. Even her standard rain gear can't hold out against this intensity. She struggles to tighten the cords of her hood, to stop the wind from battering it back and peeling it away from the buttons on the collar of her jacket.

Her world is reduced to the feel and sound of rainfall and the de-sire to escape the deluge. She senses something behind her on the road, dips her head and angles it in order to squint back. A dark high vehicle is traveling slowly toward her, headlights flickering against the waves of rain. It's a jeep, but she can't make out its color in the gloom. Somebody's beeping a horn. It stops and the driver leans across to open the passenger door. She recognizes Eugene. "Hop in," he says. Without thinking, she hauls herself up into the passen-ger seat.

"I've never been so delighted to see anyone in my life. Thanks," she says, leaning against the headrest.

"Lucky I spotted you. Actually I didn't know it was you, just saw the outline of some poor mutt caught in the downpour and thought I'd rescue them. What are you doing out in this? You're a glutton for punishment." He grins and shakes his head in amusement.

She throws off her hood and runs her fingers through her damp hair. "Obviously, I'd never have come out if I'd known. The forecast was for showers, not torrential rain."

The air is full of moisture. Everything in the jeep smells clammy. She's aware of her clothes steaming in the seat. They reek of damp. She hears the roar of water cascading through the ditches at the edge of the road. The rain lashes the jeep's bonnet and condensation mists the insides of the windows. The wipers exhale like asthmatic bellows, slapping the surface of the glass and beating out a slithery rhythm.

Visibility is atrocious. She longs to be cocooned in her own house, wishes she could be transported there by magic, to huddle in fresh dry clothes in front of a blazing fire in the living room. Instead her body shakes with cold from head to toe. "Could you drop me off at the village?" she shouts.

He shakes his head. "Can't. It's three miles away, and there's a lot of surface water on the roads. I'm afraid of flash floods."

"Then where are we going? Where are you taking me?" she asks.

He glances at her and mouths, "What?"

They turn up a steep narrow side road. She can hear the slush of mud against the wheels, the rush of water on the surface of the road, and feel the pull and dip of uneven terrain against the vehicle. The landscape is a gloomy blur. If they come off the road, they'll get bogged down in a ditch. She doesn't know how he can possibly see where he's going. He has to be driving by instinct and memory.

"God, it's very remote. Is this where you live?"

"What?"

"You're miles from anything," she shouts.

"I thought you knew where I lived." He doesn't look. His concentration is given to navigation.

"Obviously not."

All pretense of a road peters out when the jeep mounts a track. The wheels strain to keep their grip on the shifting surface. The engine whinnies and gives an oily cough. She can imagine it sput-tering out. Every moment she's sure they'll get stuck, but the jeep keeps going.

Suddenly she has the impression of being close to an edge that falls away steeply. Her horror of heights kicks in. Instinctively she leans into him.

"Scary, eh?" His left hand grips the steering wheel, while the other wipes the windscreen with a cloth. His face is pressed up against the glass, and he peers through a small clear opening that is always on the point of fogging up again. The heating is on full but they can't open windows to clear the condensation, so he has to wipe the glass continuously to see. And so on, again and again. His arms must ache.

The vehicle lurches and they appear to stop. "What's wrong?" she cries. She has a vision of them having to abandon the jeep and trying to make it on foot. She imagines the deluge buffeting her, sweeping her over the edge of the mud into a treacherous bog that will gulp her down greedily.

"Luckily, I know what I'm doing," Eugene says, and she realizes that the jeep is moving, albeit at a crawling pace. She vows never again to complain about anything if they get out of this.

"It must be impossible here in the winter."

"Never had to contend with the likes of this before. I'm getting the whole track gritted and tarred next month."

"I can see you really need a jeep in these con—" The track dips down sharply, the vehicle lurches and she fears it will tip over. Her hands shoot out involuntarily and she finds that she has latched onto his arm.

"Easy, easy," he says, undoing her grip. "It's not as bad as you imagine."

"Sorry. Lost my nerve. I thought we were going to topple over."

"Not a chance. It's okay," he says and grins. He looks to be al-most enjoying her fear. "Hold on to me all you like."

Then they're arriving in what's probably a yard. Relief washes over her. They park outside a wooden building and he turns off the engine. It's possible to discern the outline of another structure to the side of them. "There," he says. "Ordeal over. We're here."

She bows her head. "Sorry. Didn't mean to grab you that time. It was—"

"I know, the pressure of the moment. It's okay. Relax, would you? Don't be so jumpy," he says, almost tenderly. The rain pelts down relentlessly. "I'll make a dash for it. You follow," he says, and darts out, slamming the door behind him. She watches him race toward a building and unlock a door.

She sees her breath in front of her. Everything is in shades of gray. The air is thick with clouds. There's something odd about the composition of earth and sky. She reminds herself that the ground is elevated.

She jumps from a height and lands in mud. Unwieldy clothes weigh her down. The passenger door hangs open. She turns to slam it shut. Her boots skid from under her and squish ominously, but she rights herself and dashes toward the building.

Then he's at her side, supporting her arm and elbow, and steadying her as he hurries her along. He propels her into a room. "In, go in," he says.

Her breathing is all gulps. He's leaning against the closed door. "I'm glad to be out of that," she manages finally.

"They could do a small feature about that on the telly, don't you think? Just the ticket for a nice little human interest story. Wonder how much damage the storm is doing? It's a bruiser."

She surprises herself by laughing.

"What's so funny?" he asks. "You were terrified."

"Sometimes it's exciting being scared. It's . . ."

"Exhilarating?"

"Yeah. Knowing the odds are against you—we could have been badly stuck—but holding off the panic."

"Humph." The look he throws her is dismissive.

"Mr. 'I know it all,' is it? Were you as calm as a mountain?" she challenges.

He grins. "I was too caught up to worry about it."

Picture windows overlook a swirling, darkening void. A dervish has been unleashed. Here in this room it's strangely calm. She's conscious of pale wood on the floors and walls. There's a sense of spaciousness and light, even with the roof windows blurred and the rain reverberating on their surfaces. She takes a sodden step forward. It's like trying to maneuver in a space suit. She's walking like RoboCop—*thud, thud, thud.* She shivers.

"You'd better change out of those clothes," he says.

"I'm okay. I'm fine. Just let me sit down somewhere."

"You have to get shut of those clothes." With the long-suffering air of a parent burdened with a difficult child, he steers her out a door and down a corridor into a bathroom. She has a brief impression of tiled floor and walls, a sink, a radiator, and a high window. He switches on the light. The bulb flickers. "Don't want you catching your death. Have a shower. Quick, in case there's a power cut." He opens an adjacent door. "Dryer's in here. Pop the wet stuff in. Just press the on switch."

"Sorry to put you to all this trouble."

He laughs. "Think of it as an adventure. I'll go get my sister's clothes. She's about your size."

She begins the struggle against obstinate buttons and zips.

Half an hour later she reappears, self-consciously tugging at a short skirt. Her skin is makeup free and slightly blotchy. She shakes out her hair to hide her face.

"Sit over by the fire," he orders. "Get a bit of heat into you." She huddles on the edge of a chair and leans in toward the blaze. The flames crackle against wood and briquettes. The warmth of the fire begins to penetrate her body and she unfurls.

"Soup's up. It's on the table." He gestures at her to take a seat to one side of him, pulls back a chair, and slides it in under her. "Now, get stuck into that," he says, putting a slice of buttered bread onto her plate. "Pity you're not here on a good day," he says. "There's a pretty spectacular view."

"Lovely homemade brown bread," she says. She tastes the soup. "Brilliant."

"Eat up. I hope you're not on one of these accursed diets."

"I keep on the move to stay trim." He laughs. Color creeps into her neck and face, prickling her skin with heat. She's annoyed with herself. Who blushes these days? She's always finding herself in situations with Eugene where she can't show the face she tries to present to the world.

He's a neat eater, genteel, doesn't slurp his soup or chew with his mouth open.

"House trained" her mother would call him.

"So what's on your mind when you're out on one of those walks of yours?"

"I just pound along and get everything out of my system. It's a great way of getting rid of tension. I always feel better when I reach home."

"Dissatisfied with your lot?"

"There's usually some niggle. For a while it was the building work in the house. Now it's normally the kitchen. I go out thinking, Why haven't I got a kitchen, vent some of my frustration with the current situation—the cooker with only one ring working, an erratic oven, the useless fridge that lets everything go off. So then I have to find the upside. I imagine it in production, almost ready to go and then on the point of being delivered, et cetera, and that calms me down. When the kitchen's in I'll pound on about something else. The garden probably."

"Hmm." His voice has changed. He's lost interest in what she's saying. "Sit over by the fire and dry out properly. I have some paperwork so you'll have to excuse me." The words are clipped, his mood different.

"I'll wash up and clear away," she volunteers, trying to recapture the bonhomie that has suddenly evaporated.

"Don't touch anything! That's an order."

She glances out the window but there's no change in the weather. "I could make my own way home if it started to clear."

He shakes his head. "It'd be a mud bath. The rain hasn't finished with us yet, not by a long chalk. Don't fret. I'll drop you home later. I'm not taking a chance on you walking home alone in the dark. I'd be up for reckless endangerment if you came to grief and ended up in a ditch."

She pokes the fire, throws on a log, and sprawls out on the sofa. Her head feels heavy and her limbs ache. She extends her fingers like a cat flexing and unflexing its claws in the heat.

When he returns an hour later, she's fast asleep, her body folded like a concertina, knees to chin, arms hugging knees, the skirt falling away from her pale thighs. He shakes her awake. She opens her eyes, starts when she realizes he's watching her, and sits up abruptly. There's a sleepy jerkiness to all her movements.

She shifts uneasily under his scrutiny. "Get all your work done?"

He nods. "Your clothes are dry. I checked."

"Thanks," she says, and scuttles off.

In the bathroom it hits her. What an idiot she is! He took offense at her remarks about the kitchen, thought she was having a go at him. How could she have been so dense? She pulls on her jeans, zips them up, and does a sprinting dance of rage on the cold tiles.

When she rejoins him, she says, "That's better. I feel human again." He looks at her and looks away, says nothing. He's staring out one of the windows. She stands beside him. "You shouldn't take what I said about the kitchen as criticism. I didn't mean anything by it."

And he turns toward her and smiles. "That's okay. It's just that the order book is full. Everybody's lining up with demands, and they all want their kitchen right bang now, immediately, before Christmas."

Suddenly he moves to stand behind her. She imagines him being close, his breath on her neck, and tilts her head sideways but he's out of view. She doesn't like this inexactness, the anxiety of being unable to place him, and whirls about. He's not as close as she imagined, although closer than she's used to. She refuses to meet his gaze. "The weather's picking up," she says brightly. Her voice is shot, comes out hoarse.

He ignores that and draws nearer, a step or two at most, but she loses her nerve, backs away and looks down. The room seems to be breathing heavily. How will she react if he touches her? She prays for a witty putdown to come her way. There's nothing but silence. No movement. Nothing. When she looks up again, he's at a distance.

"Must put on my boots," she says. Awkwardly, she pulls them on and laces them up. The leather is still damp.

"Ram some rolled up newspaper inside those boots when you get home and they'll dry out. I think we'll chance driving you home now," he says.

"Yes."

"Okay. Let's away." His voice is brisk. "Want a quick look at the workshop?" he asks unexpectedly.

"Sure. Might as well, I suppose."

He strides ahead, unlocks a sliding door and pushes it across. It shuttles open with a magnificent mechanical crash. When she reaches the outsized shed, he's turning on lights, flicking switches and opening shutters. She sees lathes and planes and sawdust on the floor. "We're under pressure with orders, but I'm making a start on yours."

"I wasn't complaining."

"Really? I thought you were going on long walks to quell your impatience with its progress."

"I told you not to take what I said too literally."

He laughs. "Got you going there, didn't I? Were you worried?"

She clenches her fists. "It's so hard to know with you. How can I tell when you're teasing? I could . . . I could . . . oooh," she says.

"Could you now?" He grins and whips away tools and cloths covering the beginnings of a kitchen. "Here it is. It exists outside your imagination."

"What do you call that? The carcass?" She examines it. "It's hard to tell what it'll be like in the end."

"The basic structure has to travel and be installed."

Suddenly there's darkness. The world goes still. She can't see a thing. She gasps.

"The power's out," he says.

"Christ!" She's afraid she'll knock over something or knock against something. She stands rigidly still for what seems an eon in time. A hand touches her arm. She gives a loud cough. The hand retreats. Suddenly the workshop is flooded with light and she's blinded.

He packs things back the way they were. There's a disoriented feel to her body, as if she's been spun too tight and suddenly unraveled. She follows him in a dazed fashion. "Better lock this place up in case the electricity goes again," he says. "There's no light left in the day." In the jeep he says, "I'm aiming to have your kitchen ready by the end of this month. Worst-case scenario sees it spill over into early December. You'll be well used to the oven when it's time to cook Christmas dinner."

"That's great, but my mother wants me to spend Christmas with her in Dublin."

The skies open as they reach the main road. He's withdrawn and uncommunicative. The scarred side of his face is toward her but the scar is lost in shadows. He glances at her, but it's as if he doesn't see her. She has the impression that he's anxious to have her gone. She imagines that she has flunked some test and leans her pulsing head and aching neck against the cool of the window beside her.

The next thing she knows is that they're in her driveway and he's shaking her awake. "Don't tell me I fell asleep again," she groans.

"Don't worry. You only drooled a little." It isn't easy to make out his expression in the gloom. She throws him a horrified look. "No, you didn't. Honestly," he says indulgently, leans across her and opens the passenger door.

She meets his speculative look with a tentative grin. "I don't drool, but thanks anyway," she says, jumps down a little too quickly, lands hard on the gravel, and swings the door shut. She regains her equilibrium as the jeep reverses out of the yard and speeds off.

The following week an Eddie Devine, deputy principal of the mixed secondary school in Killdingle, leaves a message on Ellen's answering machine: *This is for Ellen Hughes. Ellen, I'm ringing in connection with the CV you left in. There's been an unexpected development here. One of our teachers, Moira O'Dwyer, is on certified sick leave and she's unlikely to be back before her maternity leave starts. I have somebody short-term to cover her classes, but we need someone full-time. If you think you might be interested, would you give me a ring?* He leaves his work and mobile numbers.

Ellen replays the message a few times while sitting at the kitchen table, her legs on a chair. She has never met this Eddie Devine. He sounds fussy, earnest, and dull, someone she imagines that she would go to great lengths to avoid, an unlikely harbinger of good news. But that's what he is. A job, an occupation, is exactly what she needs, even if she's a little work-shy after months of idleness.

She opens a bottle of red wine and pours herself a glass. The phone rings but she allows the answering machine to field the call. There's a sound like an exasperated sigh and then a click. Later, as she watches television in the dark, the phone springs into action again but the person hangs up.

Before she goes to bed, she rings Eddie what's-his-name's mobile and gets his messaging service. "Hi, Eddie. This is Ellen Hughes returning your call. I'd be interested in that job, but I have to be in Dublin this weekend. I'll ring you Monday when I get back. Okay?" There, it's done. Her extended sojourn may be coming to an end. She's willing to sell her soul. If she's offered the job, it will mean that she'll be working in the lead up to the Christmas holidays.

The next morning she swallows a glass of tap water, locks up the house, walks to the car, slings her weekend bag into the boot, and drives off in the direction of the main road.

Six

"WHERE TO, LADIES?" the taxi driver asks in heavily accented English as he starts the meter. He speaks with what Ellen takes to be a French accent.

"City center. Drop us off at Stephen's Green," answers Maureen. Ellen is relieved to see that Maureen's hair has reverted to its former brown. With the exception of Maureen, she hasn't met up with former colleagues since the end-of-year staff lunch the previous June. "Remember the early days, when we all used to adjourn to Whelan's after work on a Friday? We haven't done that in years. It's the mad lives we lead," Maureen says.

"It's marriage, Maureen. You've had pregnancies, kids, and held down a full-time job. It's all a drain."

"Plus I'm married to the greatest slob of all time. On the other hand, you had Christy."

"We didn't have kids. I was free to come and go as I pleased."

"Ah, but you were miserable. You can smell unhappiness. It's like body odor." Maureen likes to scratch the scab of what remains of Ellen's feelings about her marriage to see if the wound is healing or festering.

Ellen turns her face to the street. "That's in the past, Maureen, done and dusted. All's well with the world. Let's just have a good time."

"Yeah, we're going to party tonight," Maureen says with the determination of a prisoner on day release.

Ellen laughs. "You don't get out much, do you?"

"Neither do you, Missy Ellen, don't forget. All I've been hearing is whine, whine about how there's nowhere to go at night in that godforsaken village. You have to come home for a dose of night-life."

The word "home" reverberates in Ellen's head. "Oh, shut up, Maureen! Amn't I entitled to a moan now and again?"

Their driver is uncharacteristically quiet, perhaps because of limited English. Directions, queries, and static buzz through on his radio. Maureen hums a popular tune, her head at an angle, a finger pressed against her right ear, as if she's listening to herself in a recording studio. Maureen doesn't know that she sings off-key.

There's such a contrast between the gloom of the village at night and the illuminations of the city, thinks Ellen. The taxi chugs along Terenure Road North, past the rundown cinema, the church, and stretch of shops. It picks up speed in the bus lane, whizzes past the triangular park, through the lights at the junction to Harold's Cross Road, and over the hump of Grand Canal Bridge. As it trundles down Upper Clanbrassil Street toward Lower Clanbrassil Street, it passes the pawnbroker's shop with its three dented golden orbs. Traffic slows in New Street. Ellen views shops, a public-housing development, and apartment blocks, built on what used to be a warren of narrow streets and little houses before they were bulldozed to accommodate a dual carriageway.

Patrick Street presents itself to view, a run of recently built apartments squaring up against what can be seen of the floodlit spire of St. Patrick's Cathedral. The cathedral and street drop out of sight when the taxi changes lane to join the queue of cars trying to turn into Kevin Street. "I always mean to visit St. Patrick's," Ellen says. "I've never been inside."

"It's full of British military flags and all sorts of stuff about the dead of the Great War, with lots of plaques to deans, rectors, and fallen soldiers. Very weird really, kind of alien. Reading all these English names, it feels as if you're in another country."

"I wouldn't mind a look. How come you were in it? It's not the sort of place I associate with you."

"Paddy and I were really skint a few years ago. My parents took the kids off our hands for a week, so we pretended we were on our holidays in Dublin."

"Where'd you go?"

"Everywhere, whatever you can manage in a week: Dublin Castle, the National Gallery, the National Museum, the Natural History Museum, the Hugh Lane Gallery, the Dublin Writers' Museum, the place with the mummified bodies—St. Michan's—the cathedrals, Joyce's Tower in Sandycove, and the Phoenix Park, including the zoo. We did a lot of sitting in pubs in the afternoon, even went on the literary pub-crawl. Mind you, Dublin's ruinously expensive."

"So you wouldn't recommend it?"

"Oh, every Dubliner should check out their native city. The best bit is going to the tourist center and looking for leaflets. You feel you should be in the know but you're not."

"And what was the highlight?"

Maureen tosses it up. "Culture-wise, the skeletons in St. Michan's—they were creepy and interesting—and otherwise, the Botanic Gardens. I can't understand how I never went there before."

Like prehistoric dinosaurs, yellow and blue cranes arch their sinister heads above new property developments, extended necks and jaws ready to dip and bite. Traffic is blocked, tailing back all the way to the Patrick Street junction. Ellen slips down into the seat, hunches her shoulders, and wedges her chin into the top of her chest. "They are building everywhere. Whenever I come up I always see a new construction site," she says.

"It never stops. I can't keep up with the changes," says Maureen. "The scary bit is driving along some route you used to know, only to discover they've demolished houses, moved the road, and rerouted the traffic. It's panic stations then because the direction signs are useless. They're written in a code nobody knows." She gives Ellen a gentle dig in the ribs. "You must miss this. All the excitement, I mean."

"I do and I don't. The towns are really coming on. You'd be surprised what you can buy in Killdingle now—designer clothes, delicatessen stuff, even the semi sun-dried tomatoes you're so mad about. It has a really good shopping area down by the river, and there's an absolutely brilliant state-of-the-art pub-cum-restaurant.

I've been in it a few times for lunch. You'd want to see the style of the young ones, swanning about in skimpy outfits, exactly like their city counterparts, plenty of navel exposure. Reminds me of Dad's cousins being shocked by jeans years ago, Mollie and Peg tut-tutting, Sarah disapproving—'So unladylike,' she used to say. 'Wear a nice *frock*.' You never hear the word 'frock' now."

Ellen sees antique shops, unfamiliar buildings, coffee shops and restaurants full of bodies, throngs of people milling about streets, and a part of her aches for the hassle and battle of living in the city. Where do all these people come from? "I miss the buzz," she concedes.

"Paddy says you need great inner resources to live in the country. There's so much happening in the city, you'll always get by. Although, I don't think he's exactly right. You can be lonely in the city. People circumnavigate each other's lives. It nearly happened to us, didn't it, till you decided to cut and run? That was the spur for us to realize that we wanted to keep in touch."

"We let it slide."

"Exactly. Anyway, I'm laying odds on you coming back, Ellen. Lots of people go to live the rural dream but most of them scuttle home. At least you had the good sense to keep the job open."

"Thanks for the vote of confidence. I'll give it a year, maybe extend it to two. It's a big culture shock but . . . it has its compensations."

"Such as?"

Ellen laughs. "Such as the walks, the views—some of them are spectacular—the quiet, although that took some getting used to, being at a distance from Kitty and Christy, and the slower pace of life. People have time for each other. In the city the clock is always ticking."

"Maidens dancing at the crossroads? You sound like one of those tourist ads that everybody laughs at."

"It's not perfect. You keep meeting the same people over and over again. That takes getting used to. Noise from traffic starts at five in the morning. Some people have to travel incredibly long distances to work."

The taxi cruises along Cuffe Street. Ellen feels a real pang when she sees the vista of Saint Stephen's Green, its trees standing proud against the darkening sky. You left all this, a voice in her head says.

"Drop us off at the Shelbourne," Maureen instructs the driver.

"No problem," he says.

"You've got the lingo," she tells him, but he doesn't respond.

They give him a big tip. "In case he thought we were trying to insult him," Maureen says. "They pick up key phrases so quickly. It's the follow-through that's problematic."

A dark-haired Romany gypsy in headscarf, cardigan, and long, full skirt—like an outdated image from *National Geographic*—approaches them. She waves a copy of *The Big Issue* with one hand and jiggles a baby on her hip. "Hello, good evening. Nice to see you," she says in a singsong patter as if she expects to strike up a conversation. "Would you buy? Nice ladies, would you like to buy?" she urges as she waves the magazine in their faces.

"No, thanks very much," Maureen says impatiently, and they sweep past her into the hotel. "I hate the way they try to ingratiate themselves to put you on the spot," she complains.

"Like telesales people?"

"Those? I'm rude to them on principle. Down with the phone as fast as I can."

"Good evening," says the porter as they pass.

The bar is packed. Ellen sees hands waving above the heaving crowd.

"They're over in that corner," says Maureen. "What'll you have? I'll get us something to drink. You go sit with the others."

"Hi, Ellen. Long time no see," a tall, slim woman says from under a swathe of flowing robes and scarves. Jane's off-duty attire is always a severe contrast to her work outfits. She pushes a chair at Ellen. "Quick! These are at a premium. We hid this one under our coats."

Ellen grabs the chair and sits down. "Thanks, Jane."

"Hello, Ellen." A deeply tanned, slightly worn-looking blonde with a weary air extends a hand. She looks as if she's no stranger to the gym or toning table. Her makeup is immaculate, her outfit so fresh it looks as if it's been purchased that afternoon.

"Nesta! It's great to see you. Glamorous as ever, of course."

"Made a special effort for you, sweetie. Family and work wear you down, but you have to keep trying."

"Don't look now," Maureen says as she deposits the glasses on the table. She squeezes in between Jane and Nesta. "You'll never guess who's up at the bar."

"Who?"

"Keep your heads down! It's Lorcan Lynch. Damn, he's seen us! Come on, girls. We're deep in conversation. Rhubarb, rhubarb, rhubarb. Oh, shite! Here he comes!"

"Hello, ladies," Lorcan says, pint in hand. He bows to them in a cavalier fashion. When Ellen turns her head, he gives a start. "Ellen! What the hell are you doing here? I thought you'd bunked off to live the rural idyll."

"Hi, Lorcan," Maureen says in the syrupy tones she reserves for him.

"So you're back, are you?" he asks Ellen, ignoring Maureen.

"Up for the weekend, Lorcan."

"What's the occasion?" Lorcan's a moderately attractive man, on the short side, thin, with an elongated face and narrow features — reminiscent of the *El Greco* painting of St. Francis of Assisi — dark hair and neatly shaped mustache and beard. He's dressed in gray shirt and black jeans. He draws up a stool beside them. A tremor of disquiet ripples through the women. They quiver like aspens.

"We're going out for a celebratory meal," Maureen volunteers.

"My birthday . . . and don't ask!" Jane says severely.

"Wouldn't dare," he sneers, and turns his attention to Ellen. "First I knew of all this was you didn't turn up in September. Vamoose, gone! What are you up to?"

"Ah, he misses you. Isn't that sweet, Ellen?" Maureen says facetiously.

Ellen grimaces. "What can I say? I'm living a different life. That's it."

"But you never breathed a word."

"She's met up with a fella, Lorcan. It's all to do with him," Maureen quips.

"You're having me on. What about . . . the . . . What about . . . ?"

Following Maureen's lead, Ellen says, "The marriage? Over. Finito. Gone. New man. New life."

Lorcan clears his throat. "You're kidding me, right? This is the back-of-beyond we're talking about. How could you meet anyone there?" He slaps his knee. "You're hitching up with a farmer, marrying him for the land. That's it, isn't it?"

Ellen can't resist the opportunity to annoy him. " 'Fraid not, Lorcan. He's a young fellow. It happened completely out of the blue."

"Toy boy," Maureen says, nodding judiciously. "He's hot." Maureen nudges Ellen, pursed lips betraying her efforts not to laugh. "Drink up, ladies. The table is booked for eight. This woman moves fast, doesn't she, Lorcan? A few months out of Dublin and she's in a new relationship. She's been yapping on about him all night. Can't shut her up. I fear we'll never see her again."

"Oh, come on. This is a joke, isn't it?"

"Are you saying that I wouldn't appeal to a man?" asks Ellen.

"I'll attest to your charms any day," he says with well-rehearsed gallantry.

"You'd attest to anybody's charms, wouldn't you, Lorcan?" Maureen gibes. "Anyone will do."

Lorcan stands up abruptly. "No need to be crude, Maureen. See you, Ellen. It's been nice meeting you, ladies. Enjoy your meal," he says shortly and heads back to the bar.

"I don't think he's ever given up hopes of making it with you, Ellen," Maureen says cruelly.

"Yeuch!" Ellen shudders. "Please, Maureen. You know it's not me in particular."

"Yeah, but he sees your coldness toward him as a particular challenge. He'd like to get you hot and salivating. We'd better head," Maureen says.

"Give us a chance to down our drinks. We'll drink to Ellen's charms. A few extra minutes won't make a difference," Jane says. "Ellen, tell us, who's this guy? I never heard a word. Have you been hiding him from us?"

"There isn't a fellow," Ellen says, smiling.

"We made him up to get rid of Lorcan," Maureen says. "Otherwise he'd have tried to tag along with us, or looked for your address, Ellen, and God knows what else. I wouldn't put it past him to end up on your doorstep in Ballindoon. He has a brass neck."

"Please, don't say such things. I'll get indigestion," Ellen says.

"Lorcan's such a wanker," Jane says. "Have a kid, Ellen. Be like all of us. He goes off women once they're pregnant. Isn't that right, girls? None of us has to watch out for Lorcan in the staff room anymore. We're perfectly safe."

"I pity his poor wife. How she puts up with him, I'll never understand. I just hope she doesn't know the half of it," Maureen says.

"He's not as obvious these days," Nesta says. "He just makes comments, nothing you could pin him down on."

"Afraid of the legislation."

"Come on, let's go celebrate my birthday," Jane says. "Maybe I'll meet the love of my life tonight."

"What about your husband?" queries Nesta.

"Sure, I was out with him the other night!"

"What age are you, anyway?" Ellen asks.

"Have you no discretion, Ellen? You never ask a lady her age. I'm forty, bloody forty," Jane says with some force.

Later, in the restaurant, Maureen turns to Ellen. "For a moment in the bar, that time you picked up so quickly about your imaginary lover, I thought you might be starting to live dangerously. No chance of something stirring?"

"I wish! No . . . same old, same old, I'm afraid."

"You've ditched the marriage. Now live the life!" Jane says. "Do it for us women with husband, kids, job, and mortgage. We need to live by proxy!"

Ellen surveys her companions. Although she's chatting away, amusing them with anecdotes about Nan Brogan and Brenda Finnegan—particularly their visit to her house, their oohing and aahing over everything, and their malicious comments to others about her décor (fed back to her by Terry)—she has an unreal sense of being on show, a raconteur inventing a life that she hasn't begun to live.

Inside the main door of St. Philomena's, one sign says RECEPTION, another STAFF ROOM. Their location mirrors in reverse the layout of the school in which Ellen taught until recently. There are other similarities—the heavy-duty vinyl floor, painted block walls, fire doors, and corridors lined with lockers. The classroom doors are windowed. She can smell chalk. It dusts the air, lingers in the corridors, clogs the skin's pores, and irritates the throat.

She holds open a fire door and peers through the glass panel of the first door in the corridor. A class is in progress. A woman is saying, "What are we being asked to do here? We're talking about differentiation, aren't we? How do we know?" Ellen watches the students. They're restless, just under control, but twitching with suppressed energy and boredom. "Come on, who's going to explain it?" the teacher says. A few students slump in their chairs with trancelike, expressionless faces, their eyes fixed on a point above the teacher's head. They look as if they've been chloroformed.

"Donal?" The teacher's voice strays perilously close to irritation.

"Don't know, Miss."

"Anybody?"

Two students stick up a hand, propping their arms up at the elbow with the other hand, as if they lack the strength to keep them in the air.

"Yes, Jackie?" Ellen recognizes hope in the teacher's voice. The students shuffle their chairs to look back at the volunteer. Desks scrape the floor and Ellen doesn't catch the answer.

"Very good," the teacher says. She's a young woman but her expression is as vacant as those of her students. Her delivery is maddeningly slow, her voice monotonous, her movements sluggish. All in all, Ellen considers it a disappointing performance. Where is the woman's enthusiasm for her subject? Why doesn't she try to provoke more of a response from her students?

"Miss?" comes a voice from beyond Ellen's range of vision.

"Yes?"

"Could you explain that again, please? I don't think I understand."

The teacher's face screws up with exasperation. "If you weren't listening, Celia, it's not my fault," she retorts. "It's your loss."

"I was listening, Miss. I don't get it, that's all. I do one sum and I think I understand it. The next one I look at I can't make out what I'm supposed to do."

"Well, I'm sorry for your troubles," the teacher sneers. "It has been explained."

"But—"

"Not another word."

"She doesn't understand the math's jargon," one of the boys ventures.

"That's enough! I don't want to hear any more. Understood?"

"Yes, Miss," Celia says meekly.

Ellen is rooted to the spot, but the woman says, "Next page," in a cold fashion and, unbelievably, there is the rustle of pages being turned.

She hears a sound and swirls about. A man is running lightly down the stairs, a broad smile on his face. She steps back into the reception area and the fire doors swing shut.

"Ellen, is it?" the man asks. "Ellen Hughes?"

"Yes." Every molecule in her body urges her to make a run for it. Instead she smiles and says, "Eddie? Eddie Devine?"

"We've only ever spoken on the phone, but Nora says she met you." He's a dapper man, tall and thin, with a full head of graying hair and unremarkable features, except for his heavy lidded eyes and washed-out complexion. The impression is of a fading imprint until he smiles. The smile colors him in.

"I ran into your principal the day I was in."

"Yes, she was impressed. Let's go up to my office," he says.

His office is surprisingly spacious. It has a desk, some chairs, a filing cabinet, and a potted plant. It even has a fridge, a kettle, and a few mugs. A year-planner adorns the wall. He blusters about, extracts a file from the filing cabinet, and sits facing her, his back to the window. She shifts in her seat.

"Daunting, isn't it," he says.

She grimaces. "I don't know if it's possible but I think I'm suffering from stage fright. It's hard to start over."

"I'd have been worried if you were overconfident."

"I'm confident, all right. Just this is all new."

"You'll find your feet quick enough. After the first week, you'll forget you were ever anywhere else."

Ellen is taken aback. "Are you actually offering me the job?"

He laughs. "Wasn't that clear? I rang your school yesterday and I was talking to your principal. She told me that we'd be lucky to get you."

He's trying to put her at ease. Whatever she says, he'll reply that it's exactly what he needs to hear. There's always a chance that she might not turn up for work. It happens all the time with substitute teachers.

"You have a fair bit of experience under your belt," he says. "It's handy you living in Ballindoon. What is it, ten miles?"

"About that."

"You're not looking for a transfer, are you?"

"A transfer?"

"Yeah, changing your workplace to here."

"It's early days," she answers uneasily.

"I know, I know. You have to test the waters. I mention it because there might be a slot here next year. The woman you're filling in for, Moira, this is her fourth pregnancy. She's finding the going tough. I know she has considered throwing in the towel for good. Nothing definite — she's keeping all her options open." He fiddles with her file, pushes it about the desk, and looks up. "I believe you're related to Matt Hughes."

"He's my uncle."

"He's a highly respected member of the community."

He is interrupted by the trill of a bell. Doors open. Voices fill the air as students move from one classroom to another. There's an incremental increase in noise as feet clatter up and down stairs, locker doors slam, and the occasional screech rends the air. Almost as suddenly as it began, the racket ceases and all is quiet, except for the sound of one or two teachers greeting a class and a murmured response before doors slam shut.

He watches her. "Feels as if you've never been away?"

"Awful sense of the unavoidable inevitable."

He smiles sympathetically. "Now, are you ready to meet one of your classes?"

"Hold on. I'd like to see my timetable, and I'll need background information. Don't want to face into them unprepared if I'm going to be here for a long stint."

He pulls a face. "I admire your professionalism. You could be here until the summer holidays. Moira isn't at all well. Let's go down to the staff room, shall we?" He jumps to his feet. "Next bell is break time. I'll nab someone to give you the lowdown." He hurries her to the stairs and, as the heels of their shoes clatter against the steps, she has an overwhelming impression of them gathering momentum, as if preparing for takeoff.

They break their flight pattern in the hall where he demonstrates the security code for the lock on the staff room door — "Can't leave it unattended" — and leads her in. "Sit down, grab a chair," he says. "Somebody will come in soon. The majority of students in this school are regular kids. Have to stamp on them a bit, of course, be somewhat unreasonable at first to make an impression, or they'll walk all over you, like all kids." He fills a kettle from the sink tap. "You have the inevitable parental split-ups — dreadful, but it's happening everywhere now — and some bad parenting — parents in the pub getting sloshed every night, kids neglected, that sort of thing. Not much of that, thank goodness. Tea or coffee?"

"Coffee, please. I'd like to be sure that I'll get backup if I decide to kick up a stink, that I won't be hung out to dry."

"Of course you'll get backup." He points out a locker to her as he passes her a mug of coffee. "You colonize this. Moira won't need it while she's away. You're going to be all right. I can tell."

The door opens and a young woman with a shock of red hair walks in. "Tessa," he says without missing a beat, "this is Ellen Hughes, Matt Hughes's niece. She'll be taking over from Moira. Could you talk her through some of the classes she'll be having? I have a copy of her timetable here." He looks at his watch. "Mrs. Feeny has an appointment to see me now, so I have to run."

"See you at break," he says to Ellen as he vanishes out the door.

Tessa surveys Ellen. "He always does that — dumps people and expects others to look after them. I'm no good to you. I'm part-time," she says. "It won't be long till the others come in. Eddie will be back, too." She plonks copybooks on a low table and sits down to correct them. Ellen takes a sip of over-strong coffee and settles in for a wait.

• • •

Ellen rushes home and rifles through the cardboard box in which she has stored her textbooks and stash of handouts, and spends the rest of the day pouring over and organizing them. She squares up to the full-length mirror in her bedroom, reacquaints herself with her body language, and psyches herself up for heckles, confrontation, and defiance. This is something that she hasn't worried about in over a decade, but she doesn't want to wake every morning to a knot of dread cramping her gut.

Ellen has seen effective teachers lose their touch, forget the knack of doing the job, and come to grief. How she behaves in front of different groups — it's a balancing act that unhinges many aspiring teachers — will settle her fate. If she underperforms or overdoes the familiarity with students, the entire construct will be at risk. It's usually an incremental collapse. At first, nothing much will seem wrong. The students will become a little restless. If no effort is made to contain the slippage, the disintegration will intensify. Unchecked, the momentum will prove unstoppable. The resultant discord will end with unruly, raucous, and finally unmanageable students. Classes on either side will hear shouts, shrieks of laughter, the scrape of furniture being moved about, even the sound of a fight breaking out, and — sometimes — the hapless shouts of the teacher. Such a situation will be next to impossible to retrieve. "What have I let myself in for?" she says to her reflection the night before her first day.

She wakes to a feeling of gloom. There's no avoiding being the new conscript. Her stomach is in her throat as she drives into the staff car park that first morning, her box of tricks sitting on the back seat of the car.

The day is a mass of impressions. Everything runs at half-speed, as if in a dream. A sea of unfamiliar faces is replaced by a sea of different faces. She moves about a lot. She asks questions. She has lists of names. Beside certain names she has penciled in comments. In theory, she knows the likely troublemakers, although these can vary from teacher to teacher. She hears the measured tones of her voice. She deals with the here and now, the immediate. They are watchful — thirty of them to one of her. She pays close attention to them and picks up on body language. She's able to infer something from the way a head swivels about or remains immobile. She returns each curious stare, forcing the eyes down.

She explains that she will take over revision of the term's work and that Moira has set their Christmas tests. She expects them to be subdued the first few days as they take her in. Two weeks into the job and classes still go without a hitch. She is overprepared. They're quiet, minded to be cooperative. They test her by lobbing challenges in the form of questions. She projects a confidence she doesn't feel — years of practice standing to her — and collects written exercises from each group. For weeks — well into the next year — she will devote hours to correcting work on the day it is handed in and return it the following day. She knows that quick feedback to students is the most effective way to inspire their confidence in her ability to do the job.

She has always been verbally dexterous with teenagers and her penchant for the dramatic is a bonus. The students are good-humored. They do their work and answer her questions. It all seems under control, but she anticipates a confrontation. Minor or major, it will happen.

But they're gentle. They rib her about her accent. She mimics theirs. They decide that she comes from Foxrock. Anybody with what they term a "posh" Dublin accent has to come from Foxrock. They rubbish her suggestion that they ought to think of her as a local. "My father was from this neck of the woods. My uncle lives near here," she tells them.

"You weren't born here" is their response.

"Next best thing," she hits back.

Sometimes she overhears them taking her off as she comes into the class. They quote back some of her phrases to her. At the end of her first week a student stands up and strolls to the wastepaper bin to pare a pencil. "No, no. Always ask," she says, shooing him back to his desk. "This isn't primary school. You use a pen, not a pencil, in my class." She stands over his desk. "That is, unless you have a problem with pencils. Maybe it's a compulsion, this thing about pencils. You should worry if you need to pare one in *every* class." Her voice drops to a mock-whisper. "I have an issue with pencils. It's wrecking my life." She smiles. "There are people who can help with a problem like that. Don't lose hope. There is a cure." The class laughs, the boy grins and takes out a pen.

The effort she puts into the job exacts a toll. Monday to Friday, she's in bed early every night. Except for essential sorties into the outer world, she buries herself in her house at weekends.

"Well, this is a real improvement," Beatrice says to Ellen. "Shows what a bit of design can do. I can't get over it. If you saw what passes for a kitchen in my place, you'd pity me — doors hanging off hinges, drawers sticking, everything lopsided, and the whole thing rammed into a corner beside the kitchen door."

"Eugene's prices are very reasonable."

Beatrice runs her hand along the worktop. "So neat, and no door into the kitchen opening in your face while you're working, or anybody getting in your way if they come in. If I even had half the cupboard space you have. It's more the layout of the thing really. Never mind, it's sinful to want things. What I have will see me out."

"Some people change their kitchens every ten years."

Beatrice smiles. "Looking to throw some business Eugene O'Brien's way? Can't say I'm not tempted, but no. I'll make the best of what I've got."

"Sit down and take the weight off your feet. I'll make tea."

"I called a few times but missed you, and then I just put it on the long finger. The days merge into each other. I can't believe that Christmas is so close. Will you be here for it?"

"No, no. I always spend Christmas with Mum."

"That must be nice."

Ellen grimaces. This year Kitty has demanded a week from Ellen's holidays. "Christmas forces you to be with family."

"Ah, go on. It can't be all that bad. I enjoy every bit of that fuss. Usually, one of the girls comes home, and I love to see the grandchildren. I wouldn't miss it for the world."

"That's because you have a nice family." Ellen sets the teapot on the table. "You know," she confesses, "when I first saw you, I hadn't a notion who you were, but then something twigged. You've no idea how many times I've had conversations with people without knowing who I'm talking to. Terry helps me out, matching descriptions to names, although I'm not always precise enough for her."

"Oh, Terry has all the news. But, sure, how would you remember me? We haven't seen each other in — what is it? Twenty years? I'm trying to remember why we didn't meet at Sarah's funeral. Oh, I was away. That's why. I can still see you as a child, Ellen. Remember when you and Paula used to go swimming? And I have a memory, as if it were yesterday, of me driving the two of you into the pictures in Killdingle."

"Great times. I'm thrilled to see you, Mrs. Furlong."

"Beatrice. Call me Beatrice. I'm glad that all that old formality is out of the way. I approve of people being on first-name terms. There are some around here who take a dim view of that, but I see nothing wrong with it."

"Imagine Paula having kids. It seems like yesterday when we were tearing about the countryside. How is she these days? Where's she living? What about Niamh? It was Niamh, wasn't it?"

"Niamh's a doctor now, married with a son. She's living in Hull. Loves it. Paula's in London, married with a son and daughter. They live in Richmond, big house and all that. She has a long commute to work. We were on the phone last night and I told her I was coming to see you. She sends her regards."

"I wonder if we'd recognize each other. I remember John and — was it Andrew or Andy?"

"Andy. Andy's in the States now." Beatrice swallows the last of her tea. "Well, I'd best be off. This was just a quick visit to set the ball rolling. You'll have to call up to me some evening."

"I don't get many visitors," Ellen says at the door. "It's nice when someone calls."

"No point in expecting invitations around here. You'd be left waiting. They're funny like that. I go into town on market day, Wednesday. Otherwise I'm generally about. Give me a ring. I'm in the book."

"I'm always afraid people will send me away with a flea in my ear."

"Well, that reflects more on them than you, doesn't it?" Beatrice kisses her cheek. "This is great, Ellen. You'll be a huge addition to the village. It's a pity Sarah isn't around to see what you've done with her house. She'd be tickled pink. She was always the one with a bit of style."

"Yes, Sarah would have approved. Remember to give my best to Paula."

"I certainly will. There's just one thing, Ellen." Her voice has changed, and something in her demeanor makes Ellen afraid.

"What's that?"

"Our John is dead."

"John? Oh, my God!"

"He — took his own life in January of last year, a few weeks before the start of the foot-and-mouth restrictions."

"Dear God, Beatrice, I had no idea. Nobody mentioned it. I don't know what to say."

"Don't worry. Nobody does." Beatrice takes her hand. "I wanted to put you in the picture. Don't let it upset you too much."

"Oh, Beatrice, I — can't — it's just so awful."

"It's okay, Ellen. I keep thinking it's a year ago but it'll be two years after Christmas. I've had time to get used to the idea, and time's supposed to be the great healer. I wish I weren't the one to have to tell you . . ."

"I'm so glad you did. Stopped me putting my foot in it . . ."

"Don't dwell on it, Ellen. By the way, you could hire out Jimmy Joe O'Dwyer to clear the back garden. He's the man for all that sort of work."

"Matt mentioned that name."

"Try Jimmy Joe. He can turn his hand to anything, and he charges a very reasonable daily rate. Remember now, don't be a stranger. I'll expect you soon."

Ellen's mind is a blur of images. She remembers John as a young boy kicking a ball in one of the farmyards, dodging close about her, whooping loudly, a rush of air past her ear and a thud against a wall behind her as she passes. Once she and Paula went to a hurling match to watch him play on the local team. He had transformed into a reserved teenager, not much given to talking, his attitude toward her changing, growing less friendly, more combative — always angling to tease her, keen to catch her out, laughingly saying,

"I bested you," and crowing and hooting if she believed some tall story he'd made up. He must have been seventeen or eighteen the last time she came across him in the village, and he had cut her as if he didn't know her.

Another ring from the bell brings her back to the present. She opens the door and finds Eugene, his right arm thrown across the doorjamb, his body stooped and leaning forward so that, unusually, she finds herself on a level with his head. His eyes gleam as he registers her holding her stance.

"Oh, it's you," she says.

"Oh, yourself. I hope you're not disappointed. Remember I promised to show you that furniture place? Would now be a good time?"

"Now? Come in," she says distractedly.

"Is something wrong?"

"It's nothing really. I've just heard some news and it upset me a bit." She stumbles over the rug in the hallway.

"You okay?" he asks.

"Beatrice Furlong has just left. She told me about John, about her son's death. I don't know what to think. It's just the shock. I'm still . . ." She gestures with her hands. "But I'll be all right."

He rubs his hands together as if trying to warm them. "That was a sad business. It can't have been easy for Beatrice but she kept going. Look," he says uneasily, "do you want to leave the outing for another day? Maybe you're not in the humor?"

She shakes her head emphatically. "No, it's exactly what I need. It'll take me out of myself. I'll only brood if I stay in the house. I drove round in circles when I tried to find that furniture place. There aren't any signposts. You should have drawn me a map."

"It's complicated. You need to know the lay of the land."

"Beats me how they ever sell anything if they don't advertise."

"It's only Dublin jackeens like you can't find them," he says glibly.

Later that afternoon he parks the jeep outside a pub and suggests that they go in for soup and a glass of something to celebrate her purchases. "You're very preoccupied," he says after the barman has taken their order.

"Oh, you know, thinking about John and what happened. It's

not as if I knew him that well, but I can't put the idea of him not being alive out of my head. I'm remembering various things, but what sticks in my mind is a particular day. We were playing some game — I can't remember why Paula wasn't there — and he told me to tie him up with a length of rope as tight as I could, bet me he could get out of it. So I tied him up and, sure enough, he got free pretty soon. And then he insisted that he would tie me up, even though I wasn't keen and — of course — he secured the knots so well that I was shouting for hours to get free. He left me in one of the sheds, well away from the house. Paula came home eventually, heard my shouts, and freed me. Beatrice was furious and gave him an earful, but he was completely unrepentant. He was grand as a young fellow, but he went off me. When he reached adolescence, from about thirteen onwards, he just shut down. I think it was mostly because of where I came from. A lot of his bravado was the country fellow showing the city madam who was boss."

He hands her a tissue. "Wipe your tears," he says.

"Tears? Isn't that stupid? And it isn't just wounded vanity. Afterward he was always hostile. It hurt that he disliked me so much." She pats the tears dry, blows her nose, and sits up straight. "Are my eyes red?" she asks, striving for a lightness of tone.

"No, no. Nothing obvious. You'd have to be up close to notice." The barman sets down their drinks. "I hardly knew John," he continues. "He wasn't a good mixer, kept himself at a distance, and was next to impossible to talk to. He'd ignore you or mutter. I always thought he had a chip on his shoulder, and he was drinking pretty heavily toward the end. Of course, afterward it seemed as if we should all have known what was coming — there were incidents, a good few things really — but somehow people never realized."

"Don't tell me. I don't want to know any of that."

"Sorry."

On the way out to the jeep, he puts an arm about her shoulders, pulls her close, and kisses the tip of her nose and then her mouth. There's the pressure of his tongue, his hand at the back of her head, and a peculiar shivery feeling at the top of her spine.

At the back of her mind is an agitation, like shock. She has imagined such a moment, even hankered after it, but now that it has happened it feels as if her body has shut down. Something within her hesitates — she's frightened of slipping into a dangerous place.

When he pulls away, the two of them are breathing heavily. He stares at her. "You didn't like that," he says in a flat tone of voice.

"It's . . . it isn't that," she stammers. "I wasn't expecting it. Don't you have somebody? Aren't you involved? I heard you were."

"You think I'm spoken for?"

"So I was told."

"I'm unattached. What you were told about broke up over a year ago."

"Right," she says. "Though I can't see why you'd be interested in me. I'm just out of a bad marriage. You could have your pick of lots of uncomplicated women."

"So uncomplicated that I learn everything there is to know more or less immediately? No, thanks. I find it easy to be keen on somebody who cries over the death of a boy who disliked her, someone who isn't obsessed with her own image. It's great the way you enjoy your own company but take fright whenever the spotlight is on you." He traces his finger along the outline of her neck. "Have I got it wrong? I feel a connection. But maybe you're not interested? Tell me if that's the case."

Emphatically not, she thinks. She opens her mouth to mention the age gap, but he's more or less forbidden that. She's dumb with confusion. How can she know what he's really like? She doesn't want to become enmeshed in another disastrous liaison. On the other hand, if she doesn't act, this moment will slip away. She has to gamble on instinct. She turns to kiss him, but her jaw hits his chin.

"Hey! Ouch!" he says with a grin, and rubs his face.

Her face flames red. "I was trying to — eh, seeing if . . ."

"Know what? I've never met anybody quite like you."

She can't meet his gaze. "That could mean anything."

"You're like a deer or something. A sudden movement and you bolt!"

"I'm sorry," she says. "I'm not any good at this."

"It's not easy. There's so much potential for embarrassment."

She smiles. "Especially if one's gaffe-prone."

Later, when he's driving her home, he says, "I'm not doing so well with you, am I?"

Her head feels as if air has leaked into it. "Depends on how much patience you have."

"I have some."

Maybe not enough, she thinks. She wishes she could open up the way other people do. She desperately wants to.

"Sure, isn't everything a challenge or an opportunity these days?" he jokes. "There's no such thing as failure or defeat."

He carries her purchases into the house. Before he goes he ducks his head and she finds herself locked into her second embrace of the day. Her brain detonates panic buttons, but she manages to lean into him and even puts her arms around his neck.

"Much better," he comments and steps back. "Practice makes perfect."

"Perfection's a long way off then."

"You know what they say about perfection?"

"Tell me."

"Trifles make perfection, but perfection is no trifle. Michelangelo's supposed to have said that."

"Sure." She laughs.

"He did," he declares. "And he was a very sensuous man." He grins. "Though not the way we'd understand it. Still . . ." He touches her hair. "You've nice hair. I like your hair." He gathers the ends into his right hand, bends his head, and reaches around to kiss the nape of her neck where her hairline ends. She shivers. "Very nice," he murmurs.

She's giddy with sensation. "What?" he asks.

"Just that spot. I must be very sensitive there."

He laughs. "So I'm getting it right?"

"Very much."

"You're a dreadful distraction," he chides. "I'm entering my busiest season, jammed up with orders. I made time today, but I'm going to be ferociously busy between this and Christmas."

"That's okay. I'm under lots of pressure with this job. It's naught to a hundred every day in terms of energy, and it takes a while to charge up. My first year teaching full-time, I was in bed every school day by nine o'clock."

"And I'll be working the production line. We'll still see each other, won't we?"

"We can keep it ticking over."

"Or tickling over," he jokes, kissing her neck on that receptive spot.

When he's gone, she's overcome by skittishness and dances about the room. "Tarumtidum. Tarumtidum," she sings and, finding herself in the hall, comes to a halt in front of a mirror. She examines her hair. "Shameful," she mutters. She scrutinizes her head from this and that angle. "What absolute nonsense," she says to the air.

Seven

*I*F, AT MORNING break time, Ellen flops down into a chair in the staff room and says "I'm bushed," or "whew!" she doesn't expect a response. Hardly anybody answers any of her overtures. A grunt is the best that can be expected.

Before coming to work in St. Philomena's, she had anticipated new colleagues being curious about her, welcoming her, volunteering to show her the ropes, offering an apposite word to the wise now and again, and displaying, if not empathy, well, then, consideration for her situation. For the most part none of this has been forthcoming. She's as good as invisible.

The prohibition on talking to her is selective. It's in the realm of inconsequential day-to-day exchanges and interactions that she is excluded. If, at lunchtime or during a free period, two or three others are chatting together, they act as if she isn't there. She sits at a table, corrects copybooks, avoids all eye contact, and suffers from a diffidence that is strange to her. However, if she makes a work-related inquiry, she will be answered. If she needs to be informed of a meeting or a problem with a student, somebody will mention it to her.

She misses the certainties and comforts of her former working life — the inevitability of knowing exactly when Maureen will head toward the trees at the edge of the basketball pitch to snatch a furtive smoke, the pleasure of watching immaculately groomed Nesta open an impeccably presented lunch box of homemade brown rolls, healthy salad, screw-top miniature bottle of dressing, and regulation portion of fruit, and her fleeting guilt at her lack of fitness when tracksuit-clad Jane returns from a games or gym session with a class. Even the prospect of an irritating encounter with Lorcan Lynch seems faintly enticing. What she really craves is a greeting or a nod of recognition.

It's a weird situation being a new teacher in another school. All her familiar props have vanished. She and the students are strangers to one another. She has no track record or reputation. Without a context, she's cast adrift.

It may be that the lead-up to Christmas gifted Ellen with a honeymoon introduction to her students because setbacks arise in the New Year. During the first school week in January only three students in a particular class turn up with the required book. For some moments she looks at them and they watch her. "Why do you think I'm here? How can we do any work when you have no books? This is unacceptable," she says grimly. Giving them no time to respond, she storms out of the classroom, finds Eddie, drags him back with her, and demands that he impose detention on the lot of them. "They're wasting my time. I can't work. I've nothing to work with," she declares, inhabiting the alter ego she constructs when teaching — everything for effect.

He's unctuous. "You're quite right, Ms. Hughes. These students are a disgrace."

"I've never come across the like of this before," she claims. "People yap on about teachers not doing their job, but today shows what I have to contend with, Mr. Devine," she says with a flourish. "Students are here to work, and it's my business to give them what they're entitled to. You understand, Mr. Devine?"

"Absolutely, Ms. Hughes. I'm dreadfully sorry about this, Ms. Hughes. Look, would you consider allowing the class to start over with a clean slate? If anyone shows up without a book tomorrow, it's automatic detention for the lot of them."

She taps her foot impatiently, crosses her arms, and stares at the floor. "I don't know," she says and sighs. "I don't like letting them off."

"I can assure you they will have their books tomorrow. Hands up those who left the book at home — there, look Ms. Hughes — that's the majority. Jenny, where's your book?"

"I have to buy it, sir."

"Immediately after school today, Jenny. Tim, why haven't you got a book?"

"Have to get a copy off my cousin."

"You need it for tomorrow's class. Understand?"

He smiles at Ellen's stony expression, as though trying to charm her, and begs her to humor him by giving them a chance. He guarantees that they will all have the book by the following day.

She agrees. When he leaves, she glowers at them, makes them take out their copybooks, and dictates notes from the missing text, talking at a speed they struggle to keep up with. "Know that for tomorrow," she says, and flounces out of the classroom.

At the end of the day she meets Eddie coming out of his office. "Thanks for the help. I had to make a stand with those third years."

"I hope you're not going to be pulling stunts like that every day," he says coldly.

She's taken aback. "Only if I feel I need to," she snaps.

"It took up a lot of my time," he says sulkily.

Her discomfiture is replaced by a cold rage. A surge of adrenaline engorges her veins. Her pulses thump. When she looks at him, this puny weed of a man, she doesn't trouble to hide her contempt. Why should she care about him or about his beloved school? "Sorry about wasting your precious time, Eddie," she snaps. "I didn't do it for fun. It wasn't a lark. I didn't do it to be difficult. It happened only because I want to get on top of things. If you don't like the way I operate, I can always leave." That's what she'll do, she thinks. Leave. No need to waste more time here. There's plenty of work in the world.

Immediately he's all solicitous concern. "No, no, absolutely no need for that. It's not something I want every day, being called into a classroom."

"If it turns into a regular occurrence then we're all in trouble and I won't be hanging around," she says, and stomps off.

He comes after her. "Ellen, Ellen," he cajoles. "No hard feelings, eh?"

She sighs.

"We all have our off moments," he coaxes.

"All right," she mutters. She's still cross with him.

The following day she calls, "Books out!" as she enters the room. There's a clatter as the books strike the desks. She does a tour of inspection—"Very good," she says approvingly. Each student present has a copy—the relief!—either battered or torn or brand new. "Page ten," she says.

Eddie accosts her at coffee time. "I had young Tim's mum in this morning delivering his book to the office and complaining about the cost. She says that there's precious little money left for school when they've paid out for fast food take-outs and hiring in movies." He shakes his head. "People and their priorities, I never get it."

"You're a tough taskmaster," he says when they meet at the photocopier one day in the second half of January. "You have them all on the run."

"You think I'm being unreasonable?"

"They're toeing the line."

Ellen presses the staple button on the photocopier. The machine clicks a sound like castanets. "I'll ease out," she says, "once I'm sure it's okay."

"It's okay. I'm telling you it's okay."

"The sixth years are still sullen."

"Sixth years are always the biggest problem. It's partly panic, and they resent losing their teacher before the final exam. They'll be the most demanding, your toughest proposition."

"I'm pulling out all the stops."

"It's not personal. They don't even see you. They see Moira's absence."

"She's a bit of a control freak, Eddie, but doing a great job," a voice from behind them says. "I've seen her in action."

Ellen recognizes the woman. "I'm Ellen," she says.

"I know who you are. I'm sure you introduced us, Eddie, but I'll introduce myself again. Joyce—Joyce O'Dea is my name," the woman says. "I saw you deal with Rosie McGann in the corridor the other day. The little madam was petrified. No harm to put manners on her. But you expend an awful lot of energy, Ellen."

"Is that bad?"

"Depends. You should watch it. Teaching takes you in, sucks you dry, and spits you out."

The bell for the next class goes. "See you," Joyce says.

At the end of the day Joyce nods as they pass each other in the corridor. Ellen is relieved. She had almost given up on establishing a bond with a person other than Eddie, and she and her aloneness have been uneasy companions.

From then on, although they don't hold conversations, Joyce greets her with a "Good morning," "Hello," "Goodbye," or "See you" whenever they meet. Otherwise, the staff still treat Ellen as an unwanted spare part, a disconnect.

Sometimes lonely days merge into even lonelier nights. Matt is elusive, and Eugene has landed a job installing kitchens in a cul-de-sac of new-build houses on the outskirts of Killdingle. She seldom sees him. "I thought you didn't take on those kinds of jobs," she protests when he tells her.

"The fellow doing the job originally is out of action. He was in a car accident."

"I wish you hadn't agreed to do it."

He sighs. "Maybe I shouldn't have, but the money's good, Ellen. I can stick it for a couple of weeks." But when he calls to see her, he's tired. He's a go-to-bed-early Eugene, a one-drink-and-he's-off Eugene, a falling-asleep-after-a-kiss-or-two man.

Perhaps the absence of romance is good, she thinks, Eugene's periods of stress dovetailing neatly into her embattled work situation. It may be that she needs to be thrown back on her own resources. Nevertheless, there are times when she'd like to drive out to his place and stand in his workshop, just to have contact with him.

The special afternoon that they spent together has taken on a cinematic quality. She can summon up a memory of what happened, but their kisses and exchanges have become unreal.

By the time Ellen gets around to painting the main conservatory wall, the original outer wall of the house, it's the last Saturday in January. She has been sparked into action by Eugene commenting that he imagines the plaster has finally dried out, and that she could risk tackling the ceiling and wall surfaces. Progress is slow, but when she eventually paints the final wall under the windows, it will be possible to apply a second coat of emulsion to the main wall.

Suddenly, from her perch at the top of the ladder, she notices Terry pushing open the side gate and making her way into the garden. It's a drizzly day but Terry is without hat or coat. Her shoes crunch on the newly laid gravel.

When the bell rings Ellen has reached terra firma. She grabs a cloth and holds it under the paintbrush. When she opens the door, there's no one to be seen. She glances down, and Terry is crouched over, head tucked in as she struggles for breath.

"Are you all right?" asks Ellen.

"I have a stitch in my side." Terry straightens up. "Have you heard?" Ellen shakes her head. "Father Mahoney was in for his morning paper when his mobile went off calling him up to your uncle's. Nan Brogan met Mona's husband at the post office half an hour ago. He had just been told. Julia's dead. She died at ten o'clock."

"Julia!" Ellen has anticipated this moment for some time, but when she hears the news — and despite her dislike of Julia — she feels a rush of sympathy for the woman, for what she had to endure before her demise. She takes a step back and spills paint on the floor.

"Tut, tut! Careful. What's with the brush in your hand?" scolds Terry, extracting a tissue from her sleeve and wiping the paint. She commandeers the brush. "Get newspaper," she orders.

Ellen gestures vaguely in the direction of the kitchen table. "There," she says.

"Apparently, Julia was due to go back into hospital for a blood transfusion, but she hasn't been good this last while," Terry volunteers.

"Oh, Christ. I have to sit down," Ellen says, and lands on a chair.

"Careful. Don't do yourself damage." Terry locates a soaking jar, into which she plonks the brush. "What are you painting?" she asks.

"The conservatory."

"Why don't you hire Jimmy Joe to do that? He'd have the whole house done in a flash. You dribbled paint in the hallway, you know."

"Don't bother about the bloody paint," Ellen says. "Ten o'clock, was it?"

Terry nods. "I thought you might know already."

"No. It's been quiet for weeks. I've hardly seen Matt. He wasn't getting out much. I called twice but . . ."

"You weren't wanted."

"Exactly."

"Beatrice said the same thing. She offered to help, told Matt to lift the phone anytime he needed anything but he never did."

"All that was Julia's doing. She didn't want people in the house."

"She was always a very private sort of person. Do you think they'll wake her from the house?"

"I've no idea. I wonder Matt didn't ring."

"He's a man."

Ellen stands up. "Sorry, Terry, I'll have to run you. I'd better head straight up. Thanks for letting me know. And I had almost finished the paintwork."

"Go upstairs and get yourself sorted. Show me this paintwork." Terry makes for the conservatory and Ellen trails her. "Sure, it's only a matter of an undercoat of emulsion. I'll finish it," she says.

"No, Terry. There's no need, none in the wide world. It doesn't matter."

"A shame to abandon it when it's so near to finished. Look, it's twenty minutes' work at most. I'm a great one for paintwork, absolutely love it. It's brilliant therapy. I'll soak the brushes and close the front door after me. Come on now, I'm very trustworthy." She steers Ellen toward the stairs. "You get changed. Leave this to me."

Matt sits slumped at the kitchen table with a tumbler of whiskey before him, a half-empty bottle beside the glass. He looks up. "So you found your way here," he says coldly.

"I came as soon as I heard."

"We haven't seen much of you of late."

"That's not fair, Matt," Ellen protests. "I called a few times but it was made clear that I wasn't needed. I felt in the way."

"So you would have been. Mona took over strategic command and ran the show. I didn't get a look in."

"Do Colum and Stephen know?"

"I rang. They pulled Colum out of a meeting, but we haven't tracked Stephen down yet. He's not answering his mobile."

"Where's? — Is Julia in the — ?"

"Is her body here, you mean? No. She's gone to the funeral parlor. She'll be on view this afternoon. The removal's tomorrow."

"Terry was wondering if it'd be today."

"Oh, was she now? Maybe you'd better ring and give her an update." The edge in his voice cuts her.

"It was Terry told me that Julia was dead."

"Good news travels fast, doesn't it?"

"What!"

"Oh, nothing," he barks. "Sit down, will you. You make me itchy looking at you hopping from one foot to the other."

Slowly she sinks into a chair on the other side of the table. "Take a drink," he orders. "What's your poison?"

"I'll have a beer."

"We've no beer. Have a proper drink."

Mona comes into the room and stares at Ellen. "Hello," she says dejectedly. There's a family resemblance to Julia, but Mona is a more substantial figure. She's taller, stooped about the shoulders, chubby-cheeked, with multiple chins, and graying light brown hair.

"Where did you get to?" Matt asks. "This is Ellen, my niece. Ellen, this is Julia's sister."

"I think we've met before," Mona says stiffly.

"At the door a couple of times. I'm really sorry about Julia, Mona."

"Oh, yes. Well, thanks." Mona's eyes are fixed on the glass in Matt's hand. "Matt, you're not drinking again!" she says in an anguished tone.

"Have you finished her room?" he snaps.

Mona faces him, legs slightly apart, her hands crossed in front of her at the wrists, like an army cadet reporting to a superior. "I've cleared everything and put on a load in the washing machine."

"That's fine. Take a rest now and go home. I'll meet up with you later."

Mona glowers. "I'm not going anywhere. I want to clear up in case people call."

He shrugs. "If they call, they call. They'll have to take me as they find me."

"She should have been waked from the house," Mona mutters mutinously. "It's what she would have wanted."

"Rubbish, woman. Why do they have funeral parlors, if it isn't for this?"

"She loved this house."

"Well, she wasn't all that fond of some of the people in it. It's only a house, Mona."

Ellen shrinks into her seat, eyes on the table. Matt looks as if he could spring into physical action, with God knows what detrimental consequences. Silently, Ellen urges Mona to give way. Then she hears an engine, looks out the window, and sees a car maneuvering to park in the yard in front of the house. "There's someone outside," she says, and there's a sudden restaging of positions by Matt and Mona. He drops his gaze, pushes the glass away from him, and she dabs her eyes with a tissue.

Seconds later, Beatrice enters, carrying a large cake tin. "I've come to pay my respects, Matt. I just heard," she says. She bends as if going to take his hand but, unexpectedly, he gets to his feet and embraces her. He prolongs the moment, and she has to disentangle herself gently. "I'm really sorry, Matt." She reaches out a hand, strokes his cheek, and steps back.

He seems torn. He gazes at her, but then either remembers the others, or is embarrassed by this show of emotion. He sits down again and pushes a glass across the table to her. "Have a drink, Beatrice, the day that's in it," he says gruffly.

"I most certainly will."

He pours a good measure.

"Steady on, Matt. Just a drop."

"It's not much. You can dilute it. It's soda water or tonic you take, isn't it?"

"Either. It's much of a muchness to me."

It's a small thing really, this revelatory familiarity between them — it's not just the particularity of the occasion, Ellen thinks — and it confirms for her what she has long suspected, that Beatrice is the woman Matt didn't marry.

"He's being completely unreasonable. He won't let me do a thing," complains Mona suddenly. "He's told me to go home. It's ridiculous, Beatrice. You can't shut up the house at a time like this. People will be calling."

Ominously, Matt says nothing. It's as if Mona didn't speak.

Beatrice takes a quick look about as if judging the situation. She leans forward and touches Matt's hand lightly with hers. "Matt, why don't you and Ellen go down to the drawing room while Mona and I give this place a bit of a going-over?" she suggests. "I know it's a nuisance, but think of it as a necessary evil."

He groans, throws his eyes to heaven, and glances over at Mona. It's clear that he wants her out of the house. "I'm sick to death of people. I'd like the place to myself."

"Of course you would," Beatrice soothes, "and in a few days you'll have everything you want. Look, you and Mona are exhausted. Will I ring Traynor's and organize a few trays of sandwiches? Lily will do soup if we ask. Wouldn't it be grand to have a big pot of soup on the go?"

"I suppose," he says gruffly. He carries the bottle and glass to the door and signals Ellen to follow. She indicates that she'll join him soon and he slams the door after him.

Mona says, "I don't believe it. You got round him. He even agreed to caterers coming in. He wouldn't listen to a word I said, dug in his heels against my every suggestion."

"He just needs peace and quiet," Beatrice says, donning an apron she found in a drawer. "Will we get stuck in, Mona? When word gets round, others will soon arrive."

"Are you sure I can't help?" Ellen asks.

Mona throws her a cold look, but Beatrice smiles. "Your job is to keep Matt company, Ellen." The phone trills into life and Beatrice runs out to the hall to answer it. When she returns she says, "That was Colum. They'll all be here tonight. Ellen, go into Matt while we tidy up. Tell him they located Stephen."

"We'd better make up a few fresh beds," Mona says.

Ellen finds Matt staring out the window at the side garden. He turns when he hears the door open. "I was too hard on you," he says. "Completely out of line."

It's as close to an apology as she's likely to get. "That's okay. Colum and Stephen are on their way."

"We all know the drill, know what's expected of us," he says tiredly.

"It must be a bit of an ordeal."

"Yes and no. At least it'll restore a bit of order. Everything's been all out of kilter the last while."

She takes his hand, suddenly aware of the coarse, dry texture of his skin. "It's all over now." Suddenly she's worried that it's the wrong thing to say.

He throws her a strange look. "Yes, it's all over. She's gone."

"She's not suffering anymore."

"No, the suffering is finished." He withdraws his hand.

They stand in silence for a long time. There's the sound of furniture being moved about. In the distance a vacuum cleaner roars into life. "My mother was laid out in this room," he volunteers. "They put the coffin on the dining table. Mona has been at me for weeks to wake Julia here." He looks grim. "Funeral homes are a great invention. The dead don't clog up the house. It tidies up the business and allows people to return to everyday living."

"But—"

"But nothing."

There's no mistaking his meaning. Ellen knows well enough to hold her tongue. She feels particularly stupid not to have gleaned quite how oppressive his marriage was.

He lapses into a forbidding silence that she hasn't the courage to break. The mantelpiece clock ticks. The room resonates as if breathing. Outside an occasional sun casts long shadows in the garden. Crows caw close to the house.

Moments pass. Matt sighs a few times and she wonders if he hears her answering sighs.

Eventually Beatrice carries in a tray with tea and cake and sets it on the table. "Here's something to sustain us. Have to keep body and soul together."

Matt manages a half smile. "Thanks, Beatrice. You're very good."

She presses a slice on him. "Come on, Matt. I'm sure you had no breakfast. You have to keep up your strength over the next few days."

Obediently he eats. Beatrice and Ellen talk about cutlery, plates, and glasses, and estimate the numbers to be catered for after the funeral. Lily Traynor's name gets a mention. "Her quiches are second to none," Beatrice says. "And as for her salads!" They measure and lob their utterances to each other and watch Matt covertly.

After a short while he stops eating, sits back in his chair, stretches his neck, sighs, and closes his eyes.

"Will people adjourn to Hegarty's after the burial?" Beatrice asks.

He answers with his eyes shut. "I suppose. Would you set the ball rolling, Beatrice? I'm past all caring. You're good at that sort of thing. The boys will take over once they arrive."

"Consider it done, Matt. How about a lie down for a while?" she asks as she collects the tea things. "I'd say you could do with a rest. Don't worry about the milking. Simon will help out there."

"I'm perfectly capable of looking after the farm," he says wearily.

"Of course you are. Nobody's suggesting otherwise, but it's the custom to help each other out at times like these."

He nods. His eyes are ringed with tiredness and his skin looks dull. "Of course, you're right. Sorry." Ellen marvels at how Beatrice can calm him.

"Go on up now. You're exhausted. We'll look after things down here. We'll call if you're needed."

He gets to his feet and yawns. "I'll grab some shuteye while I can."

Suddenly he's gone. Beatrice looks at Ellen. Her shoulders sag and her head droops. Whatever animated her expression has evaporated. She looks to have aged ten years.

Ellen touches her arm. "Are you okay?"

Beatrice almost pulls off a smile. "I'll be grand in a moment. I just have to pull myself together."

Ellen realizes what she means. "I'm an eejit. You're thinking of John, aren't you?"

Beatrice compresses her lips and nods. "I find these occasions unsettling. A death, any death, sets off so many associations and memories. I have to keep whipping myself to go on."

"I don't know how you do it."

"It's simple really. You have a choice. Go on or give up. I decided to keep going." She stands up and flaps the tea towel as if fanning herself, and her face regains some of its sparkle. She has sourced some reserves of energy. "Now, do you mind being put to work?" she asks.

"Not at all. I'm only delighted. Won't it upset Mona? By the way, where is Mona?"

"She's in the kitchen. She wasn't up to facing Matt. Look, Mona will have to accept the way things are. We need to pull together to keep Matt on an even keel. And why wouldn't you be here? You're family. I'm the odd one out, if you want to look at it that way."

When Mona sees Ellen clearing out the fireplace in the drawing room, her face closes down with repressed irritation.

By mid-afternoon the house is clean. A van draws up to the kitchen door. "Well timed, Lily," Mona says. "We could do with some of what you have."

It's raining outside. Lily's son rushes in carrying a huge pot and places it on the cooker. "Vegetable soup," he says. They unload trays of sandwiches covered in foil.

"I'd say you'll have a fair crowd up tonight," Lily says. "There's egg, salmon, ham, tomato, salad — you name it, we have it."

"I hope Matt's happy with what I ordered."

"He won't notice anything except there's a bill to be paid," Mona says.

"Give us a shout if you're running low," Lily says.

"I'd say this will be ample, Lily."

"You should have let me take care of all this," Mona says in a whinging tone. Her expression says that she feels sidelined.

"Would you prefer me to go? Is that it, Mona?" Beatrice asks.

"No, not at all," Mona says, her eyes darting about nervously. "He'd kill me if he thought I ran you. It's not your fault the way things are. You're very good to help out, I have to say." She can't keep the querulous note out of her voice.

"It's no bother. I'm only too happy to have the chance. Anyway, we won't be on our own for long."

"Once all the baking is done, they'll be up."

Lily has watched the exchanges with interest. "How's Matt taking it?" she asks.

"He's like a dog!" Mona complains. "He hasn't said a civil word to me in weeks."

Beatrice starts. "He's drained, the poor man," she says. "The last while has been rough. We sent him up to rest."

"And you, Mona? You must be worn to the bone," Lily says.

Mona puffs up like an affronted hen ruffling her feathers. "As well as can be expected. Everybody asks how Matt is doing. They forget she's — she was my sister."

"Nobody's forgetting that, Mona. You've been a trooper the last few weeks, practically living over here. I'm sure Matt's grateful."

"If he is, he never shows it."

"You know what men of that generation are like."

Mona is mollified. "I could do with some of that soup, Beatrice," she says. "I don't know when I last had a proper meal. The last few days have been dreadful. We were run off our feet looking after her."

"It's no wonder Matt's on a short fuse," Lily says.

"I did most of it," Mona says. "Well, he did the shopping and some cooking," she concedes, "but I nursed her. Still, better that she died at home. If she'd gone into hospital, that's where she'd have finished up. It all worked out in the end."

"Didn't you have help, Mona?" Lily asks.

"Oh, sure we had to at the end. Julia was all against it, but we'd never have coped without agency nurses and backup from the hospice. We had a hospice nurse in every night. They couldn't have looked after us better. Still, we hardly got a wink of sleep the last three nights. She was very low. I was afraid to leave her. She took a turn for the worse this morning, so we got hold of Father Mahoney after morning Mass, and he got here in time to give her the last rites."

"Take the weight off your feet, Mona, and I'll heat up soup," Beatrice says.

"I'll away," Lily says. "See you, Mona." She looks across the room at Ellen.

"You know Ellen, don't you, Lily?" Beatrice says. "Matt's niece."

Lily does a double take, swinging her platinum blond locks. "I've seen you about. If I'd paid proper attention, I'd have realized that you're Brendan's daughter. I remember your mother. When's she due to arrive?"

"Oh," Ellen says, flustered. "I haven't told her yet."

"Aren't you the one?"

"All in good time," says Beatrice.

"I'd best be off. Good afternoon to you all. You're the image of your father, God's honest truth," she says to Ellen.

"So they say."

Beatrice heats up soup, ladles it into a bowl, and sets it on a tray. "Open the door into the hallway, would you?" she asks Mona. "I'll bring some up to Matt."

"Didn't he eat cake?" snaps Mona.

"I think I hear him moving about. He needs something more substantial. He hasn't eaten properly in days—neither of you has. Would you mind opening the door, Ellen? Thanks. You're a love."

Ellen follows her into the hall and watches her climb the stairs.

The front door is open. The drizzle and mist have lifted and the sun is out again. Light floods the dark hallway. She steps out into the yard. To the left of the front porch, beyond the tarmacadam yard, is a patch of lawn dotted with evergreen shrubs. The sun's futile rays glance off her. She breathes in. The air singes her skin with cold and she steps back smartly into the hall.

"He's out for the count. I hadn't the heart to disturb him," Beatrice says from behind her, placing the tray on the hall table. She moves toward the door and steps outside. Ellen follows. Beatrice makes for the lawn and peers at some of the shrubs. "Hard to believe that they'll be in bud soon," she says. "We can't see it, but it's all starting to kick in, the engine of renewal. Marvelous, when you consider it. But we could be in for more cold snaps yet. I can remember snow in May."

"I was just thinking how long ago Christmas feels, yet it's only a few weeks."

"Paula was disappointed to miss you."

"If I hadn't stayed with Mum over the holidays it would have been death by a thousand cuts." She shrugs off her thoughts. "I'm so glad you're here, Beatrice. We'd never have managed Matt without you."

"It's difficult after a death," muses Beatrice. "Nothing tops it for making people feel disoriented and alone."

His mother had suggested the marriage. She had gone to school with Julia's mother and the two women remained firm friends, meeting up for Mass and Benediction, playing cards in the same group, exchanging books and gossip, bolstering each other's widowhood.

Mrs. Hughes thought the world of Julia. "What's your problem with her?" she asked. "She's a shopkeeper's daughter. The nuns educated her. She's of good character. She can cook and sew and do all the chores. What's more, she's strong. Besides, she's supposed to have a soft spot for you."

"I haven't the slightest interest in her."

"You should. She'd be an asset to us. The family's well-off."

Chary of incurring his mother's wrath through continued resistance, he took to calling to Julia's house. His mother set the agenda and turned it into a culinary courtship, giving him milk or eggs or salted meat to bring to the house, and, through the medium of her son, offering her friend a goose at Christmas and a leg of lamb at Easter. She courted Julia by proxy.

As the months wore on and a year went by, Matt showed no sign of proposing. Julia tired of him sitting uneasily and mostly silently on a chair in her mother's parlor. She took over the business of courtship, became the energizing force in their dealings with each other, and tried to spur him into action. At home his mother wore him down with her eulogizing of Julia. She told neighbors that he and Julia were "walking out" with each other. People began to ask when the big day was planned.

Julia was small-breasted and slim-hipped, her mouth always slightly open because of her bucked front teeth, a long, bony face — her head a fuzzy curly mop — nothing to look at, thought Matt. Could he tolerate her day after day, year after year, decade after decade? Would it drive him mad to have to listen to her inane chatter, or would he become immune to her?

He'd been working up to taking a stance, breaking it to her that they should go their separate ways, when Beatrice married Jack Furlong and that threw him into turmoil. He hadn't even been aware of the wedding plans.

His mother crowed. "Jack Furlong must have been lovesick. What had she to bring to the marriage? Her family hasn't two pence to rub together. Her father's a small farmer, hiring himself out to make ends meet."

"Don't you say anything against her," he warned.

"If she was so wonderful, why did ye break up?" she taunted. "Who wouldn't pull? All your secret comings and goings — don't think I didn't know what was happening. Did she give you the shove? If only Brendan were here. He wouldn't be hankering after a common little madam. Can't you see the squalor she comes from?"

"Squalor, is it? There was never a more respectable, clean-living family. They might have to scrabble about to make a living, but they're decent honest people. You're an almighty snob, Mam. Look, Brendan couldn't get out of here fast enough. He wanted to put as much distance as possible between you and him. Your beloved son couldn't stomach the idea of knuckling down under your yoke. Vocation, my eye! It was his pass out of here!"

"Don't you badmouth your brother. If he had stayed, you'd have had to sling your hook. And if you don't watch your step, I'll will the farm to somebody else."

He laughed shortly. "And who will you leave it to, Mam? The church? Get away with you."

"Don't underestimate me."

"That I'd never do. I have the utmost respect for your spite."

At teatime that evening, in a more reasonable tone, she said, "Get shut of all those romantic notions, Matt. Don't be pining after what you can't have. You need a wife. I won't be around forever. If you don't settle down, you'll rue the day. You'll be like one of those pitiful old bachelors who still drive down to the creamery with their asses and carts."

There was something to what his mother said. The woman he had wanted was spoken for. There was nobody else. Emigration had taken care of that. Most of the young women had left the place. Julia was probably the best of those still living in the parish. He didn't want to end up like one of those half-mad fellows on a dilapidated farm. He'd seen them at Mass with their dirt-encrusted skin and stained fraying suits. He'd sniffed their odor. He'd been in their stinking, filthy kitchens. Would he finish up like that? Could he endure it?

He confronted his reluctance to marry. It should have been merely a matter of resolve, but it wasn't a decision he came to easily. He reminded himself how few expectations his parents had for their own marriage, and how little happiness it had delivered to them.

Julia's good points? He rehearsed his mother's arguments again and again. God willing, there would be children who would dilute their enforced intimacy. They would surely make an accommodation with each other.

When he proposed, she accepted immediately, almost as if she were afraid he'd withdraw the offer if she gave him a minute to think about it. There were no pre-wedding intimacies. Once or twice he forced himself to deliver a chaste peck to her cheek, and Julia initiated some awkward hand-holding in public.

As the wedding date approached, Julia's attentions to him slackened. This reticence revealed itself for what it was on the night of the wedding. They were in their hotel bedroom in Galway on the first of two nights away from the farm. The weak light from the single lamp in the room muddied their complexions, draining any color from their faces. He sat on a chair by the window, restlessly smoking a cigarette, trying to decide whether she was too nervous to be touched, but wondering if she expected it.

"Let's get one thing straight," she said as she pushed their cases under the bed. "I can't abide the idea of you laying hands on me. I'll do my duty as far as having children is concerned. Don't expect me to like it, that's all."

He stared at her. He'd been worried about trapping her into a marriage where love was absent. Once he'd even said, hesitantly, that he wasn't in love with her, but he supposed they'd grow fond of each other and make a go of it. They were standing at the door of her mother's house. She said nothing, looked down at the ground.

He thought it odd at the time and then forgot it. Now it was clear that there was no love on her side. He stamped out the cigarette butt on the floor. "So a roll in the hay is out of the question?" he said challengingly.

She met his unwavering stare with a look of disdain. "Don't use that tone of voice to me! It's disgusting. How could you talk to your wife that way?"

"You mightn't mind it too much when you get used to it."

"Don't corrupt your tongue by talking that way."

"Why did you agree to be married if that's the case? Didn't you know that sexual intercourse is part and parcel of marriage?"

She shook her head. "Bodily lusts. Carnality. The thought of it disgusts me."

"Come on," he cajoled. "We have to be companions to each other."

She turned away. "I know there has to be some of it," she said. "It's unpleasant to even think about. The main business is the running of the farm and passing it on to the next generation." She sat calmly before him in the other chair, confident of her power.

"The marriage isn't consummated. We could have it annulled. That'd bring us back to square one."

She blinked quickly a few times, as if in shock. Then she recovered herself. "You wouldn't have the guts for that. You'd have to face down people at home and have them all talking about you. You'd know there'd always be sniggering and speculation. Sure, your mother wouldn't stand for it." She smiled her thin-lipped smile but there was no friendliness in it.

She'd outmaneuvered him and played him for a fool. She and his mother could augment each other's pride. They could connive against him, the man.

He was overcome by a feeling of rage. He wanted to hit her. His arm ached to whack her or throttle her. He could send her flying. The force of the blow would upend her chair and she'd be propelled against the wall. He pictured her on the floor, stunned, imagined taking her by force, imposing himself on her. He felt sickened by these thoughts. No, he wouldn't belittle himself by hitting her. He wouldn't bully her into submission. He looked at her in disgust. She looked ugly. Whether it was because of what she had said, or because of the unflattering light, he didn't care. He would always be repulsed by her.

"Why did you want this marriage?" he asked.

She frowned. Perhaps the question had never occurred to her. Marriage, any suitable marriage, was enough for her. Whom she married was immaterial.

"Didn't you realize that you'd be expected to be a wife?"

"A wife!" she spat. "Don't upbraid me for that. I know I'm not the one you wanted. I know full well that I'm second best for you."

Such resentment, such sanctimonious intransigence, made him sick. "Hardly even second best," he said cuttingly. "If it weren't for my mother, you'd never have got a look-in. Tenth best, tenth rate is what I think you are, and that's only because there isn't any competition."

Just a slight inclination of her head indicated that he had got through to her. That had torn it. He had done it. There would be no mending of fences.

He had to get out of this situation and away from her. He jumped to his feet, knocking over his chair, and rushed out of the room. He hardly noticed where he was going.

What if he disowned her? He knew the arguments against that. Her reputation would be damaged. Soiled goods. That's what they'd say. What did he care about that? He'd be shut of her. In his heart he knew that he had to care. She was tenacious. She might sue him for breach of promise.

He looked about and realized that he was on the beach. He kicked a few pebbles and scattered them, grabbed a smooth flat stone and skimmed it across the top of the water. It bounced and hit the surface twice before it sank. He picked up another stone and aimed it.

His mother wouldn't back him. That the marriage was a sham would be of little import. He knew what it would boil down to with her. The preservation of outward appearances was paramount in all her dealings with the world.

He considered walking into the sea, the dark, dark sea. What would be the point of that? He knew he'd turn around and come out again. He had only one good suit and he was wearing it. He'd have the problem of explaining how it got wet, and the trouble of attempting to dry it.

He walked up from the scrunching shingle across the road to the hotel and spent the night on a seat in the lounge. The bar was long closed. One of the waitresses woke him. At her urging, he ate a full Irish breakfast. The girl seemed sorry for him. She was very attentive to his needs. He knew she guessed that things hadn't gone well in the bedroom. Such occurrences were common in those days. She didn't know the half of it. She couldn't comprehend what he had tied himself to.

He spent the next day in a bar in the city center. At night he walked back to Salthill and again slept in a chair. The following morning he paid the bill and she came down for breakfast. She deposited the packed cases in the hall, and he threw them into the boot. They maintained a hostile silence all the way home, even when the engine overheated and they had to wait for it to cool. The first words she spoke were to his mother.

Eight

KITTY SWEEPS INTO Ellen's house. As always, she looks fresh. "Hello, darling," she says, holding her daughter at arm's length. "Let me look at you. I think you've lost weight. That's a blessing. At least you're wearing a decent ensemble this morning. You're perfectly capable of looking like a tramp. What time is this wretched funeral?"

"After eleven o'clock Mass."

They air-kiss each other's cheeks — a carefully controlled maneuver — and Kitty springs away from contact. Almost four weeks have passed since Ellen's return to Ballindoon following their first Christmas alone together in Dublin. During the enforced isolation of the holiday, they found themselves in unending opposition. Kitty reproached Ellen on a daily basis for moving to Ballindoon, and Ellen countered by going out a lot. The predictable quarrel erupted the day before New Year's Eve when Kitty claimed that the least Ellen could do for her was to spend more time in her company and less socializing with Maureen and other friends.

"Funeral Masses are always so late," Kitty complains, sitting at the kitchen table and looking about. "Still, it could have been midday. Thank God for small mercies." She purses her lips in a critical fashion. "Your place is a bit bare, isn't it? There's hardly a stick of furniture. It's possible to overdo the minimalism, you know. You haven't gone all Buddhist or contemplative, have you? I hope not." Kitty is a repository of small talk, a bottomless reservoir of commonplace sentiments on any subject. It's as though no topic holds her interest for long. She and Ellen have never indulged in any mother-daughter confidences, and if she has any deep convictions, Ellen has yet to discover them. They are disconnected and unaligned, Ellen thinks, clinging tenuously to a relationship that could easily fall apart.

There was a time when Kitty's actions concerned Ellen greatly. All through her childhood and teenage years her mother produced various men friends, claiming them to be cousins or in-laws who, nevertheless, shared her bedroom for weeks or months before departing on good or bad terms, or simply suddenly absenting themselves — sometimes taking monetary souvenirs or mementoes with them — never to be mentioned again. As a teenager, Ellen worried about the fallout from others branding her mother a slut. She knew that priests had stopped denouncing wrongdoers from pulpits but that didn't stop her worrying about repercussions arising from Kitty's behavior. However, Kitty led a charmed life and no such difficulties ever arose. As she aged her supply of admirers thinned somewhat, although the aging process has been kind to Kitty and makes few depredations on her appearance. She's a slim and elegant woman in her early sixties, today dressed smartly in a deep blue dress and light cream coat. Her simply styled short hair is dyed a light brown and her makeup, though minimal, has been carefully applied. The scent of her perfume pervades the kitchen. "Christy's parking the car on the main street," she says.

Ellen's internal organs contort. "What! Christy! You said Christy, didn't you? What's he doing here? How come? I don't understand. I mean, there's absolutely no need for him to be here." She paces about in an agitated fashion. "He's not coming into this house," she declares.

Kitty sends an exasperated look her way. "Don't be ridiculous, Ellen. Calm down. If he's not allowed in, then we'll turn right round and drive back to Dublin. Don't be cross. He's being such a sweetheart. Offered to drive me down when I rang him. My old jalopy is in for repairs so he insisted on giving me a lift." She stands up. "I have to do a little tour of the house, dear. I want to see what's what."

Ellen stirs herself and leads Kitty into the front room. Kitty moves about briskly. "Oh, my dear, this is still very drab. But the conservatory is such a good idea. See what a difference color on the walls makes. That's a nice shade of yellow. I know conservatories are being built all over the place now, but this one is properly positioned." She peers into the garden. "You haven't done much out there, have you? It's a jungle."

Suddenly Christy joins them, and the room darkens. For Ellen, he's the focus of energy-sapping negativity. She says nothing but she can't bring herself to look at him. He moves as if to embrace her, but she sidesteps him, and he smiles sheepishly when he sees her scowl.

Kitty turns. "Grace under pressure," she says, her face taut. "Be civil, Ellen!"

Ellen recovers quickly. *Grace under pressure* — one of her mother's favorite sayings, almost her motto for life. "Hello, Christy," she manages. "Want a cup of tea or coffee? Tea is very big in these parts. Why don't you show him around, Kitty? Have a look yourself." She's delighted that her delivery is pat.

In the kitchen she breathes in deeply, trying to remember a yoga instructor's directions about how to control one's reactions through controlling one's breath. *"If the breathing's right, then you're all right."* She hears the shrill of her mother's voice conducting a full tour of the house and pours water into the kettle, only to realize that it's already full. "Shit," she mutters as she tries to catch the overflow with a cloth. The water drips onto the floor. She mops up furiously. Damn Kitty, damn her interfering nature, and damn and doubly damn Christy for not having the sense to stay away.

Kitty shows Christy into the kitchen. "I like this room. It's rural but not twee. I love the handles on the units, they remind me of an apothecary's shop."

"When were you last in one of those?" Ellen asks.

Christy stands at a remove from Ellen, his hands jammed into his jacket pockets, his shoulders frozen in a shrug, lips shaped into a grimace that could be a smile. Seeing him like this, hunched and round-shouldered, separated from his normal milieu and without his usual props, makes him look vulnerable, like a mouse poking its quivering, alert nose out into the world. There's something deeply offensive about his pale weak face. Once, she thought him good-looking, but now that she knows how lily-livered he is, she finds him distasteful.

"Nice place," he says. "I wouldn't mind it myself."

Ellen sighs noisily but bites down on a sharp rejoinder. She must keep herself under control. She calculates that she'll have to tolerate their company for more than an hour before they'll be able to set off for the funeral Mass. It'll be hard work, grueling really, but she reckons she can endure anything for an hour.

"Where's the jacks?" Christy asks.

Ellen signals the direction of the downstairs toilet. "What did you think you were playing at by bringing him down?" she snaps at Kitty when he's gone.

"Bringing Christy down?" Her mother feigns puzzlement. It's one of her standard tactics.

Ellen explodes. "Don't try the innocent with me. I'm up to all your tricks, remember? Did it ever occur to you that it wasn't the thing to drag him along, that he's the very last person you should have brought? We're not separated all that long. What were you thinking? Did you lose your reason? Don't you dare tell people who he is!"

Kitty removes her coat and hands it to Ellen, who accepts it automatically. "Hang that up, would you, darling?" she says and arranges the skirt of her dress to sit down. "Don't be ridiculous, Ellen. I'm not going to pretend he's a stranger. People know he exists. Anyway, it's difficult enough for me to remember day-to-day things, never mind the nuisance of a deceit. We're not part of a farce."

"Don't introduce him to anybody outside the family then! I've managed not to mention him. It just complicates everything."

Christy returns and Kitty invites him to sit at the table. Ellen hangs up Kitty's coat in the hall. For a second she contemplates slashing its quality lining. Instead she rests her head against the coat for a few moments. Her forehead feels hot. She's sure that her face is flushed. On her return to the kitchen she slams a plate of sandwiches and cut cake on the table in front of them. The plate survives. "There's a reception in the pub after the burial," she says.

Kitty nods, but then she and Christy are discussing how soon they will be able to make a getaway after the funeral. They are easy and intimate with each other, full of casual banter and practiced phrases, with Kitty — a dedicated flatterer of men — chuckling flirtatiously every so often. Their calm demeanor maddens Ellen. It's an affront to her. Her jaw aches from clamping it down on intemperate words.

"We'd better show up at the pub. Wouldn't do to skip off after the burial," Christy concludes.

Kitty sighs. "There's no avoiding it."

Ellen sits away from them and listens. She watches Kitty push the sandwiches toward Christy and hears him laugh at something she says. Their voices sound far away, as if the volume has been turned down. She can't tune in to their wavelength. There's even a static buzz in her ears.

Christy faces Ellen, his pasty face intent. "How long does the business in the pub last?" he asks.

"The immediate thing with food goes on for about an hour. Then it thins out."

"Quite the local bumpkin, eh, Ellen?" Kitty says. "You know it all."

"Sit here, Ellen. I've poured coffee," Christy says, doing his best to be gracious. Somehow she manages to comply. He pushes the milk toward her and offers her a sandwich. He's deferential, his head low by way of apology. He's taller than she remembers and wears his clothes better. It's odd to be on the receiving end of his conviviality, disconcerting even, like viewing different presentations of him on a split screen and being unable to choose the definitive version.

"I never expected you to turn up, Christy," she says. "Last person on earth I thought would be eating sandwiches in my kitchen."

"Told Kitty I'd give her a lift as she'd no other way of getting here. Should have thought through the ramifications, I know. Sorry. Anyway, how are you, Ellen?" His voice compels her to be civil.

"I'm well." She hopes she says it with conviction. "Yourself?"

"Can't complain."

"He's had dreadful luck since you two split up," Kitty says. She fiddles with a bit of cake on her plate.

"Is that so?"

"Yes, the agency folded and he lost his job. Luckily, he had the apartment all sorted out — no mortgage — so that's a blessing."

"That's a shame, Christy. I'm sure you'll pick up something."

"Let there be no panic, I always say. Something will turn up. I'd have jumped ship if I'd realized that the place was going to close down, but it happened suddenly. I'm not destitute or anything. It's no trouble to pick up bits and pieces of part-time work. There's always a need for a good PR man. A bit of slack between jobs is natural. I'll just have to wait it out."

Ellen nods. "You'll be fine," she says coldly.

Kitty darts an irritated glance at Ellen. "How's Matt coping? How's he taking it? I always thought that he and Julia were mismatched."

"He's not great."

"Years since I last saw him," Kitty says, patting her hair. "Is he still as dashing as ever? Brendan was a fine man but he wasn't a smasher like his brother."

"Smasher, Mum? That word is so passé. You should get your terms up-to-date. You'll have to judge his looks for yourself. You'll see him soon enough. He wants us to sit in the same pew as the family."

"That doesn't include me," Christy says.

"No, no, not you, just Mum and me."

"Why can't Christy —" Kitty begins, but a shake of Ellen's head silences her. "Oh, I suppose not." She shudders. "If we must." She leans forward in her chair and places a hand on Ellen's elbow. "And it's only because you insisted that I agreed to come. I'm sure I could have found some excuse to get out of it."

"You're dreadful, Mum. Absolutely dreadful."

"Call me Kitty. Don't call me Mum. I don't want people guessing my age."

"I'll tell them you had me in your teens."

Kitty looks around. "Burying yourself down here. It's madness really. Don't you agree, Christy?"

He coughs a few times and manages not to answer, looks as if he'd choose to be anywhere but in Ellen's kitchen. "Would you listen to what you're saying, Mum? You're interfering again. It's none of your business."

"Surely I'm entitled to my opinions?"

"Certainly, but that doesn't mean you have to express them."

"It's not right that my only child is living so far away from me. Why don't you move back to Dublin? You and Christy should hook up together again. I can't understand why you didn't make even the teeniest effort to patch things up."

Ellen thumps the table and her mother gives a theatrical start. "Mum, back off. Stay out of things that are none of your business. Since when did you become the great advocate of the moral order?"

"Well, I never—such impertinence!"

"Your mother thinks it a shame we broke up," Christy says. He fiddles with the sugar bowl, lifts a spoon of sugar into the air, tilts the spoon, and pours the sugar back into the bowl.

Ellen snatches the spoon and pushes the bowl away from him. "Best thing ever happened to us," she snaps. "We were miserable together."

"Ellen," her mother says brokenly. "Ellen. How can you say such a thing? Christy's a lovely man." Ellen has to admire the intensity of her delivery. She has often thought that Kitty missed a career as an actress.

"You don't know what a marriage is like unless you're in it, Mum." Ellen looks at her watch and jumps to her feet. "Time marches on. Do you need to freshen up?" she says.

Kitty fixes her with a resentful glare. "I'll call you Kitty all afternoon if you keep your face out of my business," Ellen says sweetly.

Kitty sighs heavily twice, and then pulls herself together. She composes her face. "Thank you, darling. I'll just nip upstairs and leave you two to talk." She jumps to her feet and glides away. Her footsteps tap lightly on the bare boards of the stairs.

Ellen begins to clear the table. She picks up the last sandwich and eats it at the sink.

Christy clears his throat a few times. Then he coughs. She had forgotten his little coughs. "I wonder did we do the right thing by splitting up?" he says.

Ellen ignores this.

"Have you ever thought about it? Maybe we were too hasty?"

"Christy!" she warns. "You were the one who wanted out."

"Maybe I was too rash?"

She walks toward him, rests her hands heavily on the table, and looks into his eyes. "Wild horses, all the tea in China, or gold in the world — nothing could make me want to get back with you, Christy. I don't care if I never see you again. Geddit?"

He's silent, his face inscrutable. Then he spreads his hands, palms up in a gesture of surrender, and smiles his engaging smile. "Got you! Don't worry, pet. I've no designs on you. It was worth a try to see your reaction."

She doesn't believe him for a moment. "You're a dreadful twit, Christy, did I ever mention it?"

He grins wickedly and eventually forces her to smile. "We don't have to be enemies," he says.

"No, we don't have to be enemies." We'll just never be friends, she thinks.

In the pub later on, she's horrified to see Christy talking to Eugene. She stands beside them, but it's as if she's not there. She tries to interject a few times but they don't draw breath. They're talking about sport, arguing the toss on whether the commercialization of sport has reduced soccer and rugby to mere businesses. She leaves them for a while, but when she comes back they have become absorbed in the analysis of goals, great saves, great tries, superb feats of athleticism, deciding how to classify or categorize them. Again, she moves away, and when she thinks they must have exhausted the topic, she discovers them discussing drug taking and cheating. She cannot believe the intensity of their contributions. They toss in arguments, kick them around, find something to disagree about and pitch points at each other. It's like a competition from which everybody else is excluded. Christy's thoroughly engrossed in the conversation. At one point, Eugene catches her eye and smiles, but he keeps talking. She wants to separate them but she's helpless in the face of their indifference.

The crowd around Matt has thinned a little. She spots Stephen — it's only in the last few months that they've come across each other again — nursing a pint. Tall, lean, and good-looking, he takes after

Matt. Colum, shorter, balding and slightly plump, is engrossed in conversation with old school friends in a corner. His wife and children are sitting at a table with Beatrice.

Kitty beckons her over. "Get me a top-up, darling," she says, holding up her glass. She's on her second or third drink and chatting to Brenda Finnegan, who's pumping her for information. Kitty's the mistress of giving nothing away while seeming to be expansive.

Ellen passes Matt on her way to the bar. He's in good form, stimulated by the occasion. He squeezes her elbow as she passes. She waves at Stephen, who calls her over. "Is your mother staying on for a couple of days?" he asks.

"Oh no, she's heading straight back. She intended to leave much earlier but then she relaxed into the moment."

"By the look of it, you may have to put her and Christy up tonight."

"I agree. They look as if they've no intention of moving. I'm getting Mum a drink. It's kind of weird how convivial funerals are."

"I've met more of my schoolmates here in the last hour than in the last ten years, plus been introduced to scores more people. Feels as if the family has just expanded. Let me get these. What's the order?"

"Not at all. We got our drink."

"Let me buy, for God's sake. Another lager for you. What's your Mum's poison?"

"Pernod and ice, half a lager for me. If I don't eat soon I'll be stupid with drink."

"There's plenty of food."

Eugene approaches her on her way back from the table and steals a cocktail sausage from her plate. "Hello there," he says. She looks askance at him. "Hey, what's up?"

"What's up? You have the nerve to ask me what's up! I don't get it. I've hardly seen you of late and then you decide to monopolize Christy."

"I couldn't let the opportunity of talking to him pass."

"And had you lots to say to each other?" she asks. Her drink catches in her throat and she's overcome by a coughing fit.

He pats her back solicitously. "Oh yes, we had a great chat. He seems a sociable fellow."

She feels that he wants to nettle her. "The man you spoke to wasn't the man I had to live with. How did you get talking to him?"

"Your Uncle Matt introduced us. I had a chat with Kitty, too. She's wearing well. Think it might be genetic?"

"Who cares? Think you know it all now, do you?" She's aware that she sounds cantankerous but she can't keep the sharpness out of her voice.

"You never said much about Christy, although you did mention your marriage."

"He's not going to be my husband for much longer," she snaps. "I didn't ask about your history, did I?"

"I seem to remember it being mentioned."

"Shit, you're right. I just didn't like to see the two of you talking. He shouldn't be here, but Kitty brought him."

"It's kind of interesting though, isn't it? What makes a couple? What attracts people to each other? It can be difficult for outsiders to understand."

"It's even difficult for the people in the relationship. It's not surprising that people split up. What's surprising is when they stay together."

He laughs. She's still cross with him, so when Stephen appears at her side and says, "Your Mum is looking for you," she replies, "Come and talk to her, Stephen. She's susceptible to handsome young men," and springs away from Eugene. He doesn't follow, and perversely she's disappointed when she looks back to see him talking to Beatrice.

Christy is sitting on a bar stool in front of her mother's table. As Ellen and Stephen approach, he stands up. "About time we hit the road, don't you think?" he says to Kitty.

"Oh. Stephen, were you coming to talk to me?" wails Kitty. "I think we're going to go."

"We'll find another opportunity," Stephen says smoothly. "Thanks very much for traveling down, Kitty. You too, Christy."

"Are you fit to drive?" Ellen asks Christy.

He grimaces. "I kept it down to a pint and ate loads. Food makes a difference."

Her mother pulls a face, stretches her arms, and yawns. "He's a man, Ellen. Of course he'll manage. I think I'll sleep all the way home. I'm so glad we made the funeral," she says to Stephen with a coy look.

Stephen hands her the Pernod.

"Drink up," Christy urges.

"I'll have to leave it," Kitty says, putting the drink aside. "What a waste. Last thing I want now is to face the drive to Dublin."

"Stretch out in the back seat if you want," Christy says.

She shakes her head. "I'll just pop on my sunglasses and lean back against the headrest. You won't know if I'm awake or asleep."

"Except for when you snore," Ellen says.

"Don't be unkind. You know I don't snore." Kitty rises to her feet. "It's been lovely to see what fine young men Matt's boys have become," she says to Stephen. She kisses him on the cheek and turns to Ellen. "Remember, dear. Come up to Dublin and call in to see your poor old mother sometime. You were out and about a lot at Christmas."

"Of course I'll visit, Kitty. Let me see you to the car."

"You're not running away, are you?" Matt asks Ellen as Kitty makes her protracted goodbyes, extracting kisses from Matt and Colum.

"I'll be back."

Christy and Kitty are in a great hurry suddenly. "We've a good distance to go and we don't want to get caught in rush hour traffic," Christy says, pointing to his watch as if it's to blame for their delay. Ellen allows her mother to kiss her cheek but repulses Christy with a fierce glare. "Well, I'm done with this village," Kitty says as she sits into the passenger seat, "unless you're going to invite me down for a visit, Ellen."

"Certainly, I'll invite you down." She glances at Christy. "Unaccompanied, I mean." He makes her an ironic little bow before he sits in behind the steering wheel.

The engine bursts into life, tinted electric windows whirring open as Kitty waves and then shutting as the car glides away. Ellen can see Kitty and Christy only as silhouettes. She waves them off. It's one of those surreal moments, as if she dreamed it.

As she goes to re-enter the pub, she finds the entrance porch blocked by Mona, deep in conversation with another woman. Her "excuse me" and clearing of throat is ignored as they hunch into each other like penguins with outstretched flippers. They're oblivious to her.

"It was awful beyond imagining, Sadie," Mona says. "At first, we couldn't manage the bloody wig. It's shapeless when it's not on somebody's head. We had the hairdresser up twice and she fixed it, but when she was gone it took ages to get it right. Then she took against it and refused to wear it—the perversity of it—but equally refused to be seen with a bald head."

"Still, you can understand it in a way. You can see why," Sadie says as they move toward Mona's car.

"But it meant no visitors, Sadie. That didn't seem right. It was a nightmare."

"Wouldn't she tie a scarf around her head or wear a cap?"

"You might as well have asked her to go to the moon, Sadie. There was no way."

"You had to respect her wishes, Mona. You had no choice."

"It was heart-scalding."

"But she wore the wig in the coffin?"

"I made sure of that," Mona says grimly. "He was indifferent. Typical man."

Mona suddenly sees Ellen and acknowledges her with a cool nod. She doesn't seem to realize that she's in the way.

"Are you off, Mona?" Ellen asks. "Sorry, excuse me while I get by."

Belatedly, Mona and Sadie shuffle out into the street. "I've had enough of this funeral. They're all in great humor in there. It's more like a get-together," Mona says bitterly.

"It's always the way," Ellen says weakly as she squeezes by.

Mona and Sadie resume their huddled conversation, their hatted heads arching low.

Back in Hegarty's, Stephen accosts Ellen and says, "Most people run away from the countryside. What makes you the exception?"

"It's a long boring story, Stephen. When Christy and I split up, it wasn't easy. I didn't want to stay in the city, but for ages I didn't know what to do. When it came to the crunch, all my history, all my associations with Ballindoon, really counted for something. I used to be so happy here. Suddenly, this seemed the only place to be."

He laughs. "Can't see how myself. I know you and Christy aren't together. But wasn't coming here a bit extreme?"

"Ah, Stephen," she says lightly. "When there's a crisis, it's surprising how your mind works. You have to think outside the box to solve it."

"And think inside another one?"

It's her turn to laugh. "That's one way of putting it. I thought archaeology, not psychology, was your forté!"

"We're going back to the house now, Ellen. Are you coming?" Matt calls.

She hesitates. "You will," says Stephen. "No arguing. It'll give you a chance to talk to Colum and Úna. You'll like them. We'll make a pot of coffee and we can make inroads into the sandwiches. We've enough to feed an army."

As they leave the pub Ellen spots Eugene in deep conversation with an attractive, tanned, skimpily dressed teenager. His face is animated, totally focused on the girl, who welcomes the attention, unfurling her body, thrusting out her chest, and leaning toward him.

"There's your kitchen man," Matt says. "Looks like he's doing some cradle snatching. He has a bit of a reputation, you know."

"Really?" Suddenly she feels sick.

Nine

*T*HE MORNING AFTER Julia's burial, on Ellen's return to
work, she doesn't expect and isn't offered expressions of
sympathy, such as, "Sorry to hear about your aunt," or the
more standard "Sorry for your trouble" from colleagues. Nora, the
principal, says, "Eddie told me there was a death in the family."

"Yes," confirms Ellen, clipping the word.

"Sorry to hear the news about your aunt," Joyce O'Dea says in
the car park at lunchtime.

Ellen nods. "Thanks," she says bleakly.

"How's Matt?" Eddie asks that afternoon when they meet on
a school corridor. "He's had a hard time the last few months." To
Ellen's amazement, Eddie put in an appearance at Julia's removal,
came and shook her hand afterward, muttered platitudes, and
offered his condolences, especially to Matt who, when nudged by
Ellen, appeared to recognize him but later claimed that he hadn't
a clue who he was.

"He talks as if he knows you," Ellen prompted. "Mentioned you
the first time I met him."

"Probably served on some committee I was on. I understand
who he is, but we don't know each other," Matt said.

"Thanks for turning up," she says to Eddie.

"Least I could do. I live out your direction," he replies, and
passes on.

However, a week or so after Julia's funeral — did it prick their consciences? — as if by pre-arranged signal, other colleagues begin to acknowledge Ellen. Oh yes, now they all know her name, where she lives, and how she came to be in the school. They chat as if they've always chatted to her, smile as if that's always how they behaved, make common ground about the weather, query her opinions on items of news, and ask her professional advice. At last she occupies space, and now she has mass and momentum. She can't fathom why she has finally impinged on their consciousness, but welcomes rather than resents the attention, relieved not to be endlessly embattled.

She's well aware of how little in common individuals on the staff have with her and that she's unlikely to strike up any friendships. However, civility and surface friendliness will do well enough.

She hasn't — what was the point? — committed a directory of teacher identities to memory. Now, suddenly, she has to remember a glut of names. It's a while before she adjusts to the strangeness of the *Hiya, Ellen* or *Good morning, Ellen* or *How's it goin'?* or *Want to come to the Riverbank for lunch?* invitations.

Matt said that Eugene has a reputation. Does he? Could he be a dissembler? She's reconfiguring him, revisiting her feelings, and weighing everything between them. She senses that Eugene is a person of integrity but how can she be sure? She's no expert on men and her track record isn't good.

However, in his presence, her powers of discernment don't work. Her only weapons against him are words and there she is vulnerable. She doesn't have full control over what she says.

"Can't you get shut of those copybooks?" he asks in uncharacteristically bad-tempered tones during a visit one night.

"You've no idea of how much stress I'm under."

"A lot of it looks self-inflicted. Ellen, you have to have down time, time off, your own time, time for me. What's the problem?"

But she can't bring herself to say "irrational jealousy" because she knows how repellent that is.

"This job, the atmosphere in the school," she says. "It's suffocating, really getting to me."

"I thought things had improved. Give it up if it's so awful."

"Don't be ridiculous." He recoils from her snappiness. "Sorry, sorry," she says.

"Hey, Ellen," he says, pulling her to him. "Poor Ellen."

She frees herself from his embrace. "I'm all on edge," she explains. "I could snap, like a twig."

He could snap me in two and discard me, she thinks. She remembers those tenuous teenage years when she fancied the boy who collected the pools from her mother's house every Friday night. Then her mortification, when a verbal slip betrayed her infatuation to the hostile cohort of pretty girls in her class, and it was relayed back to her that he knew she was besotted with him and found it amusing, if somewhat pathetic. And the care those girls took to ensure that she knew precisely in what terms he had dismissed her — in all its grubby, and no doubt enhanced and distorted, detail.

Then the agony of knowing that she would have to face him at the door the following Friday night. But she carried it off, handed the money over with aplomb, took the sheet from him, cracked a joke (cracked a joke!), and closed the door firmly in his face. From then on she had engineered being out on a Friday night and encountered him only once again, at one of those hideous discos that, occasionally, her mother forced her to attend with Teresa (whatever happened to Teresa, her fellow sufferer?). When he approached and asked her to dance, she turned away.

"Well, obviously, you can't fit me into your busy schedule," Eugene says, inviting contradiction.

She sighs heavily. "Maybe we'd better cool it for the moment."

He gives her such a look that she's afraid she has pushed him too far. "Perhaps that's best. Let me know when you decide to rejoin the world," he says in a voice taut with exasperation.

Ellen collapses into a seat in the staff room after a parent-teacher meeting in mid-February and sits with the other washed-out souls. "How did you get on?" Joyce inquires.

"Kept my end up."

"I'm going to treat myself to a stiff drink tonight."

"Good idea," Ellen says. "I'll buy a tipple on the way home."

"Entertaining?" asks Terry, when she presents her bottle of wine at the till.

"Unwinding after a parent-teacher meeting."

"You call that work?"

"There's more to it than you realize, Terry, same as there's more to your job than meets the eye." She's more circumspect with Terry now, conscious of the woman's appetite for the lowdown on everybody.

"Your uncle's in Hegarty's," Terry says.

"What?"

"Matt has been drinking all afternoon."

Ellen has been dreading an encounter with Matt. He's a tinderbox of emotions, touchy, quick to take offense, and easily fired to anger. Nothing placates him. She has been giving him a miss of late, although he's on her mind constantly.

"That's as may be, but I'm going to get a burger and chips from the take-away, go home, and hit the sack. I'm good for nothing tonight."

"Take a quick look in at your uncle."

"Matt's business is none of my business, Terry. He's a grown man. He'd be furious if he thought I was checking up on him."

"It'd do no harm to say 'Hello.'"

"Any other evening, but I'm just whacked."

"Pop over to him—there's a good woman. Take over the till, Bart, would you?" Terry calls. She hustles Ellen out of the shop. In a low voice, she says, "Matt was never one of those drones propping up the bar. He's always been able to hold his drink, but this time he's out of it altogether, polluted drunk. It's a crying shame. For his own sake, try and persuade him to go home. I'm terrible fond of him, as you know." She registers Ellen's look of irritation and shrugs. "I'm only doing it for the best."

"Are you sure you're not exaggerating?"

"I most certainly am not. He needs someone in his corner. Go and give him a hand."

"Fine," Ellen snaps. "This is ridiculous, you know." She opens the car, drops the newspaper and wine bottle on the back seat, and locks the door.

A passerby watches them curiously. "Evening, Mrs. O'Sullivan,"

Terry says. "Your magazine will be in tomorrow. I rang the distributors." She throws Ellen one of those loaded looks and scuttles back into the shop.

"Damn," mutters Ellen as she enters the pub. At first, she can't see Matt. Then she realizes he's wedged in behind a pillar, his cap at an angle and a few days' growth of stubble on his face. He has lost weight and there's an unkempt air about him. She's working up the courage to approach him when a hand is laid on her arm. She turns to find Eugene blocking her way. "Out and about again? And about time, too," he says with a grin.

Meeting him is like a punch to the stomach. "Oh, Eugene," she says, winded.

"You never got back to me," he accuses. "I'd almost given up on you."

"I know, but I'm getting on top of things finally."

"This coming out of purdah is long overdue. What'll you have? I heard a great report of you today."

"I'm sick of all this scrutiny," she says. The words are no sooner out than she regrets them.

"Hey!" he protests. "It was intended as a compliment. Customers of mine are the parents of one of your students. The wife mentioned that her daughter loves being in your class."

"That's very nice but . . . Look, I'm sorry. This isn't a good day." Out of the corner of her eye she observes Matt raise a finger and order another drink. Even at a distance, it's obvious how drunk he is, how out of sync his body is. Her whole being contracts with tension. Her breath is constricted. "I can't talk now, never mind have a drink. I have to go over to Matt."

Eugene's face darkens. "If this is more of giving me the runabout, just say."

"Nothing like that," she protests. "Anyway," and she can't shake off a caustic tone, "where's your young friend? I don't see any sign of her."

"My young friend?" He looks genuinely baffled.

"The one you were talking to the day of Julia's funeral," she says lamely. She imagines how she must sound.

"The one I was . . . ? You've got me there. I don't know what you're on about."

"It doesn't matter." Nothing she says is right. She pushes past. "Look, I have to talk to my uncle."

"Okay. Be that way then."

She pulls her disordered thoughts together and lays a hand on his arm. "This is a bad time, Eugene. There's a bit of a situation. I can't leave him on his own."

"Oh." He's inscrutable.

"I really do have to go."

A moment's hesitation will sap her resolve. She had better whip herself into action. She sits up on a bar stool beside Matt and orders a glass of lager.

Matt balances himself on the counter with his elbows, his head sunk close to the whiskey glass. For all the world he's like a wasted, decaying artist, but his shambling appearance doesn't entirely mask his natural elegance. Although he appears on the point of collapse, invisible threads somehow maintain the vertical.

"Hiya, Matt," she says. "I haven't seen you in a while."

There's no response. She's not sure he heard.

She tries again. "Hello, Matt. How are you?"

He turns his head and gives her a disturbingly blank look. It's as if he doesn't recognize her.

"It's Ellen," she offers.

"Ellen," he says in a sluggish voice, mangling the middle consonants of her name. "Hiya there, Elim." She's torn between disgust and sadness.

Another voice intervenes. "Ellen?" Tom, the owner, is busily wiping the countertop. He's a small skinny man, with a brick-red pock-marked face, almost completely bald but with voluminous curling hairs in his nostrils and ears. He edges a cloth toward her till it touches her elbow. His eyes and mouth twitch and work to catch her attention. He's like a mime artist. She's mesmerized by the performance but can't decipher his message. "Could I have a word?" he asks eventually.

"Now?"

"Yes." He steps out from behind the bar and she follows him across the floor into a darkened room packed with metal kegs, a door of which opens out into a yard. The room reeks of damp and alcohol.

"Yes?" she asks.

"I've served him his last drink today," he says with a pious air. "I can't be responsible." He shudders. "He's been drinking steadily since I opened up. I've never seen the like of it. He was stacking them up like skittles. Worse still, others were buying him drink. Is there any way to get him home?"

She hesitates. "I dunno. I'm not sure he'll come. You know how stubborn he can be."

"Cussed stubborn, but you can see he's beyond caring."

"You didn't have to serve him."

He clicks his false teeth. "It's difficult. He's usually a gentleman to his fingertips. Never an ounce of trouble up to recently. I had plenty of delaying tactics. Believe me, I tried to persuade him to go home but he says he can't abide the place." Tom slaps the cloth down on a barrel, hunches his shoulders, and rams his hands into his trouser pockets. "It's hard to know what to do. If I'd refused him earlier he'd have gone elsewhere, and there are no guarantees they'd look after him. If you can persuade him to go home, I'll organize a lift — or drive him myself."

She shrugs. "I'll try," she says. "I can't see it getting us anywhere but I'll give it a bash."

"Good woman." He picks up the cloth and pats her as if dusting her with it.

Matt has fallen into a stupor. He lists from side to side. "Matt," she says. No response. She catches his arm. "Wake up, Matt. How about going home?"

She shakes his arm vigorously. "Come on, Matt. You can do better than this." He opens his eyes, and she's shocked by the dullness within. It's not clear that he recognizes her. "Matt, it's Ellen. Your niece, Ellen. Time to go home. Have you had anything to eat?"

"He's eaten nothing," Tom says. "Packet of crisps early in the afternoon. That's it."

Matt grunts something.

"Do you know me?"

He sways alarmingly and looks as if he could slither directly from seat to floor. He makes as if to raise his glass to his lips but misses. Whiskey spills on the counter.

She passes his drink to Tom, who dabs the counter clean. "Matt, we have to get you home. You've had a lot to drink. You need to recover. Do you understand?"

He mutters something she can't make out. "Yes, it's me—Ellen," she says, like a hearty nurse to a difficult patient. "We're going home, Matt. I'm going to drive you."

They maneuver him off the stool. Suddenly he slumps against her, an impossible weight. His arms are rubbery and inert. She sags, recovers, and struggles to right him. He exhales noxious fumes all over her.

"I've got him," Tom says, dwarfed by Matt's height. He manages to right the swaying form into a vertical position. "Get his arm around your shoulder—hold on, hold on—good—don't let go! —I've got him on this side. We'll have to drag him between us. Let's get him to the door."

"Not so fast. I can't get a grip." Matt has slumped. The toes of his shoes drag along the floor. Her knees give but she recovers. "He's a ton weight."

Suddenly Eugene is beside her, uncoupling her from Matt and taking the load. "I've got him," he says.

"Ah," is all she can say. She's out of puff.

The cold of the evening air assaults them as they leave the pub. Matt is comatose. "Put him in the back seat?" asks Tom.

"We need to get him home," she says.

"We'll have our work cut out for us," says Eugene.

"He's not getting any lighter," pants Tom.

"If you bundle him into the back seat of his car, I'll drive," she offers.

"How would you get him out again? Think about it. I'll do any driving has to be done," Eugene says. "Tom, you go back and mind the bar."

"The missus can hold the fort. It's slow now, won't pick up till about ten."

"Is home the best place for him?" Eugene asks.

"What about taking him up to your house, Ellen?" suggests Tom.

She's horrified. "He wouldn't like that."

"It's certain he won't like it, but at least you could keep an eye on him. I'd be worried about leaving him on his own at home. If he vomited or anything. You never know."

"Okay. Okay."

They drag Matt along the street. She's conscious of stares and of comments being made. Why are so many people out and about? Let them all go to hell. She runs ahead to open the front door.

"Bring him upstairs to the spare bedroom," she says. "The bed's made up."

They haul him upstairs, remove his coat, shoes, and jacket, and stretch him out on the bed. "We'll take it from here, Ellen," Eugene says. "We'll call you when we've fixed him up."

"I've no pajamas."

"Men don't wear pajamas nowadays," Eugene says with a grin.

"Vest and pants will do him," Tom says.

"Push the bed up against the wall, turn him on his side, and tuck him in tight," Eugene says.

"Good idea."

She leaves them to it and goes downstairs. The clock says seven. She sighs.

Presently they join her. "He's out for the count. He won't move till morning," Tom says. "I'd best go and relieve Hannah. Don't want the punters drinking the place dry."

"'Night, Tom. Thanks very much for all your help," she says.

"Mind if I use your facilities?" Eugene asks.

"You know where to go."

"I'll be off so," Tom says. He pauses at the door. "Give us a tinkle tomorrow to let us know how he is."

She smiles. "Okay. Will do. Thanks again."

She runs upstairs, slips into the darkened bedroom, and listens to Matt's ragged breathing. As she looks down at him she realizes that her chest feels tight. She's full of dread. He has always been part of the backdrop to her life, gruff, usually undemonstrative, an erratically attentive godfather—postal orders on the birthdays he remembered—but always accepting of her in her own right. His approval, which she prized, was shown in the packets of mints he always brought her on his visits to the cousins, and the two telephone calls he made, the first to see how she had fared in her Leaving Certificate, the second to congratulate her on her first-class honors degree—followed on each occasion by a generous check enclosed in a congratulations card.

Matt is the nearest approximation she has to a father. Her real father she remembers in images—his laugh, one or two outings together, a meal with him and Kitty, probably in Dublin, sitting in the passenger seat as he drove the two of them to Ballindoon and being greeted by a radiant Sarah. Some of his sayings have been passed on to her—"Hop to it, jump to it!," "Rome wasn't built in a day," and "I'm sick of telling you, I'm tired of warning you"—and four photographs of father and daughter survive, the last taken on the day of her Holy Communion. He was dead long before her Confirmation, but she has lived off memories and stories and happily made do with Matt.

What if this uncle, who means so much, has changed irrevocably? What if he has slipped away from her? If this new Matt is all that's on offer, how will that change their relationship? The world will be a sadder and more lonely place.

Eugene's in the kitchen when she comes down. "I'm exhausted," she complains.

"How's that?"

"Bloody parent-teacher meeting ran late and I got delayed by road works on the way back. I feel peculiar, kind of light-headed, as if I might float away." She sits down at the table, shakes her head wearily, and places it in her hands. "And to cap it all, I'm going to be in the bad books with Matt. He'll be furious when this is all over the village tomorrow."

"Don't worry about that. Matt will ride it out. Nobody's out to get him." He draws a chair close to her and sits down. "Sometimes you have to make allowances for people. I'd put money on it that this is a phase he's going through."

"Maybe, but maybe not. That's what worries me."

"No jumping the gun. Wait and see."

She smiles a watery smile. "By the way, thanks for your help." It's hard to get out the words.

"What's the matter? What have I done? You're so short-tempered with me."

She's really not equal to this conversation. There's a tightening at the back of her eyes and it's becoming more and more difficult to fight her tiredness. "Why would I be out with you?"

"You tell me."

"It's nothing really. I'm just tired, Eugene. The job —"

"Feck all those excuses. They don't wash anymore. I feel this cold air between us."

"Could we talk about this another time?" she pleads.

"You've been dodging me since Julia's funeral."

"I know. I know. I've been thinking about things. We've nothing much in common, have we?"

He stands up, scraping the chair behind him. "I knew it," he says angrily. "Just because I never went to university or got a degree."

"Oh, my God, no. Where did you get that idea?" she says, startled. "It never even crossed my mind —"

"Then why?"

She can't answer. He's close. The clean, sawdust fragrance of him. She breathes him in.

He touches her on the arm, the wrist, the back of her hand. She panics. "Don't!" she says, and pulls away.

There's a silence. "Is that it?" he asks. He waits for a while and then she hears "Goodnight." The tone of his voice tells her that he's reached a decision.

"What am I supposed to say?" she bursts out. "I don't have the words." She lifts her head but there's no sign of him.

"What was that?" He rushes back. "I didn't hear you."

"You have to help me," she declares, agitated.

He holds her, murmurs things against her hair and ear, and kisses her brow. "Oh, Ellen."

She looks up. "You remember that young one you were talking to at Julia's funeral? Matt said you had quite a penchant for young flesh."

She feels a change in the way he's holding her. He pushes her away in order to look at her. "Did he really say that?" he asks.

It's ridiculous to push for an answer, but she has to know. "Words to that effect."

"All these accusations." He throws his eyes heavenward. "Wait. I've got it! The skimpy top, bare midriff, fake tan madam. Is that who you're on about? Good God!" he says passionately. "Well, unlike some others I could mention, she was very keen to talk to me." He laughs. "Do you know who she was? A niece of Mona's husband. She was practicing her charms on me, before her father claimed her."

"You were obviously susceptible."

"Ellen, please," he says with a grimace. "I was talking to her for fifteen minutes, twenty tops. She's across the pond, studying art in an English college. She's lovely, and doesn't she know it, but nothing she says is worth listening to. You didn't seriously think? You did! You were jealous," he exults.

"Of course I was."

He presses in against her. The ease of him. The grace of him. The feel of his touch.

"Oh, God," she says, remembering the earlier part of the night. "The wine. It's — I left it in the bloody car."

"Forget the damn wine. Just kiss me."

Out of nervousness she dodges him.

"Ellen!" he admonishes. "This is becoming a habit. Is it so terrifying?"

"Sorry, sorry. I'm so sorry," she apologizes breathlessly. Then she laughs.

He catches her close. "Is this safe? You're not going to head-butt me again? Put your arms around my neck," he orders and she complies. "That's more like it." He locks her into a grip, his hands tightening about her pelvis, rocking her back and forth.

How do people manage this? It's weird. She's all starts and awkwardness, a novice. Nothing has prepared her, she thinks, neither her initial exposure to inept fumbling and strip searches by would-be lovers in dank bed-sits or back seats of cars, nor, certainly, the effects of being mauled by Christy. How could two men be so different? Her hand comes into contact with his hair. She feels the back of his neck, the boniness of his vertebrae. "This is ridiculous," she murmurs.

"How is it ridiculous?"

"I'm so much older than you."

"Only in years."

She laughs. "True."

"I'm available for any instruction you need."

"Stop laughing at me."

He places her hand on his heart. "Feel that," he says. "It's hammering away." He edges her toward the stairs.

"Oh, God! Christ!"

"What?"

"Matt's in the house."

"He's dead to the world."

"What if he wakes up?"

"He's not going to wake up. Have courage."

"You've no idea how much courage I need."

"It'll come to you."

"I hope so."

He laughs. "You're hardly afraid of me, are you?"

A part of her is alive to the incongruity of what's happening. "I don't know about this," she says, her voice rising in distress. "It isn't what I planned."

"Nothing ever is. It'll be all right. Matt's almost in a coma."

This can't be happening, she thinks, but as from a distance. She clutches him. He brings her upstairs. She's beyond speech. They fall onto her bed, and it creaks alarmingly. He pulls away, walks across the room, closes and locks the bedroom door.

Through the window she can see the moon, a full moon. Something in her has given way — a trapdoor has opened and she has dropped right through. She lets him undress her and kiss each revealed part. She's lost in the beauty of his throat, his shoulders, and his chest. His torso, that muscular slenderness, undoes her. It doesn't seem quite real that she can kiss any part of him. In the mirror she sees the shadows they make. He is responsive to her every move. She feels thrusts from his limbs, hands, and fingers. He repositions himself so quickly that she feels he is everywhere.

"Are you there, Ellen? Are you with me?" he asks, and she's amazed to hear him say her name.

She hears a cry — for a wild moment she thinks Matt has come into the room — then realizes it came from her.

He lifts his head. "Ellen," he says. "Ellen?" His voice is molten. His breath scorches her face.

She hears herself say "Yes, now."

Ten

*T*HIS NEW MATT rustles up tension in pubs, pushing it to the extreme of almost being banned on a few occasions — although clued in enough to hang back or ease off at the last minute, as if he's gauging how far he can go — and having to be dragged out into the street and driven home. When he accuses Ellen — as he does on several occasions — of being a "conniving, interfering, judgmental cow," she finds herself full of loathing for this boorish, drunken bastard.

The comments of others she finds hardest to bear. Terry lectures her on family responsibilities. According to her, Matt will "have to be taken in hand and sent away to dry out," that there can't be "any more of this carry-on." In addition, Terry wonders how long his drinking has been "undetected" and "undiagnosed." Ellen has taken to shopping in James O'Flaherty's store — nowadays sparsely stocked and gloomy — to avoid Terry.

A visit to Beatrice proves of no avail. "Could you talk to him, Beatrice? He has great regard for you. He'd listen to you," is met by a sad smile, a shake of the head, and an unnerving silence.

"I don't know where to turn," Ellen says in desperation. "He pays no attention to me."

Beatrice stirs tea. "Do you mind if I say something?" she asks.

"I wish you would. I'm at my wit's end."

"I hope you won't take offense —"

"Why would I take offense?"

"It's a delicate situation. Often people in trouble don't want help. It feels like interference to them and they resent it. They most resent the person who gets them out of a jam. Puts them under a compliment."

"That sounds like nonsense to me."

"If you harry Matt and persuade him to stop drinking, he could turn on you. You'll be a reminder to him of the worst times, when he was at his weakest. He'll associate you with all that and maybe take to avoiding you. Your relationship may never recover."

Beatrice offers her a scone. Ellen waves the plate away. "That's crazy. What am I supposed to do? Just let him get on with it?"

"Well, it could be the price you have to pay."

"Obviously, I don't want that, but equally I don't want him the way he is. This is a catch-22 scenario, is it?"

"Damned if you do? Damned if you don't? Why not hand the problem over to his sons?"

"I haven't seen Stephen or Colum in weeks."

"Contact them. Contact Stephen — I know he rings Matt on a regular basis — leave it up to them."

"But that's dodgy too, isn't it? What'll I say?"

"As little as possible. Then it's their problem. Take a scone, Ellen. You're too thin these days."

Ellen accepts a scone and bites into it. "I don't fancy having to ring Stephen. I'm not even sure I have his number."

"They won't be able to claim they didn't get fair warning."

"I don't want my relationship with Matt to go down the tubes."

"You can't control that."

"God, how is it you know so much, Beatrice?" exclaims Ellen.

Beatrice shakes her head. "If there's one thing I've learned, it's how simple it is to dish out advice. Easiest thing in the world. Acting on it is what's difficult."

People think that Matt is out of it, but he's conscious of what's going on, aware of it all, not calling the shots anymore, as if he's an onlooker watching his own performances.

The house is quiet. Now that he may do as he wishes, he's like a freed bird, flailing and fluttering about, panicked by the opened cage door, unable to take advantage. He has lost the knack of pleasing himself, has forgotten how it feels. The difficulty is coping with each day, trying to find ways to kill time, skid past the maddening crawl of the clock, and defeat torpor.

He wakes up each morning, his swollen tongue furled in his mouth, his teeth covered in a caked layer, his red-rimmed eyes sensitive to light, his skin exuding a noxious nicotine smell, the bedroom fetid and stinking of staleness, decay, and old socks. As likely as not, his head won't be clear and he'll have slept through the alarm. He'll linger on the edge of consciousness — it's a tossup between dipping back into a doze or resolving to get up — stumble to the bathroom and face that all too familiar reflection in the mirror. When did getting up in the morning become such hard work?

"Flotsam" and "jetsam" — the words drift through his mind — bits of ship's wreckage. The tide has washed him up on an isolated little island. Nothing is as expected. Release feels remarkably like loss.

He wipes his face down with a hot flannel. The pores on his skin are enlarged, the lines more pronounced. The whites of his eyes look yellowed. He looks wan, his features a mask, his expression without vigor. Alcohol emphasizes every defect of aging.

He turns on the taps, fills the sink with tepid water, lathers his shaving brush, applies it to his face, catches his razor, wets it, arches his neck, dips his head and shoulders, and shaves. No nips. His hand is steady. He splashes on aftershave, towels the skin dry, rinses out the bowl, and then sets about cleaning his teeth.

The workings of the heart are a mystery. Since Julia's death he has been staggering about like a person truly bereaved. Why doesn't he feel what he wants to feel? It's as if he's possessed by a demon. The demon speaks through him. He is its thing. He belongs to it.

Even when awake and sober, he dips in and out of consciousness. He's seldom in the moment, as it were. He doesn't participate or respond to stimulation. So much of him has closed down. He is of himself — in himself — at this precise moment, but this is no longer the norm for him.

He reviews fragments from recent times — the month's mind for Julia — Colum, wife and children, Stephen — they all came — stayed over, looked after themselves and looked after him. He barely registered the commemorative Mass or the gathering in Hegarty's for tea and sandwiches. He was sunken into himself and incommunicado. They tiptoed about and fell away at his approach. He was conscious of their comings and goings, their whispered asides, their tentative words. He loathed their attentions, not least because he felt temporary and inconsequential. He snapped at Stephen because he offered to make him a cup of tea.

As usual, Colum's children ran a little wild at Sunday lunch in the local hotel, and he took them for a walk between courses. They skipped along beside him, their piping voices full of questions for "Grampa." A vague memory of the little girl throwing stones into the pond in the hotel grounds, and her elder sister climbing a tree. The boy watchful, restful, his unruly curls, the bottle-end spectacles pressing down on the tiny bridge of his nose. The rest a void.

Stephen dropped him home, but they all trailed back to the house. Faithful attendants, a subdued retinue. He remembers their departure — Stephen first, then Colum, Úna driving — thinks he managed a farewell wave from the door, had to have. Habit. Ingrained.

Ellen has gone to ground recently. As well, really. Just as well. Her anxious eyes and fluttering hands. They haven't seen much of each other since that time he woke in a strange bed that happened to be in her empty house. He must have been in some state to end up there.

The market-day bus is full of shoppers, bags laden with the day's purchases. The bus slows — its indicator flashing — and pulls off the dual carriageway onto a secondary road. As it turns the corner, Beatrice spots a dark column of smoke rising from one of the old cottages behind the hedgerows.

"Is that Jim Kilfeather's place?" asks Dan Tuohy's widow, Stella.

"I think so."

"A chimney fire?"

"Probably — can't tell. The smoke is very dense." To the side of the cottage can be made out an ambulance, fire brigade, and Garda squad car.

"It wouldn't kill the driver to slow down so we could get a good look," Brenda Finnegan says in an aggrieved tone.

The bus driver cranks up the grinding gears as the vehicle gathers speed.

"It's more than a chimney fire," Nan Brogan says with a certain amount of relish. "The place looks gutted."

"God between Jim Kilfeather and all harm," Stella says. "He never did anyone a bad turn."

It's Stella's first excursion on the bus since Dan's suicide last August, almost seven months ago. The previous night she rang Beatrice to ask if they could sit together on the journeys to and from town. "I'm not fit to drive the car," she explained. "I could lose concentration and crash. Still, I can't keep depending on the goodwill of neighbors. They must be sick of helping me out. I'm going to have to brave the world. However, if I end up sitting beside Brenda or Nan on the bus, I won't be held responsible for my actions."

"No problem, Stella. Any time you're going in on the bus, let me know. They'll never take on the two of us."

"No, they usually single you out before they hunt you down," Stella says with grim humor.

Stella has lived at a remove from people in the village since Dan's death. She keeps her children indoors. They seldom play on the street.

"How are the children?" asks Beatrice.

"Bewildered mostly. I wasn't much good for anything for the first few months. The school called me up last week to tell me that the little one, Orla, is being bullied."

"You're not serious. How?"

"Wicked stuff. Taunts about her father. Jeering her. The works."

"But that's terrible."

"I've been talking to the teacher. Supposedly it's being taken in hand but I have my doubts. Bullies are devious. Could you believe it? Aren't people cruel?"

"They have to nip that in the bud, Stella. It won't be allowed to go on."

"I don't blame the kids so much as the parents. Whatever the kids come out with is what they overhear at home. I couldn't repeat some of it, it's so awful."

An ambulance, siren whirring, hurtles past on the other side of the road. A collective moan ripples through the bus. Stella makes the sign of the cross. "Please God he'll be all right."

"I'd say he knocked over one of those old paraffin heaters or the chimney caught fire. These old bachelors aren't the best to look after themselves."

"Or the fire sparked."

"Something like that."

Earlier in the day Stella and Beatrice met up for lunch in O'Reagan's restaurant and delicatessen. "I've wanted to talk to you for a long time, Beatrice," Stella said. "Just wondering how you cope. It's very dark for me now. The only thing keeping me going is the children. The life I had before all this happened didn't seem to amount to much. But there isn't anything I wouldn't give to turn the clock back."

"We'd all turn back the clock if we could."

"What do you do to keep going? I feel I could lie down and die sometimes."

"It'll be slow but you will find ways and means."

"Does it ever get easier?"

Beatrice let out a long sigh. "Can't say it does. It becomes more manageable, that's about it."

Stella sank back into her seat. "That's what I expected, but I was hoping beyond hope that you'd found a secret solution, and that you might let me in on it."

"Put one foot in front of the other. Keep going. I find doing things helps. There are times when you forget completely."

"My head is full of it. And I'm so angry, Beatrice. He left us in the lurch. So selfish. If you saw the bills that have to be paid."

"You have to assume that he wasn't in his right mind when he died."

"Well, I can see certain things now. The company were going to let workers go, and Dan was sure he was in for the chop. When I think back, it's obvious he was paranoid. He thought everyone was out to get him. He had changed. If only I'd my wits about me I might have prevented it."

"Avoid those thoughts, Stella. Hindsight is treacherous. Don't trust it. Don't let it blight your life."

"Oh, I don't know. I swing this way and that, but I can't figure out where I am."

"One day at a time. You could go for counseling, bereavement counseling. I'm sure it's on offer."

Stella was on the verge of tears. "At a price. I suppose you're right. Take every day as it comes."

Beatrice patted her hand. "That's it, I'm afraid. If you want a listening ear, I'm here."

"Thanks for the chat at lunch," Stella says on the return journey that afternoon. She stands up to get off the bus. "I won't rest till I know if Jim survived the blaze" is the final thing she says. She waves back to Beatrice from the road.

"How's Stella these days?" Nan calls over.

"As well as can be expected."

"You're no good for bits of information, Beatrice."

"The world's worst, Nan. The world's worst."

The bus slows to stop at the creamery. Beatrice picks up her bag of groceries. "See you next week, Nan," she calls. Nan scowls.

On her way into the house, Beatrice notices the tractor in one of the lower fields. There's no sign of Simon. She unpacks the groceries, kicks off her shoes, and stretches out on an armchair.

She wakes to find Simon shaking her. "You were out for the count," he says.

She sits up and yawns. "Sorry, Simon. I'm tired these days."

"It's only March. Take a tonic. You might need a pick-me-up."

She yawns. "I'll make a start on the dinner right away."

"No rush."

"Town was packed. We saw smoke coming from one of the cottages at the crossroads on our way back."

"Old Jim Kilfeather's place."

"How did you know that? Bush telegraph?"

"One of the lads was driving by, stopped to have a look, and rang me on the mobile. Old Jim knocked over the paraffin stove. Some newspapers caught fire and the whole place went up. He's in hospital suffering from smoke inhalation."

"Lucky he wasn't trapped."

"Neighbors got him out. It was pure chance they spotted the smoke."

"I'll have to get one of these mobiles, Simon, so I'll always be in the know. Poor Jim. I expect he'll end up in the county nursing home. Once they land in there, the old lads don't last long."

"He's tougher than he looks, plants his own spuds, digs all the rills himself, and puts down the seed potatoes."

"That's finished now."

"The Feeneys will take him on. He's a distant cousin of the wife's, and they've always been good to him."

Beatrice smiles. "That's the best news I've heard today." She yawns, flexes, and extends her arms and looks out the window. "The days are starting to stretch out. It lifts the spirits." She's still yawning as she fills the kettle.

Being close to someone is a new experience for Ellen. She's unpracticed, clumsy with the etiquette, a stranger to the habits of intimacy, and of being continually at ease with herself in another's company.

When, as frequently happens, Eugene turns up with a bottle of wine and food and proceeds to cook dinner for them, she finds herself at a loss. Sometime after the meal, often on the flimsiest of pretexts—she'll cite work to be prepared, tests that she should correct—she'll suggest that he might like to go home.

"You don't have to make polite chitchat with me," he'll say. "I'll read the newspaper, watch the telly, or listen to music while you get on with it."

"You'll be bored."

"How could I be bored in your company?"

She's exasperated by his displays of affection, patting her hand, holding her arm, touching her on her shoulder, kissing her hair, smiling at her if their eyes happen to meet. She can't shake off this double take of wanting to be wanted but not wanting him near her. She has trained herself to repress gestures and anticipate snubs.

After the initial physical encounter, she isn't able to recapture that impetus to give of herself. Indeed, in retrospect she's amazed that she was so readily available. It's like a blip on the monitor of her consciousness, a skewed reaction. Now her wretched watchfulness has reasserted itself. She is her own audience and detractor.

• • •

"This is a mistake!" she says one night. "I'm sorry."

His hand strokes her back. "We'll have to arrange relaxation classes for you," he says lightly.

"It won't make any difference. I'm not cut out for this," she laments.

"Of course you are. There's fire in you. I'm not going to let conditioning get in the way of what we have."

"I don't know if I can do this. Everything was fine the first time. That was a fluke."

"We know it's there, the kernel of you. You don't want to let everything go because of stage fright, do you?"

"Stage fright? Isn't that what happens before the performance?"

"You were a natural the first time, but now you're thinking about it too much."

"Stop thinking, is that it?"

"Start thinking in a different way. Think of bodies — mine, yours — and what they're designed for, what we can do for each other."

She laughs. "If only."

He distracts her from her preoccupations, soothes and cajoles her, and her body surprises her by easing out. Each incremental relaxation is hard won and precarious, the eventual union achieved out of a determination on his side and exhaustion on hers.

"A younger woman wouldn't be such hard work," she says another night. "They're so at ease. They have confidence in themselves."

"Confidence can easily tip over into arrogance. It's not always attractive."

"There's less to cope with."

"If people were all straightforward, life would be boring. I like the Ellen I see when she forgets herself. I'd like to see more of her."

"It's amazing what a man and woman can do for — to — each other," she volunteers after a more successful encounter. "I would never have believed it."

"I don't get this. Unless you and Christy had an extraordinary arrangement, you had sex. Didn't you relax with him?"

"Christy just did whatever he wanted, and it wasn't always very nice."

Eugene looks as if he's been set a riddle without a solution. "Why marry in the first place? If there wasn't an attraction, I mean."

"Sure, what did I know about anything? I married the first man who asked. He said, 'Marry me,' and I said, 'Yes.' By the time I realized there was nothing between us, it had gone too far to turn back."

"It's never too late to change your mind."

"You need courage for that. And Kitty thought he was great. Even the cousins liked him, so I didn't want to disappoint them."

"And you married to please others?"

"Exactly," she says in surprise. "I expected nothing and got nothing. You're the closest anyone has ever been to me. You put yourself out for me."

He sits up. "It's what people do. Like what a mother does for a child, that sort of stuff."

"Not my mother. Being a single parent didn't suit her. I was a burden."

"But . . . the natural bonds of affection?"

"Kitty isn't demonstrative," she says with a smile. "Dad was the one who doted on me and took me places. I could do no wrong in his eyes. I don't remember a lot of things, but that's the feeling I have about him. He was the real mother. He'd have liked more children. She didn't know what to do with a child. I got in the way of her enjoyment of life."

"What about the cousins?"

"I was the apple of Sarah's eye."

"Thank God for that."

She finds his solicitude endearing. "Don't sound so cross," she soothes. "It's me. I never know how to react to affection. I'm not sure that everybody is entitled."

"You're not used to it, that's all. That's why you're not at ease."

"I'd give anything to change that."

He kisses her forehead. "I can give you all the warmth you need. It's easy for me. I grew up with it. I'm used to it."

"Well, lucky you! But I'm not looking for any concessions."

"Look for things, Ellen. Want them. It's your due." He sounds angry again.

"I'd hate to turn into a needy type."

"If you need me, what's wrong with that? If I need you, where's the harm? It's part of being human."

"It's easier for you."

"It should be easy for all of us. It's just a bloody shame it took so long to happen for you."

She laughs but finds it difficult to be reconciled to appetites. Passion is a double-edged sword. She feels everything might be taken away again. If she gives of herself entirely, and if he changes, she could be left alone with those desires.

It feels as though she's wrestling with herself. She's the laggard, withholding, stalling, and keeping a distance between them. She knows that she needs to let go, and it feels like being poised to jump from the Eiffel Tower. She could hurtle past the safety nets.

But Eugene is resolute. He is a constant presence. He humors her. He's on a mission.

One night she watches him as he sleeps and reaches out to touch him, experiments with kissing and stroking his skin. He appears to be in a deep stupor but turns suddenly and draws her to him. His appetite for her fascinates her. It's so straightforward that she's disconcerted. Something gives way, and what she withheld previously she now bestows. For the first time in her life she can forget herself thoroughly and behave in an unconstrained fashion. She is bemused, breathless, and surprised at herself.

It's early on a Saturday night, and the cars are lined up along the side of the street, parked in irregular patterns. From the pub by the petrol pumps comes the *thump thump* from whatever band is booked for the night. The takeaway is open for business. Straggly bands of youths, incontinent with drink and desire, linger outside, their shouts and bursts of laughter hanging on the air. The smoke from their cigarettes rises above them like a mist. Occasionally one of the boys shuffles into the off-license to buy a few cans of cider, which are then passed around the group. One boy, slightly younger than the rest, supplies soft drugs to anyone who comes looking.

Earlier in the day they all attended the funeral of Denis Scope, a brother of one of the youths. Three nights previously he had emerged from a remote mountain pub after closing and challenged Ted O'Driscoll, a married man in his thirties, to a car race. Only on certain sections of the twisting roads could they attain high speeds, but, when they reached the wide three-mile-long stretch on one of the approach roads into Ballindoon, each car took a side of the road.

They were traveling at over eighty miles an hour when a van suddenly emerged from a gateway. Seeing Denis's car hurtling toward him on the wrong side of the road, the driver hastily reversed the van, but Denis had slammed on his brakes and his car went out of control. It crashed into a wall, killing him instantly. Ted's car spun about and landed upside down in a ditch and—miraculously—he survived, although he is expected to spend a long time in hospital.

A large crowd has stayed on in Hegarty's long after the funeral reception, partly because it's not a working day and partly because the funeral has changed the nature of the day. Denis was twenty years old and well liked.

In the pub Beatrice meets up with Ellen. They sit together at one of the low tables to the front of the pub. "I won't stay long," Ellen says. "I didn't know the boy, but I thought I'd put in an appearance under the circumstances."

Eugene joins them. He brings cutlery for Ellen. Beatrice is struck by the ease with which they talk to each other.

"I'll call up soon, Beatrice," Ellen says, as she and Eugene rise to go. "I'm starting to come to terms with the job. The energy levels are better."

Eugene steers Ellen through the door onto the street. Something in the solicitousness of his manner makes Beatrice nostalgic for the —admittedly brief—carefree days of her youth. All that potential, she thinks. She spots Simon's former girlfriend Angie, smiles and waves at her. Angie gives a little wave back but doesn't join her.

She has almost given up on meeting Matt—if he's missing, it's a bad sign—when she spots him at the back of the pub on her way out of the ladies. He's alone, standing by the bar with a pint in his hand. There's something forbidding about him. He's frowning and biting his lower lip, glowering almost. To her eyes, he's still attractive, different — weary, older certainly — but still compelling. Although she's well aware of his shortcomings, she can never write him off. She expects more of him than he can ever concede.

She approaches him. "How are you these days, Matt?" she asks.

He gives her a dark look, gulps his pint, and swills it about in his mouth before swallowing. "How am I?" he says caustically. "Bad, very bad . . . if you must know."

"I'm so sorry."

"Ah, sure, everybody's sorry. I've lost count of the number of people who are sorry."

"Well, it's hard to put it another way. I am genuinely concerned. It can't be easy —"

"Of course it isn't — that's obvious, isn't it? But it's difficult in unexpected ways. The big stuff, the removal and funeral, are straightforward. The things that trip you up you imagined would be uncomplicated." Some of the anger in his voice evaporates and he sounds more normal. "I thought I had a handle on it — turns out I don't. I didn't expect all this — reaction."

"Frightening, isn't it, Matt, how little control we have over events?"

"You never spoke a truer word. Life is a cold-blooded business."

His words find an echo in her heart. Julia's dead and buried. His sons have gone back to their lives. He hasn't shed tears over Julia and he won't. His marriage, like many of the time — her own included — offered little by way of comfort or camaraderie, but he's likely finding that he misses the presence of another person about the house, the companionship — however uncongenial. Julia kept the house clean, cooked meals, did the laundry and shopping. Notwithstanding her many flaws, she was company. He might even miss the passionate presence of their dislike of each other.

Before Simon came to work and live on the farm, Beatrice endured a few weeks where, on most days, she went without hearing another voice about the place. When Jack died she missed him. She didn't love him — he was too irascible, stubborn, and self-obsessed for that — but she could tolerate him. In his better moments he loved occasions and excursions and was given to impulses.

He could surprise her by presenting her with tokens of approbation: a book she had mentioned or an item of clothing or jewelry she had admired. When she remembers him, she feels exasperation mixed with fondness. If he had lived, would they have reached beyond limited accommodation of each other's foibles to acceptance and tenderness? Could they have forged a genuine alliance? No point in tossing that one up.

Older people's lives are all about absences, she thinks, people missing, people dying, little defeats and losses — Beatrice waiting for a visit from one of her daughters and their families — and from now on, Matt isolated, getting used to his own company, dependent on his sons for attention and visits. She can't see him asking people up to the house for tea or lifting the phone to ring somebody for a chat, much less joining the card club in the village and heading down to the community hall of a Thursday night. How unremittingly dismal their prospects are, she thinks. There's little respite or consolation.

"Funny how things turn out," he mutters. "If life had gone differently, you and I would have ended up together. That would have been a better bet."

She shakes her head. "Don't. Don't rake over the past. It doesn't do any good."

"I'm not sure about that. Wouldn't it be nice to retrace your steps and take the right rather than the wrong turning?"

"It's the life you chose, isn't it?"

"If there's one thing I didn't have in my life, it was choices," he says with feeling.

After a while she says, "You had one or two, I think." All the sorrow of her youth is in her voice.

He looks startled. His shoulders drop and he reclaims his pint from the counter. The dour expression is back. "That's very harsh," he says. "One mistake."

She's sorry she let that sharpness into her voice, but she's tired of people blaming others for options they themselves selected. Matt's mother was always against Beatrice, but she wasn't responsible for their breakup. That he engineered on his own.

The chatter in the pub resonates in her head. They're standing close together but there's an ocean between them. The anger of betrayal burns for a long time. She's surprised to discover its cindered embers still warm. "I'll leave you in peace, Matt. I hope you feel better soon. This will pass, remember," she says abruptly and walks away. Shortly afterward she sees him leave without a word to anyone on his way out.

As the pub empties, Beatrice finds herself having to talk to Brenda Finnegan. Suddenly she notices some youngsters trying to drag a particularly drunken and hysterical girl out to the street. The young woman is pretty, slight, and small. She thrashes about wildly.

"That's the one," Brenda says, with a knowing look.

"I've no idea what you're talking about."

Brenda casts a cantankerous glance at her. "Don't you know anything? That's young Sandra Dingle. Denis used to hang about with her. They say she has a bun in the oven."

"Somebody could take advantage of her, the state she's in."

Brenda sniggers. "Somebody already has. I mean," she continues, perhaps anxious not to seem too harsh, "that's what they're all saying. It's well known that she's loose."

Loose. Easy. Game. Those terms have lost currency. They don't wield the power they used to, Beatrice thinks. Feeling it pointless to comment, she sips her lemonade.

"You have to think of your baby, Sandra. Come on, now," one of the girls urges. They manage to drag her outside.

"The young have no self-respect these days," Brenda says grimly.

"There was plenty of that happening in our day too, Brenda, don't forget. Only then the girl was bundled off into one of those homes to have the baby, or the couple was forced to marry. Now the women often end up going it alone."

Brenda puts on her coat and does up its buttons. "The more I hear from you, Beatrice Furlong, the more I wonder what planet you're on."

Beatrice waits outside the old creamery for the shopping bus into Killdingle. The creamery, where old-time farmers used to drive their ponies and carts, with a "Whoa-there" or a "Gee-up," is closed.

The roof is falling in, and the lock on one of the boarded-up doors has been forced. She's heard that teenagers use the place for Friday night drinking parties.

She remembers childhood trips to the creamery with her father, the unloading of the milk churns, the companionable murmur of the men's small talk, the crude jokes of the creamery manager, and her impatience for the promised treat. She can still see her father's contemporaries, those long-dead farmers, sitting in the snug of the pub, bottles of porter on the table, plugging the bowls of their pipes with tobacco from their leather pouches. Her father would suck on the stem of his pipe as he pressed a lighted match against the weed, and smoke would drift across to where she sat at the counter, hugging her glass of lemonade.

The bus appears and she waves it down. The only other person getting on is Sandra Dingle. The little bump on her belly is hardly noticeable. Beatrice smiles at her. "Hello," she says, but the girl keeps her head down. The driver loads Sandra's case into the boot of the bus. At times during the journey into town the sun flashes through trees and Beatrice can see the reflection of the girl's hunched, slumped form in the windowpane.

That afternoon, Nan plonks down in the seat beside Beatrice. The doors wheeze shut and the bus begins the return journey to the village. "Young Sandra's gone over to England for an abortion," she says.

Beatrice braces herself for an onslaught of speculation. "Couldn't blame her if she did decide to have an abortion," she says.

"God almighty, Beatrice, trust you to take a contrary view."

"Have to keep you on your toes, Nan . . . but I think she's gone to stay with an aunt until the baby is born."

"That's all a cover story." Nan lapses into an aggrieved silence but it doesn't last long. Soon she nudges Beatrice's elbow and begins to talk.

Beatrice tries to let the rumors and stories she hears pass her by. She lets out an occasional "I see" or "Really?" or "Aha" as she looks out the window. The day's light has a strange quality. Thick clouds line the pale gray sky, which shimmers with a yellow luminosity.

"It looks as if the weather's going to give us a blast," Nan says. Beatrice nods.

The bus lets them off at the creamery. It's half past five and the light is beginning to fade. She spots Simon standing by his car at the edge of the square.

"You didn't come down specially to collect me, did you?" she asks.

He grins. "That wind would skin you, it's so cold." He nods over at Hegarty's. "I got a bit sidetracked, but I'll run you home."

"Not at all. Stay put, Simon. You take very little time away from the job."

He reaches down for her shopping bags "Have you forgotten? The cows need to be milked." He deposits the bags in the boot of his car and opens the passenger door for her.

"The milking is an awful bind," she comments as they set off.

"It's the nature of the beast, never bothers me. I was in O'Hara's earlier buying tools and wiring when I got waylaid by an old pal. You know how one drink turns into two?" he says with a grin.

She laughs. "With some people it can turn into four or five."

"That's the beauty of your farm being the closest to the village. If I'm the worse for wear, I can always walk home. See, here in record time," he says as he parks the car to the side of the house.

She follows him through the back porch into the kitchen. "It has that advantage. Thanks," she says when he drops her bags on the kitchen table.

"Don't cook any grub for me," he says. "I'll go straight from the milking and grab soup and a sandwich in the pub. My pal's on his way back to Leeds first thing tomorrow morning and I don't want to miss him while he's about. I could be very late tonight. Oh, the forecast is for the wind to drop in the early hours of the morning. We're in for a cold spell. They're expecting snow tomorrow." There's a sudden breeze as the back door slams after him.

She sees the message light flashing as she passes the phone, presses the play button, and hears, "Mam, it's Paula. Ring me on my mobile the minute you get in."

"Great! You got my message," Paula says. "I've news for you!" Her words are rushed. She sounds either drunk or excited.

"Is everything okay? Are the kids all right?" Beatrice asks.

"Mam, I saw him!"

Instantly she guesses what her daughter is going to say, but she asks, "Who?"

"Andy, I saw Andy! I met him on the underground today."

"My God!" The temperature in the room dips. She feels her shoulders shaking. Everything has gone out of focus. She can hardly wait to hear what Paula will say next. "Were you talking to him?" she asks. She's finding it hard to breathe.

"I held back. I was afraid he'd run off if I spoke, so I waited until we were in the carriage. When he saw me, he recognized me before I opened my mouth. He remembers me as plump, the way I used to be before I slimmed down."

"What was he like?" She has to speak briefly or her voice will break.

"He was asking after everyone. He knew Dad has passed on but John's death was a bit of a shock."

"Is that all?"

"Well, I got off at his stop, even though I was dead late for a meeting. So we went for a drink."

"I see."

"You sound peculiar, Mam."

"I just can't imagine it."

"I can't believe it happened. He's over in London for a conference. He's married to a Yank and living in New York. They have a child. We exchanged addresses."

"Was he friendly?"

"He was just lovely."

"And how did it end?"

"He had to go. We exchanged phone numbers too. Then I had to ring my boss and explain why I was so late."

Beatrice checks the room around her. The ceiling, walls, and floor have settled down again.

"Will I give you the number?" Paula asks.

"I'll get it off you again."

"Aren't you pleased? I thought you'd be pleased. You sound disappointed."

"I don't know what I am. It's hard to take it all in."

"He may be in touch, Mam. He might even come on a visit."

"We'll see."

"Don't be skeptical. He could surprise us. Look, got to go. I'll ring you tomorrow."

"Bye, love."

She stands at the kitchen window. It's almost dark outside. The wind whistles round the gable end of the house. The bushes in her garden shake. She shivers. She hears the click of a switch as the central heating boiler turns itself on.

Simon has set a place for her at the table. She picks up the dinner she left out that morning and places it in the microwave, fills the kettle with water. The air in the room feels heavy and inert. It's as if the kitchen is smothering her.

The microwave signals the end of cooking time with a ping. She doesn't touch the food. She has forgotten it. She longs to tell somebody her news.

Eleven

OUT OF THE BLUE, Stephen starts to come down for weekends, and Matt resents the intrusion. He takes exception to feeling obliged to invent a routine whenever Stephen is about, and dislikes the shopping, cleaning, and cooking that having a guest entails.

After three such visits, Matt realizes that this might be setting a pattern. "Don't feel you have to keep me company. I manage perfectly well on my own," he says, but Stephen pays no heed. His cheery determination to create a pleasant atmosphere wins through, shaming Matt into a semblance of normal behavior. He scrubs up and makes an effort. On Friday nights in the pub he confines his intake to two pints and insists that Stephen meet up with friends on Saturday nights.

Stephen voices disappointment on finding Matt retired to bed on an early return from the pub, so Matt begins to wait up, watching the flickering screen of the box or scrutinizing a newspaper. This is more show than anything else. Most of the time, his mind is a vast panoramic vacancy.

They go through the hoops of attending Mass on Sunday morning, and Stephen rewards him with a roast for lunch — chicken, beef, lamb, or pork — initiating Matt into the mysteries of cooking roast spuds or making Yorkshire pudding, reminding him of the minor triumphs and pleasures of life.

Matt knows full well what his son is up to — he won't have anything put over on him—but he can't pretend that it's easy. Stephen is so unrelentingly upbeat that he's irritating. That tedious cheeriness grinds you down. Anyway, he's skeptical about his own adaptability. Old dog, new tricks? He may not have the resources for a start-up, never mind a follow-through.

Stephen's always telling him he has choices, is forever saying that life's not over. It's all very well for him. He's young. It's all ahead of him. He has energy, courage, and reserves.

Matt could continue to wallow in bitterness, bemoaning his bad luck and drowning in self-pity. He could backtrack, let things slide, ease up on the maintenance of the farm, forego the little jobs, retreat from all his responsibilities, and run everything down. It's tempting. However, farming is all he has ever known and all that he's likely to know.

He's sixty-four years old. "That's no age nowadays," Stephen says. "You have to be well into your eighties before we allow any concessions." What can he look forward to? Peace of mind would go a long way. At some stage in the future his strength will ebb. But not yet, not yet. No sense in giving in for the moment. He's seen people wait around, sometimes for decades, for death to claim them. Living death. No, he has to keep going and maintain a routine, if only from inverted cowardice.

When Stephen's around he's always rattling on about how the farm needs modernization to cut down on physical labor. It amuses Matt to see his son sizing things up and seeing them properly for the first time. Stephen investigates machinery and equipment, examines outbuildings, walks fields, scrutinizes cows and calves—actually helps out with milking the cows and feeding the calves, seeks out other farmers and chats to them about recent developments, intent on easing Matt's workload. Stephen's no slouch when it comes to research, reading *The Farmers' Journal* and ringing up farm organizations for information. It almost puts Matt to shame. He jeers his son, terming him a "gentleman farmer" or a "part-time farmer" and cautions him that he'll develop muscles if he's not careful. Stephen takes it all in good part, and Matt enjoys a rekindled interest in the business the times his son is about.

As he eats toast and swallows tea one morning, he realizes that he has felt less like a delicate fossil of late. There are moments when he lifts his head, enjoys the warmth of the sun on his back or savors the tranquillity of the day. There's an intermittent sense of purpose as he goes about his work.

Last weekend, they moved the bookcase from the study to the living room. It was Stephen's idea. They sorted and arranged books on the shelves. Matt has gone as far as to single out a volume, extract it from its position, and open it. Reclaimed books lie about the house. It gives a great but thoroughly misleading impression. His concentration isn't what it once was, and he needs a new pair of reading glasses. He knows that he only has to say the word and Stephen will ring up the optician and make an appointment, but he hangs back.

"You'll enjoy this," Eugene says. "We were lucky to get a seat." He balances two drinks as he wedges himself in beside Ellen on the bench. The barman tops up the musicians' drinks when they take a break to go outdoors to stretch their legs.

Ellen can't take in enough of the pub. "It's tiny," she marvels. The room is about three times the size of an average living room and crammed with people. She's enthralled by the rough plaster on the walls, the traditional dresser in a corner, old signs and sayings on the walls, the knickknacks on the deep windowsills. From outside, the car park looks like an old-style picture-postcard yard enclosed on three sides by a thatched cottage and outbuildings. She would have driven past without a second glance, and was amazed when Eugene turned in.

"They come from miles around on a Saturday night. It's a great session."

"This is a real education. It's like time travel, going back forty or fifty years. It's brilliant. The bar could have stood there for centuries. No mock anything. I can't get over it."

"You didn't know about this place?" She shakes her head. He catches her hand. "It's up to me to reveal these hidden treasures."

The musicians return and start the second part of the session. They launch into a few reels, and then one of the men sings a Bob Dylan song, accompanying himself on an acoustic guitar.

"This can go on till two or three in the morning," Eugene says. "It's a great mix of Irish traditional music, American folk, and the occasional rock tune. I've even heard a jazz version of a traditional tune. Only once, mind you, when there were visiting musicians."

"I feel sorry for car drivers, having to sip soft drinks most of the night."

"There's no problem with having a few drinks. They lay on a taxi service."

A young man with a strong true voice belts out a Neil Young song, followed by a woman singing an unaccompanied ballad. The predominant instrument is the guitar, followed by tin whistle, bodhrán, and ukulele. One man plays a flute.

"Have you any song?" a woman asks Ellen.

She shakes her head.

"Go on. You can sing," Eugene urges.

"If you have a voice, there's no point in shouting down a well," the woman says.

"I don't sing in public," Ellen hisses, but she's spared when attention moves away to a girl who agrees to play the tin whistle. After each performance — and most are good — there's roaring applause.

"Don't deprive us of your voice," Eugene whispers, but she quells him with a severe look.

"Shut up," she says emphatically.

Inadvertently overhearing her rendering of "Carrickfergus" in the fledgling days of their relationship, an impressed Eugene had asked, "Where did you learn to sing like that?"

"Concerts and listening in on traditional music sessions. I did music at school," she answered. Ellen sings when she's happy or sings along to music, and now she sings for Eugene, but she has never had the confidence to sing in front of a crowd.

Now, she slips away from him. "Back soon," she promises. In the queue for the outside toilets, she hears a voice say, "That's Hughes, isn't it?" She has no idea who's speaking but she doesn't turn to look. It's clear that some student has seen her.

Another voice answers, "You're right. She's nice, isn't she?"

"I don't know about her being so fucking nice. The bitch got me into trouble," the owner of the first voice says. Ellen gazes at the floor to avoid eye contact with anyone. She's wondering if she should just make for the bar, grab Eugene, and beg him to take her home. No, she can't. She needs to go to the toilet. The trouble with avoidance is that they can see her, but she doesn't know them. She'll have to hope that whoever it is isn't intent on causing trouble.

She's jumpy when she rejoins Eugene. She knows the dangers of this situation. Provocation followed by confrontation, if they have the nerve. One of the girls was okay, the other hostile. But first she has to know who they are. Eugene catches her scanning the crowd. "What's up?" he asks.

"I think that some of my students are here." She looks again. "Christ! At least three of the sixth years."

He puts an arm about her shoulder and she throws it off. "What're you doing?"

He gestures angrily. "Back to that, are we?" he asks. "How can it matter? You're off duty."

"Humor me. I'm not happy about them being here."

"They've seen you. So what? It's not such a big deal. You're just the bitch who stands in front of them every so often."

"Thank God you didn't kiss me."

"You know you're neurotic about this? You do know that, don't you?"

"Even if there's no threat, it's not good from a discipline point of view. I can't afford to give them any ammunition. I earn every cent of my money trying to sweeten those bloody sixth years, the troublesome ones."

Her eyes rake the room again, and she breathes a sigh of relief when she fails to locate them. Perhaps they've gone? Not their scene really, this place. Boy bands are what they're after. Eugene places a discreet arm about her waist. She directs a warning look at him. He grins and, with his free hand, raises her fingers to his lips. "Don't!" she says sharply, pulling away, and he laughs.

In the early hours of the morning, as Eugene and Ellen push through the crowd on their way to the exit, Ellen notices a slight, dark-haired girl talking to a sixth-year boy. It's Isabel Hussey, Ellen's harshest critic. The girl's mother is known as a professional complainer. Isabel throws a venomous look Ellen's way.

After a quick final visit to the ladies, Ellen finds the doorway blocked by the little madam. "Hi," Isabel says.

Ellen swivels her neck to look and spots two of Isabel's retainers in the shadows to the side of the toilets. Away from Isabel's influence, the girls are nondescript, polite and well behaved. When Isabel pulls their strings, they mutate into sullen, gum-chewing thugs.

"Hello."

"Enjoying the music, Miss?"

"Sure," she says, and dodges past Isabel.

"Nice boyfriend. Good-looking. You like 'em young," Isabel calls after her.

Ellen laughs dismissively. She longs to say "You bitch" to the sour-faced cunt but contents herself with "Goodnight." The girl's two companions are mute. Conscious of being under scrutiny, Ellen forces herself not to make a run for Eugene's jeep.

Isabel says something under her breath to her friends and they snigger. Ellen won't allow herself to look back.

Eugene starts up the jeep, revs the engine, and turns on the headlights. The yard floods with light. She levers herself up quickly and he drives away immediately. "Were they annoying you?" he asks. "I was going to come over."

"Small stuff. Snide remarks. I could handle it."

"You shouldn't let them spoil the night."

"I didn't. What's the name of this place?"

"Kill."

"What's that? 'Cill'? Church?"

"Yes. It's about ten miles from Ballindoon."

And ten miles farther on is Killdingle. Twenty miles doesn't put sufficient distance between her and Isabel Hussey. Young people have money and cars now. They can turn up anywhere.

Suddenly she's exhausted from the effort of the draining self-control she had to show tonight. The Isabels of this world shouldn't have a walk-on part in her private time. She huddles close to Eugene. "I'm tired," she says.

Briefly, his cheek rests against her head. The impenetrable darkness across the sharply undulating terrain makes driving hazardous. He takes it slow, and she's glad he's at the wheel. The narrow road across the bog is like a thin strip of ribbon fluttering against unruly, coarse hair. It would be remarkably easy to career off and into a ditch on any of the sharper bends.

· · ·

Some weeks after her phone call to him, Ellen spots Stephen on the main street in Killdingle. She registers his height, his loping stride, his trademark calf-length coat, and the shoulder-length hair that Matt is so strangely dubious about. Instinctively, she ducks her head as if she hasn't seen him, but he steps out to block her. "Ignoring me?" he asks.

"I thought you mightn't want to meet me."

"Life's too short for that sort of messing about," he says in a dismissive fashion. He catches her arm and leads her down an alleyway into a coffee shop by the river. "It's hard to believe this place used to be so run down," he says. "You'd wonder where all the old warehouses, garages, and workshops went."

"I don't remember much about this part, except that it was a bit grim."

He orders coffee and smiles, but he's not his usual self. A tension in his face, a particular tautness about the eyes and jaw, makes him look severe.

"Look, I'm sorry about that call," Ellen says.

"Not at all. You did the right thing."

"I don't know any longer what the right thing is. It must have come as a shock."

"Bit of an eye-opener," he says harshly.

She recalls their exchanges on the phone, his cordial "How're you, Ellen?" and the invitation to "fire away" with whatever it was she had to say. He didn't query anything she told him about Matt, but she became conscious of heavy breathing at his end. She heard equivocation in his cough and in the silence that followed. "I hope you won't think me too interfering," she had said.

"I hear what you're saying," he answered in a tone so chill it sent a reverberation down her spine. "Thanks for letting me know," he said and put down the phone.

"I can't figure out — I don't understand why Matt's doing this," she says now.

"Why he isn't happier in himself now that my mother's gone, you mean?"

"I wasn't suggesting that. I'm not even sure we should be talking about it."

"You rang me," he says dryly.

"I feel like the great betrayer."

"You think I've taken offense."

"Well, of course. I'd understand. Strictly speaking, it's none of my business."

Stephen studies his hands. "I'm very glad you rang, Ellen. So is Colum, for that matter. It's not easy to get under my father's skin, and I owe him a lot. He headed Mum off about me taking over the farm . . . and it cost him."

"Do you ever regret not taking it on?"

There's a self-contained element to Stephen that makes him complicated and difficult to gauge. Although he's always perfectly friendly and polite when they meet, she feels that they never connect properly. If he comes across her in the pub in Eugene's company, he'll join them for a drink, but he has been in her house only once, and that was because Matt asked if he wanted to see the place. Ellen wouldn't dream of suggesting they meet up as she has no idea how he would react. For all that, she likes him.

He shrugs. "Farming? Not really. It's a hard life. Costs keep going up and income keeps coming down. It's harder and harder to make a living from it. Plus, there's more physical work than I'd ever want to do, and Dad hasn't modernized much. If I had a family and a working wife I might feel differently. Then there's the question of what's likely to happen in dairy farming. Our farm will seem small by the standards of how big farms are going to become."

"I know nothing about farming."

"Where's that coffee?" he says, looking about. He signals the waitress. "The way it is, Ellen, it'd be fine in the summer, when the place is full of visitors, but I couldn't hack it in the winter. The old way of life is gone. The neighborliness has vanished. It's quite an isolated existence."

"I know what you mean. And we get more extremes of weather here. Dublin didn't get any of that snow we had recently."

He nods. "At least you're living in the village. Farms are cut off from the general run of things."

The waitress delivers the coffees and smiles. Girls smile at Stephen all the time. He's a handsome man, and that suggestion of remoteness is intriguing.

"You're a hit there," teases Ellen. "She'd go out with you if you asked."

He turns to have a look. "No, thanks," he says, then smiles. He has a slightly distracted air. She suspects him of being uneasy about the topic of his father. "You don't have to discuss Matt with me," she says.

He shakes his head. "That's not it. I've been thinking about what you said, all that stuff about Dad. It got to me. There's something about his generation. I've been trying to put my finger on it."

"That particular generation, you mean?"

"Yeah. So different. From us, I mean. But then again, the bloody economy was down the tubes in the world they grew up in. The politicians were almost worse than useless. Nobody was given any quarter, unless they were part of an elite — the Church, the judiciary, the politicos — and those boyos were very adept at defending their power base. Loads of people were forced to pack their bags and take the boat. What hope was there? Where were the opportunities? Neither my dad nor yours got any breaks. The choices were toughen up or go under, effectively one choice. I never knew my grandmother, but I believe she was one goddamn awful bitch, a strong woman, ruled the household with a rod of iron. Your father's escape route was into the priesthood — it was that or take on the farm. Dad had no prospects, no way of staying on in school, and no way of escaping unless he ran away. He didn't want the farm, and he wasn't keen on marrying my mother, but he ended up being landed with both." Stephen leans forward, controlled, impelled. "I try to get inside his head, Ellen. I try to imagine it. But it's impossible. It must be almost surreal for him to see how circumstances have changed for us — the immensity of it — bloody difficult to accept."

He is silent, as if he's fallen into a reverie. "It's weird, isn't it?" she says to rouse him. "They might as well have been living on a different planet."

"Exactly. The Church ruled the roost. And we know how it reveled in all that power. A priest, bishop, brother, or nun lurking around every corner, ready to swoop down if you deviated a centimeter from the prescribed course and expel you into outer darkness. If you dared to cross them, they could block your promotion, cost you your job or position, disgrace you socially, hold you up to ridicule, and effectively ruin your life. Bloody awful country then, full of things that couldn't be said, full of silences, the confessionals doing the work of spies, the thought police. And it took the sex- and child-abuse scandals to weaken the hold they had over people." He cradles his mug, as if for warmth, and accepts a refill from the waitress who is hovering, perhaps eavesdropping. "I know you know this, Ellen, but bear with me," he says. "It must be galling for Dad to see our generation having it so easy, expecting to have a say in how we run our lives, demanding certain things as rights. Rights? The concept didn't exist in their day. Nobody gives a damn about values anymore. Nobody agonizes about things. Young people thumb their noses at authority, go gadding about, hardly aware of their good fortune, indifferent to everything really. What his generation suffered is forgotten, unappreciated, and unrecognized. Their world, their touchstones, just disintegrated. They have nothing to show for all that loss."

"Whole lives an exercise in denial."

"Well, here's the riddle." He jabs an index finger into the oilskin tablecloth. "What do they do with all those emotions? They're difficult to expunge. How do they come to terms with that?"

"I haven't the foggiest."

"Rhetorical question. I'm doing the talking. Keep up." He waves an admonishing finger at her and looks mischievous.

"I can see how you ended up being a lecturer," she sneers.

"Okay. They fall into two camps — accept or deny. Tough choice whichever route you take. Some of them can't bear to acknowledge it. It's too painful. They don't want to come to terms with the way life used to be — so they re-create the past, reinvent it. Think of Mrs. Gormley. You know her, don't you? She suffered an atrocious marriage to a waster of a husband. He battered her, drank, and gambled any money he could lay his hands on. She survived whatever way she had to, used all her cunning against him. She had nowhere to go, no one to turn to. No respite, except whatever satisfaction she got from the children. Decades of misery she put in, and there was no love lost between them. She hated him, hated the misery he inflicted on her and her children. When he fell ill, she was thrilled because she realized that he was going to die. There was no reconciliation, no big coming together. He was an awful man. Difficult to the end. I'd say she didn't relax till he breathed his last. Signs on it, she never shed a tear for him. Nevertheless, once he was dead and buried, she began to change her tune. Now that he was definitely out of the picture, she began to pretend that he hadn't been so bad."

"You're joking." Ellen has met this Mrs. Gormley, a stooped little woman with wiry gray hair and a singsong voice.

"No, I was struck by it at the time. Happened about eight years ago. It began with little things. She'd startle someone by coming out with the like of 'Con was very partial to classical music' or 'He loved nature' and everyone would be flabbergasted. Complete fabrication. The man was a stranger to finer feelings. His only talents were drinking, gambling, and terrorizing his family. I think she couldn't come to terms with the notion that decades of her life had been flushed down the drain because of that man. Over the years she has reinvented him so that he's become a kind of saint. She keeps a photograph of him in the hall. She says not a day passes but she misses him. She makes out she's deprived because he's not around. She attributes little sayings to him, invents nice little touches, composites of things she's heard other women say about their husbands. She wants to be able to boast about the wonderful life he gave her. She needs to claim back her due and keep her place in the pecking order. The truth is she'd wither away if he were to come back. But I suspect she half believes her fictions — she needs to believe them. They're what keep her going."

"But that isn't true of Matt," Ellen says. "That's not the way he copes."

"Too honest. That's his trouble."

"He must be desolate at the moment."

"It's like a cancer eating him up."

"Is that what you think, Stephen? I do too." She sees no hope for Matt, just unremitting bleakness, his face set against the world.

Stephen sips his cooling coffee. The waitress materializes, and he asks for the bill, throwing a careless, charming smile her way.

"If he could just let go — stop hanging on to his anger."

"There's the challenge," says Stephen. "How do we encourage that? He's a healthy man, fit and active, nobody's fool. There's no way I could mention any of what we've been talking about. He wouldn't tolerate it for an instant."

"It's all very grim, isn't it?"

"I'll get this," he says as Ellen fumbles for money to pay for her coffee.

"It's easy for us though," she says as he walks her to her car. "Even if things aren't going our way, we've got a good chunk of life ahead of us. He's probably wondering how much time he has left."

Stephen nods. "Exactly. For the next while I intend to come down fairly regularly at weekends. He has to keep himself in check when I'm about, puts up a big front. Colum can't get away so easily, young family and all that, but he's promised to visit the occasional weekend."

"That'll give Matt something to look forward to."

She sits into her car. He leans on the open door and looks down at her. "It's early days yet. We'll give him a chance to come round. Look, I'd better go. I said I'd help out with the milking."

"You're having a working weekend?"

He smiles. "I don't mind that. Nice talking to you, Ellen. See you next weekend."

Beatrice presses the doorbell but there's no reply. She calls out, "Hello" and "Is anybody here?" Following the sound of voices, she finds herself at the top of the steps that wind their way through Ellen's back garden.

She peers down and can make out two forms, one half-hidden by the dense foliage, another taller person feeding a fire in front of the boundary wall with discarded branches. Beyond the wall surges the swollen dun-colored river, its steep banks edged by trees. The branches of a willow tree trail in the water as if on the point of plunging in.

Close to the clamorous water, Eugene and Ellen work in harmony, she chopping brambles and weeds with large shears, he raking and forking up after her. He carries a load to the bonfire, throws on the vegetation, and aerates the fire with a digging fork.

He looks up and catches Beatrice watching them. "Hello there!" he shouts, and bounds up the steps two at a time. "Ellen thought she heard something a while back but we were too engrossed in the work. We're clearing the lower levels, hacking it all back."

The steps are strewn with displaced earth and grass. Beatrice picks her route carefully, trying to step on the clear spots. Ellen grins from under a wide-brimmed straw hat. Her fingers are dirty and her face is grimy with streaks of clay. She looks like something out of a hillbilly show, her hair tied back in an untidy ponytail, a coat covering torn jeans and Wellingtons. She's wearing gloves with no fingers.

"It must be decades since anyone turned a sod in this place," Beatrice says. "How'd you rope Eugene in?"

"He's the driving force behind this, said he was sick and tired of looking out at a wilderness."

"You two didn't waste much time getting together, did you?" declares Beatrice.

Ellen flushes but Eugene looks happy. He heaps hewn branches and dead weeds onto the fork and offloads them onto the fire. Ellen rests the blade end of her shears on the ground.

"You never gave any indication, Ellen," Beatrice accuses.

"We started only yesterday."

"I don't mean the work, I mean *him*," she says, pointing at Eugene.

"That's only very recent," Ellen says, looking uncomfortable. "I'm being low-key about it."

"Yeah, it's very private," Eugene says. "She has a furtive side to her nature."

Ellen looks annoyed. "Discretion is the better part of valor. Teacher in a Catholic school and all that."

"She makes me look for permission to put my arm around her in public. I keep telling her the Church isn't a power broker anymore."

"Some of those changes are only skin deep. Lots of squinting windows still about," Beatrice says.

Ellen nods. "People can be very prickly."

"You're just substituting for somebody else. How can it matter what you do in your free time?" Eugene says. "They should be thrilled to land someone of your caliber."

Ellen smiles. "He thinks I'm good at my job because he's heard a few stories."

"I've heard good reports too. They're very pleased with you."

"See what I mean. There are no secrets here. What if I wanted to transfer to the school here? There might be an opening later this year. Don't want to blot my copybook, do I?" Ellen works the shears energetically and shuts them with a snap. "Fancy a cup of tea, Beatrice? I could do with a breather."

"I'll dampen down the fire and join you," Eugene says.

"I'll be stiff tomorrow," Ellen says, massaging her lower back with her hands. "I haven't done physical work like that in years."

"I can't but think of the cousins. Sarah would be delighted with this clearance. She was the force behind the garden."

"I like to think she'd be pleased."

"So, tell us about Eugene," Beatrice says with a playful nudge.

Ellen flushes. "Nothing to tell."

"Come on."

"It's been brewing since the time he came to quote for the kitchen."

"Instant attraction?"

"Sort of—although I fought it. He says I was hard won."

"I love a romance. There's less of it about than people realize."

"It's not so straightforward. Me being older for one thing." She grins. "I can't believe it. I'd given up on all that."

"Is it serious?"

They enter the kitchen by the back door. Ellen prizes off her Wellingtons. "One day at a time, Beatrice. That's the way we're taking it."

"You're looking well."

"He likes me with my hair longer," Ellen says dreamily. She laughs. "You'll think I've gone soft in the head."

"Not at all. I'm delighted for you."

Ellen puts on the kettle. "It's nice here, isn't it, the house and everything, the privacy?"

"Fantastic outlook over the back wall." Suddenly, Beatrice can't pretend an interest she doesn't particularly feel. She can't contain herself any longer. "Ellen, could I tell you something?"

"What is it?"

"It's not something I'd want known generally."

"Don't worry. I won't go tittle-tattling around the village."

"Paula rang last night. She ran into Andy in London."

"I remember him but I didn't know him as such. How is he?"

"You probably don't know, but he hasn't been in touch with any of the family since he fell out with his dad years ago. Typical of Jack to choose the wrong moment to bring up the subject of money. We were on our way to a restaurant in Cork to celebrate Andy's graduation — Andy had to repeat his final year — when Jack began to taunt him, going on and on about how much extra his education had cost us. It might have been meant as a joke — Jack had an odd sense of humor — but Andy took it badly, reared up, and stormed off. He drove straight home, cleared out his room, and . . . we haven't seen or heard from him since. Anyway, Paula broke the ice. He's married and has a son, and she thinks he's going to get in touch. I probably shouldn't say anything —"

"Wouldn't *that* be wonderful!" Ellen hugs her. "Of all people, Beatrice, you deserve to have this come right. Are you going to make contact?"

"Oh, I couldn't. He has to make the first move. I'd be afraid he'd slam the phone down."

"I'm sure he wouldn't."

The front doorbell rings. "Damn," Ellen says and goes to answer it. She makes a surprised face at Beatrice when Matt follows her back into the kitchen.

"Beatrice! I didn't mean to interrupt," he says and stops.

"There's nothing to interrupt. Come in."

"Sit down, Matt," Ellen says. "Tea or coffee?"

"What about a drink?"

"I'm afraid the cupboard is bare."

"Coffee so."

Eugene comes in the back door and Matt stares at him. "You do gardens now, do you?" he asks.

"He's helping out," Ellen says.

Matt sits at the table. "This is an unusual little gathering," he says and looks about. "I haven't seen the house in a good while. It looks finished."

The last time he was in Ellen's house was weeks before, the night she consummated her affair with Eugene. By the time she got home from work the following day, he was gone. They met at young Denis Scope's funeral, but he avoided her eyes and discouraged any conversation.

Today he looks more like the old Matt, freshly shaved, hair washed, skin and clothes clean. "Didn't expect to find you in this neck of the woods, Beatrice," he says.

"I get about, Matt. Don't let the grass grow under my feet. I must say you're looking very spruce."

"Stephen's coming tomorrow. He's very particular about how I look—as bad as any woman!"

"It's great he can come so often," Ellen says.

"How do you know how often he's been about?"

"I ran into him last week in Killdingle. We had coffee," she says, a touch defensively.

"How did you persuade Eugene to knuckle down to work in the garden?" says Matt.

"Ah, sure, love is a great incentive," Beatrice says, and smiles.

"What's that? I'm sure I misheard you," Matt says.

"Not at all, Matt. Spring is in the air."

Eugene notices Ellen's tense stance and moves to be close to her.

"Are you telling me that these two are—whatever it's called now —going out with each other?"

"I most certainly am."

"Eugene and I are good friends," Ellen mumbles.

"Very close friends," Beatrice says.

"Is this true, Ellen?" asks Matt flatly.

She shrugs. "It is and it isn't."

Eugene makes a sharp movement. "It is, Ellen. Don't deny it."

"Well, it has to be one thing or the other, doesn't it?" Matt says crossly. "Let me get this straight. You're separated, on your way to a divorce. Right?"

"Yes." She wants to shut him up but can't think how.

"In the meantime you've taken up with this fellow?"

She nods.

He points at Eugene. "He goes through women like — you're just one in a long line. Do you know that?"

"What?"

"He's one of those serial — what d'you mecall 'ems? . . . One at a time, but he always moves on. I warned you, but it seems you didn't listen."

Eugene glowers at Matt. "Take that back!" he says. "Take it back!"

"Why would I take it back when it's true?"

"The gloss you put on it, but there's no truth in it. None whatsoever. I've heard of pig-ignorant people but this beats all. You're out of order, Matt!"

Matt looks at Ellen. "That's not as I heard. He's had numerous women. You must know that."

"Stop this, Matt!" snaps Ellen. "Just stop it!"

"Matt, I haven't heard any of this," Beatrice says. "Where did you get hold of it?"

"It's well known."

"Whenever I hear that something's 'well known,' I know nobody has a clue what's going on," Eugene says crossly. "Tell us about the swath I'm supposed to have cut through the womenfolk here!"

"You came here with a woman. Then you were living with another. There was a third, I think. I don't want you adding my niece to your list of conquests."

"Why not check your facts before making wild accusations, you ignorant bastard. I'll make allowances, because I assume that you're acting from the best of motives —"

"You're the bastard!" Matt says.

"Matt, that's enough now," Beatrice says. "Hush."

"God help me, I'm trying to answer him civilly instead of beating him down on the ground but I could lose the run of myself here," Eugene says.

Matt stands up. "Try me, and you'll get more than you bargained for."

Ellen rushes between them. "None of this macho stuff," she orders. "This behavior is ridiculous."

"Ellen's right. Would the two of you back off? You're like stags in the rutting season," exclaims Beatrice. "It's between these two, Matt. Sit down, for God's sake!"

"Thanks, Beatrice," Eugene says. "For your information, Matt, I followed the first woman here —"

"You don't have to explain," interrupts Ellen. "Don't say anything, Eugene."

"It's all right, Ellen. He has some false idea of me — I don't know how he picked it up — but because he's your uncle, I'm anxious to dispel it. I had *one* girlfriend, Matt, and you've misinterpreted the other situations. I've told Ellen everything. She knows all about me."

"Well, she knows your version of the story. But what about Ellen, Eugene? You can't run a cart and four through her. What are your intentions there?" Matt barks.

"Matt!" Ellen says, mortified. "He has no right to ask," she mutters to Eugene.

"I don't mind at all," Eugene says. He looks at Beatrice, who's squirming on her seat. "How're you doing there, Beatrice?"

"If I could disappear now, I would," she says with feeling.

"Good woman. Hang in there." Eugene turns to Matt. "My intentions toward your niece are honorable."

"So you're not sleeping with her?"

Ellen gasps loudly. She rounds on Matt. "Next you'll be talking about fallen women and damaged goods. I must be dreaming. I can't believe we're having this conversation."

"I'm trying to look out for you, Ellen. That's all. I don't want you shacking up with some lowlife who'll toss you aside like a —"

"Like a used teabag — is that it?"

Matt gives a snort of laughter. "Not the way I'd phrase it, but it'll do."

"It's a different world," Beatrice says in an exasperated tone. "Times have changed."

"Exactly," agrees Ellen.

"You like Eugene, don't you, Beatrice? That's why you're sticking up for him," Matt says.

"Well, I do. I've always liked him. And I think Ellen's well able to take care of herself."

Matt laughs. "So ye all think I'm an interfering old git, is that it?"

"In a nutshell," Ellen says. "Although I know what's behind it."

"It's to the forefront, Ellen. Life's not as uncomplicated as you'd like."

"No, I know it isn't, Matt. I understand that. But this isn't your call."

"If you mess my niece about, Eugene, I'll knock your block off. Do you understand?"

Eugene squares up to him. "Perfectly."

"Could we change the topic of conversation, please?" begs Ellen. "You haven't heard Beatrice's news, have you, Matt?" She realizes her gaffe when she sees a horrified expression on Beatrice's face.

"Shush, Ellen! Remember what I said?" hisses Beatrice.

Ellen puts her hands to her head. "I'm desperately sorry, Beatrice. I didn't think you'd mind me saying it in front of Eugene or Matt. But I shouldn't have opened my mouth. Forget anything I said, everybody."

"It was meant to be confidential," Beatrice says crossly.

"Is it about Andy? Is that it? Have you heard from him?" Matt guesses.

For the first time in — it must be decades — Beatrice feels that he is tuned in to her wavelength and really sees her. She shrugs. "Nothing solid, Matt. Paula ran into him in London, that's all. Don't know how it's going to turn out."

"I'd go for that any day," Matt says. "It's better than a slap on the face from a wet fish."

"Will you all promise not to breathe a word? Nothing may come of it."

"Quiet as the grave," promises Matt.

"If either of the two of us opens our gobs, Beatrice, we'll have Matt to contend with," Eugene says.

"Watch it, Eugene," Matt says, but the hostility has gone out of his voice.

Twelve

EATRICE IS WATCHING the late night news from an armchair, feet propped up on a footstool, a supper tray wedged in on the small table beside her. She sips coffee into which she dunks her own homemade gingernut biscuits.

Behind the chair, close to the range, Shep dreams. His nose quivers, his paws twitch, and he emits an occasional whine. The phone rings and he barks. "Shush, Shep," she orders as she lifts the receiver. "Hello." There's a silence at the other end. Wrong number, she thinks, and is about to put it down when a voice says, "Hi there, Mom. It's Andy."

The biscuit hits the floor and she nearly drops the phone. "Andy!" Her voice is hardly recognizable to her. Another silence follows. "How are you?" she asks, afraid he'll hang up.

"I'm okay."

"Where are you ringing from?"

"The States."

"I believe you're living there now," she says politely. How odd to be talking to him as if he's a stranger.

"That's right." She recognizes an American intonation in his voice.

"How are things?"

"Okay."

"It's great to hear your voice again. I'm told you got married."

"Yeah, we're living in New York."

"And you have a son?"

"Correct."

His voice is unengaged, neutral. He sounds vaguely bored. Talking to him is like wrestling with a shadow. It's perplexing that he acts so distant when he has gone to the trouble of phoning.

"What did you call him, your son?"

"Scott."

"Scott?" Scott Furlong. Too American, she thinks.

"Yeah, Scott . . . after Kerry's dad."

"That's nice. Kerry's your wife?"

"Yeah, she's a New Yorker. We met in the Big Apple." Beatrice suspects that somebody — Kerry? — is beside him, egging him on. She imagines a whippet-thin woman with dark long hair, an expressive face, and lively brown eyes, dressed in jeans, plaid shirt, and clean sneakers, a pretty woman probably. Andy always had an eye for the pretty ones. She imagines this woman convincing him to ring his mother. *Andy, you gotta make the first move. You made the break.* She's probably full of therapy-speak and sees her shrink on a regular basis. No, no, not fair, she could be perfectly normal, a rock of common sense.

"Paula told me about meeting you in the underground."

"Yeah, we had a long talk. It was good." The American drawl makes him sound like a stranger. "Hey, I was over in London last week and I called in on them, stayed over. She has a big house and the kids are great."

"Paula never breathed a word," Beatrice says indignantly.

"She was on at me to ring you, but I made her promise not to let the cat out of the bag until I got in touch. She said she gave you my number, so I kinda expected you to call me," he continues.

His matter-of-fact tone nettles her. He presumes so much! Seconds tick by, a minute perhaps, before she finds her voice. "Well, I didn't know what to do, Andy. I wasn't sure you'd want to hear from me. To be honest, I was in two minds about what was best."

"Hey, Mom," — sounding so like a Yank — "all that stuff was to do with Dad. It was never you."

Then why didn't he make contact in all those years? A letter, a postcard, either would have made the world of difference. Better not ask. No reproaches.

"What age is Scott?"

"Five going on six."

"And who's he like? Does he resemble anyone on our side of the family?"

He laughs. "There you go, all that stuff about likenesses. Typical. He's like himself, Mom, like himself." For the first time he sounds warm.

"Just trying to get a picture of him in my mind. I'd love to see a photo."

"I'll post you one. I guess you don't have e-mail."

"Well, I have a computer but I haven't hooked up the e-mail. Paula is always on at me about getting into it."

"Jeez, there must be some changes about the old place if you've got a computer!"

"I use it for the accounts. There's a very handy program, speeds up the whole thing."

"I thought you'd be pressing me to visit, Mom."

"Well, would you come?"

"Sure. Kerry's been working on me to vacation in Ireland. She thinks it strange that we're not in touch. She wants to see the place I'm from."

Beatrice can't imagine this daughter-in-law. She's even hard put to construct an image of Andy. Has his appearance changed as dramatically as his accent? "Well, you know you're always welcome. I'd love to see you."

"We might come in a month or so. We're due some time off. How would that be?"

A month? Such a turnabout, from nothing to everything in the space of a few minutes. His directness is new. It must come from living in the States. She imagines this wife, who has suddenly metamorphosed into a brash, blond woman with blood-red talons for nails, saying, *It'd be great for Scott to see where you grew up. I just love the idea of going to Ireland.*

"You'd be more than welcome," she says, casting her eye about the room, which suddenly looks shabby. "A month. Did you say a month? Around Easter you mean?"

"Yeah, Easter time. April. I kinda thought it would be good, before the fares go up."

Alarm swamps her. Little or no time to . . . well, to . . . she is bolt upright in the chair. "Of course, whenever suits." Her voice sounds like the squeak of a rusty gate.

"That's good. We'll ring with dates when we've booked flights."

Too fast, this is moving way too fast. "How long do you plan to stay?"

"I guess about three weeks, but we'll travel around a bit. I want to show Kerry the sights."

"With a name like that, you'll have to show her the Lakes of Killarney and Dingle Bay."

He laughs. "Hey, Mom, you haven't lost your sense of humor." He talks to somebody. "You wanna talk to Kerry, Mom?"

"Em—I suppose." She hears the phone being handed over. "Hello," she says. Her throat tickles ominously and she feels a strong urge to cough. What is it about nervousness and coughing? There's nothing from the other end. "Hello?" she tries again.

"Hi, Mrs. Furlong," comes a fresh voice. It's soft, high, and hesitant. Beatrice thinks of Jackie Kennedy Onassis and reactivates the more sympathetic image of this woman.

"Hello, Kerry. Nice to hear from you. My name is Beatrice."

"I've heard a lot about you."

"Well, I know next to nothing about you, except that you're a New Yorker—"

"I'm originally from New Jersey. I live in New York."

"Lots of Irish people in New Jersey. Lots in New York too. Have you any Irish connections?"

"No Irish in the mix. My mom liked the name. That's all. I guess I'm just your average American."

"You should get Andy to post me a picture of you when he's sending Scott's photo."

"Sure." Kerry sounds deflated. It's difficult to manufacture phone talk with a perfect stranger.

"Well, I'm looking forward to meeting you in the flesh."

"Me too, Mrs. Furlong, me too."

"None of this formality, please. Call me Beatrice, Kerry. Everyone does."

"Okay then, Beatrice. Talk to you soon."

There's a click and the phone goes dead. She holds the receiver in her hand. What if that's it? Say she doesn't hear from him again? She glances up at the clock. Half past eleven. It's half past six — six-thirty — evening time in New York.

Before she realizes what she's doing she has phoned Paula. She gets her husband. "Barry, I know it's very late but could I speak to Paula?"

"She's in bed, Beatrice. She's asleep. I'll get her to ring you tomorrow."

It's too late to ring Lily Traynor. She's like the birds, early to bed and early to rise. Her fingers type out Ellen's number but she cancels the call when Eugene answers. Is Eugene living with Ellen now, she wonders?

She's still in a stupor when Simon arrives. The dog greets him with an ingratiating whine. "I must have dozed off," she says. "Did that cow calve?"

"Eventually. No problem in the end," he says pleasantly. "At least I don't have to stay above tonight. It's been hot and heavy the last week."

"The most grueling time of the year."

"The sleep deprivation's the worst. I'm going to make myself a cuppa before I turn in. You want some?"

"No, thanks. I don't know how you keep these late nights and still get up first thing in the morning. You must have the constitution of an ox."

"It doesn't bother me."

"Give me the stamina of youth," she says, getting to her feet. "I'm away, Simon. Goodnight. Will you lock Shep in the shed?"

"Sure thing. 'Night, Beatrice."

Ellen tilts the tube of the pregnancy testing kit to read the result. Negative. Her shoulders slump and her stomach settles. It's a strange moment, like relaxing after a high-altitude ride on a fairground attraction and savoring the relief of not having to view the world from a peculiar angle anymore.

Were she to examine her life and draw up a list of regrets, missing out on being a parent wouldn't get a rating. She believes that divine intervention saw to it that Christy and she never had any children. What a mess that would have been. Would she now be a single mother? Or, miracle of miracles, would Christy have taken care of them?

She remembers comments from the early days of her marriage, "Any news?" inquiries, and pointed looks at her stubbornly unexpanded stomach. Even Kitty got in on the act, although she would have been hard-pressed to cope with the idea of being a grandmother, involving as it must an acknowledgment of the aging process. "I'll never agree to being called 'Granny,'" she had said. "I'll be known as Kitty." Of course, as years went by, interest in the hypothetical child waned and finally atrophied.

"Do another test in a week or two," Maureen advises. "You have to be sure."

They're in Maureen's kitchen on a Saturday morning, the rays from a late March sun bathing the room in a low-intensity glow.

"I think I'd travel to England if it tested positive."

"Would you though? Would you have an abortion?"

The features on Ellen's face twist. "Would I? I don't know! I'd have to do something."

"Really? I know there's an element of shock. Mind you, I don't know if Paddy and I would have married without the incentive of the baby. We hadn't a notion of getting hitched."

"Just as well I'm not pregnant then because Eugene and I aren't getting married."

"Does Eugene know about this?" Ellen shakes her head vehemently. "Will you tell him?"

"Why would I? It was a false alarm."

"You should say to see how he reacts."

"Why? To scare him off?"

"Giving him a jolt would be a good test, if you're serious about him."

Ellen snorts contemptuously. "You have babies on the brain,

Maureen. Man — woman — love — commitment — baby, that's the way your mind works."

"Tick tock, tick tock, biology's clock is ticking away. Maybe Eugene would like children."

"We've only started to be a couple, Maureen. It could end tomorrow. I've no intention of tossing babies into the equation."

"You think it'll end?"

"Can you see a future in it?"

"Why do you think you'll split up?"

"I don't know that we will, but it's the age thing. Twelve years, Maureen. It's no joke."

"I wouldn't worry. The French writer Colette seduced a seventeen-year-old when she was in her fifties, and he was heartbroken the day she died. An American writer — I can't remember the name — was married to a woman he thought was ten years older than him. When she died, turned out she'd lied, and there was an age gap of eighteen years, but it didn't matter. He never recovered from her death. We're always trying to put people into categories. It's much more random and haphazard than we imagine."

"Well, obviously, I'm in favor of that theory."

"But, Ellen, what if you were pregnant? Imagine that there's a high probability you'd never be able to conceive again. For argument's sake, say you are, and that this is your absolutely one-time-only shot at motherhood."

"It's early in the day for this sort of speculation."

"Your only opportunity. Forget Eugene. Forget your job. Forget everything else. Now, do you want a baby?"

Ellen frowns. "I don't suffer from baby hunger. I've seen you going 'Coochie, coochie, coochie' and tickling babies you haven't been introduced to. Remember when Nesta had her last baby? I pretended to admire him, asked her to let me hold him, all the stuff you told me, but I didn't feel anything. It was all show."

"Are you sure that you're not going to end up being one of those women who 'forgot' to have a baby?"

"Well, I can't take out my crystal ball and have a good old rummage about in the future, can I? Besides, babies are trouble. Children are a worry. Then they bugger off and dump you in a nursing home. What's the point?"

"Is wanting a life that is nothing but comfortable the best course of action?"

Ellen shakes her head slowly. "Of course, silly me! Why didn't I realize? My life's way too perfect. I should bugger it up by having a baby to make Maureen happy!"

"Don't turn all snooty on me."

"Why you have to keep banging on about it. We know I'm *not* pregnant."

"But what if you were faced with it?"

"Well, then I'd know what I felt."

"You're like a blind person where children are concerned," Maureen says impatiently.

"You've always liked kids, Maureen. You're programmed to want them."

"I'm glad I had them . . . because they broke me open."

"Broke you open," Ellen says caustically. "Bits of Maureen here, there, and everywhere?"

"Emotionally, put me through the wringer. Brought me to life in a way I'd never been alive before."

"So? So what? Hurrah? Look, I know about the old-style Catholic idea that people improve through hardship and suffering. But I'm not sure about it. What about the woman who gives birth to a physically or mentally disabled baby?"

"Challenged."

"What?"

"A physically or mentally challenged baby," Maureen says.

"Yeah. Okay. Well, that woman's suffering would heighten her awareness of life, but does it enhance her quality of life? It might be detrimental to her."

"We all make choices," Maureen says, clipping her words. "I happen to think the more you experience of life, the more you confront what's difficult, the more alive you end up being. You evolve. Isn't that what it's all about?"

"That's the greatest load of balls I've ever heard. I'm surprised you didn't suggest that I'd live on forever in the child and its descendents."

"You're still a child, Ellen."

"Haven't you heard of prolonged adolescence, Maureen? We

don't grow up now. We don't accept the responsibilities of adult-
hood. We don't want to grow old. Life's too sweet."

"I never thought I'd see a resemblance between you and your
mother, but I do now," Maureen says glumly. "Self-obsessed, not
wanting anything to disturb the calm of your life. You'd resent a
child."

"Were I to have a child, I'd know to make it feel loved, but it'd
be bloody irresponsible to produce offspring just to see how I'd react. What if I rejected it? Lots of 'what ifs.' In the end, I'm me and
you're you. And I resent the implication that I resemble my mother.
All the other stuff I don't mind."

"I take that back, but you're not necessarily out of the loop with
the pregnancy thing. Do another test next week."

That night, Ellen dreams that she's staying in Maureen's house.
She's on the point of discarding the testing kit and its packaging
when she notices a wavering blue line in the glass part of the tube.
She shakes the tube and the line breaks up. She wonders what that
means. Is she really pregnant? False reading, she thinks. It has to
be. The line re-forms. She's mesmerized by it. What will she tell
Eugene?

Maureen laughs. "That's putting it up to you," she says.

Now Ellen is awake. She sits up in bed. The room is unfamiliar.
She can't find the light switch. She can't see anything. Her hand
knocks something over. Her heart is running its own Olympics.

"Are you okay, dear?" comes Kitty's voice. "You cried out."

For a moment Ellen thinks she has blundered into another dream
until she remembers that she's staying in her mother's apartment.
"I'm okay. I'm grand," she says.

"'Night, dear."

"Goodnight."

Kitty puts down her paintbrush. "Stop being so fidgety, darling. Just
another few minutes."

Ellen sighs. "Why didn't you stick to landscapes?"

Kitty purses her lips. "Portraiture has always interested me. My
tutor suggested I give it a go."

Kitty must be the tidiest painter ever. Her overalls are, naturally enough, spotless. When she finishes, she'll wheel her easel into a corner and clean her color palette. The tools of her hobby will be stored unobtrusively beside the dresser in the kitchen.

"Your mouth is turning down again."

"I'm wilting."

"Lift the edges of your mouth. I'm trying to give you a nice expression."

"It doesn't matter if I have a scowl."

Kitty clicks her tongue in irritation.

The apartment is full of Kitty's paintings — her early botched representations of vases of flowers, the worrying gradients of the horizons in her first landscapes, and later competent renderings, when she had mastered drawing and perspective. She has sold a number of paintings at the summer exhibition on Saint Stephen's Green. Her work graces walls in the houses of quite a few friends who haven't chosen to hide the paintings in obscure places.

Ellen respects her mother's limited talent but she doesn't like the palette of colors Kitty works from. When not doing watercolors, she uses pastels. Still, the portrait will be recognizably Ellen. "My daughter," Kitty will say to anyone who asks, and they'll probably imagine a close relationship.

"Christy has picked up a job," Kitty says as she dabs at the canvas.

"I knew he would. I wasn't worried."

"Aren't you going to ask about it? You wouldn't care if he disappeared off the face of the earth tomorrow."

"I'd attend the memorial service. Anyway, who's he working for?"

"You've a heart of stone, Ellen. No finer feelings. He's with Sergeant and something or other. It's a big company, not as exclusively arty as the previous place, which he's disappointed about, but they're less likely to fold than a small firm."

"And how's his love life?"

"He's with a very nice girl. Why? Are you jealous?"

Ellen laughs. This is typical Kitty. Conversations with her take little twists and turns. They're a scenic route of impressions, jumping from this topic to that, a mishmash of random provocations.

"There, you can move."

Ellen yawns, stands up, and checks her watch. "You said half an hour — that was nearly two hours!" she complains.

Kitty smirks and stands back from the canvas.

Ellen ponders Kitty's rendering. An abstract of an angled head and torso — three-quarters angle — is daubed with light brushstrokes of pallid grays, yellows, and orange, light hair, dark brows, and lurid spots of consumptive color on the cheeks. Still, it's a pretty Ellen. It corresponds to Ellen's idea of how she looks, perhaps how she always looked but didn't realize, but certainly how she sees herself now. "That's good," she comments. "You're in control of your material."

"Do you really like it?" Kitty asks. Ellen can tell she is flattered by the praise.

"Indubitably. I look weird but I like it."

Mother and daughter smile at each other. Ellen would like to stretch this moment, to eternalize it, before its inexorable deterioration, before Kitty lobs in an undermining comment, or makes some outrageous statement calculated to throw Ellen into a frenzy. She has learned to receive all her mother's taunts with surface equilibrium and knows how to fast-track a conversation back into the shallows of small talk.

Often Kitty is disappointed when she can't elicit extreme reactions from Ellen. Sometimes — rather wistfully — she'll say, "We used to have such fights, darling" or "You've iced over, Ellen. I think you don't have any feelings at all." It's not for lack of trying on Kitty's part — teasing, she calls it — but Ellen is adamant that she won't be drawn into a row.

"I'll heat up a nice little something from Marks and Sparks tonight. There's another bottle of Chablis in the fridge," says Kitty.

"I was going to treat you."

"Wouldn't hear of it, dear. Let's be frugal."

"Frugal it is."

Kitty isn't normally an aggressive woman, but a persistent lingering disappointment — with life or with Ellen — makes her fractious in her daughter's company. Ellen is the butt of all her nastiness, that insidious awfulness that nobody else witnesses. For as long as Ellen can remember, her mother has been dissatisfied with something or other concerning her daughter, sighing over Ellen's outfits, figure, friends, and interests. Ellen has never cracked the riddle of what exactly her mother wants from her, but she knows that Kitty won't ever find her satisfactory.

The previous night they went to a film and ate in one of the Temple Bar hostelries, a lively Italian-owned restaurant Kitty had booked. They were given a table by a window that faced out onto the River Liffey with a view of the constant comings and goings of natives and tourists. Kitty fancies herself as a Bohemian and likes to wander about Dublin's self-styled Latin quarter whenever she can. At heart, however, she's a suburbanite, nursing her prejudices, cultivating her image, fond of her comforts, and dabbling in the arts.

She has a satisfactory time of it, meeting friends for lunch, regularly taking short breaks for the over fifty-fives to France, Italy, Portugal, and Greece. She suffers a distinct shortage of family. Originally from a public housing estate in Crumlin, she is the only child of long-dead parents who were themselves solitary children. Their legacy to Kitty was an education. Kitty's contribution to her social elevation was to cultivate a middle-class accent. A dead husband, a live child: that is her lot. Ellen is her only kin, Matt her only in-law. She often reminds Ellen of this, with her "You're all I've got now, dear" and "We two will have to stick together." Ellen foresees this phrase being used with increasing frequency in years to come, and dreads the apocalyptic moment when Kitty will beg her to live with her, or insist on living with Ellen.

"And how is Matt getting on?" Kitty asks over salad and rolls at lunch. She has never bothered much about Matt although she claims to find him attractive. Ellen suspects that she doesn't fancy the idea of being associated with a farmer. Kitty has an instinctive disdain for anything that smacks of hard labor and a horror of finding herself in a situation which wouldn't satisfy her yen for material comforts.

On the other hand, Brendan's profession as a teacher gave him social standing and respectability. He didn't survive long enough to clock up a pension, but an insurance policy paid off the mortgage on the house they were living in when he died. Reluctantly, Kitty returned to work in a public library. It was better than being a shop assistant.

Everything Ellen has been told about her father makes her think of him as the strong one in her parents' marriage. Kitty, with her pretty ways and feminine wiles, would have latched on to that strength. She sometimes wonders how they adjusted to each other, or if they did. Were disagreements and rows a feature of their union? Ellen has a vague memory of her mother crying, but whether that was because she'd had a fight with her husband, or because her husband had died, she has no idea. Matt wouldn't have borne Kitty's machinations. They would have irritated the life out of him.

"Matt's okay now. He was off form for a while after Julia's death but he's coming round."

"He should never have married Julia. She wasn't fit to lick his boots. It was an arranged marriage. The mother forced him into it. Brendan told me."

"It certainly wasn't a happy union. Still, he's free to make something of his life now that she's gone."

"I don't understand why you choose him over me," Kitty says petulantly, with one of her sudden mood swings.

"Choose Matt over you?" Ellen echoes with a carefully constructed frown. She's on immediate alert, her neck so tight it feels brittle.

"Yes, throwing in your lot with him, instead of being here with me. I can't think what I've done to deserve it. It's quite a slap in the face, I can tell you. Humiliating, in fact."

"Don't be ridiculous, Kitty. It's not as if I see that much of Matt. Be honest. You and I don't get on. It's best when we live at a remove from each other."

"Oh, darling, that's not at all true," Kitty protests. "We make a great team. Wouldn't it be lovely if we could hang about like sisters?"

"Too much rivalry, Kitty. We'd kill each other!"

Kitty laughs. "A shame, isn't it?" she sighs. She sounds wistful.

Ellen hopes that Kitty isn't coiling up for another attack. She knows that at the back of all of this girlish posturing is a deep loneliness. Her mother's life is mostly surface. She wants everything to be right but feels emotionally isolated.

Kitty once hinted that she had suffered many disappointments in her time. Ellen supposes that her mother's glooms stem from the realization that her life has failed to live up to her imaginings. She offsets this by fabricating a virtual world in which she plays an improbably important role. The cultivated, sensitive, intelligent, beloved, and moneyed Kitty — her best self — lives this life. Bits of it she salvages through her interest in books and art. She compensates for lack of money by dressing well and eating little. However, she's convinced that she has been cheated out of an alternative life, where — Ellen is sure about this — she lives in one of the grand Southside city houses with a fawning husband, successful children, and healthy bank balance. Kitty is always anxious to establish her superiority to others, convinced of her greater sensitivity, refinement, and taste in relation to other people. She's like a waitress who has tried and failed to make it in acting, treating her customers disdainfully because she knows that she will outshine them the day her talent is recognized.

"You'd find it an awful drag having to live with me," Ellen says. "It'd be a letdown."

"I suppose that's true," Kitty says. "You've let me down in many little ways."

"Well, I'm glad they're only little ways," Ellen says vigorously. "I'd hate to be a big disappointment."

"Don't sulk, dear. Sit down and pour another glass of wine."

In less than twenty-four hours Ellen will sit into her car and drive back to Ballindoon, blessed peace, and Eugene.

"I'm your mother, darling, but you never confide in me," complains Kitty. "You're a closed book. I don't know anything about your hopes and dreams. I don't even know if there's romance in your life."

"Nothing to tell," Ellen retorts cheerily. "My life is boring." She can't bring herself to reveal anything to Kitty. She can almost hear her mother's shriek of "You so-and-so. Never breathed a word. Now, you have to tell me everything about this Eugene," and her unconscious pouting as she grooms and preens, imagining herself as a rival for the affections of Ellen's new man.

Eugene said, "Haven't you told her yet?" when Ellen and he kissed goodbye the previous day.

"Have you said anything to your family about me?" she had asked, and was disconcerted when he said, "Of course I have. They're dying to meet you."

She'd laughed. "Ha, ha, ha," she'd said.

"Wait and see," he'd answered with a grin. "My regards to your mother."

Ellen's mobile screeches out arrival of a text message from Eugene: "miss u," it reads.

"What's that, darling? Who's sending you messages?"

"Just one of my friends wondering if we could meet up."

"Well, you know I've never stopped you doing anything you want, darling. I don't stand in your way. Are you going to meet this person?"

"No. I was hoping to see Maureen, but she's away this weekend. It'll do me good to have a quiet night in."

"But we're going to the Gate, darling. I have tickets for that new production."

"But you said—"

"What did I say, dear? I'm sure I didn't mean it. Nearly forgot about the tickets. I was lucky to get them. It's completely sold out, and the reviews are very positive. If we pre-book drinks, we won't have to queue at the interval. Pierce O'Hagan is in it. You've heard of him, haven't you? Another Irish actor made good. And the cast mingles with the audience in the bar afterward. It's a lovely night out."

"You're a demon for springing surprises."

"Tush. I forgot. That's all. And I went to such trouble to get them. Wouldn't it be a tragedy if I'd forgotten completely and we missed it? It makes me weak to think of it."

This is Kitty at her animated best. Ellen has always appreciated the aspirational and artistic side to her mother but can never admit it, for fear of providing her mother with more of an entrée into her life.

Ellen thinks her features have softened and plumped up under the influence of love. Her complexion has cleared itself of blemishes. People tell her she's "blooming" or "looking particularly well." Her body feels reinvigorated. It's all to do with attention, the giving and receiving of it, being alive to somebody and knowing she's alive to them.

Eugene has an affectionate way of touching her hair, cheek, or throat. Sometimes she catches a surprising tender expression on his face.

They have almost finished work on the garden. Eugene's dense planting of shrubs on the terraces subverts the previous cottage-style flowers, but Ellen thinks that Sarah would find lots to please her.

Sarah's is the spirit behind Ellen's house. Neither Mollie nor Peg appreciated the beauty of the site. Peg, in particular, like many of her contemporaries, hated anything old, associating it with poverty. The sisters fretted that their house wasn't "modern." They dreamed about low-ceilinged rooms with brick fireplaces and central heating. They slavered over brown and orange color schemes. They ached for a smart new fitted kitchen. They lusted over 1960s and 1970s bungalows — cramped and small by the standards of today.

However, the sisters could never persuade Sarah to sell the house in the village. "What'd I want with cleaning out septic tanks?" was her unvarying response. "This is a grand house. It has character. We're hooked into the water and sewerage system. The shops are within walking distance. We have our little oasis of a back garden. All we have to do is maintain the place. It'll see us out." Minor skirmishes were waged over modernizing fireplaces, doors, and windows, installing beauty-board panels on the walls or buying a Formica-topped table, but Peg and Mollie lost each and every tussle. They fumed and sulked and fantasized about what they would do when Sarah, the eldest, was gone, but in 1985 Mollie suddenly succumbed to a rampaging cancer that she hadn't complained about until it was too late, and Peg failed to wake up on Christmas morning in 1991. Sarah pronounced herself willing to die in 1995 and was duly dispatched in March of that year.

Ellen knows about those battles of long ago because she and Sarah corresponded until Sarah's hand became too unsteady to hold a pen. Today, a dry day in late March, she and Eugene are trimming the hedge close to the river. Eugene has sandblasted the old stone steps and they've come up remarkably well.

Matt suddenly appears at the top of the steps. "Hello there!" he shouts down, funneling his voice through his hands.

Ellen hears the call and waves up. "I'll put on the kettle," she yells, but Matt puts a hand to his ear and shakes his head. "We're due a break," she says to Eugene.

"Are you going to the meeting tonight?" Matt asks when she joins him.

"What meeting?"

"About the motorway."

"Motorway?" She stops, puzzled.

"Don't you ever get out? There's a meeting about the proposed route."

"Well, how does that affect us?" she asks as she removes her coat.

"Affects everyone. You'll maybe have to drive all the way to Butler's Pass to get to it, if the access roads aren't sorted out properly. Farmers are worried they'll lose land or have it divided up. There are all sorts of issues."

"This is news to me."

"Living in a dream world, are we?"

"Do you know about this motorway?" she asks Eugene when he comes in.

"Yeah. There are three proposed routes. One could pass very close to the old Protestant graveyard, depending on which direction the Killdingle bypass takes."

"But that's within walking distance. A motorway would never be let run so near to the village."

"That's progress for you. It leaves nothing untouched," Matt says.

She sits down. "I'm shocked, you know. Thoroughly shocked."

"It's easy to shock you," Matt sneers.

"As long as we don't end up as a commuter town," she says. "Can you imagine?"

"No avoiding that sort of thing. Housing estates are springing up in every two-bit town near a main thoroughfare. Villages are being swamped. You hear of it everywhere."

"But not here, surely? We're off the beaten track."

"Not as much as you'd like. Remember there's a big city just forty miles away, and it's expanding all the time. You'll have to go to live in Leitrim if it's isolation you want," Eugene says.

"Is this a setup?" she asks suddenly, eager for them to be playing a trick. She's met by silence. "It won't come that close, will it?"

"Could come to within a mile of us," Matt says.

"You're joking."

"That's the worst-case scenario. Better turn up at the meeting tonight and find out."

"They're testing out reaction to the various routes. We'll have to hope we don't get a bad deal," Eugene says.

"He who shouts loudest is heard longest," Matt says. "If we don't like what we hear, we'll have to raise a racket."

"Will it really affect us?" Ellen asks.

"Don't tell me you're lamenting the decline of old ways," Matt teases. "Prosperity comes at a price."

"But you're just as unhappy about it."

"I can live with it once it passes clear of my land. They'll be handing out maps tonight."

"How did this suddenly come out of nowhere?"

"You just haven't been aware of it. This is change. No avoiding it."

"Don't look so distressed," Eugene says. "It's not the end of the world."

"The end of the world as I know it. It threatens all the things I like about here."

Eugene takes her hand. "You're such a sentimentalist," he says.

"Well, I am," she wails.

"Come on, you like all those trendy shopping places in Killdingle. You love that new walkway by the river. You're delighted that there are Chinese, Italian, and Indian restaurants there. You want all your mod cons. This is the next step. We just have to protect our territory as best we can, try to ensure it isn't messed up too much."

"Everything happens so quickly now," she complains. "Why can't they leave things alone?"

"That's the only thing I envy the Brits," Matt volunteers. "They know how to plan for change. They have systems that work. They don't make a dog's dinner of it the way we do in this country."

"Bloody county councilors lining their pockets, assisting this and that developer," Eugene says.

"I don't think that happens anymore," Matt says.

"Dream on," Eugene says crossly.

Matt falls silent. "Matt's right," Ellen says. "That sort of corruption doesn't happen now."

"Nonsense!" Eugene says.

There's an incendiary feel to the moment. Ellen wishes Eugene hadn't stated his views so uncompromisingly. Matt was once a county councilor.

Matt sucks his lower lip and stares at the floor. Suddenly he lifts his head. "Word has it that Beatrice is getting a new kitchen," he says.

"That's right. It's going in next week," Eugene says.

"All in honor of Andy's arrival," Ellen says.

"Nothing wrong with the kitchen she had," Matt declares.

"You can't have seen it recently. It's over thirty years old and falling apart," Ellen says.

"Sure, if she does up one part, it'll be laughing at the rest of the house," says Matt. "She should leave well enough alone."

"She hasn't gone mad," Ellen says. "Just replacement cupboards and a new tiled floor."

"It's going to cost her."

"No," Eugene says. "It covers a small area. She's not getting a solid wood kitchen. We rejigged it a bit with one or two additions."

"Have you no shame?" Matt says to Ellen. "Touting for business for your new boyfriend."

"It had nothing to do with me."

"Baloney. You fed her the envy potion. I saw it myself."

"That's rubbish, Matt. If you're suggesting —"

"He's winding you up," Eugene interrupts.

"Falls for it every time," Matt says.

She sits back against the seat. "You're a terrible tease."

"You're such a good subject, I can't resist." He stands up. "Will I see yez tonight?"

"Wild horses wouldn't keep us from it," Eugene says.

Ellen stands to walk Matt to the door. "No, don't anybody see me out. I know the way."

She places the mugs in the sink and washes them. Eugene stands behind her, encircles her waist with his arms, and drops a kiss on her neck.

"I thought Matt was going to lose the rag with you," she says.

"Yeah, there was a moment when I felt I'd overstepped the mark."

Thirteen

*Y*OU'RE VERY COY about Simon," Brenda Finnegan says to Beatrice on the way out of Mass one weekday morning.

"How's that, Brenda?"

"All that talk about him and the Callow girl."

"This is all news to me."

"I hear it's very serious."

"Who's this girl? This is the first I've heard of it."

"You know, Celia Callow. Her people have land out Glenfee direction. Her father was left a farm by his uncle a while back."

"In the next valley?"

"Yes. Your Simon is supposed to be great with her. There's talk of wedding bells."

"Beats me, Brenda. I can't enlighten you."

"Word is that's why he dumped Angie Fitzsimons. He's on the make with the Callow one."

"I don't think I know her."

"You do. Plain with glasses. Very quiet. Wouldn't say boo to a goose."

"She must have some pulling power."

"They say he's after the farm. She's an only child. He's steeped."

"It's a small farm, isn't it?"

"Forty acres."

"That doesn't make sense. He'd be a part-time farmer. Simon's a good lad, Brenda. I can't see him doing that."

"That's the word. The girl thinks her ship has come in."

"Brenda, listen, nobody wants a farm nowadays." As she speaks she realizes that, of course, Simon would want a farm, or the association with one. "Are you sure that this isn't one of those mad rumors that do the rounds every so often? They're very good at totaling two and two as five around here."

"Supposedly they've agreed to sign the farm over to him."

"Now that's nonsense, Brenda, pure unadulterated spin. They wouldn't sign, seal, and deliver so quickly. It's a risky business handing over farms nowadays, what with divorce and the danger of breaking up a property if a marriage fails. The family would hedge their bets."

"But this is the clincher, Beatrice, she's a nurse. See, ideal. Her salary will keep the farm afloat. He'd be a fool to pass up the opportunity."

Their paths divide at this point. "I'd nearly bet this is one of those tall stories, Brenda."

"If you're so certain, why don't you ask him?" Brenda throws back as she turns down the lane to her house.

Beatrice ponders Brenda's words all the way home. Simon's talking to the vet at the back door when she reaches the house.

"God, you're looking fit, Beatrice," Bob McGovern calls out. "Why is a perfectly good car sitting in your garage?" Bob is pale and plump with mottled red cheeks and blond curls that give him the incongruous appearance of an overgrown baby. He's a kind man, a reformed alcoholic, but reputedly foul-mouthed when dealing with recalcitrant animals.

"Need the exercise, Bob. This is my fitness regime."

"Masochistic is what I'd call it. You shouldn't let that incident in Killdingle put you off. We all have bumps and near misses."

"I hit the child, Bob. Didn't see her."

"You did feck all harm, Beatrice. The car was almost stationary. She had just a few bruises and was a bit shocked."

"Still, it gave me a fright."

"Time to bury that now, Beatrice. Nothing too wrong with your calf. She's feeding and I've given her a shot. You're doing well. You haven't lost any so far."

"A good run. I hope it keeps up. Anybody for a cup of tea?" she asks dutifully.

"I'd best be off to my next port of call," Bob says. "The weather is great these days, good and dry, but there's still an edge to that wind." He climbs into his jeep. "So long," he says, and drives off.

Simon follows Beatrice into the kitchen. "Did you bring back anything nice?" he asks.

"Some of those doughnuts you like."

"Good woman."

"Brenda Finnegan was full of rumors about you this morning."

"Not my star turn at the karaoke night in Killdingle, was it? You shouldn't believe any of that stuff. It's all malicious. I can sing in key."

"Much more intriguing, Simon."

He laughs and sits down. "There's always some story. What have they concocted this time? I suppose Nan Brogan was in on the act too?"

"No, Nan's at home with a cold."

"Ah, there is a god!" There's a challenging, almost angry expression on his face. "Well, what was it? What were they on about?"

"Speculation about your love life. You're supposed to be taking the matrimonial plunge. They've even lined up a prospective bride."

"I'll keep you posted if there's any news, Beatrice. Don't you worry," he says grimly. Suddenly he gets up. "Save my doughnut for later," he says, and hurries away.

Afterward Beatrice can't get Brenda's words out of her mind. The more she rehashes them, the more she's inclined to believe there's something in what she said. There's an unknowable part to Simon. He's full of guarded concealment. His secretiveness rankles with her, and yet she has no right to resent it. Life charges on. One can't slow down time or stop the clocks.

She tries to dodge her thoughts but they catch her anyway. It's ridiculous to jump to conclusions on the say-so of an unreliable dirt-raker, but she can't help wondering what it would mean were Simon to marry this girl. How would it affect her? It's obvious. He'd move away. She would lose him, and her dreary old life would come back. The vigor would go out of her days.

Simon's very affable. The rhythm of their lives is deeply agreeable. He's so reliable that she can trust him with any aspect of the farm. She's come to depend on him, on his being about, has become fond of him and would miss him terribly. She shivers as if she's caught a chill. The chill lies in the chambers of her heart.

Still her mind races. Neither she nor Angie can offer Simon what he hankers after. Beatrice's farm gives employment: he can never own it. She knows that his family isn't well off, and Angie comes from a poor background. Their collective income would hardly finance the purchase of one of the new semidetached houses on the outskirts of Killdingle. She doubts that they would be able to buy a site — the days of cheap sites are long gone — and fund the building of a house. Probably their only option would be to look for a county council house. Beatrice can see how Simon could be tempted by the prospect of marrying into the Callow family. Sheer economic self-interest would make it an attractive option.

She can see it all, recognize the dreadful logic, and her heart surges painfully. Her feet are cold, and she rubs them vigorously to warm them. When she stamps them on the ground they hurt. She closes her eyes and feels dampness on her hands. Her eyes start open. Shep is licking her hand. "Off you go, Shep," she says, and shoos him out into the yard.

When she comes to again, she's sitting at the kitchen table. She has no memory of getting there. She stays without moving for a long while. Eventually she gets up and walks about but she can't settle to any task.

Simon will look out for himself. He won't consider her situation. Why would he? When there's something to say he'll tell her. He said so. She can hope that the romance, if there is one, will fizzle out. She can wish for that, and pray that she'll have him on loan for a little longer. She'll bite her tongue and bide her time.

She smiles. Isn't she, in her own way, as conniving as she suspects Simon of being, and as attentive to her own degrees of comfort? We're all at it, she thinks, putting ourselves first.

• • •

Nan and Brenda are standing by one of the mini-market checkout stalls talking to Terry. Ellen gets the strong impression that she has interrupted a crucial stage in the pooling of tittle-tattle and rumor. "Hi," she says, and receives muted hellos in return. The trio bestow their full attention on her as she fills her basket. Their compacted physical presence puts her in mind of a judging panel, a cluster of scowling individuals who award marks for suitable and unsuitable purchases. She's tempted to hold up individual items and call out, "Okay to buy this?" or "Will I lose marks by choosing that?" to see if she can shame them into looking away.

"Everything all right?" she asks. "You're all very quiet."

"How's the job going?" Terry calls out.

Ellen shrugs. "It's going," she says. "Where are the baked beans?"

"Top shelf. To the left of the eggs." The air is rancid with tension, as if they're in possession of classified information and are toying with her.

"Is this a test?" she asks.

"An inquiry. What's wrong with a civil inquiry?"

Nan and Brenda are still in a huddle, their Judas eyes scrutinizing her.

"Work is fine," Ellen says, and intercepts a knowing glance between them. "Don't let me detain you, ladies," she says with a beaming smile. "You mustn't let politeness delay you." She stares at them until, reluctantly, they move toward the door.

"We're not in any rush," Nan says with a begrudging display of false white teeth that struggles to pass itself off as a smile.

"It must be a lot different from Dublin," Brenda calls over.

"What must?"

"Teaching in the country."

"Not that much."

"Sure, teaching in the city's supposed to be a fright. The students are all out of control," Nan says.

"To be honest, I don't find much difference. I've heard of people finding country kids quite a handful, depending on the area. Some villages and towns are very rough. The kids I'm teaching in Killdingle are mostly okay but they're no pushovers. I have to be on my toes with them, same as in Dublin."

This seems to annoy them. "I wouldn't dream of bringing up

children in the city. Sure, you could never rest easy," Terry says.

"Terrible environment. You'd never be able to relax. You'd always have to be on the lookout," Brenda says. They're sullen almost to the point of hostility. Something has put them out of sorts, but it's difficult to guess the nature of their gripe. Most likely it arose out of whatever was being discussed before she arrived.

She expects an occasional outburst or rebuff because of a residual local hostility against cities, in particular Dublin, and the people who live in them. She has never quite figured out what motivates such flare-ups, whether it's jealousy of the perceived better lifestyle in the metropolis, a feeling that small communities are constantly disadvantaged in terms of government funding, that they are consistently looked down on, or if it's simply an unfocused hostility requiring an outlet. "Did some big story break on the news? Has something happened?" she asks.

"No, nothing," Nan says. Nothing that they intend to share with her.

Ellen plonks her basket in front of the till, and the two watch as Terry scans and transfers each item to Ellen's shopping bag. She feels she could demand a performance fee. They're like dogs watching sheep, and Ellen has the horrible feeling that there's a mark on her face or her skirt is tucked into her knickers, only they won't oblige her by telling her.

"That'll be twenty-three, seventy-one," Terry says. She can just about bring herself to nod. Her usual persona has been replaced by something altogether more remote and calculating.

Ellen hands over the exact amount. "Well, I'm off. Good day, ladies," she says breezily.

Of course, she is baffled by the episode. She understands that she hasn't grasped fully the essentially conservative nature of the people, even if she pays theoretical respect to the differences between them and her. There's something almost tribal about their anger at times. It's usually a matter of attitude or emphasis. She tries to bear in mind that what they have experienced in life is radically different from what she has known, so she lets whatever grievance they're voicing pass without comment. She doesn't want to be perceived as the know-all city one when she knows so little about them.

She thinks she has the measure of Terry. The woman believes

that Dublin is dangerous, promiscuous with criminality and replete with libidinous perverts. She assumes that Ellen is glad to have escaped city life. Terry used to connive with her when they pretended that Ellen knew everybody. Now, probably antagonized by Ellen's disregard for the role allocated her by Terry's concept of what constitutes acceptable behavior, Ellen has been reconfigured as a "blow-in," a permanent outsider tainted by the evil of cosmopolitan influences, somebody who will never slot into village life, despite family connections. Every so often Terry likes to pull rank and to remind her of her status, prefacing remarks with phrases such as "Of course, not being from here, you wouldn't understand" or "You couldn't know about that."

On her way up the street, she passes Father Mahoney, who frowns and ducks his head as he nods. He doesn't bestow his usual cheery comment. She's definitely at odds with the world today.

That evening Eugene doesn't call over, hasn't left a message, doesn't ring and, when she tries his landline and mobile, she gets answering machines. It's so unusual that she wonders if it is a cause for worry. She decides to wait for what the next day will bring, makes an early night of it, and is rewarded by endless dreams of chasing through tortuous tunnels and gloomy corridors.

The following day at work, it's back to the exclusion zone. Ellen's verbal sallies are met by blank looks. It's as though the news of some person's death is pressing down on everybody. She scours the newspapers for information on a local or global catastrophe but there's nothing.

"Honestly, I'm at variance with everybody," she complains to Eugene when he turns up on her doorstep that evening. "Where were you last night? Are you part of this terrible secret?"

He laughs. "I was out with my mother and sister and left the mobile at home. You forgot they were coming, didn't you? And they're treating me to dinner tonight. I booked all four of us into Duffy's Hotel tomorrow for Sunday lunch. They're mad to meet you."

Ellen feels the old dipping sensation in her stomach. "It slipped my mind that they were coming. Look, don't feel you have to include me tomorrow. I don't need to be there."

"I want you to meet them."

She dons a black outfit and jewelry for lunch and feels over-dressed when she sees his mother and sister in trousers, casual shoes and tops. Eugene has told her that his mother is just sixty, but this tall woman with the well-cut blond hair, strong features, and excellent skin could pass for somebody much younger. She has the daunting look of one of those formidably brusque and efficient women who manage dogs and horses, an impression that is immediately dispelled by her smile and handshake. "You must be Ellen," she says warmly, instantly conveying the impression of being a dependable and good-humored person.

"Ellen, meet my mum and Cora," Eugene says, his hand pressing up against the small of her back, propelling her toward his mother.

"I'm delighted to be able to put a face to the name at last," Mrs. O'Brien says. "I knew someone was bleeping his radar."

Cora grins and says, "Hi." Even taller than her mother, she is all thinness and angles. She hasn't yet grown into her looks.

Ellen manages an answering "hi" although, afraid of close scrutiny and an interrogation, she avoids eye contact.

"Sorry we deprived you of Eugene the last two nights," Eugene's mum says. "We were supposed to arrive in the afternoon but we were late starting out." Mercifully, she doesn't seem interested in vetting Ellen. She hands her a menu and works to make her relax. She's all gestures and smiles. They survive the lunch on small talk, surface explorations of each other's opinions, and family jokes. Despite Cora's coltishly provocative outbursts, there isn't a mention of Ellen's great age.

Eugene speaks rarely during the meal, happy to let his mother make most of the running. Ellen is conscious of him opposite her at the table, his knees pressed up against hers, his hands now and again brushing hers as they pass around condiments, vegetables, and sauces. He eats at a leisurely pace, not especially interested in the food, intent on what's being said. Every so often he sends her encouraging looks, a conspiratorial wink, or nods of approval when he thinks she has acquitted herself well.

Cora drops a potato on the floor and manages to spill gravy on her napkin. Occasionally her interjections are puzzling when delivered without introduction or context, and punctuated by nervous laughter. Ellen tries to tease out meanings and finds herself on the receiving end of grateful looks from the girl.

"Don't mind anything Cora says," Mrs. O'Brien advises after one particularly baffling contribution. "She speaks before she engages her brain."

"Mum!" screeches an outraged Cora.

"She's very bright, Ellen, has started first year at Cork University, but she's nineteen going on fourteen."

"Mum thinks I'm an emotional retard, liable to embarrass everybody," Cora says crossly. "Never mind, Ellen, I like you, even if I am in danger of causing an international diplomatic incident."

In the following days Ellen is very glad to have them about. They provide a welcome distraction from the tedium of work where, even though Ellen isn't being cold-shouldered as such, there is a noticeable reduction in conversational engagement.

"I expect everyone's worn out because Easter is so late. Easter Sunday falls on the twentieth of April this year," she complains to Eugene's mum. "People are too tired to talk."

"It's spring. The change in the weather affects people's moods," Mrs. O'Brien says. "By the way, call me Mel. This 'Mrs. O'Brien' is very formal."

"Fancy a trip to Cork tomorrow morning?" Cora asks. "I can show you about, and you can treat me to lunch at one of those posh restaurants poor students can't afford."

The following day they come across Terry in one of the little alleys off Patrick Street, and she barely manages to rise to a "pleased to meet you" when the introductions are made. Ellen is surprised by how effectively Terry has become another person. She has lost her ability to engage with people in a natural way.

"Is she the one who runs that mini-supermarket in the village?" Mel asks.

Ellen nods.

"Well, she has neither the personality nor the manner for it."

"Normally she's okay."

"She could do better. A lot better. You can be certain I won't be spending any of my money in her shop."

• • •

Eddie closes the door of his office and turns to face Ellen. He acts as if he expects secret state police to burst in and drag him off. "You know I'm a teacher representative on the board of management? Your name got a mention at last night's meeting," he says harshly. "One of the parents brought it up."

"Brought what up, Eddie?"

His eyes are evasive. "Your situation," he mutters.

"My situation?"

"You know well what I mean," he says irritably.

"You're not making any sense, Eddie."

"Mrs. Hussey — a dreadful woman —"

"In plain English, please."

"The irregularity of your lifestyle. That bloody woman tried to talk about it — made an attempt to bring it up under any other business — but she was shut up."

"What's all this about, Eddie? You'll have to explain."

"Bloody ridiculous, it is. You're living in fairyland, Ellen. How is it I didn't know about this? I had to find out from the other staff rep."

"What did you hear?"

"Not a bother on you," he complains. "Carrying on as if you're still in the city. Well, it won't wash down here. You've no idea who's connected to whom. Let me fill you in on some local color. There are wheels within wheels. Brenda Finnegan is great friends with the arch bitch, Hussey, mother of your favorite student, Isabel Hussey. They went to school together. They're in the same branch of the ICA, and they've been keeping an eye on you, monitoring your behavior," he says crossly. "Separated, heading for divorce, and now having a . . . well, carrying on an open relationship."

"Somebody's interested in my personal life. Is that what you're saying?"

"Yer woman, Hussey, was up to the office first thing this morning but, luckily, Nora was away at a principals' meeting, so she had me to deal with. You're an eejit to be giving her ammunition."

The warning bell for first class goes. "That woman has you in her sights because of those battles you've been having with Isabel," he continues. "I know her type. She bears grudges on behalf of her daughter. Anyway, watch it. She's out to do you harm, although there's no mechanism through the board of management."

"It doesn't matter, Eddie. Let her do what she likes. I don't care."

"And you're good at your job, that's the pity of it," he mutters. "I get someone who can teach, and then this. Couldn't you pull back, lay low till we know if Moira is going to resign? Be discreet. It is a Catholic school after all, and the trustees like surface piety."

She's surprised that he's taking it so personally and lays a hand on his arm. "Don't worry about it, Eddie. I'll get back to you."

He opens the door and she brushes past him into the corridor. "I'll see you at break time," he calls.

The first group she meets with are sixth years, and Isabel Hussey's is the first face she sees. The girl is sprawled across the desk in front of the teacher's table. Ellen looks at her, and the girl returns the look scornfully. A seething viper's den concealed in pretty enough packaging, Ellen thinks.

She fills in the attendance sheet and hands back corrected exercises. There's a gasp at the back of the classroom. "I got an A!" a pleased Rachel Gorman exclaims. "My first."

"You deserved it," Ellen says. "Great work. Replicate that standard in all your answers and you'll fly the exam."

Ellen is aware that Isabel Hussey is scanning the red pen comments on her work. The girl rarely achieves more than a top C grade. Isabel's hectic social schedule leaves little time for concentrating on schoolwork. Her infamously awful mother blames teachers for her daughter's results. She makes appointments to meet most of them and tries to bully them into giving her daughter better grades. Mrs. Hussey has been in twice to see Ellen — unannounced the first time and offended that Ellen couldn't meet her — and then for an arranged meeting.

Ellen remembers a slim, dark-haired woman, mid to late forties, whose good looks have held up well, but whose expression of inordinate and permanent dissatisfaction is deeply unattractive. It's rumored that though she and her husband live together, relations between them are anything but cordial. "I'm on the board of management," she began, sidelining introductions, courtesies, and small talk, and launched into a tirade of complaints against Ellen. When she drew breath she looked as if she'd like to start again.

"This is so rude. We haven't been introduced," Ellen said. The woman declined to shake her outstretched hand and, even though Ellen gave her a chance to rethink her aggression, refused to meet Ellen's eyes, crossed her legs — the top one twitched with agitation — and stared out the window.

Ellen took each complaint in order and rebutted every one, but it was clear the woman wasn't listening. She ranted some more and repeated herself endlessly. In a heart-sinking moment, Ellen realized that she was up against an irrational force, that nothing she could say would penetrate this woman's hostility. It was obvious that Mrs. Hussey saw the world through her daughter's eyes. If Isabel claimed she was working for her exam, then that was the case. Her daughter's friends were her mother's friends. Her daughter's enemies were her enemies. If Isabel thought her teacher had taken a dislike to her, this was indubitably true. "I don't have favorites," Ellen said, but Mrs. Hussey threw her eyes heavenward. "If Isabel were to start working, she'd do very well. She's winging it so far but still managing to get C's."

"She studies very hard," Mrs. Hussey declared, "but she's up against it with the teachers in this school. You seem to have a grudge against her."

"I've never borne a grudge against a student or acted out of malice. You'll just have to take my word for it and respect that," Ellen said finally, bringing the interview to an end.

"You never gave her a B, even once," Mrs. Hussey hissed on her way out.

"Be assured that when Isabel's work is B standard, I will be delighted to award her a B grade."

"Useless talking to you," Mrs. Hussey said bitterly. "You don't have my child's best interests at heart."

"That's quite a serious charge, Mrs. Hussey, and it's not true. I have every student's interests at heart. I won't, however, top up marks. You'd be the very first to complain if I awarded her high grades and she only scraped through on the exam."

"God knows, I can't stand her daughter but it makes no difference to the marks I give. She won't achieve high grades if the information isn't there, or if the answers are too short," Ellen said to Eddie afterward.

"Often when you meet the parents, you understand the children," Eddie said.

"If she comes in again, I want someone to sit in on the meeting."

This morning Isabel has a smile on her face. She watches Ellen when normally she stares down at her hands. She looks radiant. She looks triumphant. Got you, the look says. Something tells Ellen that the little sweetheart has been working on her case ever since the encounter in the mountain pub.

Ellen knows that she can't spend the time locked in eyeball-to-eyeball confrontation with Isabel, so she says, "Start us off, would you, Isabel? Read the first verse from the Hopkins poem." Isabel looks mutinous, and Ellen anticipates a delay and some shape throwing. At last, with a cough, an irritated look, and much throat clearing, the girl begins to read. "I caught this morning morning's minion, kingdom of daylight's dauphin, dapple-dawn-drawn Falcon, in his riding . . ."

"Very nice. Good articulation," Ellen says when she finishes, and is rewarded by a look of scorching hatred. She turns to another student. "Pick up the next verse, would you, Dermot? — 'Brute beauty and valour . . .'"

After the final class of the day, she finds Eddie waiting, leaning against the corridor wall, arms folded. "God, you're persistent," she grumbles.

"Think about what I said."

"What are you suggesting?"

"It's that old thing. You can get away with anything once you pretend to be playing by the rules. The appearance of the thing, how it's perceived, is what matters. It doesn't have to be right but it must look right. That's always been the way. The most important thing is not to get caught. You've broken the cardinal rule. No discretion, Ellen. No discretion."

"This wouldn't be an issue if I were living in Dublin."

"Of course it wouldn't. But you don't have the anonymity of the crowd here."

"I don't want to sneak around hiding things." Suddenly she feels weary. "Does this matter, Eddie? Maybe it won't matter to all the people you think it will. Ireland has changed."

"Not as much as you'd like, Ellen. You're in a vulnerable position."

Ellen has discussed the matter of being groomed for this hypothetical job with Matt. "No point Eddie harping on about it all the time" was Matt's comment. "They say he's the real power in the school, but it's not in his give."

"I suppose he thinks he can influence the decision," Ellen had hazarded.

Matt looked dubious. "Perhaps. Come to it, I know some of the people who sit on those interview panels. But he's right about agendas. The interviewers will have worked out priorities. Often it won't matter who's the best candidate. It'll be a question of who conforms most."

A part of Ellen is in cahoots with Eddie's plans to fast-track her into a teaching position in the school, but today she's fed up with all his fussing, all this prying into her business. She says, "My job's waiting for me back in Dublin, Eddie."

"I got the impression you were anxious to put down roots here."

"Nothing is settled, Eddie."

"My interest is purely professional," he says at the front door of the school. "In any given area, there's a small pool of teaching talent. Not everybody can impart knowledge, but you can."

She has a headache from listening to him. "You're a tonic, Eddie," she says with feeling. "If ever I need my ego bolstered, I'll come to you."

Ellen is switching off lights and on the point of making an early night of it when the doorbell rings. She debates carrying on as if she hadn't heard the bell but decides she'd better open up in case Eugene or Matt decided to call.

She opens the door to find herself looking at Eugene's mother. "I expected you to be back in Enniscorthy by now," she says.

Mel proffers a box of chocolates. "Cora came down with a bug so we've put off going till tomorrow. No," she says, when she notices Ellen looking beyond her, "there's no Eugene. He's keeping his sister company."

"Well, come on in."

Mel smiles. "You're wondering why I called?"

"You could say that. Would you like a drink?"

"Don't mind if I do. Make it a small one. I'm driving so I'd better be careful. You know, I never got a chance to see your place. Eugene said it was worth a visit and sent me down to have a look."

"That's nice," Ellen says, but she suspects that Mel may take the opportunity to air some of her concerns about her son's liaison with Ellen. So far, Mel has been remarkably sanguine about their relationship, but good breeding and even better manners have probably placed constraints on her tongue. Ellen wonders if the charm will break down, and if she's about to experience the deadly thrust of a few sharp observations. For the moment Mel seems content to walk through rooms and express appreciation of the décor. When they come back into the hall, she says, "I have the dinkiest mirror I think would go beautifully here. I'll send it back with Eugene next time he's home, and you can decide if you like it."

Ellen still suspects that the woman's friendliness is superficial or artificial, so she decides to plunge in. "I expect you're here to discuss your reservations about Eugene and me."

Mel dazzles her with a smile and shakes her head. "Not at all. I'm very happy with the way things are turning out. You're such a relief after the last 'friend' he had. We were worried about that liaison."

"But aren't you worried about the age thing? Isn't that the problem?"

"Oh, there isn't a problem as such, Ellen. I've long given up trying to influence Eugene. There's no gainsaying him. He's the only boy and he's always been single-minded. His sisters are all academic high flyers, but he hated school with a passion and refused, absolutely refused, to consider third level. He has brains to burn, though he was never bookish, but he was determined to do carpentry. At the time his father was very unhappy about it, but it's all turned out for the best. Of course, we lent him the capital to set himself up. That's how he managed it so young. Still, I've learned to let him go his own way. He doesn't take direction."

"Is that it?"

Mel purses her lips and Ellen braces herself. "It isn't my business, Ellen. You and Eugene are going to have to work it out between you. You're in the early stages of a relationship. If the gloss hasn't worn off in the next year or two, I expect you've as good a chance as most of making a go of it. I know all about your separation and divorce. It'd be very convenient if everything in life was tidy, but that's not the way it happens."

"And that's all you have to say?" Ellen asks.

"No." Mel lays a hand on Ellen's arm, and Ellen wonders if what she's been expecting is finally going to come out. "Actually, I came to invite you to visit us in Enniscorthy. Come along with Eugene next time he's due."

"God, you're a very tolerant woman, Mel. That's the last thing I expected to hear."

"I know my son, Ellen. He's really keen on you, and it's a relief to know you're not going to make him miserable. Do you expect me to map out Eugene's life for him? Give me some credit. I'm his mother, not his warden. And if I did really object to you, do you think he'd pay the slightest attention? No, he's my heedless, head-strong son, and that's the way I like him." Mel looks about. "This really is a grand little house. You did a fantastic job on it."

"If it weren't dark I could show you the garden. Eugene was a great help."

"So I hear. This house has a charm all its own. I like the mix of old-world and modern."

Later, over a cup of coffee, Mel says, "He's no angel, of course, my Eugene. He has a temper. I can see from your expression that you haven't had the pleasure of him going off the deep end, but he will. It blows over very quickly, fortunately. Then he's so pernickety about things, always tidying up after people."

"That I know about. Stacking newspapers and cleaning surfaces. He says I'm slovenly about the house. But I say he can't complain. It's the only thing I'm relaxed about!"

"There's an upside. Your house will always be clean!"

"You've taken a load off my mind, Mel. You don't know how much I appreciate it. It's been so nice meeting you," Ellen says as they make their goodbyes.

"Likewise. So, stop worrying. I'll do my best to remember that mirror. Send it back if you don't like it."

"Safe journey," Ellen calls out.

It's only as she's getting into bed that Ellen realizes that Mel and Cora's visit has not only regularized and legitimized her relationship with Eugene, but has probably catapulted awareness of it in Ballindoon into the stratosphere. Poor Eddie's concerns about respectability and containment lie tattered and in ruins.

Fourteen

EATRICE ADDS finishing touches to Andy and Kerry's bedroom. Their flight is scheduled to land in Shannon in the afternoon, and Simon has gone to collect them. The freshly painted room with its laundered curtains and new bedclothes is transformed. Finally she satisfies herself that there's nothing other than fiddling and rearranging to do. This is now the best room in the house.

Her eyes range over the hallway and calm deserts her. Cleaning and painting can do only so much. The furniture is shabby and the carpet threadbare. The sitting room is somewhat better. It too has been painted. She replaced the broken lamp, steam-cleaned the carpet, and laid a rug to disguise a frayed piece in the middle. The westerly sun breaks through the bay window, warming the mahogany of the tables and tipping the gilt of the picture frames. The piano will be fine once nobody tries to play it. She hopes that the house exudes a dignified if dilapidated grandeur.

What if Andy disapproves of the changes she's made to the kitchen? What if he's possessive about the old things? He was never sentimental but maybe he has become so.

She moves through the house in a trance. All morning she had been dreading the phone call to say that they've decided not to come. Even now, it wouldn't surprise her if Simon returned empty-handed, saying they weren't on the flight. She has to trust that it will turn out right. Should she have been there to greet them when they got through customs? But no, she had decided it was best to stay at home, stoke the fire, and keep an eye on the dinner.

She lifts lids on pots, adjusts the temperature settings, checks the roast, and counts the parboiled potatoes. They go in the oven the minute the guests arrive. Gravy can be made later.

The clock taunts her with its sluggishness. Every moment is an agony. She goes to the kitchen window to see if she can spot the car coming. How can the minutes have such a stretch in them? Time feels taut, quivering and paused. She, by way of contrast, feels speeded up. She has stymied herself by leaving nothing to chance. It will be another while before there's a hope of anybody arriving.

She pours a sherry and gulps it down. It fails to relax her, feels as if it's having no effect, as though she metabolized it instantaneously. Fool! She should have strung that out, slow sip by slow sip. She's wound too tight. Can't have another. Could lead to a succession of . . . well, could lead to her being found on the floor! She's heard of that happening, people getting drunk through nervousness and making a show of themselves.

She finds a packet of mints, tears it open, and swallows one. She doesn't want them to get a whiff of alcohol from her. Still, she could do with something — a tranquilizer, a sleeping tablet — anything to slow her down.

Ellen, Matt, and Eugene know that Andy is coming and she's sworn them to secrecy. It's difficult to believe that she will soon be able to see and touch Andy, and that he will sleep in this house tonight. For nine years she tried to make him dead to her and stored him in a seldom-opened compartment in her mind. This was easier than continually tormenting herself as to why he continued to cut himself off.

If there is a hell, it will be a place of waiting. The house is confining, closing in on her. It's suffocating. Unbearable. She makes for the back door, heads out, and takes off up the yard. The day is good, windy, sunny, and slightly cold. Shep follows, slinking and weaving in and out behind and in front of her, body low to the ground as if he's working the cows, tail wagging furiously to show he's off duty. She throws a stick to give him something to fetch, but she tires of the game. The yard is immaculately tidy. She wanders about the outbuildings, poking at this and that, but there's nothing to do. The calves have been watered and fed. Everything is in plumb order. She strolls across to a gate and leans against it. The cows are grazing in the lower field. They pay her no attention. The mountains look far away, a sign of continuing dryness, their purples and blues hazed and muted in the sunshine.

It's chillier than she thought, too cold for standing around. She should have worn a jacket. She hurries back down to the house. No sign of Simon's car. Where can they be? She returns to the sitting room, puts another log on the fire, feeds it with coal, and warms her hands. She turns on the telly and searches for flight details on tele-text, the way Simon showed her. The plane has landed. Something else has delayed them, road works, diversions, an accident — no, not an accident — slow clearing through customs, problems with luggage, that sort of thing.

She searches the phone book to see if she's written in Simon's mobile number, hears the car engine, shoves the book back, and rams the drawer shut. She listens for voices, frozen like a novice actress.

This has to go well. How could it not? Jack's no longer about, tense and touchy, ready to fly off the handle at the merest perceived slight. She won't have to referee the occasion and salvage it. But part of her is sorry that Jack won't be present to witness Andy's return, to meet his wife and child, to rejoice in Andy's success and maybe — because Jack had moments of generosity — to write off the treacherous debt, the wretched university fees. "We'll say no more about that, son." Glossing over the pseudo-row and wrong-footing Andy. A pause while Andy digested the implications of his father's expansiveness. And then? A reciprocal graciousness on Andy's part? That might have happened.

But in her heart she's afraid, scared that the visit will end on a sour note. It isn't just Andy she has to think about. There are the unknown entities of his wife and child. A lot depends on what they're like. She replaces the guard on the fire and makes her way to the kitchen.

The kitchen is empty, not a sign of anybody. Voices drift past the side of the house. She makes for the porch and follows the sounds outside. Where are they off to? She hurries to the upper yard but they're not there, listens again for voices. This time she gets it right. They've headed for the garden. She can make out forms beneath the apple trees. They've stopped to look at one of the views. Andy — is it Andy? — is pointing out the flowerbed he made for her when he was fifteen.

She wipes her palms on her apron, unties it, and folds it into a neat shape in her hand. Simon and Andy are talking. Andy turns. His hair has darkened to a light brown. He's filled out. He's taller than she remembers, a good bit taller than Simon. She'd hardly know him. She'd pass him on the street.

He sees her. "Mam!" he says. He catches her and swings her about. "Whee!" he says. She laughs at the silliness of it and settles a little dizzily on the ground, holding on to his arm when he lets go. Purple and green spots blind her. Of course they don't kiss. That famous old-style Irish reserve about kissing. She's one of the worst offenders.

"You don't look a day older!" he declares.

"Get away out of that."

His arm rests lightly on her shoulder. He pushes her toward somebody. "Meet Kerry, Mam. She's heard all about you."

"Hope it wasn't all bad," she says lightly, and shakes hands with a shadow.

The woman laughs. "Hi, Beatrice," she says, and Beatrice's eyes begin to adjust. This daughter-in-law is whippet-thin but considerably shorter than Andy. Hair — what's the color of the hair? Light brown? Fair? Blond? She's not sure. The features of the face catch the light but she couldn't say what Kerry looks like. It's too much to take in.

Then she can see again. The little boy — the sun catches his strawberry-blond hair — hangs back, clinging to his mother's leg, hiding his face. "Scott, this is Granny Beatrice," Kerry says. Scott's small for his age. "Say hello to Granny Beatrice. Scott, come say hello!"

He stands like a floppy straw doll, shaking his head. He has the face of an elf with a little pointy chin.

"Scott!" Andy sounds annoyed.

"He's shy!" exclaims Beatrice. "Take no notice of him. He's probably tired after his big long journey. We'll let him calm down." Then, because she can't take in much more, she says, "Welcome, welcome" to them all, and Andy links her back to the house. "I had spots in front of my eyes," she says. "Couldn't see a thing."

"You don't miss much," he says.

Simon has fetched the suitcases. He places them on the floor in front of the range. "Will I bring them upstairs?" he asks. He squirms in his jacket, his big brown hands emerging like canoe paddles from the cuffs of his shirt.

"That'd be great, Simon. Thanks. We'll all have a drink when you come down."

"I'd better change into my working clothes and round the cows up for milking."

"I'd forgotten about the milking. Is that the time? It's later than I thought. That's a shame, Simon. I'll keep your dinner for you."

"Does he eat with you?" the woman asks, as if she doesn't approve, when Simon is gone.

"Simon's like one of the family," Beatrice says.

Kerry grimaces and all goes quiet. "Why not sit down for refreshments," Beatrice suggests.

"The kitchen looks different," Andy comments. "It's not the way I remember."

"The old kitchen? That whole thing was falling apart. I had to replace it."

"Yes, but you've moved things. The sink used to be over by the wall."

"It's much better where it is now. What'll you have to drink, Kerry?"

"She'll take a sherry," Andy says.

"Do you have white wine?" Kerry asks, ignoring Andy, who casts a reproachful look at her.

"There's wine in the fridge. Sauvignon Blanc okay, Kerry?" Beatrice cuts in. She's bought enough alcohol to stock a mini-bar.

"Thanks."

"This is a bit late for dinner. It's usually in the middle of the day here," Andy says to his wife as they sit at the kitchen table.

"That was in your father's day. Now it's variable. Depends on what Simon's doing," Beatrice says.

"Get a load of all those new houses we saw on the way here," Kerry says. "Nothing but mansions all over the place — five and six bedrooms. Not a thatched cottage in sight. Right, Andy?"

"Haven't you heard about our economic miracle?" Beatrice asks.

"I've seen changes on business trips to Dublin, but the fact that it's all over the place didn't hit home till now," Andy says.

Dublin? Business trips? He's been so close and she didn't know. Beatrice fights down her anger and hurt. This is a new start. She mustn't sabotage it.

Fortunately, there's a distraction. Scott disappears under the table, his food untouched. "How's the little fellow doing?" Beatrice asks.

"Hey, Scott?" Kerry says. She lifts up the tablecloth and looks in underneath. "I think he's asleep," she says.

"Hardly. Are you sure?" Beatrice asks. "Maybe he's pretending."

Kerry slides from the chair onto the floor, gets down on all fours, and crawls in under the table. Andy and Beatrice lean sideways, lift the edge of the tablecloth, and peer in. Their upside-down faces watch Kerry touch Scott and shake his crouched form gently. Mother and son have the reddish-blond hair and pointed chin in common. "Yup," Kerry reports. "He's out. What a shame. I wanted him to see the cows after dinner."

"He can see them another time," Beatrice says.

"I'll take him up to bed," Andy says.

"Maybe best to put him on a sofa in case he wakes up and takes fright in a strange place," Beatrice suggests.

"That's probably better," agrees Andy.

Kerry reverses out and sits back up at the table. "Let him be for now, I guess. He might wake up. This is a big house, Beatrice," she says. "I dunno. I guess I was expecting low ceilings and small rooms."

"It was originally owned by a Protestant."

"Pardon?"

"She means it was built by an Englishman. That's why it's sizable. The natives had to make do with mud huts."

"I can't keep up with all this history. Andy keeps telling me this stuff, Beatrice. I guess you Catholics bought out that Protestant guy."

"My husband's grandfather, that'd be Andy's great-grandfather, made his money in the States and came back to Ireland. That's how we got the house."

"How long ago was that?"

"Mid–eighteen hundreds."

Kerry raises her glass and says, *"Sláinte."* When Beatrice laughs in surprise, she says, "That's right, isn't it, Andy? That's what you told me to say?"

"It's exactly right, darling. You even got the pronunciation!"

"You know you're called after an Irish county, Kerry, don't you?" Beatrice asks.

"Guess it must have been prophetic. Like, I married an Irish guy, didn't I?"

"You'll have to show me where you milk the cows. I had a peek at the yard and the place is unrecognizable," Andy says to Simon, who's wolfing down his microwaved dinner.

"He's transformed it," Beatrice says.

"Had to be modernized," Simon says. "The new milk hygiene regulations left no option. Come up tomorrow morning and I'll give you a guided tour."

Beatrice rinses out the washing bowl in the sink and rubs the stainless steel basin. To her left saucepans tilt like a declining tower of Babel. She feels winded, as if tiring at the end of a long race. Now that the threat of the feared row and walkout by Andy has evaporated, she has lost her puff. Simon is seated at the kitchen table, his back to her.

Andy appears at her side. "You okay, Mam? Need a hand?" he asks.

"Just have to get my breath. This is a big day, Andy. We're going to have to get to know each other all over again."

"I know, Mam, I know."

"Kerry seems really nice."

"She's afraid you won't like her."

"What I've seen looks fine to me."

He hugs her. "Sorry I took so long to break the ice," he says. "I just kept putting it on the long finger. It was Kerry said I had to contact you."

Took you long enough. I might have died, she thinks, but says nothing.

The following morning, Andy accompanies her to the village for Mass. "Fastest way to meet people," he says. Kerry doesn't go to Mass. She's Episcopalian.

"Are you still a Catholic?"

"Practicing? I kinda shrugged off being a Catholic in New York. I go to church with Kerry sometimes. Episcopalian is like what Church of Ireland would be here."

"Anglican, you mean."

"Sort of. Religion is a big thing with a lot of Americans. Her folks are devout but they're not fanatical."

"Not too many attend weekday Mass now. The old regulars are dying off. Saturday night attracts the best show."

He drives slowly through the village. "They've filled in a lot of — correction — they've rebuilt all those derelict sites that used to be on the streets. No harm. They were an awful eyesore. The place looks half-decent now. What have they done to Mundy's shop? It looks like a mini-mart."

"Terry and Bart Fitzgibbon did it up when they bought it. It's about twice the size it used to be, the best shop in the village now. There's even a customer car park behind. What keeps James O'Flaherty's shop open is the post office, that and the custom of a few regulars."

"I'd have expected him to be retired by now."

"He'll retire only if forced to."

"What's this?" he asks outside the newly built health clinic. "That used to be Johnjo Byrne's house."

"Johnjo's dead, long gone. They knocked the old place down and built the clinic."

"And who lives in those houses?" he asks as he spies the county council houses down Mart Lane.

"That's a new public housing scheme."

"I hope the village hasn't turned into a dumping ground for white trash. They'd better not ruin the place."

She hasn't heard him use the term "white trash" before. Will she have to introduce him as my son, the snob?

"Most of them were renting old places, Andy. They're perfectly ordinary decent people. They've been on the housing list a long time."

At Mass, Andy is restless and shuffles about in the pew. Were he a child, she'd have a word in his ear.

When they emerge, she sees Matt hurrying toward them. "Welcome home," he says warmly, and crushes Andy's hand in a firm handshake. "*Céad míle fáilte.* A hundred thousand welcomes." He turns to Beatrice. "I bet you're delighted to see this fellow back, the return of the prodigal. You're looking well, boyo."

"Hello, Matt. You haven't changed a bit."

"More than I can say for you. You left a young fellow and now you're a man. Looking prosperous too."

"Not doing too badly."

"Doing well, boyo, doing well!"

"Listen, I was really sorry to hear the news about Julia. Mam told me last night."

"That's the way, boy. There's no avoiding it. Comes to us all," Matt says, shrugging off his sympathy.

Word spreads and Beatrice and Andy are surrounded by a gaggle of people. Even Father Mahoney stops on his way across to the presbytery. "You're from before my time," he murmurs when introduced, "but you're more than welcome. A fine son you have there, Beatrice."

"You're a dark one," Nan Brogan says. "Not a word about him coming home."

"I wanted it to be a surprise."

"That it is. You could have knocked me down with a feather. It must be a great comfort to have the surviving son back again."

Andy stiffens, and Beatrice senses a few people awaiting her reaction. The usual dull anger against Nan stirs. "Come on, Andy," she says loudly. "If we don't get a move on, we'll be here all day."

She takes a cloth, wipes the morning dew from the seat of the bench, and sits down. The day is only getting started. The sky is an unbroken blue, the pale gray of early morning dispersed by sunshine. The blue-bronze patches of bog and heathers on the mountains are etched with the clarity of a painting against the splashes of yellow plants and gray rocks, with the multitudinous greens of arable land below.

She hears a sound and turns to see Andy. He's standing under one of the old beech trees planted almost ninety years before by his grandfather, the father-in-law she never knew. "Morning," he says, and joins her on the bench.

"Where are you lot off to today?"

"Kerry and Scott have gone to Waterford. I've done enough sightseeing."

"You packed in a lot this visit."

"We haven't seen much of each other."

"You've been away on those trips."

"Yeah, I know we've been a bit touristy. Kerry's really taken with Ireland. She wants to come back."

"Well, there's an open invitation to stay here anytime. You know that."

"You'll come see us in the States?"

"It's a long way away."

"Not nowadays. The world has shrunk."

She hesitates. "Come to see Scott," he urges. "You're a real hit there. It's Granny Beatrice this and Granny Beatrice that, and 'Granny Beatrice says' all the time. You've made a big impression."

"I hardly hear a word out of him."

"That's what he likes. You're not always at him to talk. Kerry's mom wears him down trying to get him to speak. You don't force any agenda on him."

"He's a good child."

He fiddles with his watch. She stands up, stretches her back, and sighs. "Better go in and do something to justify my existence."

"What's your hurry?" he asks.

"Things to do, people to see," she jokes.

"Mam?"

"Yes?"

"Where did John shoot himself? Will you show me?"

She groans. Here it comes, the inevitability of having to talk about it again. "I avoid the place."

"I'd like to see it."

"You don't know what you're asking. What's the point? He's dead. Seeing where he died won't change that."

"Please."

"If you must," she manages.

The dairy tanker roars past as they make their way across the upper yard to the barn. She leads him to the exact spot the policeman showed her. "This is it. There's nothing to see."

He clears his throat. "We used to play chasing and hide-and-seek here as kids. I can see it clear as yesterday."

"There was nothing to stop you coming home after Dad died," she says. "If you had, you'd have seen John, noticed what he was like, what he became."

"You're not blaming me, are you?" he asks sharply.

"Don't get me wrong. That isn't what I meant. Just . . . it might have . . . explained it a bit better. It might have been easier for you to understand."

"I know. Kept putting it on the long finger."

"He smoked a cigarette before he died. They found the butt. Imagine that. Of course, there was alcohol in his blood. And antidepressants. I didn't know about the antidepressants."

"I often speculate about why he did it."

"There are all sorts of theories about why people kill themselves. He wasn't happy in himself. I think he was in this place he couldn't get back from, that the loneliness wore him down. He couldn't reach out for help."

Andy says nothing. He looks about him as if trying to impress everything on his memory.

"I question it every day, wonder why he didn't feel he could talk to me," muses Beatrice.

"It wasn't your fault he killed himself."

"Oh, I know that. Still, one of my sons left home. The other killed himself. I'm sure that speaks volumes to some."

"I meant to stay in touch."

"I'm sure you did." He probably did. Just careless and thoughtless. No malice aforethought.

She's surprisingly calm. The barn is merely a structure. It hasn't any hold over her. "Have you seen enough?" she asks.

"Quite enough."

"I'm glad you asked."

"Can you forgive me?"

"Forgive you?"

"For not being around."

"It's not a hanging crime."

He laughs shortly. "It sounds dreadful when you put it like that. Makes me sound pathetic."

"It's the callousness of youth. You're growing out of it."

"Everyone's trying to hold on to their youth in America. They put a premium on it," he says. "There are no dispensations from growing old."

"I think they're deluded in that. What a horrible way to live. Will we go?" They make their way back to the house.

"Let's go out for lunch some day," he says.

"Only if you're buying."

"Of course I'm buying."

"Where did this Simon guy come out of? How'd he get the job? Is he related to you?" Kerry asks the next morning at breakfast. She's eating a plain cracker and sipping water. Kerry talks about food as if she wolfs it down, but when it comes to a meal on a plate she picks at it.

"No relation," Beatrice says, adding honey to her porridge.

"So he's an employee?"

"Yes."

Scott is out in the garden running up and down with the dog. Shep is ever ready to retrieve sticks and Scott never tires of throwing them. Beatrice has no idea where Andy is, but he's not in the house.

"The son inherits the farm, right?"

"The son inherits the farm?" echoes Beatrice. A trick Beatrice has learned over the years is to fall silent when someone says something challenging. It usually makes them explain themselves. She has Jack to thank for this. His complaints used to falter when he couldn't elicit a reaction from her.

"That's how it works, right?"

Beatrice shakes her head. "Say again," she says.

Kerry takes a sip of water. "Hey, I'll just shut up now."

"Sorry?"

"I'm done." Kerry gets to her feet. "I was just curious," she says uneasily. "That's all."

"I'll just check and see if Scott and Shep are okay. Shep's quiet but he's not used to children."

"I'll go," Kerry volunteers.

"I'll do it. I need the air."

Scott and the dog are sitting on the steps that lead up to the old granary store, the dog flopped devotedly at Scott's feet, panting, tongue out.

"What about coming in for breakfast?" Beatrice calls.

"Uh-uh. I ate."

"Wouldn't keep a fly going what you ate this morning."

"I'm not hungry."

"You'll never grow if you don't eat."

Scott looks irritated. "I will grow," he says fiercely.

"No, you'll end up a little pishameen of a man."

"A pissawhat?"

"A stunted little runt of a man."

"What?"

She smiles. "A tiny little man."

"Yeah, right," Scott says eventually. He grins. Barely six years old and he doesn't believe a word of it.

Andy comes out. "He's fine, Mam," he says. "He doesn't have much of an appetite but he won't go hungry."

"He picks at his food."

"He's a finicky eater."

"I was hoping the fresh air would give him an appetite."

"I thought the air would knock him out but it hasn't had that effect."

"It's not pure the way it was years ago."

"I guess you're right."

She goes inside, up to her room. She has a headache. Was that why he came home? To check out the inheritance? To put his spoke in?

241

Later Andy appears beside her when she's taking washing in off the line. He unpegs some of the clothes. "Kerry told me she put her foot in it this morning," he says.

"How so?" She's unwilling to make it easy for him, for either of them.

"She was asking you about the farm."

"Are you interested in taking it over? Is that what she was on about?"

"No, no. Not at all. I told her she shouldn't have opened her mouth."

"The farm reverted to me when John died."

"So, what will happen to it?"

"I often wonder the same myself."

"We won't be here for dinner today. We're heading off after lunch."

"Showing them the sights? Don't forget the view along the back road. It's spectacular."

"No, we're going away for a day or two. We're booked into a hotel in Killarney. Kerry just arranged it."

"I thought you were going to stick around for the last few days." She turns. "I'm disappointed, Andy. I was looking forward to having you for a bit longer."

"It's difficult with that Simon guy about. It doesn't feel like home somehow."

"I won't hear a word against him. He doesn't put in or out on you. He's a fantastic worker, Andy."

"Still, kinda spoils the place a bit. Oh, I know that's not reasonable, Mam. It's caveman stuff. I'm sorry. Can't help it." He pats her shoulder. "It's not a big deal, Mam. Don't fret. We'll be back soon."

"But then you'll be leaving almost immediately."

"You'll be sick of the sight of us before we go. It's Kerry really," he confides. "She has so much energy. The pace of life here is too slow for her. She gets restless. Besides, she wants to cram in as much as possible."

Is there an atmosphere, she wonders? Is Kerry annoyed that she wouldn't discuss the succession with her? "I hope you'll be lucky with the weather. The forecast is good."

Kerry calls Andy into the house. Beatrice finds Scott perched on the gate to the nearest field. "You'd better go down to your mum and dad. They're packing. You'll be off on your travels, off to see the sights."

"Can I stay with you?" he asks.

"There's not much to do around here. You'd be bored."

"I like Shep, the cows and stuff, and feeding the calves."

"Do you really?" she asks. This little grandson is reserved, self-contained almost. The language they have in common connects them tentatively. If he speaks quickly, she finds it difficult to follow him. If she uses colloquialisms, he's lost. They cling to the shared parts of the English language.

Before Andy and Kerry drive off, Beatrice hears raised voices in the car. Andy steps out from the driver's seat. "Scott's being difficult," he complains. "Says he wants to stay here with you."

"He's more than welcome," she says without thinking. All of a sudden her mind is full of speculation. How would they fill up the days together? Would he, like her other grandchildren, be enthralled by bread-making and cooking, getting eggs from the few hens she keeps, feeding the dog, and exploring old farm machinery in the sheds? Would he instead pronounce himself bored with everything and demand to be entertained with videos, toys, and games? She thinks not. She's noticed a stillness in him, a quietness that is given to listening.

"Don't tell him he can stay," Andy says, alarmed. "Kerry wants him to come with us. Would you have a word with him?"

"Of course." She sits into the rear seat of the car beside Scott. "When you come back, Scott, we'll walk all the fields with Shep and feed the calves. You can watch the cows being milked and, if he has the time, Simon might let you sit up on the tractor."

His voice is tremulous. "I want to stay with you." Beatrice's chest spasms and tightens.

Kerry shakes her head vehemently, her lips thinned. Behind her sunglasses, her expression is unreadable.

"Wouldn't you hate to miss all the interesting places you're going to see?" urges Beatrice. "You can go home to the States and tell them all the attractions you've been to. Come on, give us a hug," she urges. "I'll be waiting for you when you get back."

His little body launches itself at her as if in a fury. She braces herself for an assault but registers his twig arms embracing her and his hot breath on her neck. He doesn't speak, then breaks away to huddle into himself, his eyes averted.

"That's my boy," she says, getting out. "You're the best in the world."

"Bye, Mam. Thanks," Andy says.

"See you soon, Beatrice," Kerry shouts, sounding resolutely cheerful.

"Have a great time!" She waves after them as the car drives off.

Scott's hand waves from the rolled-down back window until the car disappears around the bend in the driveway.

That pressure of his little head burrowing into her. The imprint of his embrace on her neck. The sudden gift of his tenderness. Years of expecting nothing, a life managed rather than lived, and now this child.

"So," says Andy, when the waitress brings dessert to their table, "there's this Irishwoman on a trip to New York with her husband. It's her first time. She's heard all these stories about people being robbed in the Big Apple and she's a nervous wreck, expecting an attack at any moment. In restaurants she insists on sitting with her back against the wall so she'll be able to duck down under the table if gunmen come in to shoot up the place. She feels she has to do some shopping so they tour the shops. She's really jumpy, not sleeping well at nights.

"The hotel, though, is nice and the staff is friendly. The couple spend a lot of time in their room or venture into the hotel bar to drink coffee.

"Anyway, Eddie Murphy, the movie star, the comedian, is staying in the same hotel. One day they meet in the elevator, or lift as we'd call it. He's with an entourage but he's really friendly, making small talk. She's frozen with fear. She's not up to date with movies and has no idea who he is. To her, this is a black man. He may be in an expensive suit, he may look rich, but he's a black man. She's seen too many television series where the baddies are always the black guys. They belong to a criminal class. They mug you. This is what she thinks. The lift is stalled, door open, because she hasn't pressed the button. She's frozen with fear.

"Eddie Murphy says, 'Hit the floor, lady,' meaning, press the ground-floor button. She misunderstands, thinks this is it, the moment she has dreaded. In desperation, she throws her bag at him and flings herself to the floor, hoping he won't shoot her or knife her.

"There's a silence, then uproarious laughter. She looks up. Eddie Murphy helps her to her feet and hands her bag back to her. Her husband explains who he is. Eddie is convulsed with laughter. His entourage, with their expensive watches and clothes, smirk. Her husband chuckles. She feels a fool.

"The next morning she insists that they check out. When they go to pay the bill, they discover that Eddie Murphy has already paid. The receptionist mentions that he said to tell her he hadn't laughed so hard in a while."

"Is this true?" Beatrice asks.

"Absolutely," Andy says.

"Ridiculous. Silly woman."

"I'm sure Eddie Murphy got a gag out of it."

"How'd you hear about it?"

"I know someone who knew the couple."

"Well, well, well, would you look at who we have here! Welcome home, stranger," Lily Traynor's voice cuts in. She has appeared suddenly out of the restaurant's lunchtime crowd, all smiles and excitement. "I didn't notice the two of you till I was at the counter paying my bill."

Andy drops his napkin to the floor as he gets to his feet. "Lily!" he exclaims. He kisses her on the cheek. "We never saw you. We were engrossed in conversation."

"Give us a good old squeeze," she says. "Don't be shy!" She tut-tuts at Beatrice. "We've been sending out search parties ever since we heard he was home but there have been precious few sightings. May I join you?"

He draws up a chair. "Sit down! Sit down, Lily," he says. "It's good to see you."

"They've been sightseeing," Beatrice explains.

"We've been baking and laying in stores of booze in expectations of a visit, but ne'er a twinkle," complains Lily. "You'll have to arrange one of your card evenings, Beatrice, so we can all meet him."

"Don't tell me that's still going on!"

"To tell the truth, that practice snuffed it long ago, more's the pity," Lily says. "Still, I thought the custom could be resurrected in your honor."

"Not a hope of that, Lily. They're flying back tomorrow," Beatrice says.

"That's a big letdown, Beatrice. You're no good at all. Don't you know all our eyes were out on stalks trying to catch a glimpse of him! I have to hand it to you, though. You've been very even-handed, very democratic. You've spurned everybody equally."

"It wasn't intended that way, Lily. You know that. Andy was keen to show his family the sights. There wasn't enough time to pack in visits."

"You should ring round a few people and ask them over tonight. It'd be no trouble to rustle up a few sandwiches. The disappointment will be mighty if they don't meet with the royalty. That way nobody's nose will be out of joint."

"Too short notice," Beatrice says.

"Who cares about notice? 'Come up tonight for an hour' is good enough for anyone. None of us has appointment diaries, now do we? We're not exactly living in the fast lane. What do you say, Andy?"

Andy laughs. "You're a terrible woman, Lily. Sure, why not?"

"There's no point in being backward about being forward," gloats Lily. "This will be mighty. It's going to be a real treat."

"It's difficult to turn you down," Andy says.

"'Tis, isn't it?" she replies with a grin.

"I don't know how Kerry will react," Beatrice says when Lily has gone.

"She'll cope. She hasn't much choice. Word will soon be out."

"I'm sorry, Andy. We couldn't refuse her."

"It'll be a bit of an education for Kerry and Scott," he says as he pays the bill. "I hope they're up to it."

"Lunch was delicious. Thanks very much, Andy."

"I should have taken you to some remote outpost," he says ruefully.

"We might have got our comeuppance there too."

He laughs. "Could just as well."

Fifteen

I HEAR THAT congratulations are in order, Simon," Beatrice says as she clears away the dinner things.

"What?" A reddening of the skin at his throat confirms that she has struck home.

"The news is that you're getting hitched pretty soon. I'm worried now that I won't receive an invitation."

"I was going to tell you, Beatrice. Really I was. I was working up to it."

"Sure, what's to tell? Congratulations." She pulls open the dishwasher and begins to stack the plates.

"There's something else," he says, his hand swatting an imaginary fly. "It means . . ."

"It means the finish of you here."

"Exactly," he says miserably.

"Ah sure, things change, people move on."

"You're not mad?" He looks at her for the first time.

"What's the point? Would it change anything?"

"No. No, it wouldn't."

"You've been here more than two years now, and that has been a great bonus."

"Look, I just couldn't bear letting you down, but the wedding date is set, and Celia and her mother have sniffed out a hotel."

"Do you think her parents will sign over the farm to the two of you?"

"They'll hold on to that. They won't want me selling it off. But *you* know I'd never willingly sell."

"I know the lure of the land for you, how much it means. You know you're one in a million, don't you, Simon?" she says. He raises his head. "Most young people wouldn't touch a farm with a forty-foot pole, but there you go running back to the land. It must go very deep for you."

"It does," he says fervently.

"Well, I hope it's worth it," she says. "It's a small holding. There isn't a full-time living to be had from it. You'll be a part-time farmer."

"That's a given with farming nowadays. I've lined up work as a driver with the factory, and I'll get other bits and pieces."

"You're a good worker. If anybody's to make a go of it, it'll be you." She pauses. "I'm worried about one or two things, Simon. When it's time to introduce the calves to outdoors, for one, and the day of the silage cutting."

"Put those things out of your head, Bee. I'll be around for a while yet. The wedding is mid-May. I'll definitely be here for the change-over with the calves, and I'll bring along my brothers, same as last time."

"They get so jazzed up, I'd never manage them."

"You need manpower for those fellows. Remember the puck one of them gave me last year? Consider it taken care of, Bee. We'll be there to keep them in order. And just give me a shout the day before the silage cutters are due. There's no problem."

"Thanks, Simon. I appreciate that."

"My pleasure," he says gruffly. He stands up and makes for the back door. "I'll just check the yard before I go."

Silly man, she thinks. Stitched up for a lifetime, and all for forty acres. She doesn't understand what compels him. It's stronger than his feelings for any person, stronger than rationality. Now, when only big farms are likely to survive, what makes him scorn everything in order to scrabble about on a few acres?

She inverts the kitchen chairs on the table, squirts cleaning fluid into a bucket, fills it with hot water, and mops the kitchen floor. Unexpectedly, her technique lets her down. The water is too sudsy, the mop too wet. The tiles will take an age to dry. What'll she do when he's gone? It's a lot of trouble to keep the whole enterprise going. She's never had the interest. The house and the garden are her domain.

If only John hadn't . . . None of that allowed. She must put the head down and get on with it, even if it feels that the dark cloud hovering over her could swallow her with one gulp.

She finds herself on the half-landing on the stairs, looking through the window at her vegetable and fruit garden. Simon clatters past her on his way down to the kitchen. "'Night, Bee," he says as he passes.

"See you later," she calls after him. She never even noticed him go upstairs.

Tonight she doesn't feel whatever it is you're supposed to feel when you're alive. She feels transparent, ethereal to the point of being almost her own ghost. It's hard to convince herself that she exists.

Their fortnightly lunch together. Originally, it was Lily's way of getting Beatrice out and about after John's death and it has become something of a ritual. Today they're trying out a new restaurant in a big old house that has been converted into a hotel. They are the only two left in the dining room. "Do you miss the Yanks?" Lily asks.

"I miss Andy. I was just getting used to him when they left. The little fellow, Scott, was great, not at all what I expected. But they phone about once a week, usually after the late night news, so that's nice."

"And how'd you get on with the daughter-in-law?"

"She's hard to get to know, but then some people take time. Plus, she's the one who made Andy get in touch, so I have to hand her that."

"What did she make of the last evening?"

"I think she was bemused. She couldn't get over people's curiosity, and some of the questions stunned her."

"I'd say she was never such a focus of attention before!"

"All in all, I think the visit went well. Andy got a lot out of it, and it made me feel whole again. It was nice to recover part of my family."

"What is it they work at?"

"Andy's in IT. She works for a bank, in taxes. She travels around to rich people's houses and works out their tax for them. She was telling me she goes into these places where the people who made the money have grown old. And the children are still living at home — forty- and fifty-year-olds — and never did a day's work in their lives. Like parasites, feeding off the money. Isn't that extraordinary?"

"There's no doubt, money's a great corrupter. Now, do you feel up to doing a tour of the grounds?" Lily asks as they finish coffee. "I think they'll throw us out if we don't move soon."

Beatrice signals the waitress to bring the bill. "The very thing to clear the head and walk off that meal."

"It's my turn to pay."

Beatrice brushes aside her protests. "Won't allow that. I haven't paid since I don't know when, so I insist." She hands a card to the girl. "You've no idea what a comfort these lunches are, Lily. A great idea."

Lily puts a hand to her mouth. Her brick-red lips contort into a grimace.

"What is it, Lily? What's wrong?"

"Ah, sure I'm heart-scalded, Beatrice, thinking of that poor boy. I'm still not the better of that news. You could have knocked me down with a feather when Terry told me this morning. And I felt sorry for her. She was so cut up about it. Seems she and the boy's mother are second cousins. They haven't seen much of each other in recent years, but the bond is strong."

Beatrice sighs. Terry's story concerned the suicide of a twenty-two-year-old man in the next parish. He had been out with friends on the previous Friday night, had gone missing, was looked for on Saturday, and the alarm was raised that night. The following Monday a forester discovered the body miles away in the next county. Apparently, the boy drove into the heart of the woods on one of the access roads, hid the car in a clump of bushes, walked the winding pathway to the lake, propped himself up against one of the trees overlooking the lake — as if admiring the view — and swallowed rat poison washed down with whiskey. The contents of the note found in his pocket are not known.

"He was only a young fellow, finished university last year, and he was earning good money with that computer outfit outside Cork. He was talking of buying an apartment in the city to save the trek into work every day," Lily says, as they begin their walk. "Why he did it is an absolute mystery, Beatrice, an utter and absolute mystery."

Beatrice says nothing. She is taken over by contemplation of what the boy's family must be going through — the wakefulness, the exhaustion, the disbelief, the despair, the reproaches, the grief, the maddening thoughts, their turmoil. And if they were to dwell on the signs they must have missed. And their anger at "how could he?" And how could anybody be so selfish, so self-obsessed? To think he had planned it down to the last detail. And what in the name of God was so terrifying, so unspeakable, so unbearable, so utterly unmanageable that he had decided this was the only way out? And what did he think he was doing by writing that letter? And if they had succeeded in thwarting him, would that have solved it? And so on, until their brains feel frazzled, and their bodies are numbed, or switched off, as they contemplate the astonishing abyss that has opened up in their lives.

And then she's aware of Lily holding her arm, her voice high with anxiety. "God, Beatrice, I'm such a fool! You'll be giving me ten out of ten for insensitivity. This is the last thing you want to talk about."

"No, no. I'm all right. It's okay, Lily," she says, though her heart feels congested, as if too much blood is trying to pump through. "Not to worry. I'm grand. Really I am. It's just that there are so many young men doing away with themselves."

"Scarifying, isn't it?"

"You'd wonder what, at the age of twenty-two, would be severe enough to make someone consider ending it all," muses Beatrice. "Disappointment, depression, inadequacy?" She needs to watch where she's walking. Pools of water from recent rain lie on the paths, and the fringes are covered in mud.

"They say he was a popular young fellow, not at all on the edge of things."

"Not like my John, you mean?" It's great to be on the move, thinks Beatrice. Movement is therapeutic.

"Not like your poor John, God rest his soul, or Dan Tuohy for that matter. They say Dan's job was on the line. He'd have found it difficult to pick up work at his age. But a young lad of twenty-two — what was that all about? He had everything going for him and all to live for."

"You can never know the workings of a person's mind."

"But he was in such good form. That's what his mother said. She's baffled. And it isn't a case of her thinking he's okay socially when, in actual fact, he's a loner. He had lots of friends."

"But did he really, I wonder? Something had to be eating him."

"He'd been out drinking the night before, but nothing more than usual on a Friday night."

"Still, he must have been facing into something on his own, whether it was spur of the moment — a sort of erratic impulse — or something he'd been living with for a long time."

Lily shudders. "I'd prefer if it was a long-standing problem. Imagine throwing everything away because of the mood of a particular moment, killing yourself on the strength of a whim."

"I often wonder if my John would have gone through with it if the shotgun hadn't been readily available."

"If he was serious, he'd have found the means."

"I suppose, if he was intent on it. Yes."

Lily is trampling ferns and grass as she keeps away from the edges of the path. "If I'd realized the ground was so wet I wouldn't have suggested a walk."

"Not to worry, Lily. If anybody's used to negotiating mud and puddles, it's us."

"I wonder if he was involved with a girl? That's what they always ask, isn't it?" Lily says. "People want to know if there was some girl."

"It's a fair enough question."

Lily plonks herself in Beatrice's way and forces her to stop. "Yes, but what if there wasn't any girl?" she asks animatedly. "What if he wasn't interested in girls? You don't hear that being talked about."

Beatrice changes course and gets going again. "Don't be silly. That might have been the case years ago, but nowadays it's all out in the open. It's legal at sixteen. It's okay to be gay. All that prejudice and discrimination is done away with."

Lily shakes her head. "You know yourself that there's a world of difference between what's legal and what actually goes on. There'll always be reasons why some people find themselves on the margins. You can change policies and laws goodtime, but you won't stamp out prejudice. Humans are primitive creatures. We're always trying to ferret out the chink—the other person's weakness."

"Come on, Lily. It's not always seen as weakness. What about gay pride and gay literature?"

Lily turns an animated face to Beatrice. "Lots of trouble as I recall, wasn't there, when the gays tried to march in the Saint Patrick's Day Parade in New York? It's probably okay to come out in a big anonymous city, but what about small communities, places like us? And the Church is no help, with all those pronouncements on the evils of homosexuality and talk of disorders."

"So, are you suggesting—?"

"I'm suggesting nothing, just speculating." They pant up the final stretch of path and reach the formal gardens, stopping for a moment to pause for breath.

Beatrice doesn't speak for a long time. She can't, and she doesn't need to because Lily will wait until she's ready. Strangely, this conversation hasn't churned up the usual intensity of emotion concerning John's death. It has prodded and poked the vulnerable spots, but the emotional scars are more resilient, less easily bled. Of course, it's an infinitesimal increment in the lessening of pain, a deregulation of its all-encompassing nature. "Whatever motivates those unfortunates, whatever sparks the urge to finish it all, there's a similar end result—well, the same result in that they're dead," she says.

"Do you remember Mr. Deasy in school, 'No two things are the same, they are similar'? I can never forget it," Lily interjects.

Beatrice smiles. "Me neither. And I still say 'elder' and 'eldest' for siblings." She brushes away an imaginary piece of fluff on her coat. "It's a sad old world sometimes, isn't it? Anyway, for whatever reason, all these men end up in a lonely place—desolate and forlorn."

"Forlorn? Now, there's a word brings school to mind. Old Deasy was always harping on about certain words. That was a regular favorite. Wasn't it in one of those poems he made us learn by heart? It killed me to memorize it. How did it go? 'Forlorn! the word is like a'... something... Let's see if I can remember..."

"'Forlorn! the very word is like a bell / To toll me back from thee

254

to my sole self!'" says Beatrice. "Remember the other bit? 'Dark-
ling I listen; and, for many a time / I have been half in love with
easeful Death, / Called him soft names in many a musèd rhyme.'"

"The very thing! Good woman."

"Keats, Lily."

"That's very apt."

"That's what they call associative thinking."

Lily nudges Beatrice's elbow. "God, I always knew you were
brainy! Why didn't you take that scholarship and go off and finish
your education, girl?"

Beatrice shrugs. "I wasn't allowed. They couldn't see any point
in wasting education on a girl when she'd have to give up the job
if she got married." She smiles. "No point in dwelling on that. You
know, there could be another explanation for that poor boy's despair. Didn't you say he was lovely looking, and that all the girls
were mad about him? Think of all these sexually active girls we
keep hearing about, voracious young ones making demands on the
poor lads, and the fellows not able to handle it! Isn't that what's supposed to happen now?"

Lily snorts. She shakes her head as if she doesn't really believe
this. "In our day the fellows were supposed to be in a state of per-
petual arousal, lurking behind hedges and walls, ready to drag
some misfortunate female into the bushes for a ride, and we were
given all the responsibility for putting the brakes on!" She pauses.
"You'll have me crying for the men next. And I can't do that. They
ran the whole show then and, by golly, they reveled in it. We were
too meek, Beatrice, always putting a good face on things. That was
our trouble. Well, the boot is on the other foot now."

Unexpectedly, Beatrice finds herself mired by her memory of the
night Matt finished with her. Despite everything that has happened
in the intervening years, a distillation of the essence of that moment survives.

"What's that expression on your face? What are you thinking
about?" asks Lily. She has always been quick to sniff out changes in
mood. Beatrice and she have honored each other with confidences
— and Lily was a bastion of support after John's death — yet they
keep their deepest feelings in reserve.

Beatrice shivers. "Somebody stepped on my grave." Suddenly realizing how cold her feet are, she stamps them briskly up and down. "We'd better get a move on. It's late, and I don't like the look of the sky. Those clouds are hanging very low, and there's still the journey home."

How alone we are, she thinks as they sit into Lily's car. How little we know of each other. Countless intersections and overlapping of individual lives, yet, underpinning it all, the mystery of the subconscious.

Eddie waylays Ellen immediately after school and rushes her into his office. He's animated and his normally sedate speech is rushed. "Moira handed in her resignation this morning. I knew it would happen."

"So you'll be advertising a position?"

He's sitting at his desk, chair tilted back, feet up. "The board of management is meeting on Friday night. Ad will be in the papers the week after next. I presume you'll apply."

"I thought you didn't rate my chances of landing that job."

"I was probably a bit hasty," he says expansively. "Why not throw your hat in? Never let a deadline pass is my motto. You're not committing yourself to anything. You can always withdraw."

"Ever the pragmatist?"

He smiles wearily. "Let's not quibble about trifles. I was nursing a professional disappointment that day because I wasn't in the know about your circumstances."

"I'm so glad it wasn't personal."

"Of course it's personal, Ellen," he complains. "You can put me down as a referee, if you want, and I'll sing your praises. I'm in your corner, but you don't seem to care."

"I care. Take that as read. But I'm thirty-eight years old — thirty-nine next birthday — I think it's time I lived a little. Anyway," she shrugs, "I know well that the job could go to somebody else. Thanks for the offer, Eddie, but it'll look bad if the principal doesn't want to give me a reference."

"Nora?" He shakes his head. "Of course she will. I'll see to that." He jabs a finger at her. "It'd be a crying shame if you were to take up something other than teaching, Ellen. You're a natural."

"Don't forget it was the mother of one of my students who tried to shaft me."

"Ah," he says, righting the chair and landing his feet on the ground, "the great conspiracy. It's a pity those bitches singled you out for attention, but who knows what, if any, damage they've inflicted. I know I tend to be old-fashioned but, even here, there are people in highly irregular unions working as teachers. The times they are a-changing. You can't pre-guess any outcome. You might just get away with it."

She can't discern what Eddie thinks of her. He's slippery that way, keeping his opinions close. All his advice is practical. Despite his encouragement, pep talks, and strategic counsel, she suspects that he doesn't actually approve of her, that a part of him wants to reform her. "I never know what to make of you," she says.

"That's the way to have it. Keep 'em guessing." Suddenly he's serious. "You want to know what I really think? What you're doing makes no sense to me."

"It's all tactics as far as you're concerned, is that it?"

"Play the game, Ellen, play the game. But you thumb your nose at it all."

"What? The way you talk about it —"

"The way I talk about it? Making a laughingstock of yourself. Everyone is full of jokes about your toy boy. Why did you leave yourself open to that?"

"I'm not going to go there, Eddie," she says coldly. She turns on her heel and leaves the room.

Immediately he's after her. "But there's no future in it. There can't be," he says gruffly.

"It's none of your business." She stops, exasperated with him. "You're very patriarchal, Eddie. Has anyone ever told you?"

He pats her shoulder awkwardly. "It has been said. My wife accuses me of it."

"Well, this is it, Simon," Beatrice says. He's fidgety, tugging at his tie, fiddling with his cuffs, adjusting his sleeves. A fine specimen of manhood, she thinks, not especially tall, about five-nine or -ten, with a compact muscled strength, no heaviness on his frame. A surprising grace of movement denotes an agility not immediately obvious. The rusted red of his hair and eyebrows emphasizes the almost transparent delicacy of his skin, softening the high ridge of his nose. Pale eyelashes frame the startling green of his irises and confer a deceptive vulnerability on his expression.

She had expected him to travel from his parents' house to church the morning of the wedding, but he said, "Here is closer than home, Bee. I don't fancy going back for just one night and then having to drive the best part of eighty miles the next morning." He's been up and down to his bedroom a number of times already. His packed suitcase stands in the hall, waiting to be collected by his best man. His family have already been and gone.

"This getting married is an awful chore," he says.

"I'm not sure how to take that."

"All this fussing and codology. It's unnatural."

"Almost at the point of no return. You can still cut and run."

"Yeah, yeah." He coughs as if something has stuck in his throat.

His best man, one of his identikit brothers — she can never tell them apart — arrives to bring him to the church and she locks up the house.

In the church, Simon's sisters wave as he walks up the aisle, but he's oblivious to everybody.

This is the day my artificial little world gets blown apart, thinks Beatrice, as the bride arrives. But hers isn't the only world being decimated. The previous day she met Angela at the checkout in one of Killdingle's supermarkets.

"I suppose there's great excitement over the wedding?" Angela said.

"Very low-key. It's strange. I've yet to meet the bride."

"That figures. He won't be in a rush to show her off."

Angela's anger was almost tangible. It hissed and crackled like a rogue electric cable, twisting and jumping and shooting out maverick shocks.

"What can I say? Men are strange creatures, Angie." What age is Angela, she had wondered. Twenty-six or twenty-seven? Probably no more than twenty-eight. The unmarked mask of youth is hard to read.

"I never thought he'd go through with this," Angela continued.

"Kept expecting he'd come back. But love is a foreign notion to these men." She wiped away angry tears.

Beatrice wanted to urge her not to waste her emotions on an undeserving recipient, to warn her against allowing corrosive anger to sour her life. "Don't let it get to you, Angela. God knows I'd be very happy if you were the one he was going to marry. But we mustn't judge. He may love her in his own way."

"The only person Simon loves is himself. Don't you worry about me, Beatrice. I'm a survivor. I'm fighting off men who want to go out with me. This time I'm being right picky. None of that love stuff. I've got a calculator instead of a heart."

The next time Beatrice sees Simon is a fortnight after his wedding. He comes armed with a box of chocolates and a piece of cake from the reception. "Howdy," he says with a big grin. She puts aside the pastry she's just made, wipes her hands, and goes to greet him. They're like old favorites, a former teacher with her star pupil or an aunt greeting a darling nephew, all shyness and delight. "Thanks for the towels," he says. "They're magnificent."

"You didn't bring Celia with you?"

"She's off shopping with her mother. You know how seriously these women take their shopping."

She looks for signs of change in him but there's nothing she can notice. He's as personable as ever, full of that easy charm.

"You're looking well," he says. "I took a notion to come over and see you."

The mistake is to take him on a tour of the place before tea. He becomes somber. It's clearly an emotional experience for him. He hardly speaks but looks a lot, at the outbuildings, the yard, the machinery, and the cows grazing in the pond field. "There's great space here," he says. They linger at her special spot by the beech trees and hedge, enjoying the vista of ash and birch trees in the next field and the mountains beyond. "What I wouldn't give to own the likes of this," he says sentimentally.

All through tea he makes competent small talk. It's difficult to reconcile the open affection he lavishes on her with the calculating coldness people suspect him of.

When she tells him she's negotiating with a neighboring farmer to rent or lease the farm, he seems genuinely pained. "That'll be a wrench," he says.

"It will and it won't. Even with hired help, I'm run off my feet these days. I'm well able to do it all — drive a tractor, handle calves and cows, manage the milking, and load up a trailer. If pushed, I can mend a fence or sort out a drainage problem. But, at this stage of my life, there's no way I'd want to be up all night waiting on a cow to calve. Except for emergencies, I never had to bother with those things. Farming is backbreaking work, even with all the equipment, the scraping machine and what have you. You'd need to be in the full of your health to sign up for it."

"I enjoyed my time with you, Bee," he says as he leaves. "It's an unfortunate accident of birth that I wasn't your son." He hesitates. "I meant what I said about coming back to help out. I'm surprised you haven't heard from the silage cutters. Are you sure you haven't lost your place in the queue? I'll give them a ring."

"It's okay. They'll be along soon."

"No, I'll phone Tom and see what's up. Sometimes they need a little reminding."

"That's very good of you, Simon. Thanks."

She watches him drive off with very mixed feelings. Would she ever want such a son, this thirty-one-year-old man with little schooling and various employments as factory worker, lorry driver, delivery man, and farm worker? None of that would count against him except that she suspects him of a serious lack. She suspects that he has no inner life, and that he has only a limited capacity for reflection. His love of the land doesn't ennoble him. She can't love somebody whose attachment is to something that is beyond human emotion. Yes, she thinks later, as Shep and she round up the cows to drive them into the milking shed, I couldn't feel for a person who values the earth above its inhabitants.

Sixteen

$\mathcal{E}$LLEN IS PACING the floor of her kitchen. "There's a sense of being held to account. What annoys me is being judged by standards that most people have given up on. There's quite an amount of what you'd call 'irregular unions' among the parents — separations, divorces, and what used to be called 'living in sin.' As far as I know that Hussey woman and the husband are separating, but she's the one shouting tally ho and leading the charge."

"It's that *in loco parentis* bind, Ellen," Matt says.

"I know all that, Matt, and the role model business. It's just that a lot of the *parentes* I am *in loco* for are rather slack in that regard."

"Catholic school."

"I know. In Dublin nobody would have been any the wiser. No prying eyes. No stories doing the rounds. There's a lot to be said for anonymity."

"Still, I have connections, Ellen. I'm well in with a lot of the people who sit on these interview boards. I'll make a few discreet inquiries. Can't do any harm."

"It's the religious trustees and meddling parents you'll have to nobble if you want to get anywhere."

"A bit of discretion on your part would have gone a long way, Ellen."

"You don't like Eugene, do you? You've never approved of him."

Matt shifts uneasily. "I don't dislike him. He's very presentable, pleasant, good-humored, but —"

"But?"

"Ah, he mightn't — mightn't — be all that serious."

"You think he's making a fool of me."

"No. Just that he's not necessarily committed. D'you know what I mean?"

"I can't answer that, and I certainly can't speak for him." She sighs. "Anyway, thanks for not giving up on me. I do appreciate that."

"The older I get, the harder I find it to pass judgment. Nothing is as cut and dried as it used to be."

"Relativism. Better watch yourself, Matt, or you'll end up on the slippery slope."

"And which slippery slope would that be?"

"Oh, the one you're always on about. The low whatever it was in high places."

"Low standards in high places. George Colley, Lord rest him, it was said that. And he was right. It was the beginning of all that chicanery in politics, public representatives out to cut deals and make personal money, the end of idealism and the beginnings of self-interest. That was over thirty years ago. You were a child."

"I heard it often enough. But you always acted honorably and did the right thing, stuck to your principles."

"And was probably a fool to do so. That's what a lot of people would think."

"But you're not bitter. Tell me you aren't."

He laughs shortly. "Bitter? Am I bitter? That comes with age and disappointment. Let's see now. Probably not." He stands up. "But one thing is certain, I'm probably jealous of you and Eugene. Whatever the outcome, you'll have had a better deal than I ever did. We didn't know we were alive, or what it was to live. Not much use discovering it now when it's too late."

"You're sixty-four, Matt. You have at least two good decades. You're fit and healthy. This isn't the last hurrah."

He puts his cap on his head. "Your options narrow as you get older," he says with some asperity.

"I'll have to get back to you on that."

"I'll be out of the picture when you discover it. You're the one causing scandal. You're the one having a fling. I'm out of the loop. Stephen will be home this weekend. Call up, won't you?"

"Saturday afternoon?"

"Perfect. We'll expect you."

"Hello, stranger," Nan Brogan says as Beatrice hauls her shopping onto the bus. "I hear you're doing a deal on the farm with Tim O'Shea."

"We're sorting something out. I hope you approve of the terms and conditions, Nan, because if you don't, I won't go through with it."

Nan gives that "huh" sound that passes as a laugh from her.

"Where's Brenda today?" asks Beatrice. In the village, they're known as Tweedledum and Tweedledee. "It's unusual not to see the two of you together."

"Haven't you heard?" Nan says with a stricken air. "Brenda's at home. She was in hospital for tests."

"Well, how am I to know what's happening if Brenda's not around to tell me? Nothing serious, I hope?"

"No, no, nothing bad. A twitching in her face, it's called Bell's palsy. It'll go away again — but there's no knowing when — and she's very self-conscious about it."

"What a shame. You must be lost without her," Beatrice says, and the words "poetic justice" come to mind.

"I don't have to depend on Brenda. I have plenty of friends," Nan says, but she speaks without conviction. The absence of Brenda lessens her vitality. Nan seems shrunken and reduced, as though she has become dependent on the synergy generated by their combined viciousness and is diminished on her own. "I suppose you heard about Sandra Dingle?"

"Denis Scope's girl? What about her?"

"She's home with her baby."

"I thought she was in the early stages when she went away."

"Not at all. It was well advanced. She carried it small."

"Boy or girl?"

"Girl. Poor mite. She doesn't have a chance."

"I don't know about that. Anything I've heard about Sandra has been good. Her teachers were heartbroken when she dropped out of school. She's got a good brain."

"Not clever enough to avoid making a complete mess of her

life. These single mothers sicken me. They're doing it because they know the council will house them. I don't feel any sympathy for them. They're cadging off the state."

"I rather think that Sandra imagined Denis would be about, and that the child would have a father."

Nan laughs coldly. "Yeah? Well, he's history now."

"Well, at least she didn't have that abortion you were on about. Mind you, it would have saved the exchequer a fortune if she had."

"Grrrh," Nan says, or something that sounds remarkably like it. "You know how I feel about abortion."

"And single mothers. Nan, you'll have to arrange your dislikes in order of priority. Those poor girls are damned if they have the babies and doubly damned if they don't."

"If they didn't get pregnant in the first place —"

"Unrealistic, Nan. That's always going to happen. When we were young, it got hushed up and tidied away. Wasn't that the case? Lots of people locked up, hidden from sight, babies adopted, false histories invented, misery all round."

"I'm sick of you and your bleeding heart, Beatrice. Anyway, I hear you're great with Matt Hughes these days," Nan says slyly.

"The rumor mill has gone into overdrive again, has it, Nan?"

"You know what they say, no smoke without fire."

"They're going to be disappointed though, aren't they?"

"It'd be a great merging of property if the two of you got hitched."

"Don't hold your breath, Nan. I'm issuing a categorical denial. There's no truth in the rumor, none whatsoever. Lily, Matt, and I are on the committee that's organizing the sponsored walk to raise funds for the children's ward in the Regional Hospital."

"That's just spin. The two of you were seen in Hegarty's the other night."

"Lily was with us earlier. You're incorrigible, Nan, determined to sniff out a story. Nothing I say will make any difference, will it?"

Nan laughs. "Divil a bit," she acknowledges.

When they reach the top of the hill, Beatrice is out of breath. "It's years since I walked this route. I'd forgotten how steep some of it is."

"You're not fit enough," Matt says.

"Most of the young ones have probably reached the finish. This seemed no distance at all when we were young."

"We were ready for anything and everything then."

"This is as good a spot as any to stop." She unzips the backpack she brought with her and extracts a plastic box, a flask, and a jar. "Time for some refreshments," she says and opens the box.

"Did Lily drop out of the walk?" Matt asks, taking off his cap and placing it beside him. He takes a bite from a chicken sandwich.

"No, but she fell a good bit behind." Beatrice is a little uneasy in his company. It's years since she found herself completely alone with him. "What happened to Ellen and Eugene?"

He frowns. "I wonder did they take the wrong turning at the crossroads?"

"If they went that way, they'll have to backtrack. Ned Roe blocked off the path by the river, and Tim Sullivan land-grabbed the track that used to run along the edge of his place. Bianconi's coaches used to travel that way. It was the original mail road. The only intact part is the walk by the old mill."

"Walks are getting scarcer by the day."

"It's vexatious, this question of access."

"Desperate. Having to take out insurance and the fear of compensation claims. The whole thing's a viper's nest."

"Still, it'd be such a shame if people couldn't go for a ramble across the countryside. It's not nice to see places cut off. I hate it when I see barbed wire."

Walkers pass by but there's no sign of Ellen or Eugene. "They must have sprinted ahead. We'd surely have seen them by now. This chicken stuff is good, Beatrice. You didn't buy it in a supermarket."

"Certainly not. Supermarket chicken has no flavor."

"Nothing has a good flavor anymore, except at a premium price."

Matt's hand brushes against her arm as he reaches for another sandwich. Beatrice starts and pulls back. The weight of their history presses down on her. She has devoted decades to avoiding him, but over the last few months the balance of their relationship has altered. When Julia died, something broke in him. He seemed wounded and was so at odds with everything in his world that she found herself stirred by something—compassion? Now that he's come through his bad patch, it's possible to recognize something of the young Matt again. Perhaps it's her vanity, but it's difficult to resist the allure of being valued, especially as a friend. Were a friendship to develop between them, it would be a good outcome.

"Funny old world, isn't it," he says suddenly.

"It certainly is."

"Here we are, your Jack long dead and Julia gone."

"How do you feel about Julia now?"

He reaches for his cap, puts it back on his head, and readjusts it so that its peak shadows his face. "It's strange. I don't feel anything much. Once I got over that reaction, I haven't looked back. It's as if she never existed." He looks up at her. "Sometimes I suspect I went out on the edge to see if I could stir real feelings. I wanted to feel alive. But there's still an emptiness."

"We feel what we feel. There's no ordering it."

His voice changes. "Do you ever think of us, of the way we used to be?"

"That was so long ago I scarcely remember it."

"I think about it sometimes."

She laughs. "You shouldn't be wasting your time."

"We're free agents."

"Except that it doesn't matter now."

"It could."

"Why would we bother?"

"Couldn't you be bothered, Beatrice? Wouldn't we be nice company for each other?" He clears his throat as if to say more, hesitates, then falls silent.

She shudders. "You're not talking about getting hitched, I take it. Friendship would be more my style. I've no problem with friendship."

"Marriage isn't so bad, not if the people are compatible."

"Who's to know who's compatible with whom?" she says crossly. "We're not the people we were." She feels a grim desperation as she tries to deflect him. "Matt," she says more gently, "we had our chance and we blew it."

266

"I don't suppose you've ever forgiven me for . . . well, how could I blame you? If you knew how much I regret . . ."

"Regrets are part and parcel of life, aren't they? Look at us, wrinkled and starting to sag. We've had the stuffing knocked out of us. Romance is a bit ridiculous at our age, but I'd settle for friendship. We could be great friends."

"Friends, is it?" he says. "How could we be just friends?"

"Can we be anything else?"

He turns away, struggling with himself. "Aren't we due some compensation for the wretched marriages the two of us put up with?" he says harshly. "For the hell I suffered with Julia, and the difficulties you had with Jack?"

"Speak for yourself!" she answers spiritedly. "Jack Furlong wasn't the easiest person to live with—he could be very trying—but he wasn't a bad man. He meant well. It was always a struggle between his impulses and his intentions."

"I never thought I'd hear you talk so kindly of him," he sneers. "Admit it. Weren't you miserable with him? Do you mean to suggest that he meant as much to you as I did?"

"He wanted me, Matt," she says quietly. "He went against his mother, told her that he wouldn't marry anyone if he couldn't have me. He found plenty of fault with me over the years, but he never once reproached me for my lack of money or background."

"Well, I have to hand that to him," he says in a subdued fashion. "But does that matter? Could you honestly say that you didn't long for me all those years, the way I longed for you?"

"Long for me, did you? You had a funny way of showing it."

"That again?"

"Yes, that." She lifts her head and looks straight at him. "It took me years to realize what a fool I was to be hankering after you. I got a very poor return for my love, didn't I? So, I wrote it off, accepted life as it was. And do you know something? It was much easier."

She waits for him to answer, but he's silent. After a while, he stretches and straightens up. "We'd want to be heading back. The cows have to be milked," he says.

His face tells her nothing. It strikes her that there's no knowing Matt Hughes. Was he trying her out to see where it would get him?

Or was he genuine? "Let's join the stragglers," she says. "We're about two miles from the finish."

They don't exchange another word during the walk to the village. Parked cars soak up the heat of the Sunday afternoon when they reach the square. The sun bounces off cement footpaths and softens the tar on the road. There isn't a soul to be seen. "The deserted village," he says. It's as if he never made a play for her attentions.

From Hegarty's open doors comes the sound of singing.

"That's where they are, in the pub." She marvels at her control.

He unlocks his car and sits in. "Want a lift?"

"I'd like to see if Ellen and Eugene are ensconced in the snug," she says, making for the pub. There isn't a sign of them when she looks in, but she spots Sandra Dingle, surrounded by friends, holding her baby up for inspection. It's the first time she's seen the girl since her return. Nothing remains of the hangdog expression Sandra wore after Denis's death. There's something intense and lively about her, a clarity and intelligence in her face that bodes well. Sandra's mother, like everyone in the group, is ogling the baby. The child's grandfather tickles her chin. Maybe there is hope, thinks Beatrice. Maybe Sandra will find a way out of the trap.

When she re-emerges, Matt is waiting. "You didn't take up my offer," he says.

"Haven't you gone yet?" she says pleasantly. "I'll head off under my own steam. It's a beautiful day, and I don't have far to go."

He watches her walk away.

She's hardly out of the village when she has to stop. Her heart races, her breath is ragged, and her legs can hardly hold her up. Again, she is the shocked creature of nearly forty years ago, standing on the bridge beside the Protestant graveyard, trying to gather enough courage to throw herself into the river. But the bridge is too low, the water too shallow, and the flow too sluggish. Once in the water she knows her instinct for survival will win out. She's hearing those words, "trollop" and "whore," over and over again. She's shrinking into herself and clutching her pain.

No Matt anymore. He's gone. His recoil on hearing her fears told her everything. She remembers his words — *Am I the father? How do I know I'm the father?* The coldness of his eyes, the cleft of his chin, and his clenched fists. He hadn't been absent during their love-making, but he made himself absent.

And, of course, he came back, ostensibly contrite but gruff and remote, a sullen suitor, so that she had to send him packing. It was a mercy when, soon after, she suffered a miscarriage. She cleaned up the mess, burned the stained clothes in the kitchen range, and made a night trek into the woods with a spade to dig a hole and bury her mistake. Not a word to her parents. Never breathed a word of it to anyone. She didn't have to go away, wasn't sent off. Decorum was preserved.

What is it that she can't forgive Matt? That he never asked what happened? That he never mentioned the pregnancy? His callousness? His cowardice? Such contempt she felt for him for years. But she no longer has those feelings. She knows that bad behavior doesn't mean that a person is bad. He doesn't have it in him to revisit that incident properly. He may even have excised it pretty successfully from his idea of what happened between them, a gruff "sorry" deemed sufficient for vaguely remembered misdemeanors. No contrite heart seeking forgiveness, no looking to start afresh. He's forgotten his cajoling, pleading, and physical forcing. He has unremembered their couplings. There's something in him that doesn't feel the need to make good his misconduct, and something in her that won't accept that.

The house feels emptier than usual. There is too much house, too much space, and not enough people. When Paula arrives home in July, her children will gad about the farm, thump up and down the stairs, and race round and round the garden. Then, in October, she'll visit Andy in the States and see Scott again. She'll learn whether their friendship will survive the change of location.

She has lots to occupy her — cooking, gardening, cleaning the church, reading, listening to the radio, watching television, playing cards in the hall, going on walks, and meeting up with friends. The book club in Killdingle is quite large and she's been thinking of joining it. She's never been to the set dancing in the hall even though she was once a great dancer. She might even develop a taste for touring about. Lily Traynor's husband, Damien, abhors travel, but Lily has suggested that the two of them team up and go away on a long weekend to Paris or Amsterdam.

She looks out the window. The tarred avenue to the house dips between hedges, trees, shrubs, and grass, and curves down to the T-junction. She can see the roofs of cars as they hum along the main road. The noise of traffic is a persistent background to the music of everyday life.

The phone rings. "Beatrice?" a voice says. "It's Ellen. Where did you and Matt get to?"

"We got tired of waiting, and Matt had to go and milk the cows. Did you go astray?"

"Yes, we got lost. Then we ran into a farmer who didn't like us walking along the edge of his land. He got very agitated. Fortunately, Stephen was with us and the farmer recognized him. It was really stupid, Beatrice. We weren't on his precious land."

"They're very territorial around here, Ellen. Don't let it upset you."

"We're down in the pub. There's a real carnival atmosphere. Won't you come and join us? Lily is here. She says she'll have to do lots more walks if the two of you are to tramp the cities of Europe!"

"I'm too lazy now. I'll stay put."

"Give me a ring soon."

"The trouble with you, Ellen, is that I never know where you're going to be."

Ellen laughs. "Try my mobile. That'll get me. You have the number."

Beatrice switches on the radio to catch the early evening news. Trouble in Northern Ireland, another glitch in the endless negotiations, a suicide bomber in Israel, a suspected banks' scandal, and allegations about some celebrity she's never even heard of. The forecast is for a prolonged dry spell. Evening temperatures will dip although it'll be warm during the day. It's a good week to catch up on work in the garden.

Seventeen

G OD ALMIGHTY, Ellen, but you're a hard woman to find," Eddie says. "I've been all over the school. Only I saw your car outside, I'd have given up. Your uncle rang looking for you. He said you weren't answering your mobile." He looks at her, hunched on the carpeted floor of the staff room annex, the contents of her locker beside her. "What are you up to?"

"What do you think? Clearing up, clearing out." She throws a book into a big cardboard box she's brought for the occasion. Her shoulder-length hair is tied up in a ponytail and she's dressed in black cords, high-heeled black shoes, and a sleeveless low-necked red top that reveals a reasonable amount of cleavage.

"Very nice," Eddie says of her outfit. "There wouldn't be a peep out of the boys if you wore that in class. How'd the interview go? I heard you blazed your way through it."

"You know, it's years since I did an interview. I did my best, but I may have overdone it. It was weird. Nothing fazed me. I had to force myself to slow down at the end. It's the times you think you've done well that you mess up."

"I heard you were running the show. You might be unpacking again."

"They didn't ask anything about my private life, didn't try to catch me out."

"They couldn't. You had to be asked the same questions as everybody else."

Desks and chairs are being set up in the assembly hall, and some classrooms have been reconstituted to act as exam centers. Throughout the day invigilators drive to the back entrance of the school, deposit the metal boxes that hold the exam papers in the strong room, assess the suitability of seating and other arrangements in the centers and sort out security and key-holder details.

Eddie looks different somehow, younger. The strain of the daily grind of work has lifted from his features and his color is better. Of course, everybody in the staff looks reinvigorated once the holidays arrive — the years just drop away. She's overheard colleagues making plans to play tennis doubles over the summer. Seems there's a long tradition of contact between some of the staff during the break. It displays a warmth that she was never able to tap into.

"We're forgetting ourselves," he says. "That phone call. Check your messages now."

She fumbles in her bag and searches the boxes. "I don't have my mobile. I bet I left it in the car."

"You'd better use the phone in my office, nine for an outside line. I'll lock up."

"Don't lock up. I have to come back here."

"Make haste, Ellen," he says, pushing her out the door, and she finally hears urgency in his voice.

"Where the hell have you been? I couldn't reach you," Matt shouts when he finally answers the phone. "I thought you were finished with school."

"There are always bits and pieces. I had to fill in report sheets, and I'm gathering my stuff. What's the matter?"

"It's Kitty. She's been admitted to hospital. Something to do with her heart."

The oddness of what he's saying strikes her. Her scalp tingles. She has never associated her mother with illness. She's not sure that she can recall a time when Kitty was properly sick. Colds and sniffles of course, but otherwise remarkably resilient. "Not an attack? A heart attack?"

"She's in for tests. You'd better get up there."

"Is it serious?"

"I'm not a doctor, am I? They're admitting her so they're taking it seriously."

"Have you spoken to her?"

"Her friend Muriel rang. I left a message on your machine. And, of course, when I was trying to find you, I was in to Terry in case she'd seen you. You can rest assured that the whole village is in the know now."

That figures. A nice little bit of excitement, people watching out for her car, little flurries as people phone around. "Have you heard?" and "Did you see?" Terry in her element regaling customers with the dramatic news.

"You'd better ring this Muriel. I'll give you her mobile number."

When she replaces the receiver, she finds that she needs to sit down. She's a little breathless. An unwelcome intruder has broken into her life. What will she call it? Mortality? Death? No, probably not death, but one or other of his myriad relations—pain, weakness, fear, illness, or decrepitude. None of Kitty's posturing or maneuvers have ever counted for much with her, but this is different. It's as if she's missing her mother for the first time.

Outside, the early June sun beats down on the tennis court below Eddie's office. She hears grunts and shouts, the twang of a ball against a racket, the thud as it hits the ground. But she feels a chill—for which she's underdressed—and sits, for how long she has no idea.

Eventually she comes to and shrugs off her inertia. Her arms bristle with goose pimples. The Muriel who answers Ellen's call to her mobile is laconic and gives practical directions. "We'll save talk for when we meet," she says. Ellen gauges the time the journey is likely to take and expects to reach the hospital at some stage of the evening.

It's oddly apt that a woman so careful of her health—moderation in all things—but terrified of hospitals and medical examinations, has earned herself a genuine medical emergency.

The incongruity of this is brought home to Ellen when, her first time in the ward, she draws back the curtain that corrals the space that she has deduced must contain her mother's bed and is arrested by the unprecedented sight of her mother's bare breasts and naked torso, her chest dotted with electric monitors connected to a machine beside the bed. Neither Kitty nor the dark-skinned medic she's talking to notice Ellen, who retreats hurriedly. It's a shock—a revelation?—to be confronted by that nakedness and to realize that the body of a post-menopausal, sixty-two-year-old woman looks reassuringly intact and firm. Her mother could still pass the swimsuit test. And yet her mother's body has been found wanting.

Ellen bolts out into the corridor and explains to Muriel that the curtains are drawn. Muriel, a diminutive busty blond woman of uncertain age, appears invigorated by the drama. "We were in my place in Wicklow—I take a house near Brittas Bay every summer—out walking along the beach early yesterday, when she began to feel unwell. Actually, she woke up not feeling great but decided a walk might settle her. She experienced this sensation down her left arm—"

"That's the classic symptom, isn't it?"

"They keep telling me that women present differently—it could be a pain in the shoulder or down the back—but that's how it was for her. So, I drove straight to my doctor who told her she was fine —it was probably just muscle strain—but that if she was uneasy he'd send her off for an ECG. She accepted that she was probably okay, but I wasn't happy. My husband died from an undiagnosed heart condition three years ago, and he hadn't been feeling well for days before, so I took the bit between my teeth and insisted we come here and, of course, the test showed up an irregularity."

"I have to sit down," Ellen says. She's just realized that she hasn't eaten since breakfast.

"You poor thing. I was forgetting the impact of the news, the shock of hearing this."

"Oh, I'm okay."

"Your mother is sleeping," an Asian nurse tells Ellen in careful English. "She is very tired," she says. "See her tomorrow."

"Irish nurses are very thin on the ground," Ellen comments when the nurse has gone.

"The world has changed. It's a regular United Nations in hospitals nowadays," Muriel says. "We'd have no health service without them." She pats Ellen on the shoulder. "You go and get a good night's rest, and I'll meet you here tomorrow morning."

• • •

The following day Ellen finds herself back on the same corridor with Muriel, waiting for the doctors to finish their rounds. "Here they come," Muriel says, edging Ellen into their path. "At least they're Irish. We'll be able to understand them."

"You're the daughter," the tall, middle-aged autocratic man in the suit and steel-rimmed spectacles says. He shakes hands with Ellen. "I'm Bill Edwards. Your mother is under my care. My colleague, Doctor Mary Day," he says, indicating the dark-haired, low-key, but reasonably attractive young woman by his side, "will explain everything. Ask any questions you like. Okay?" At which stage he gives a barely perceptible nod and rejoins a group of what Ellen presumes to be trainee doctors, some wearing traditional white coats, others dressed casually but clutching charts and stethoscopes.

"Hi," the woman says with an engaging smile. "Call me Mary. I'm the registrar. Professor Edwards is a cardiologist and he's your mum's consultant. He wants me to let you know what's going on."

"So what's the story?" Ellen asks.

"We're running a series of tests on your mother at the moment. We know there's a blockage. It's a question of location and degree. We've put her on anticoagulants as a precaution against clots."

"A blockage? An artery, you mean?" It's extraordinary to be having this conversation about her mother.

"She smokes," the woman says, sotto voce, as if to spare Ellen's feelings.

"She used to, but she gave them up years ago. She takes the occasional cigarette. Adds up to — ten or twelve a year at most."

"Still, people tend to understate —"

"No, she wouldn't understate. She never understates," counters Ellen. "If she smokes a cigarette once every six weeks, that's as much as she does. She's quite abstemious, watches her intake of food, takes regular exercise, and never overdoes it in any regard. This will put the frighteners on her. I can guarantee she'll never touch a cigarette again in her life."

Mary shrugs in a noncommittal fashion. "That's as may be. For the moment we're treating her as unstable. We need to establish the precise nature of what we're dealing with. After the angiogram, we'll have a much better idea of how things are," she says, and begins to move away. "We'll talk again," she calls over her shoulder.

For a moment Ellen can relate the word "unstable" only to explosive gases or to extreme mental or psychological conditions, which gives rise to a fascinating take on her mother's predicament — Kitty careering about wildly, dipping and weaving her way along a corridor, in danger of detonating.

"There's nothing to worry about," Muriel says in a clucking, hen-like fashion. "It's all under control. You know, your mum wouldn't let me contact you until yesterday. She knew you had an important meeting."

"The final staff meeting? That was last Friday. It wouldn't have been a hardship to miss that. Oh, I know what she means. She was thinking about the job interview the previous day again."

"You'd better go in and say hello. I'll wait outside."

"You come in too, Muriel. I've you to thank for Mum's condition being picked up."

Kitty is presentable, modestly attired in a nondescript hospital gown. She seems to have shrunk into herself, to be physically smaller. She greets Ellen with a self-deprecating grimace. "Hello, darling."

"You've pulled a bit of a stunt. Touch of the dramatics, eh?"

Kitty looks tired, her features a little drawn. "They're talking about this balloon thing," she says. "I don't like the sound of it."

"They put it into the artery and inflate it," Muriel says helpfully. "It's very successful," she says, patting Kitty's arm. "But it could be a bypass, Kitty. Don't forget. Depends on the extent of the blockage."

Kitty groans. "Anything but that. That'd really put me out of action. Oh, Ellen, why did this have to happen?"

"It mightn't be so bad, Mum. How do you feel?"

"No pain. They gave me painkillers. But to think of me having a heart condition makes me feel quite old."

And all that Ellen can think of, as she draws up a chair to sit by her mother's side, is that Kitty couldn't have engineered this better if she had planned it. Whatever the outcome of this scare, she'll forever be able to flaunt the episode and put it to good use. "My heart," she will say, delicately patting the area around her breastbone. "My daughter," she will say. "She's so good to me. She's moving back to Dublin to keep an eye on me." Ellen begins to feel weak. Her legs tremble. She feels like a character trapped in a gloomy novel about unreasonable and unspeakably controlling families. Kitty will suck her dry.

Suddenly she realizes how ungenerous she's being. Her panic feels contrived. Kitty has shown no inclination to milk the situation. She's anxious and fretful, certainly, but nothing more than that.

"I'm finding it hard to take all this in," says Kitty. "Overload." She turns to Muriel. "I'm spent. I shouldn't have taken that sleeping pill last night."

Matt looks out of place in a hospital setting, walks as if constipated. She notices his country ruggedness, his weathered face, the old-fashioned haircut, the awkwardness of the ill-fitting suit, the unnatural whiteness and crispness of the newly bought shirt, the faded tie, and, most of all, those outsized, tanned, nicotine-stained hands — one clutching a supermarket bag — hanging awkwardly by his sides.

She runs to him. "Matt! I can't believe you're here."

"When I was offered a drive up —"

"A drive? Who drove you?"

And, to her horror, she sees Eugene stepping out from one of the lifts at the front of a crowd. "What are you doing here?" she asks. She's wondering how she can explain him to her mother.

"That's a fine welcome," he chides. "You just took off without telling me." He catches her close and lands a kiss on her mouth. All at once she's full of shyness, but Matt doesn't seem to mind.

"I can't believe you two drove up together."

"Sure, I had to put in an appearance, and he made the offer."

She laughs. "I wouldn't like to have been with you on that journey."

"Eugene's okay, actually," Matt says. "Now, where's this sister-in-law of mine?"

"This way. I'll come in with you. You stay put," she says to Eugene.

"None of that now. I'm coming," Eugene says firmly.

"Kitty has to find out about him sometime. Best place for it to happen is here. Plenty of doctors and machines about if it provokes a reaction," Matt says.

"Well, I won't pretend to understand any of this," Ellen says. "I thought you two could just about tolerate each other."

"He improves," Matt says. "He knows more than you'd think about the War of Independence and our neutrality during the Second World War."

"Courting him?" Ellen hisses at Eugene as they follow Matt into the ward. He winks at her.

"Matt, how lovely!" Kitty enthuses, perking up. Her eyes widen when he produces a bag of grapes and a bottle of Lucozade from the bag. "You're so good to think of me," she gushes.

"Couldn't come with one hand as long as the other. Sorry to hear you've been in the wars."

"Oh, it's not as bad as it might have been. I've been sent from pillar to post with all the tests they've given me. They might do a bypass or this angioplasty thing. That seems my best option."

"Beats a heart attack," Matt says deadpan.

"I'd forgotten how blunt you can be." She can't keep her eyes off Eugene. "You'll have to introduce me to this young man," she says coquettishly. "At first I took him for Stephen, but he's nothing like him. Who is he, Matt?"

"This is Eugene, Kitty. You've seen him before but you probably don't remember. He'd have been in the pub the day of Julia's funeral. He's my lift, but he's also Ellen's young man."

Kitty's mouth falls open but she remembers to shut it quickly. "What's this, Ellen?" she says querulously. "Why haven't I been told?"

"Pleased to meet you, Kitty. I'm Eugene O'Brien," Eugene says.

"Likewise I'm sure, but why didn't anybody tell me? Ellen?"

"I was waiting till the summer holidays."

Mention of the summer holidays triggers something in Kitty. "I forgot about the job. How did the interview go?"

"It could be a while before we know the outcome. The board of management will have the final word at their next meeting. It's bound to go to a local."

"Well, you're at one remove from being local," Matt says as he sits down.

"And who? — who exactly are you, Eugene?" asks an unusually helpless Kitty. "You've just been sprung on me."

"He's a carpenter . . ." Ellen begins.

"A cabinet maker. Fitted Ellen's kitchen for her," offers Eugene.

"Let there be no panic," soothes Ellen. "We're not getting married or anything."

"Well, you can't, can you? You'd be breaking the law!"

"Nothing to worry about, Kitty," Ellen says.

"Well, I don't know about that. You never even told your mother," she accuses. "That's very hurtful."

"I was going to," Ellen lies. "This just fast-forwarded it."

"He's very good-looking," Kitty says, sounding slightly winded. "Have you been in touch with Christy? Does Christy know about me? Poor Christy."

"I'll contact him, if you like."

"You'll never go back to him now, now that you've taken up with another man."

"Eugene has ears, Kitty. He can speak. Talk to him!"

"Of course I'll talk to you, Eugene. It'll be a pleasure. How could I not?" Kitty says, switching on the charm.

"You were always a man's woman," Ellen says tartly.

Kitty smiles. "You always say that as if it's some sort of insult. And it's true, a handsome man always gets my attention. It'd be unnatural otherwise."

"Enough of this guff," Matt says. "What's the story, Kitty? What have they said? There's no risk, is there?"

"There's a risk with everything, Matt. Even I know that," Kitty says crossly.

"The medics give you a big spiel about risk factors nowadays, Kitty, worst-case scenarios, remote possibilities, the works," Eugene volunteers. "They have to. It's all to do with insurance. But it's nothing to worry about. I know that because my father had a bypass the year before last."

"A heart bypass?"

"A triple one actually. It took him a while to recover his fitness."

"And how is he now?"

"He's grand. He made a good recovery and he gets a lot out of life."

"You're healthy and you're fit, Kitty," Ellen says.

"All the same, I can't believe my heart has let me down. It makes me feel so delicate."

She looks quite put out when Matt says, "Nothing delicate about you, Kitty. You'll see us all out."

Eugene and Ellen have seen Matt off in a taxi bound for the nearby university campus. Matt was keen to see Stephen's office and joked that, if he got lost on his way to the Department of Archaeology, he would dig himself out of trouble.

They are eating lunch in a pub near the hospital. Ellen sips a glass of white wine. The two of them have ordered salmon. Eugene is drinking water. He's in a quiet, preoccupied mood. "I've no problem with you staying with your mum after they discharge her," he says in answer to what Ellen has told him. "It's obvious why she'd want that. As for her coming to stay with you later, that's all in order." He leans in close. "Don't worry about this tendency to feel sorry for herself. You heard the doctors. She'll be flying soon."

Ellen bites her lip. She can feel a pressure down one side of her neck like a knotted muscle or a protuberant vein. "She was on again about moving in with her after you left last night. She thinks she has the whip hand now."

"Don't give this thing legs. Let's be reasonable. She's had a bit of a fright. Can't argue with that," he says, scrupulously fair. "From what you say, she's been hamming it up a bit. Obviously, she missed a vocation as an actress."

"Like *Louise*, you mean? I used to teach that story."

"Louise? What's that?"

"It was a text on the English course, a Somerset Maugham story. It's about a woman who has a heart condition and who's supposed to be delicate, except when she's having a really good time. She outlives two husbands who are worn out caring for her, and tries to thwart her daughter's chance of happiness by insisting that the girl's forthcoming wedding will finish her off."

"How does it end?"

"The narrator accuses Louise of being selfish and manipulative, much healthier than she lets on, says she's sabotaging her daughter's happiness, and shames her into letting the marriage go ahead. On the morning of the wedding Louise has a heart attack and dies."

"You're joking!"

"No." Ellen grins. "Trick is not to get married."

"Thing is to decide in advance what you're going to do. There probably will come a time when Kitty will land in on you."

Ellen can visualize that scenario — her mother arriving with a small suitcase, a short visit extending into an interminable stay, a welter of spats and disagreements, an intractable impasse with a high misery quotient, and Kitty's unshakable resolve. Ellen shudders. "I'll go insane if I have to live with her!" she declares. "It always ends with her trying to undermine me. We don't like each other all that much."

He gives her hand a reassuring squeeze. "There's really no point in worrying, no sense in getting all worked up. That's not going to happen today or tomorrow."

"You said yourself that she's liable to move in."

He smoothes the furrow on her brow. "Stop fretting. Look, she's basking in all this attention just now, loves being at the center of everything, but I can never see her settling for a quiet life. She's too lively. There's still plenty of go in her. She'll get bored. She'll want to be out and about. Once she gets over this fright, and stops being careful of herself, she'll get itchy feet and be off on one of her jaunts." He pulls her to him in a quick hug. "Then it'll be just you and me . . . and the occasional visit from her highness."

Ellen looks skeptical. "So you think it'll be all right?"

"Of course it will. Don't worry. There's no need to look so woebegone. Anyway," he adds with a conspiratorial smile, "if anyone can make her watch her step, I can. She won't want to fall out with me."

"Why not?"

"Because I'm her golden-haired boy!"

"Yeah!" In general, his relaxed attitude to life is a great antidote to Ellen's anxieties, but today his flippancy grates on her nerves. She frowns.

"What?" he prompts.

"It's all right for you," she says crossly. "Whatever happens, you'll get away lightly. There's still another dilemma. My school in Dublin isn't expecting me back, but my chances of getting the teaching job in Killdingle are pretty slim. I'm worried about how I'll earn an income."

"You don't have to teach, do you? Stuff that job. Come on, think laterally. How about doing something else?"

"All I've ever done since I was twenty-three is teaching. Slap open a book, roar at them, entertain them, confuse them, and keep the show on the road. It's all I'm fit for."

"What about VEC schools, adult education places?"

"Mostly part-time, and I've never worked for a VEC."

"Why don't you do the rounds with your CV?"

"I put together a new one for the job interview. It felt like I was making myself up."

"Why not let your house out for rent and move in with me?" he says impishly.

"Stop joking!"

"I'm not joking. I'm serious," he says, as if offended.

"Live with you?"

"Short-term, for starters. It would give you an income. Your place is in great nick. Why not?"

"You really mean it?" She frowns. "I don't know how that would work."

"Come on. I'm sick and tired of all this coming and going between houses. One week your place, the next week mine. I can't settle. The arrangement doesn't really work."

"You want to have an easy life, don't you?" she accuses. "That's what this is all about. But can you imagine what moving in with you would do to my reputation? It'd be flittered!"

"You haven't any reputation to defend, Ellen. And that's good, not bad! Of course, it will make some people uncomfortable. In the old days they'd have tried to run you out of the place. But they can't do that now. They don't have any leverage over you. There's no momentum behind them."

She looks at him. "Are you serious about this?"

"Yes."

A waitress picks up their empty plates and asks if they want to see the dessert menu. Eugene waves her away and asks for the bill.

"Why?" asks Ellen.

"Why not? You can't deny that it makes sense. Anyway, it's been on the cards for ages. It's just a question of formalizing our situation."

Ellen is confused. What is their situation? She knows they have an understanding but she has no idea of what it means. "Excuse me," she says hastily, and makes for the ladies. She finds herself in one of those mirrored rooms with seats at counters, toilets in a farther room. She doesn't really take in much at first. She's trying to work out why she is so discomfited by Eugene's suggestion. What has upset her? Did he assume too much? Was he too cocksure? Is it something else? She knows that many people are pretty blasé about moving in with each other. It can be a decision that ranks in importance with something as trivial as deciding which color to paint their walls. She stares at her reflection, multiple images of her bouncing off the mirrored walls.

Suddenly, she's aware that she's not on her own. Two women in late middle age are sitting in easy chairs in a corner of the room. They stare at her. It doesn't take long to figure out that they are sozzled. Their lipsticked mouths hang slackly, their eyes are glazed like marbles, and their blond, high hairstyles tilt like windblown haystacks. They have collapsed into the seats, and it looks as if they will never be able to stand up again. They watch Ellen dully for some time before picking up their conversation. It's obvious that they had been talking about the breakup of one of their marriages. There's something a little disconcerting about them discussing their business directly in front of her, but they pay her no attention.

She thinks about what Eugene said. Somehow, she imagined that they would drift along indefinitely. She escapes into the farther room and locks herself into a cubicle.

"We're going through the contents of the house, item by item," she hears one of the women say. "Thirty years married and we're fighting over effects. I never imagined I'd be getting worked up over an ornament, Cecily! I mean, what is wrong with me?"

"It's the associations, Maria. Everything has associations."

"To hell with associations!"

"Let's drink to that."

"I'll drink to disassociations!" the bereft woman says, and Ellen hears the wooden legs of the chairs scrape against the floor tiles as the women struggle to their feet, and a thud as the exit door swings shut behind them.

So many breakups and so much heartbreak, Ellen thinks. She has shaken off her own unsuccessful relationship and established a new life. She likes having her own place and the feeling of independence it gives her. Sarah's house has always been special for her. After all the work that went into doing it up, she doesn't want to abandon it. It's far too soon to be moving in with Eugene. She's not ready to invest in him yet. That's the truth. She sinks her head into her hands.

When she rejoins him in the bar, he looks uncharacteristically nervous. "Well?" he asks.

Until she speaks, she's not sure how she's going to phrase what she has to say. "I'm not quite ready to move in with you, Eugene. Maybe it's a residue from my marriage, but I'm afraid it might feel claustrophobic. I like the arrangement we have at the moment. Also, the way things are with my mother, I don't feel up to making a decision like this." She can't bring herself to look at him, so the silence that follows unnerves her.

"You're saying no. Don't you want us to be together?" he says eventually. She has to look up to see the expression on his face.

"This is going to sound dreadful, but it's me — it's all to do with me — I can't just jump in like that. I have this fear of everything souring. I'd be so apprehensive."

"You expect things to go wrong?"

She can't make out if he's puzzled or annoyed. "It's not rational. It's not based on my experience of you. It's like a —"

"Phobia?"

"Nooo. More like a doubt, a reservation."

He smiles tiredly, as if humoring her. "Hesitation?"

"Deliberation."

"That's fine, your prerogative," he says briskly. "Look, I have to go. Matt's expecting me to pick him up in ten minutes. We want to get out of the city before the Friday afternoon rush."

She walks him to his jeep. "Is this the end of us?" she asks.

His expression is hard to read. "I don't know. Is it? You're the one who backed off."

"Is that how you see it?"

"I'll tell you what," he says, sitting into the driver's seat and sticking the key into the ignition, "when we have time to talk, why don't you explain it to me? Fair enough?" He slams the door shut.

She knows that this is him being angry. How he'll react when he's had time to think about this, she has no idea.

"Okay." She watches him drive out of the car park. Before the jeep leaves the footpath, he gives a brief wave. She could weep. She crosses the road to the hospital entrance on the other side.

Eighteen

*D*ESPITE HER RESOLVE to avoid Terry's, Ellen finds herself in the shop one July afternoon. It's a Wednesday, James O'Flaherty's shop is shut, and she and Kitty are out of tea bags. She grabs bread and a packet of tea bags and makes for the checkout.

"I haven't seen you in a while, Ellen."

"I haven't been in," Ellen says shortly.

"Matt told me about your mother. That must have given you a turn," Terry says with something of her former friendliness. "I hear she's staying with you. How is she?"

"She's well."

"I'd say it'll be some time before you'll be able to relax about her."

Terry's return to friendliness is irritating. "Mum had an angioplasty. It wasn't a serious blockage. Anything else you need to know?"

Terry lowers her gaze as she drops the change into Ellen's palm. "Is something wrong, Ellen?" she asks quietly.

Ellen tries to shake off her hostility. "Why should anything be wrong?" she asks coldly.

Terry looks flustered. "I have a fair idea of what's eating you, and you're right. Look, I know my tongue runs away with me at times, but I think a lot of you for helping Matt to get back on the straight and narrow, and you've been good to your mother."

Ellen sighs. "So you're prepared to let me off the hook on other things? Is that it? You'll be putting me up for canonization next."

"It's all too easy to rush to judgment, Ellen. Let's make a new start. Give your mother my regards and tell her I was asking after her," Terry calls out.

Ellen is on the point of saying that Kitty has no idea who Terry is when she notices Terry's expression. The woman is making an effort. She looks contrite.

Will they be reconciled? Is that what Ellen wants? Instinctively, she'd opt for humiliation — Terry, Nan, Brenda, Mrs. Hussey, the lot of them, biting the tough crust of penance, clothes rent through, ropes around their necks, being paraded through the streets. She'd like to out them for their machinations, hypocrisy, and bad-mouthing of her. It wouldn't solve anything, but it would be balm to her fractured soul. All the same, she is weary of conflict. No point in torturing Terry. They're never going to be close. There'll always be an element of disappointment and disapproval in their relationship, she about Terry's reactionary views, Terry about how Ellen conducts her life. People let each other down.

Ellen rises to a smile. "I'll tell her that. She'll be chuffed."

"See you, Ellen."

The teaching job has gone to someone else. Ellen keeps the news from her mother when the phone call comes through. Muriel, fitter and trimmer looking than Ellen remembers, arrives and whisks Kitty off for a few days in Kinsale, and Ellen is enjoying a respite.

Eddie calls to the house to commiserate with her. "The chairman of the board of management rang when I was staying with Mum," she says. "And the letter arrived."

"I told them not to bother you much after all that business with your mother, but they have to go through the motions," he says as they sit sipping whiskey and looking out over the garden from the vantage point of her conservatory. "Your replacement's a young pip-squeak, four years out of college, with qualifications to beat the band, of course — a list of degrees in this and diplomas in that — but no sense of authority about him. He looks about fifteen at best. Limp handshake, limp personality," he says. "I've no doubt but that he's a diligent type. He'll spend hours preparing classes, and I'll have the privilege of breaking him in, stepping in to prevent mayhem, detaining the little misbehaving bastards after school, threatening them with God knows what retribution if they continue to make the poor sod's life a misery. Seven years, they say, isn't it, that it takes to make a teacher? The first year a write-off, after that wait until each class he's made mistakes with has left the system. That is, firstly, if he turns up in September and, secondly, lasts the pace. His nervous system mightn't be up to it."

"You're being wonderfully indiscreet, Eddie. Or are you saying all this to make me feel better?"

"You know I'm not because you know the score. We'll have to revamp the timetable to keep him away from exam classes, and load other people. That won't win me any popularity contests. Maybe I'm wrong. Perhaps he'll surprise me, but he's very wet behind the ears. Bits of subbing work here and there, no continuous work. Only four people applied for the job — including you — and one of those didn't turn up for the interview."

"It's all right, Eddie. You've massaged my ego nicely. I'm not heartbroken. I might have been but, oddly enough, my mother's illness brought everything into relief. It doesn't seem important."

"Ah, but I'll miss you about the corridors and in the staff room, Ellen. And the way you might look at me."

"What?" His occasional lapses into innuendo puzzle her. Still, the parries are delivered and withdrawn with the quickness of a blade attack. She thinks he does it for effect. Regardless, she won't be deflected from what she has to say. "You're the only one who made me feel welcome, Eddie. Thanks for all the support. The rest of the staff couldn't muster an identity between them. I've never come across such an unresponsive bunch. The atmosphere in the school would scald anyone's heart. I won't be pining after them."

"Lots of staff all over the country are like that. I've never quite understood it myself. Individually most of them are fine people — some couldn't teach to save their lives, but that's something you either have or don't have — but as a group they're poison. They never rise to anything. There are about two or three of them — if you'd stayed you'd have discovered whom — with some spark. The rest set just like cement."

"Maybe they're the ones who have got it right. Perhaps the only way of going about teaching is to dampen yourself down so that hardly anybody notices you."

"I suppose that means you aren't interested in part-time work next term?"

She laughs. "After everything that happened? How could I?"

She offers him another drink but he declines. "I'd better go soon."

"Well, I'll miss you, Eddie," she says.

He looks at her in a strange way. "You never gave me any encouragement, Ellen."

Again that play on words, that duality. How does one react to such a declaration? "I wanted that transfer, really did want it. I'm even more certain of that since the drama with my mother. But that didn't mean I wanted the job beyond anything else."

He shakes his head. "You didn't hear me. I said you never—"

"That's what I thought you said." She forces herself to look him straight in the eye. "Look, I don't know where this is coming from."

"From where these things always come. How do you reckon you got so much of my attention?"

Her impulse is to run away, but there's no running away. "I'm amazed," she says. "I thought with you being married and me so involved—"

"Word is that you and Eugene O'Brien split up."

For a moment, she's so enraged by the efficiency of the local rumor network that she finds it difficult to speak. "You shouldn't believe all the tittle-tattle you hear, Eddie. You know how inaccurate these stories are. Eugene is the only man I'm interested in." Her words ebb away. A horrible thickening silence lies between them. He finishes his drink.

"See how I've turned this around," he says quietly.

"What?"

"Had you going there, didn't I? You were in a pickle."

"What are you playing at, Eddie?"

"Little games. I like games. Ambiguities. Word games. Psychological dilemmas. It's my hobby." He smiles quite a malicious smile.

"Tell me, how would you have reacted if I'd been — I don't know — flattered — suggestible or susceptible?"

He puts down his glass and stands up. "Aha," he says. "There's the mystery." He watches her with those oblique eyes and impassive face, his famous inscrutability in place again, that is, if it ever slipped.

"I'll never know what to think of you now," she says at the door.

"There you have it," he says brusquely. "Let's leave it."

When he's gone, she pours herself another whiskey and adds just a little water. Did she unwittingly send out signals? Was he joking, or trying it on? Or did the exchange between them reveal something ominous about him? Would he have proved an arch manipulator, even a bully, if she had ended up working with him?

Ellen pauses on the top step of the old Protestant graveyard wall, admiring the view of the mountains. It's July, a warm day, but she has an ache like a stitch in her side. Her walks have become a kind of penance for her, no longer enjoyable because she is miserable, but essential as a means of escaping Kitty's continued presence in her house. Wincing, she takes the steps and reaches the ground, then stretches up and down in an attempt to dislodge the pain in her side. This gives some relief and she walks toward the bridge, stopping to watch the water surging over a natural weir where salmon return every year. Sometimes she comes across fishermen on the bridge or the banks of the river, but today the place is deserted. The village is over a mile away. At her present rate of progress, it will take hours to reach home.

When, finally, she makes it to her gate she notices Matt's car parked on the grass verge that skirts the laneway beside her house. She walks around to the back. As expected, Matt and Kitty are sitting at the kitchen table.

"We thought we'd have to send out search parties," Kitty says.

"I got a dreadful pain in my side."

"I'd have picked you up if you rang."

"I dropped in to say goodbye," Matt says. Of late, he has changed his hairstyle and updated his clothes, something Kitty puts down to the influence of Úna, his daughter-in-law.

"Goodbye? Where are you going?" Matt never goes anywhere.

"I'm off tomorrow to London for a week. It's the first time I've used the relief scheme for the farm since Colum's wedding."

"And he's spending a week in Rome in October," volunteers Kitty.

"Kitty was suggesting Tuscany, and it looks great in photos, but it's the eternal city I'm after. I want to see it in the flesh."

"God, you're getting very grand."

"Jealousy will get you nowhere, Ellen," Matt says with a smile. "I don't know why you haven't taken off somewhere."

"My situation, I expect," Kitty says. "She's had her hands full with me."

"It must be six or seven weeks, more, since your spell in hospital. When is it you're going back?" Matt asks, winking at Ellen.

"Sunday morning. It's nearly the only time that the roads aren't packed with traffic."

"You'll fly it. Where's Eugene, Ellen? Is he on holidays?"

"He's in Portugal."

"I wonder you didn't go with him."

Ellen swallows hard. Most likely, Matt would be pleased to hear that she hasn't seen Eugene in a while, and Kitty must suspect the truth, but she can't bring herself to tell either of them that it's probably all over with Eugene.

"He called to visit me a few times," Kitty says, "but we don't see that much of him, do we, Ellen?"

"Well, he's away at the moment."

Matt finishes his cup of coffee and stands up. "That's it, I'm off. Have to pack up my bits and pieces. Hope you're doing all the necessary to keep the medics happy, Kitty."

"I was doing most of it before my troubles," Kitty says sharply.

"No problem then. You know the ropes."

"I'll see you to the gate," Ellen says.

"You've been putting in long stints with Kitty," he says when they reach his car.

"Under the circumstances, and all that."

"She's well ready to be launched now." He scrutinizes her face. "Everything all right, Ellen?"

"I'll be fine once I have the place to myself again. I could do with peace and quiet."

"I expect Kitty's pretty high maintenance."

"She has a low boredom threshold. It's all a bit frantic for me."

"Your father used to find her a full-time job. She was always — how to put it? — attention-seeking." He winks. "She'll be gone soon. I'll send you a card from London."

"You do that," she says, waves goodbye, and walks back across the gravel to the open front door.

Kitty is at the sink washing up. "Matt's much improved from years ago," she says. "Of course, when we first knew each other it wasn't under ideal circumstances."

"How do you mean?"

"Neither he nor Julia came to our wedding, and Julia banned Brendan and me from the house. Your father was the renegade priest and I was the wanton hussy who'd tempted him away from God. It didn't matter that I met him after he'd left the priesthood."

"I remember going to the farm with Dad."

"Visits were allowed after a while. I refused to cross the threshold for ages, and we never stayed over. Matt and Brendan had to meet surreptitiously. Your dad would send Matt tickets for a game in Croke Park and they'd go together, or they'd meet up at a hurling match in Thurles. Matt stayed with us once or twice, but it was all hush-hush. Julia mellowed a bit when you arrived on the scene."

"Is that why you're not keen on visiting here?"

"One of the reasons. I was only twenty-four when you were born, and I was a widow at thirty-three. My parents were dead by that stage, but Julia wouldn't let Matt invite you down for a holiday. I'd have been lost if Brendan's cousins hadn't helped out because I never had enough money to take us on holidays."

"No wonder you didn't want to come down for Julia's funeral!"

"I didn't mind that too much. She and Matt turned up at Brendan's, and Matt contributed to the cost of the funeral and headstone. I was very grateful."

"Did Dad and Matt get on?"

Kitty looks to be giving the matter some thought. "They were very different. Matt was more reserved, diffident, more cowed by their mother, I suppose. It was the same when he married Julia. He wasn't wearing the trousers."

"But he bested her a few times," Ellen says, remembering what Stephen had told her.

"So you won't come up with me on Sunday?"

"No. I've a lot of catching up to do here."

Kitty throws her a speculative look. "I hate to be a party pooper, darling, but I have to say what's on my mind," she says.

Something in Ellen's chest dips. She knows what's coming, but takes a leaf out of Beatrice's book and says nothing.

"I know you won't like it, but I'm going to call things as I see them, sweetheart." Kitty's overuse of endearments is always a prequel to one of her self-serving pronouncements. Ellen sits at the table. "Are you listening, Ellen?" she asks sharply.

"I'm listening."

Kitty sits facing her. "It's hard to know with you. Hear me out, anyway. You're going to have to face facts. In the first place, coming to live in Ballindoon was a half-baked idea. Your natural setting is Dublin. You'll never get a job in any school here now. And—don't bite my head off—the business with Eugene is finished, isn't it? Amn't I right?"

"Go on," Ellen says resignedly.

"Haven't I guessed right?"

Ellen nods. "We're going through a bad patch just now."

"It's over."

Ellen smiles and shrugs. "Maybe, maybe not. I don't know, Kitty."

"We'll take it that it is. There's no reason for you to be here now. Come back to your native city. It's easier to pick up work there for one thing. Sell this place—you'll make something on it—and then—"

"I know what you're going to say."

"If we pool our resources and buy a bigger place, we don't have to live in each other's pockets. You put money aside, didn't you? That's just devaluing with low interest rates. It makes more sense to invest in property."

"Some of it is in that government savings scheme, but that's neither here nor there."

"The big adventure didn't work out, Ellen. You have to see that."

Ellen pushes back her chair to stand up and makes for the kettle. "I'm going to brew some coffee," she announces. She spoons coffee into a pot, pours hot water over it, and dips the plunger.

"Well?" Kitty asks. "Really, you're most infuriating, Ellen. You haven't answered."

"Are you and Christy still close?" Ellen asks tiredly. "That's not on, you know. It's almost two years since the separation."

"It can't be that long! But, of course, you're here the best part of a year. Anyway, forget Christy!" Kitty says with unusual vehemence. "He never once came to see me even though he knew I was sick. He's a fair-weather friend."

Ellen can't but laugh. "The scales have finally fallen from your eyes," she says. She leans back against the worktop and sips her coffee. The stitch in her side is back. A band of pain is indenting her brow, and it feels as if there's too much pressure on her neck. Suddenly she thumps the mug down on the counter. "I can't do this," she says.

"But, but—what?" Kitty asks, bewildered.

"I have a thumping headache. I'll burst if I don't get out of here!" Ellen grabs keys and runs out to her car. She's almost worried that Kitty will follow, but there's no sign of her. She reverses, narrowly missing Kitty's car, and drives out from the laneway. A car nearly collides with hers, and the motorist hoots as she shoots out onto the main street. She's so full of pains and sensations that she's half afraid that she's in danger of suffering a heart attack.

She drives about in a daze, not terribly sure in which direction she's going, until she finds herself back outside the old Protestant graveyard. She parks the car, gets out, walks about, and kicks a few pebbles onto the road. The things she finds attractive about the location—its quaintness, English names that are no longer current in the locality on early tombstones, the strange inscriptions, the preponderance of Irish names on twentieth-century gravestones right up to the closing down of the graveyard in the 1940s, and the eerily beautiful setting—serve only to heighten her sense of being at a remove from everything and without a purpose.

What had she been thinking when she turned Eugene down? Why did she hesitate? How come she got it so wrong? All her dilly-dallying. It was insulting to him. Christy failed her but it doesn't follow that Eugene would let her down. All this trying to determine whether people have the natural prerequisites for a role is nonsense. She sees that now. It's clear that the madness was in rejecting the arrangement suggested by Eugene. She should have gone with that.

She paces up and down before the wall in front of the graveyard and doesn't notice a car slow down and stop.

"Ellen, are you all right?" she hears. It's Beatrice, her engine running, her driver's window down.

"Oh, Beatrice," wails Ellen.

Beatrice stops the engine. "I happened to see you when I was passing. Sit in. You look too agitated to be wandering about on your own."

"I'm so miserable, Beatrice," she says when she gets into the car, shivering despite the heat of the day. "How are you?"

"Not a bother, as it happens. But what's the matter with you?"

Ellen pinches the bridge of her nose with the thumb and index finger of her right hand. She looks to be praying or lost in contemplation.

"Is it Eugene? Is it your mother? What is it?" persists Beatrice.

"It's everything, Beatrice."

"There's a rumor doing the rounds that Eugene finished with you. I didn't dare ask."

"A rumor, eh?" Despite her best efforts, Ellen smiles. "As usual, they got it wrong. I finished with him."

"You, Ellen. But why?"

"He asked me to move in with him." The silence from Beatrice is unnerving, forcing Ellen to take away her hand and open her eyes. "Did you hear me?"

"Yes."

"What do you think?"

Beatrice clears her throat. "I think I need more information."

So Ellen fills her in. "For the first time in my life I'm independent, Beatrice. Eugene happened too quickly. You can't jump from one man to another. I haven't had time to enjoy my freedom."

"It's a scheduling problem, is it?"

"What?"

"He put pressure on you at the wrong time?"

"The timing wasn't good."

"And you don't want to live with him?"

"I do but not in his house! And I know he needs his workshop."

"So it's geography."

"That makes it sound trite. I don't know if I can be myself if I'm living with him."

Beatrice shrugs. "Who are you going to turn into? Would Eugene make you compromise yourself?"

"No, he wouldn't. Anyway, it's academic now, Beatrice. I'd better go home to Kitty. She's going back on Sunday."

"When she's gone, call up and see me. Don't get into a rut now," Beatrice says as Ellen gets out of the car.

"What do you mean 'don't get into a rut'? I'm in one."

"You can't manage life, Ellen. It manages you."

"Well, I can try!" Ellen says defiantly. The minute Beatrice has gone she sits back into her car. More than an hour passes before she starts the engine.

She bypasses her house and heads off—where else but in the direction of Eugene's place?—and drives into his deserted yard. She jumps out and runs to the side of the house to take in the view. A wind pummels her hair and T-shirt but the air is balmy. She walks around his house looking in through the windows. It's probably her last opportunity to take a look at what she turned down. She feels physically ill as she takes it all in.

She notices that she has left the driver door wide open and goes back to close it. Suddenly, Eugene drives his jeep into the yard. She had been so engrossed that she missed the sound of its engine. She stands between the door and seat of her own car, transfixed with embarrassment. He gets out and strolls toward her, and she decides to sit into the car.

"Ellen?" He's tanned from his holiday.

"I thought you were in Portugal," she stammers.

"I'm back since yesterday." He has a quizzical expression on his face.

"Mum is going home on Sunday. I wasn't sure—I was going to leave you a note, in case you were about and wanted to say goodbye."

"Come in. Have a cup of something."

She shakes her head. "I won't. I'm not feeling so hectic." It really does feel as if her throat is closing up. "Anyway, if you want — you know — to make your farewells to Kitty."

"Come in to the house, Ellen. I insist."

She surprises herself by getting out of the car. "Ah, why not?" she says, struggling for an elusive nonchalance. "How's your own mother?" she asks.

"She's well. I take it that Kitty is fully recovered?"

"Yeah." He opens the door and waves her in ahead of him. This is all wrong, she realizes. She's not going to be able to carry it off. She's in danger of breaking down and making a show of herself. He's still somewhere in the vicinity of the door. "You know, I'd better not," she says. "I've been out all afternoon. Kitty will be wondering where I am. I'm late enough as it is."

He's silent for a while, and she wishes that he'd do some talking while she fights with herself. "Ellen," he says eventually, "are you coming in or not?"

"Look, I'm really sorry I said no that time," she blurts out. "It was so stupid. I just couldn't get my head around the idea of living with you." And she's striding toward the car, but he's beside her, and he catches her so that she's forced to stop.

"What are you saying?" She doesn't recognize his voice. It doesn't sound like him. "Have you changed your mind? What happened?" he asks.

"It took till this afternoon for me to realize — that you're the best thing that has happened to me. I've been so stupid," she says unhappily.

"What do you mean 'the best thing'? Better than Kitty, a better bet than Dublin, handy to have about — is that it?"

She's shocked. "Those are dreadful things to say. It's nothing like that. Not a bit of it. I mean I got stuck, afraid to move in with you because I thought I'd lose out. I've just copped it. There's been way too much playing safe in my life. The move here was the first breakthrough. Then I got hung up on being independent. It took a while to see that I needed to break away from that."

His expression is unreadable. "Do you want me?" he asks. "Will you live with me?"

A cough catches in her throat. "I think so, but do you still want me? You've hardly been about this last while."

"That's a bit rich. You and Kitty have been living in each other's pockets, and it's very daunting. Don't forget that you shot me down the time I made a move. That doesn't boost a fellow's ego, now does it? And you don't send out signals. You can be very enigmatic, you know."

"I'd never have had the courage to come here today if I thought you were back. It's a big thing putting yourself on the line."

"Tell me about it," he says gruffly. "I thought I couldn't have been plainer about wanting to move our relationship up a notch. And I was even congratulating myself on the timing, imagining that it would help you to put the Kitty conundrum behind you."

"You thought you'd help me?" she says.

"Now, don't tell me I'm patronizing you," he says exasperatedly. "What can I say that's right? I love you — want you — need you? What's the politically correct way to negotiate all this stuff?"

"I've been agonizing over everything this last month."

"Well, I'm glad to hear that. But we're still on your 'no,' remember?"

"May I change that?"

"Honestly, even when you're under pressure you remember the difference between 'may' and 'can'! And of course you can change your mind. So, finally, is this a 'yes'?"

"Yes, to everything. Will that do?"

"I'm glad to see some positivism — or is that positivity? — at last. And I warn you that I intend to take every advantage of you. Come here," he says, gathering her to him. "It was awful you not being with me in Portugal. I was miserable. You're never to do this to me again."

"There's no danger of that," she manages to say before he drags her back with him into the house.

Nineteen

EATRICE COVERS PLATES of sandwiches with foil, counts out crockery and cutlery, checks the apple tart and jam sponge, and stands back to admire her handiwork.

The doorbell rings. She whips off her apron and makes her way out to the hall. "Evening, Matt. You're the first," she says. There's a tricky moment as they size each other up. When she rang and invited him to the gathering, she anticipated a brusque turndown. Instead, he seemed glad to be asked.

"You're a sight for sore eyes," he says, and indeed a recent haircut and color touchup, application of light foundation and lipstick, and stylish deep green dress with matching shoes take years off her.

"I'm not working a farm now so I can indulge myself. Come in, come in." She ushers him into the sitting room where she has set up chairs around an oval table. Flames hiss and spit from the fireplace. "The wood in that log is damp," she says, explaining the fireguard.

Matt warms his hands by the fire. "Funny how you need a fire to take the chill out of the old rooms. It's years since we had a game of cards in this house, in any of the houses for that matter. There was a time when we were always playing. Fair dues to you, Beatrice, for resurrecting the tradition."

"We'll see how it goes. It may happen only the once."

The doorbell goes again and Beatrice hurries to answer it. "Brrh, that's a cold night," Matt hears, recognizing Ellen's voice. "I warn you that I'm not a great card player," she says as she comes into the room. "You'll have to make allowances."

She's followed by Eugene. "I'll help," he says.

"Huh," she says dismissively. "He was supposed to show me how to play a hundred and ten yesterday, but the minute I started to get the hang of it, his competitive instinct kicked in and he trounced me every time. There isn't much incentive to learn."

Eugene grins. "Once you've mastered the basics, you need a bit of a challenge to advance you."

"You ensured that I'll be thrown in at the deep end is what it is."

"Typical. They can't bear to lose, these men, can they?" Beatrice says with a smirk.

"He very nearly put me off completely," complains Ellen.

"I'll watch out for you tonight," promises Beatrice. "Eugene can take his chances."

Ellen makes a face at Eugene. "I don't need you now!"

"That's women for ye!" says Eugene, shrugging amicably. "They never show any appreciation."

"Are there many coming?" Matt asks as Beatrice mixes drinks.

"Lily and Damien Traynor and Denis Foynes. You don't know Denis, Ellen. He's a farmer, lives over Carrigeeshal way. He's one of those confirmed bachelors, a nice man, very dry, you'll like him."

"Know Denis? Of course she knows him," Matt interrupts, and Beatrice looks nonplussed.

"He used to deliver logs for the fire. I'd hang about when he arrived with the tractor and trailer," Ellen says. She looks about. "I was half afraid that Father Mahoney might be here. You know what he told me? He said he'd noticed that I don't receive Holy Communion at Mass, that it was appropriate considering my circumstances. I'm very tempted to present some Sunday to see how he reacts."

"He was praising your sense of propriety," Beatrice says. "Technically, what he said was right."

Ellen snorts. "Them and their rules! I think that the Church concerns itself too much with the minutiae of people's lives."

"Saving our souls. Isn't that the point?" Beatrice says cheerily.

"They can save your soul, if you want." Ellen grins. "I'll look after my own."

To change the subject, Matt says, "Father Mahoney's a devil for the cards. Forgets all his Christian charity in the heat of the game, enough cursing from him to beat the band. Whatever your opinion of our priest, Ellen, were he here now, he'd be a gentleman."

"Have you seen my new kitchen, Matt?" Beatrice asks. He shakes his head. "Want a look?" He follows her across the hall.

"Must have cost you a fortune," he says when he sees it.

She shakes her head. "Doors that open and drawers that shut are a great novelty. Lost the run of myself, though. I'm stink with mod cons, built-in this and that, gadgets galore."

"Don't expect him to be impressed, Beatrice. He's only humoring you," Ellen says from behind Matt. "He's not into kitchens."

"Ellen," protests Matt. "I happen to like Beatrice's kitchen. Nothing wrong with yours either."

"He's full of eloquence, isn't he?" Ellen says as she leaves the room.

"Pay her no heed, Beatrice."

"Oh sure, I know full well not to get stuck in the crossfire."

"So, you invited Eugene," he says.

"Eugene? What's the problem with inviting him? Don't you like him, Matt?"

"He's fine, but I'm still uneasy about that business between him and Ellen. It's getting very serious."

"There's a new world order, Matt," Beatrice says crisply. "They'd have been ostracized years ago, but I'm not going to treat them as if they're social pariahs."

"Don't get me wrong. That's not what I mean. I've no time for the way things used to be, but I have trouble with some of the adjustments. What if they were to have a child?"

"So? They'd muddle through, like most people."

He laughs. "Can't please me. I suppose I'm too anxious."

"Said with feeling. Do you still find the going tough?"

"Yes and no. Difficult, but also strangely" — he searches for the word — "liberating."

"You're lucky with Stephen."

"He's very dutiful. I told him that he doesn't have to look out for me any longer."

"We all have to move on. I kept postponing things after John's death, but then I realized I had to start up again. It's the only way."

"And I'm delighted with this venture. Yours was always a great house for occasions."

"Yes, Jack was sociable. I blame the TV for some of the fall-off, makes us all lazy."

"Julia didn't like having people in the house. She did it to keep up appearances. If so and so had an event, she had to have one. Then, she wasn't a great card player and she was a poor loser."

"She wasn't alone there. Lots of people get sore."

The doorbell gives a strident bleep. Beatrice opens the door and finds Damien and Lily Traynor shivering on the doorstep.

"Your bell isn't working," Lily complains. "We had to ring it three times before you heard. We're perished standing here." She hands Beatrice a large white box, the usual pavlova, as she rushes in.

"You shouldn't have, Lily. Thanks. Sorry about the wait. Go and heat up in front of the fire."

Damien takes his and Lily's coats and hangs them on the coat stand in the hall. "You're great to revive the card games," he says.

"I don't know about reviving them," Beatrice says. "I was looking for an excuse to set up an occasion."

"This beats the cards in the hall. It has the personal touch."

"We must all be here now," Lily says, counting the chairs at the table. "Or are we missing one?"

"Denis Foynes," Beatrice says.

"Denis will be late for his own funeral," Lily jokes. "None of us has a prayer if Denis's in good form. It'll be 'winner takes all.' I didn't know you two were into playing," she says to Ellen.

"Eugene plays in the hall, but I'm almost a complete novice. I probably took part years ago when Sarah, Mollie, and Peg had people in for cards, but that's all forgotten now."

"I wonder will ye stick at it this time?"

"You want her to take some kind of loyalty test, do you?" jokes Matt.

"This could be my first and last card game," Ellen says. "I'm feeling very daunted."

"Don't worry, Ellen. We're very kind the first time. It's the second time we get tough, lots of verbal abuse," Matt says.

"Otherwise known as bullying and harassment?"

"Correct."

"Don't mind any of them, Ellen," Beatrice says. "They have to abide by house rules here."

"The cards used to be great," Lily says. "A different venue every week. Terrible rivalry—very hot and heavy at times—and then catching up on all the gossip over a cup of tea afterward."

"Has everybody a drink?" asks Beatrice. "I'm a dreadful hostess."

"Let me do barman," Matt offers.

"Work away."

"What about the motorway?" asks Eugene. "Word is that a decision has been made."

"There's another meeting next month. They're saying now that it's all being set back a few years because of—how do they put it?—pressures on the exchequer," Lily says. "They're supposed to have settled on the route, and the Killdingle bypass is sorted out. It won't come as close as we feared."

"So we're off the hook," Matt says.

"There'll be a heavy turnout at that meeting, and a good few spats before it's finally sorted," Damien says.

"Whoever thought when we were growing up there'd be a motorway nearby?" Lily says.

"I still think it's awful," Ellen says.

"Ellen's a Luddite," Matt says.

"Can't turn back the clock, Ellen. This is the price we pay for success," Beatrice says. "But I agree in a way. We have to guard against some of the excesses."

"We may as well sit down," suggests Lily. "We could be waiting a long time for Denis. Who's dealing?"

"I will," Damien says.

"Five euro a head," Matt says. "That's the bank."

"Living dangerously," Damien says.

Damien splits the deck, shuffles and reconstitutes it, doles out two cards per person, then three, dealing a spare hand on the table. "Five cards each," he says.

"What are trumps?" Ellen asks.

"There's no showing the top card on the deck," explains Beatrice.

"If somebody thinks they can make a lot of tricks, they'll make a bid for the spare hand and pick the best five from the two hands. Then they make the call."

"You can go down as well as up in this game, Ellen, so you have to be pretty confident to call it," warns Matt.

Ellen groans. "Shouldn't I just watch for a while? I think I'd be better off watching."

"We'll help when you go wrong," Beatrice says.

The doorbell goes. "Just as we were about to start!" exclaims Lily. "Denis Foynes never lost it." They throw the cards into the center of the table and Damien shuffles them again.

Matt lets him in. "Fix him a drink, would you, Matt, before he sits down?" Beatrice says. "Denis, I was going to introduce you to Matt's niece, Ellen, but I'm told there's no need."

Denis, a dapper little man in his seventies, with gray hair and chapped rosy cheeks, gives a toothy smile. "Ellen and I are well acquainted. Isn't that right, Ellen? I remember her as a child playing on the streets. Pert as you like. But this is the first time we've been formally introduced."

Ellen smiles. "We're always bumping into each other coming in or out of shops." She turns to Beatrice. "When I was a kid, he'd buy me a toffee bar or give me the change when he bought cigarettes."

"Proper little madam she was but she had ways of getting around you." Denis places his drink on the table, sits down and rubs the palms of his hands together. "I've arrived, lads," he says. "Let play commence!"

"What are you working at these days, Ellen?" Lily asks at the end of the first game.

Ellen laughs. "It's the funniest thing. I'm coordinating an adult education program in Killdingle. The previous coordinator landed a full-time job and left suddenly. That seems to be the way with me. I fall into jobs."

"It probably suits you better than the secondary school," suggests Beatrice.

"How's that?" Ellen asks, suddenly uneasy.

"You'll be a free agent there. Nobody's going to be on your case."

Ellen relaxes. "I see what you mean. Actually, there is a good atmosphere in the place. I've been there only three weeks, but the people on the staff are friendly."

"They appreciate quality when they see it," Eugene says.

"Don't be silly," Ellen says, hushing him.

"Next game," Damien announces.

"You're not doing badly, Ellen," Beatrice comments.

"Beginner's luck," Ellen says with feeling. She stays close to Beatrice, keeping an eye on her and following her lead.

Once or twice during the night, as she scrutinizes the play, pays attention to her companions, exchanges words with other players, and observes Eugene's almost unnerving ease in the company, she feels a peculiar sense of dislocation, almost a double take on the evening, but concludes that this tension, this unsettled feeling, this strangeness, might be more properly termed relocation. And if she's locked into a tableau that mimics a social occasion from thirty years before, what does it matter? It's an optical illusion. Life couldn't be more different.

The evening breaks up at eleven. Denis drives away first, followed by Lily and Damien. "When is it you're off to the States?" Matt asks Beatrice.

"October."

"That's only a week away now."

"She's mad to see that little grandson," says Ellen.

Beatrice laughs. "Wait till we see how we get on."

It's a cool, still night. The four of them stand in front of the house under a starry sky looking across the darkness to Ballyowen and Anglestown.

"You can see lots of lights from the houses on the other side of the valley," Matt comments.

"More and more lights all the time," Beatrice says.

"You'd wonder where all the people come from," Ellen muses.

"People like you, Ellen," Matt says playfully as he sits into his car.

"And Eugene," adds Ellen. Eugene's hand rests lightly on her shoulder. She feels his eyes on her. "You'd better get used to it, Matt," she says. "You're stuck with us now!"

ACKNOWLEDGMENTS

For their generous advice, information, and support, I thank Pat and Carmel Clancy, Margaret Clancy Noonan, Anne Dodd, Frank McGuinness, Johnny O'Donnell (for the title), Sheila O'Hagan, and the Saint Stephen's Green Workshop.

Particular thanks to my agent, Betsy Lerner, for her unstinting encouragement and assistance, and to my editor, Anjali Singh, for her insights, patience, and rigor.

I am deeply grateful to my husband, David Murray, for his support.